TALKING TO THE MOON

TALKING TO

THIE MOON

JOHN JOSEPH MATHEWS

Foreword by Elizabeth Mathews

University of Oklahoma Press
Norman

Chapter headpieces by Paul B. Sears

Text illustrations by Mr. Mathews

TO MY MOTHER
EUGENIA GIRARD MATHEWS

CONTENTS

FOREWORD

THIS IS JOHN JOSEPH MATHEWS' *Walden*. IT IS A BOOK THAT A THOREAU or a Muir might write, but it is a *Walden* of the plains and prairies, of the 1930s and 1940s, by a Native American.

The book was first published in 1945 and "lost" to most readers, who were occupied with war. It is a book that may be more meaningful to today's more knowledgeable readers than it was during the war years. Yet it needs some introduction. I am pleased that the book is being reissued and that the publisher has asked me to write this brief foreword.

The author was born in Pawhuska, Indian Territory, in what is now northeastern Oklahoma, in 1894, and died there last year. By any measure, John Joseph Mathews was an exceptional man—Oxford educated, well traveled, widely read, a pilot in World War I, student of his people, long-time member of the Osage Tribal Council, gifted writer, and brilliant conversationalist. A visit from or to his friends— George Milburn, J. Frank Dobie, Paul Sears, Joseph Brandt, for example—might lead to a conversation that would continue for hours, days, weeks. Out of one such visit developed his first book, *Wah'Kon-Tah*, Book-of-the-Month Club selection in 1932. That same year he "returned" home to stay.

"I have come to the blackjacks to live, as one climbs out of the roaring stream of civilization onto an island, to rest and to watch," he explains in these pages. On his ranch among the blackjack trees in his beloved Osage country, he built a sandstone house and lived in solitude for ten years.

"I wasn't attempting to escape anything," he says, "when I came to the blackjacks; I was possibly disturbed by something deeper, and I wanted to get my feet on my own bit of earth, as one might arrange one's body comfortably in bed or in a chair. I wanted to express my harmony with the natural flow of life on my bit of earth. . . . Physical action and living to the very brim each day in harmony with life about me were exhausting and therefore completely satisfactory."

For ten years he lived in harmony with the teeming wildlife about him and, in his book, shares his unique experiences with us. While his account is based on the accepted seasons, it is extended to new dimensions by the Osage concepts of Grandfather Sun, Mother Earth, and especially the cycles of the Moon. With a mixture of rare sophistication and disarming simplicity, he reveals Mother Nature and the "force" controlling all her children.

He writes with sympathy and understanding, and with obvious and shared pleasure, about his beloved blackjack country. Few writers have written so tellingly of the life of the plains and prairies, from the bluestem grasses to man in nature. His observations of the blackjack tree, the crow, and the coyote, their characteristics, behavior, and personalities are revelations. For the readers who can still experience the excitement and horror of the hunt—animal against animal for survival, and man against animal, for the thrill of the chase—the descriptions are striking and memorable.

There is writing here that reaches the level of poetry. There are passages of poignancy and sadness. There are accounts of delicious humor. And there are incidents—such as the midnight convocation of owls, under the chairmanship of Louie, a Cherokee neighbor—that would be unbelievable in a work of fiction. From it all comes an appreciation, perhaps forgotten by all except those who live close to nature, that needs to be kept alive.

"I didn't presume that I could come out of the blackjacks with the banner of truth flying but that I might be able to devote a few years to pleasant, undisturbed living. I had thought, incidentally, that I might find some connection between man's artificial ornamentation and the useless ornamentation among the creatures of my little corner of the earth. I realized that man's artistic creations and his dreams, often resulting in beauty, as well as his fumbling toward God, must be primal, possibly the results of the biological urge which inspires the wood thrush to sing and the coyote to talk to the moon."

I am glad that this beautiful book, after being out of print and

unavailable for more than thirty years, will be available again and
to a new generation of readers.

Elizabeth (Mrs. John Joseph) Mathews

Pawhuska, Oklahoma
June 3, 1980

THE SANDSTONE HOUSE

THREE RIDGES ROUGHLY BOAT-SHAPED PUSH THEIR PROWS SOUTH INTO the sea of prairie. In the spring when the grass is short and the leaves have not yet come to the blackjacks, they are boats ridiculously stuck with black masts on a sea of green, copper, and mauve. The green for the green grass, the copper for the dead grass of the last season, and the mauve for the cloud shadows. In summer the forests of the headlands grow down to the emerald, wind-rippled prairie sea, and in the autumn they flash with the loud brilliance of a color film—a color film from a strange land which the observer knows he will never see. In the winter the boats, the headlands, and the incredible color are gone, and only the space and voices remain. Then the dead brown leaves of the trees on the ridges blend with the copper of the prairie with its snow patches gleaming in the sun, and the black boles of the trees add that touch which makes undisturbed nature ever constant in subtle beauty.

There is a flat, open deck on the middle ridge around which the blackjacks and the postoaks are well spaced, so that one can see for miles in three directions. To the north their growth is dense, as it should be in our country of high winter winds. Beyond this growth of blackjacks the three ridges melt into the high prairie. At the head of the canyon which lies between the east and the middle ridges are the white ranch house and the big red barn.

My father had built the first house in the blackjacks by the spring at the head of the canyon, and before that there had been nothing from the beginning of time to upset nature's balance. The scars of the old Cedarvale stage road were still visible two hundred yards from where I was sitting, but the buggies and the stage wagons and the occasional freight wagons stopped in the area only to let the horses blow after the climb or the driver take a shot at the floating white tails of deer vanishing through the black boles of the blackjacks. This spot was the last shade the drivers would find before reaching the little town of Cedarvale in Kansas, and the last chance to get a shot at a deer on the trip from the Osage agency to the States.

The driver of the stage and others must have stopped here often to rest their horses or shoot at deer, but they halted only a short time, since there was no water on the ridge over which the sand-filled wheel tracks wriggled. Hence nature had paused and waited until the creaking and the rasping of the tires on the sandstone outcrops had died in the breezes of the prairie to the north, to resume the drama— the constant tragedy which is a part of nature's balance.

Thinking of these things, the feeling was strong about the stoppages of the cinema film of natural drama that came every day as the workmen arrived from town, and the long suspension of activity during the working day by the inhabitants of the ridge; pauses which must finally end in adjustment to me and my little house. For I had decided to live on the middle ridge, and my little sandstone house was being built.

My coming back was dramatic in a way; a weight on the sensitive scales of nature, which I knew would eventually be adjusted if I lived as I had planned to live; to become a part of the balance. However, my house was not disturbing a state that had been constant throughout the years, since there had been no absolute constancy to disturb. No two seasons and no two days had been alike through the years in the flow of earth's life toward some mysterious fulfilment, and I wanted to become a part of the flow in so far as I was able; to learn something of the moods of the little corner of the earth which had given me being; to learn something of the biological progression and the mysterious urge which inspired it, until the biological changes within myself dimmed the romance of it. I had kept my body fit and ready, but my perceptive powers had been dulled by the artificialities and the crowding and elbowing of men in Europe and America, my ears attuned to the clanging steel and the strident sounds of civilization, and the range of my sight stopped by tall buildings and walls, by neat gardens and geometrical fields; and I had begun to worship these things and the men who brought them into being—impersonalized groups of magicians who never appeared to my consciousness as frail, uninspiring individuals.

I had long realized that these wonders of civilization, as well as war and unnatural crowding of men, slavery, group fanaticism, and social abnormalities, were inspired by the biological urge manifesting itself in progression, as were the dreams of the few who had created beauty, comfort, and tragedy. By the realization of such dreams men had begun to think that they were cutting their bonds with the earth; that they had torn themselves loose from the restrictive laws of biology.

I was not interested in facts and so-called truths for the purpose of attaining them and then proclaiming to the world that I had them. I was thwarted by my own informality and defeated through my own inability to reason with those who had formal training. I could not begin with the upper branches of a tree and follow one to the trunk, but must go to the roots, and beyond the roots to the reasons for nature's encouragement of the seedling; the conditions that made its growth acceptable. I thought that there was so much evidence of the herd-and-pack law in man's groups and cliques, within the confines of which one had to remain or find one's self beyond recognition, like the member of the herd or pack in nature who strays off, endangering all, or at least drawing to himself their disapproval and bad will. It seemed to me that the herd-and-pack law obtained here as in many other aspects of civilization, and I had begun to be interested in these tendencies ascribed to "human nature." These tendencies had a much broader application and are found throughout the animal world at least. It seems that, in order to survive, man has to follow the laws of the earth in all categories of his complex existence—his dreams notwithstanding.

I didn't presume that I could come out of the blackjacks with the banner of truth flying but that I might be able to devote a few years to pleasant, undisturbed living. I had thought, incidentally, that I might find some connection between man's artificial ornamentation and the useless ornamentation among the creatures of my little corner of the earth. I realized that man's artistic creations and his dreams, often resulting in beauty, as well as his fumbling toward God, must be primal, possibly the results of the biological urge which inspires the wood thrush to sing and the coyote to talk to the moon.

I came to the blackjacks as a man who had pulled himself out of the roaring river of civilization to rest for a while; out of the flood where formerly only his head had been above the surface. Stopping for a time and looking back, he could better appreciate the sweep of the river and the spectrum in the mist above the falls which had battered him. From his island he could perhaps see the natural *raison d'être* of the mad whirlpools with their deadwood and drift, endlessly gyrating, as well as the naturalness of the eddies and the stagnant bayous. He could see everything with better understanding, even though he would be no closer to the sea toward which the river was rushing, and would be unable to see around the next bend. He would only see that the river which carried him flowed with great urgency toward some deeply mysterious objective and that he would soon slip back into it like a turtle from his log, but with a clearer idea of the relationship between turtles and rivers.

So after years spent in many other parts of the earth, I had come back to the very spot where I had lain as a boy, watching the circling of the red-tailed hawks and actually shedding tears over the fate that had made me earth-bound, the spotted bird dog and the flaxen-maned pony indifferent to my tragedy. As I sat in the shade of the same old postoak watching the stone walls rise, I was again alone with my thoughts. But this time they were happy and as colored and inconsequential as butterflies in a prairie breeze. Just as the spotted dog and the flaxen-maned pony had not guessed my tragedy, in their absorption with the practical working-out of the maze of field-mice trails and the grazing of the rank bluestem, so were the workmen unaware of my happiness and my reasons for building the little house in the blackjacks.

In the little area on the middle ridge I built my sandstone house, after drilling a well to make sure that I should have a supply of water.

I talked with several well-drillers about the possibility of finding water on a ridge several feet above the thousand-foot contour. One said: "Could a man git holt of a peach fork, I could witch you all the watter in the country—if they's airy bit of watter 'round here." Another said: "You'll hafta go to the white sand, and I jist ain't got the tools to do 'er." I eventually contracted with one to drill until he struck water.

"I can go to China," he said, "if you'll tell me where you wanta drill."

"Right on top, on the flat in that opening."

"You're the doctor," he said, looking at me with that self-confidence of those who know their work and do it well.

One day when I was riding over the pastures my attention was drawn to a white object gleaming in the sun. When I climbed to the top of a rounded prairie hill, I saw that the white object that had demanded my full attention and had imperiously called me was not a single white object but the scattered bones of a horse. As I stood looking down at them, I remembered that during my long absence the last colt of my favorite mare had been killed by lightning on that hill. Tony had stood on the porch of the ranch house and pointed the spot out to me, saying, "That's where you went out of the horse business."

I remembered the colt, an iron-gray and a veritable outlaw that only a bolt of lightning had been able to subdue. But I grew nostalgic thinking of the flaxen-tailed mare and my boyhood. I picked up two of the leg bones and examined them, then mounted and rode to the middle ridge. I sat on my horse for some time just dreaming, then realized that I still had the leg bones with me. I dismounted and laid them one across the other.

Later when I drove over the route which I decided would be my road, following as it did the sandstone and limestone outcrops, I saw the drilling derrick and the men about it. When I came up to them, I noticed that the driller had picked up the crossed bones and had laid them carefully aside and had spudded in on the exact spot where I had whimsically put them several days before.

I had left no location sign for the well, so the conscientious driller had assumed that the carelessly dropped bones were the marker. The well was down twenty-four feet, and I felt that I had to accept the area as the location for the house, and if the well were to be conveniently located only a few feet from the kitchen door on the west, then the house must perch on the edge of the ridge. As I looked again at the bones, I became even more whimsical in the realization that white had imperiously played its part as well. It had attracted attention and had inspired acute interest and activity as it ever does on the prairie.

I drew the plans for the house; a simple thing; a one-man house. It was to be of the native sandstone, with the stones picked up off the ridges, with moss and lichen and ripple marks left by Carboniferous seas intact. The plans called for a house thirty feet long and fifteen feet wide over all, with a single room and a box kitchen. Because of its six-by-twelve dimension, the kitchen was supposed to discourage the assemblage of guests.

I told the contractor that I wanted the house built with eighteen-inch walls, with weathered stone on the inside as well as on the outside, and with the spaces between filled with chipped sandstone; the whole to be built around a fireplace of limestone and firebrick. He was very eager to begin; this was in 1932, and my contractor was worried. He said that it was "a hell of a thing that a depression would come along durin' sich hard times," and he thought that if he had not received the contract to build my little house, he might resort to eating "Hoover hogs," which was the name given to rabbits by the valley farmers.

"This fireplace business is serious," I said, as the contractor and I sat under the Blackjack to discuss the matter. "I want a real fireplace; one that will draw; one that will work. I want the house sorta built around the fireplace—see what I mean?"

"Sure," he said, "I know; I been buildin' the goddam things for years, and they ain't airy one of 'em I ain't proud of—I'd be 'shamed to show to a man." He picked up a twig from the tree and began cutting it into little sections, using his flat, calloused thumb as a stop for the blade of his knife.

"Well," I said, slightly annoyed with his assurance, "I just wanted you to know what I expect in the way of a fireplace; I am sure you can build one or I shouldn't have asked you. I checked on you at the agency, and you have been conscientious in the building of Indian houses—only a good honest man could resist certain possibilities there, you know."

He jumped to a defense of himself. "Hell," he said, "if I never earned another dollar, I wouldn't do nothin' crooked....."

When he had finished, I continued: "You see, men have been building fireplaces for centuries, and still they have not perfected the art. Some of them are all right until the wind swings into the southwest, then you have a family evacuation until the wind changes—see what I mean? A man can build a house and say it's good, but it seems to me when he builds a fireplace, he is gambling—not even he knows whether it will work—no draft; throat out of dimension with the depth, or something."

He looked at me steadily. He feigned slight annoyance, to indicate the uselessness of attempting to impress on me, who apparently knew little about anything, that he could build a fireplace or anything else that pertained to the building trade. He changed his tobacco to the other side of his mouth, spread his hands with the twig in one and the knife in the other, and spat straight out between them. He looked straight into my eyes, then said:

"You got airy cat?"

"No," I answered, "wouldn't have one on the place—why?"

He looked back at the twig and cut two more sections before he answered, perhaps for dramatic effect.

"I was jist figgerin'; when I git that fa'r place built, she'll work, and if you had airy cat that you thought right smart about, you'd better keep the sonofabitch away from that fa'r place, 'er it'ud suck 'im up."

I had, of course, forgotten my compass, so I stood blinking into the sun that rested daintily on the tops of the blackjacks of the east ridge. It was expanding and contracting as though out of breath from its struggle out of the earth to appear above the blackjacks at the appointed time.

I stepped off fourteen feet from the pump of the new well and laid a cow chip where the kitchen door would be. From this chip, I faced the sun and extended both arms, north and south, then stepped off fifteen feet straight south. At these extreme points where I dug into the ground with my boot heels, I placed two little piles of sandstone rocks, then found the other corners.

When I arrived several days later to begin the work of hauling the stone, the conscientious contractor looked worried.

"Say," he said, "is that all right? We're down to live rock."

I looked at the rectangular excavation: "Yes, looks all right."

"She'll hold tel hell freezes over," he assured me. "Whin you set them walls on that live rock, you got a anchor that reaches plumb to hell and back." He grew more serious. "Say, me or you—one 'er the other is off. This outfit aint gonna face due east 'cordin' to my figgerin'. We followed your lines, then I checked, and one of us is off, somewhere."

"Is that right?"

"Yeah—the way your lines are a-runnin', she's gonna set kindy cock-eyed—toward the north some; the way I figger it."

"Oh, yes," I said; "I ran my lines by the magnetic north—that's the reason."

"Oh," he said.

When the sun comes up over the ridge, it sometimes catches me in bed on the front porch and hits my eyes directly, but I note that the very first thing it hits in the summer is the picture of a black panther on a purple limb which hangs on the end of a bookcase just inside the south window. I also notice that when the snow slants out of the north, it hits the front of the east-porch screen on a tangent; and when the rain comes from the east, I must shut the south window.

I got a span of mules from the ranch, borrowed a wagon from my neighbor, and took Virgil off duty to haul rock. He and I went over

the ridges hand-picking every stone that went into the house. When we had a great pile for the masons, I asked the contractor to tell me when we had enough. He looked at the pile, spat, and then said: "Ever fool with stone much?" He knew very well that I hadn't, but he waited for an answer.

"No."

"Well, I tell you; haul 'er up here tel ya got enough, then haul 'bout five, six loads more."

Virgil was small and as hard as a piece of twisted, rain-weathered rawhide and, incidentally, the best workman we ever had on the ranch. He didn't know how to rest. He never squatted to talk with the men at noon hour as they ate their lunches, or at intervals between loads when the mortar mixer sometimes stood invitingly unemployed for a few minutes. However, he would start cursing the mules as he stood high on a load of stone and braced against the lines, in order to attract the men's attention. He would pull back on the mules and stop them with a flourish at the building site, spit out to the side of the wagon, and say triumphantly, "Whur ya want it?"

He chewed tobacco continuously, even holding a chew in his mouth as he slept. He said that he had to chew all the time to keep his teeth from aching. The only time that he slackened in the least with his heavy work was the day when I forgot to bring out the plug of tobacco which I had promised him. As a matter of fact, he was so miserable I had to go back to town to get it.

I went out with him to select the stones and help him load them. Some of the special fourteen stones for the two doors and the five windows were what he called "three-man stones," but it was necessary for four of us to go out and load them. When he and I worked over the stones, the sweat from my face and bare upper body would drip onto them, sinking into the grains immediately; but he never sweated. His sweat might have come out with the tobacco juice, as in the slavering of a dog, his tough hide being impervious.

I would sometimes point to a large stone lying on the prairie, with the iron rust showing on its surface, and say, "That's a three-man stone." He would spit, say "Hell," with contempt, and attempt to load it without aid. After he hurt his back with such heroics, I said, "Look, you don't have to impress me—I know what you can do; take it easy." After that he was more careful.

One day as we sat panting after loading several heavy stones, he pulled out a big knife and started to strop it on his shoe sole. He felt the edge significantly, looking up at me as though we shared an understanding. He spat to one side and said, "Reckon them fellas 'ud be wantin' to work whur I'se at if they knowed I carried this?" When I smiled knowingly, he looked at me significantly. "Don't guess you've told 'em anything, have you?"

"No."

He put the knife back in the sheath inside of his levis, climbed into the wagon, and started with his heavy load to the building site as I cut across the prairie to help him unload.

One day after he had unloaded his stone, he dropped his knife. He looked up at the men on the scaffolding, and when he noticed that they had failed to see it, he stood rubbing imaginary dirt from the blade. One of the men, finally seeing him, said: "Say, fella, you must be mad at somebody?"

He didn't say anything for a while, then as he put the knife back in its sheath, his face expressing mystery by a sort of heroic glow, he smiled patronizingly at the man on the scaffolding: "Naw, ain't mad; jist tar'd a-bein' pushed around." He climbed back on the empty wagon, spat, then continued: "Fella owes me; when I git through with this job if he don't pay me, might hafta cut it outta his hide." He drove off cursing the mules as long as he was within hearing of the men.

It was noon hour, and, as he drove off to water and feed the mules at the ranch barn, I sat down with the men in the shade to eat lunch. One of them said, "That fella a bad actor?"

I was fond of Virgil; I didn't like the implication in the question. "Oh," I said, "he's one of the best men we ever had; he can do anything and do it well; never has to be told. He has known nothing but hard work all of his life and he is honest and straight as a die." I hoped that this would be sufficient as an explanation, but the sly, patronizing smile on the man's face led me on until I out-Virgiled Virgil.

"Well," I added with damning hesitation, "he .... well, as a matter of fact, he's been a sorta soldier of fortune, in a way; you know, he .... a man like that might have his enemies. You can't tell who might come prowling around the ranch house at night. A knife has to be used by an expert to be effective, you know. Seems he's been mixed up in a couple of revolutions in Mexico and South America. He told me one time that one of the closest shaves he ever had was during a mix-up in a Mexican revolution. Seems as though every man in a little scouting party was picked off except himself, and he managed to take cover behind a large anthill. His description of those snipers' bullets kicking the dirt from that anthill was certainly exciting, but the worst thing was when the ants kept biting him all the time; ants biting and bullets zipping—imagine yourself in his place."

"What happened?" asked one of the men.

I looked up into a group of interested faces; the story had done justice to Virgil's heroics. "Well, as a matter of fact," I said, "just at the point when he was telling it I had to leave—I don't remember now."

I watched the walls rise with a deep satisfaction. The quail whistled from all over the ridge, and scissor-tailed flycatchers chattered over the trees in intricate nuptial flights, their extremely long forked tails in the movements of a pair of scissors, opening and shutting. The wary crows sometimes finding themselves almost immediately over the walls, before they were aware, would swerve sharply in their flight, gain altitude, and warn all crows within hearing that something strange was happening on the middle ridge; later to come back cautiously to determine just what that very interesting, extremely dangerous creature, man, was up to.

The titmice and the chickadees came as well and chattered about the marvel, and the bluejays, constantly seeking out that which is strange and sensational, came in flocks of four and five to watch with the interest of gossips all over the world and wait patiently to investigate the lunch papers clinging to the tall grasses.

As I rested under the hot shade of the postoak and watched the masons, I had a vague feeling that there ought to be some protest to the building of the house in this corner of the ranch that had been unmolested for as long as I could remember.

I knew that the workmen had been wondering why I should build a house on the high middle ridge, far from arable land, and why I should wish to live alone. They didn't ask, and if they had, I couldn't have told them, since my real reason would not have been considered practical, and one had to be practical to be respected. I knew that they would come to one of two conclusions: either that I was a "bit off" or that I was a playboy who probably had near-by Tulsa as a hunting ground. Their exploring thoughts came down from the heights of conjecture into the highroad of the business of life one day when a young carpenter looked down from his scaffolding and smiled at me with that man-to-man understanding of man: "I bet these ole rock walls is gonna see more classy gals than I could dream about in a year. Don't reckon they could ever learn to talk?"

I smirked and lit a cigarette.

Thus I had come to the blackjacks to live, as one climbs out of the roaring stream of civilization onto an island, to rest and to watch, but that is not the only reason why I came; therefore, the explanation is inadequate. I do know that, after ten years, things now passing my island on the flood are a little strange, and that the things with which I floated and with which I was familiar have passed the island, and that I must occasionally stop to take note of this fact. I wonder sometimes if I have been left on the island, and if the falling-back into the stream will be as easy as a turtle's falling off a log. What if eddies have formed around the island and I can't swim away from it?

I shouldn't have thought of these things five years ago, or six, or seven years ago, but the change within me that is making miracles like the first morning-glory of the season, the first red leaf of the sumac, the first V of Canada geese, the visit of a painted bunting to the yard, the song of the wood thrush, into just pleasant matters of fact, seems to be hinting at some sort of accounting. There is an accounting to nature which must be made by those who leave the herd or the pack to run alone without responsibility to the pack or the herd, and that accounting is hard for all except the most able, the strongest. Whether one is stranded on an island in the river of man's civilization or has lived for a few years outside the associations of the herd and the pack, which after all is much the same thing—and could be classed as a confused metaphor—he is never divorced from either. Back into the river, he finds that he has forfeited his place among familiar things, where he was recognized and valued, and must adjust himself in his brittle state. Back into the herd or pack, he finds that he has forfeited seniority rights and that he must adjust himself to the leadership and virility—a new virility with the strength which he has spent in the enjoyment of his isolation.

This accounting business may be a feeling rather than a fact, but it comes to me now on the sixteenth of each November, at the tragic hour of three o'clock in the morning, since my last two or three birthdays, but seldom lasts out the darkness.

I have nothing to account for as far as the first two primal laws are concerned. Primarily, man is so constituted by nature that she seems interested in him only as a reproducer of himself and as a protector of his offspring until they can care for themselves. Her chief interest is in the survival of the species. I have an idea, as unflattering as it may seem, that she is little interested in him after he has performed these functions. The importance of old men, like the collective expressions of senile nations, may be self-assumed in an artificial society, unless through their experience they might have a natural importance in the tribe and in the larger units of society. They may play a much more important role in the future stages of man's spiritual development, the fires inspired by the other primal laws of survival and reproduction having become dimmed to allow a fuller play under the influence of the newer law or force which has inspired man's mental development.

But, after ten years in the blackjacks, I had begun to feel a vague responsibility; perhaps to myself. My friends put it another way. They said it concerned a certain group of literate people they called my "public." They attempted to make it appear that these people were waiting for another book from me. They even implied impatience on the part of these people, and when I was with my own thoughts again, I attempted to visualize these people, my "public." First, I thought of the men and women of my own craft—"craft" was convenient for the purpose of thinking only, since I had never thought of myself as a writer, as being within the intimate circle. I know very few writers. They surely couldn't be perturbed about my silence.

Then the men who work in offices, read the papers, play poker and golf and become soggy at the nineteenth hole, go back to work, read the papers, play poker or bridge and golf and become soggy at the nineteenth hole again. I had played both poker and golf with these fellows, and as long as I dressed in well-appearing clothes, spoke "American" without an accent, kept my mouth shut, and held my Scotch, they didn't seem to be distressed about my barren years. Most of them had been unaware that there had ever been any fruitful ones.

I thought next of their receptionists, their stenographers, and their clerks, with their red fingernails and their business courtesy; those who greeted you as a susceptible male, with a manner which declared, "I am a desirable woman," then asked you your business. I never knew much about women's souls; they seemed to play a role in my presence which was designed to fit into what they believed to be my beautiful idealism. I was sure that these people were not recalling that I existed.

Lastly, I thought of the wives, the gallant club women, and they immediately became the symbol of my friend's "public." I remembered how indulgent they were when I spoke to them, how charmingly they accepted my "message," and how charmingly some of the older ones, careless of their aging contours, full of lunch, went to sleep, their fixed and comfortable smiles still showing their indulgence.

These are the angels who buy your books, talk about your books, send your books to friends at Christmas time, and give teas in honor of your books and your authors. I felt vindictive and was about to say these things to my friends but realized that I had no point. I was defensive because the world represented by my smug friends was saying that I had wasted some of the best years of my life mooning over birds, riding after bear hounds and coyote hounds, shooting deer and quail, attempting to raise the standards of learning in the state, and trying to make more comfortable the assimilation of the Osage Indian—and just horizon-gazing.

Several years ago I should have brushed the idea away as I brush away the confused horsefly, but now it clings momentarily like a wood tick and can't be brushed off; it must be picked off, leaving the head to cause irritation.

But those remembered conversations and accompanying thoughts come only when I take stock on the sixteenth of November, when I am a year older; nine or ten years older than when I first came to the blackjacks to live. Each year I find that I have written in my diary a garbled quotation from Tagore on this day: "I shake my head and there is no fruit; only green leaves." It is the mature urge to ornamental expression.

Coming back to the blackjacks was so natural that I didn't want to have a definite reason for coming. I wasn't running away from anything and was certainly not vindictive. I had been comfortable and had access to all the mechanical comforts and had appreciated them deeply. I had not been compelled to live where coal smoke settled on the curtains and on my face and hands, nor had I been compelled to live where the streams ran with varicolored chemicals and stank as Styx might have stunk. I could live beyond the screaming of steel and away from the regions which were made desolate by industry, and I could enjoy the result of industry by my appreciation of the marvels of American architecture and the large cities which it made imposing and overpowering, and the other marvels which a mechanical philosophy had inspired.

I hadn't become uncomfortably annoyed because the great mass of the public had taken the place of the monarchs of early Europe and Asia here in America and must be pleased by the struggling creative artists. I was happy that they should be the ultimate judges of a creative artist's efforts, even though I personally was not amused by revived vaudeville jokes and manners over the radio and catchwords from the East Side of New York which had no meaning or application west of the Ohio River. The same corner drug store from Maine to California was not disturbing, and the bathing beauties on the signboards, coquettishly demanding that certain products be bought, were as natural as a red flower summoning a bee with the addition of sex, which was pleasing to both sexes: by glorifying the female body, a vicarious triumph for the women and a delightful emotional suggestion for the men; both the primal laws being satisfied, in economic survival for the producer and in serving the reproductive force in the buyers.

I could never be disturbed by the struggle of social groups in America who waved ideological banners, but I had thought that certainly the government owed them protection against exploitation, just as a very young government had paternally protected the first struggling industries in America from the acquisitive industries of Europe. I had believed that any changes in social government should be evolutionary and had been quite satisfied that such changes would be under the natural laws of progression. The fact that I had lived to see the end of a period in this progression when the exploitation of natural resources of a continent had reached a saturation point, under the berserk methods of economically, socially, and politically liberated Europeans called Americans, was very interesting; and even though I came to the black-jacks in the middle of the depression, I could not be too disturbed. I had seen the flush production period pass in the mid-continent fields and had seen the exploiters compelled to adjust themselves to retailing gasoline and satisfied to make a half a cent a gallon, if they were virile enough in their thinking to make the necessary adjustment. I knew that the European in America must make the same adjustment at the end of the period of "flush production," and I felt sure that sanity would avoid unnatural social, economic, and political convulsions.

Because I had lived in Europe, I was not disturbed; my thoughts of Americans who thought themselves to be in social, economic, and political difficulties did not raise the mercury of my sympathy. I could feel no unhappiness, when looking through the windows of a Pullman, in seeing the cars parked running-board to running-board and bumper to bumper around the smoking factories. I could feel no sympathy for the industrialists with whom I chatted and smoked in the club car when they talked of "that man in the White House" because they believed that he had interfered with their vested interests and had let them down. They seemed too shortsighted to realize that they were experiencing the end of an era and must start thinking of the international position of the unit of society that protected them and of the human element which had become important in the beginning of a new era. They wanted that shibboleth called *status quo ante* and thought only of selling more and more, and shinier and shinier, buttons.

My friends began to talk with bitterness about social struggle at this period, and many of them became free-lance champions of those they considered to be the underdogs. Tranquil men and women quite suddenly would turn delightful conversation into a series of militant statements which made me uncomfortable. I kept thinking of Europe and Asia and could not enter into their spirit.

We Americans were like Steinbeck's Okies, who in "flush production" had eaten the frosting from the cake and had never been taught by real struggle that the layers underneath were edible. I had known many of these people called Okies and was fond of them as men and women and had some sympathy for them inasmuch as their disaster was the natural result of man's shortsightedness in ravaging the land, but Europe and Asia were in my mind, and the thought that Steinbeck's Okies had actually gone to California in their own truck would not be subdued.

So I wasn't attempting to escape anything when I came to the blackjacks; I was possibly disturbed by something deeper, and I wanted to get my feet on my own bit of earth, as one might arrange one's body comfortably in bed or in a chair. I wanted to express my harmony with the natural flow of life on my bit of earth by physical action. Word symbols couldn't satisfy me as an expression; there was too much that was inexpressible; there were flying in the moonlight, the Grand Canyon, desert sunsets, riding over the Osage prairie in June. Word symbols seemed futile and pale when confronted with civilization's material magic. Physical action and living to the very brim each day in harmony with the life about me were exhausting and therefore completely satisfactory.

But deep in my consciousness was the conflict between man's dreams which create the magic of his civilization as well as his fumbling toward God; the dreams which create and nurture his ideologies and create beauty; the conflict between these dreams and his slavery to the primal laws of survival and reproduction. Perhaps my impressions under the influence of this deep consciousness during the ten years of my life in the blackjacks may not be worth recording; those things which I found for my own comfort; but the consciousness of this conflict did develop into the background for the impressions which I received and which crystallized during that time. These thoughts and emotions finally demanded an expression that physical activity could not satisfy when the worries and ornamentations of maturity arrived.

When the house was finished, there were at least three loads of the "five, six loads more" scattered about the place, and the heroic Virgil went back to the regular duties of the ranch and his pulp-magazine dreams, and the workmen left the ridge to me and the coyotes. The house with its stone colored by nature was nature's own, and, to bear out the impression, a coyote came trotting across the ridge without even looking up from his hunting, just as darkness fell.

It was nature's own except for the composition roof, which to this day startles me as I approach from the high prairie, for the roof's inharmonious battleship gray resists all the wild furies and the sweet cajoleries of temperamental nature over the blackjacks, and remains an alien.

‖‖   THE BLACKJACKS

LONG BEFORE I CAME TO THE BLACKJACKS AS AN INSIGNIFICANT BIT OF life, made powerful by a birthright resulting from man's progress through the centuries, the ridges had no topographic importance but were a part of high lands capped either with sandstone or a later member of the carboniferous limestone, now a part of the Mississippi Delta, or resting on the floor of the Gulf of Mexico. The sandstone ridges are simply the survivals of the ancient sandstone cap of my area, and the lower prairie the limestone that underlay it. It was a forest area at one time in its history, but the dramatic processes of the earth have made of it an open-woods country of limestone prairie and sandstone ridges. Through the prairie part runs Bird Creek, with the tops of its walnuts, sycamores, pinoaks, hackberrys, redoaks, and elms showing above the undulating green of the prairie. It looks like a complacent snake, arrested in his purposeless motion; and the canyons and ravines with trees and bushes in their bottoms are like hairy fingers spread across the prairie toward the sandstone ridges, groping fingers jealously tearing at the ridges to bring them to their own level.

The blackjacks grow only on the sandstone but use every square inch of it to spread to the contact line between sandstone and limestone. When the hairy fingers of the canyons have torn the ridges away, the blackjacks will go, but they hold to their domain tenaciously, delaying the end by covering the ridges with their seedlings. When a blackjack is chopped down, or blown down by tornadic or cyclonic winds, a hundred "running oaks" will spring up to take its place and give no other seedling a chance to gain a foothold in their empire. They send their roots into crevices of the sandstone and fan out from a few inches to two or three feet below the surface, but, oddly enough, only extremely high winds can tear them from their anchorage.

Sometimes the bulls kill or distort the running oaks by rubbing their heads on them and thrashing them with their horns, but when they become older and larger, the lower limbs die and slant downward, forming a perfect protection against anything large enough to harm them. These dead limbs are as hard and as tough as steel lances, capable of tearing hide or clothing. They twist in black masses, reaching almost to the ground, and have the characteristics of hard rubber when an ax is applied to them. One who knows them is extremely chary about approaching them with an ax.

Where they grow thickest the wary crows roost in them. The dead brown leaves hang on to them until the buds of spring push them off, thus providing protection from the cold winds, and the stiff black lances discourage many a marauder. Even if a prowler could manage to climb laboriously through these lances, he could not do so silently.

In the spring when the blossoms are like the tassels of a serape, the crows build their bulky nests in them. They choose the ones apart, usually those that have ventured near the contact line between limestone and sandstone. Here the canny black barbarians can see in all directions and enjoy the protection of the panoplied tree. I have often tried to get at such nests; I have tried to get close enough to swing from my saddle into the green limbs above the armament, but this is difficult. While I am high enough standing in the saddle, I cannot get the horse near enough. I have tried the same thing from the top of my station wagon, but I have the same difficulty. I succeed more often when I start from the ground with a cautiously wielded ax, cutting my way up.

I have often wondered why such effective protection. Certainly when the protective armor has been cut or broken away, the cattle will rub against the tree, but they can do little harm to a full-grown one. The only apparent effect is that the bark is highly polished by the constant rubbing. In the spring the buffalo used to leave some of their shaggy winter hair on the stiff arms in attempting to relieve their itching hides by rubbing against them. Sometimes their hides were torn, thus inviting screw-flies. Perhaps the buffalo bulls were the chief enemy of the blackjack, and one cannot readily see any other reason for this very elaborate and effective protection. Certainly they thrashed the saplings with their horns and distorted thousands of them just as the range white-faces do today, but the running oak has no armament; its only protection is its resilience and quick recovery. One season it may be thrashed and stamped into the ground, only to raise its head and sprout new branches the next.

The defense of the adult blackjack through its punishing dead branches certainly had reason for existence. Perhaps it was originally a defense against the stamping of deer and buffalo that sought the tree's shade during hot, dry weather, thus removing the top soil and exposing the area under the tree to erosion, eventually exposing the roots and causing death or allowing the tree to slant and finally fall.

I owe my hundreds of young hackberry trees on the ridges to the fact that blackjacks keep their leaves all winter, thus giving protection from cold winds to the birds.

Several years ago in January the cold breath of the Arctic floated down the Mississippi Valley, driving snow and sleet before it. The glass went down one night to 26 below zero and remained below zero for most of the month. White hunger stalked the blackjacks, and the cold winds rattled their winter-dead leaves and screamed across the prairie. There was little drifting; the snow and sleet held a glazed surface and thus covered the fruit of the earth. The coyotes stood out against the whiteness as they posed like statues, their long winter hair rippling and their bushy tails held close against their hind legs. They were not aware that they had lost their protective coloring against the gleaming whiteness. Hunger-dulled, they stood testing the air as they gazed, awaiting some movement in the white desolation. The crows, blacker than ever, lost their wariness and sat with feathers puffed for the benefit of the air-pocket insulation against the cold, as they waited for a chance to investigate the dogs' food pans at the kitchen door.

In the bottoms along the creek the coldest air rested, the warmer air remaining high along the ridges. Birds that didn't appear on the ridges during the other seasons, or if they appeared, rarely, came to the blackjacks to huddle among the brown leaves.

In all this world of hunger there were only two sources of food supply above the glazed snow, food supplies that had not been stored by rodents or woodpeckers. Only the prairie chickens succeeded in breaking through to the ice-coated heads of the kaffir. I carried as much grain as possible about the place on foot; I couldn't use a horse on the glasslike crust. I carried the grain on my back and spread it under the tops of fallen trees so that the hungry marsh hawks could not get at the quail as they fed. This fed the quail, chickadees, cardinals, and juncos. The only other source of food was the hackberry trees in the creek bottoms. This year they bore abundantly. Their reddish berries shone brightly, and apparently every bird that did not share the grain with the quail ate these berries; accustomed or not, they ate them. When they had fed, the cardinals, bluejays, flickers, and winter robins flew up to the ridge and sat miserably and puffed-up among the leaves of the blackjacks, the hard seeds of the hackberries falling intact with their droppings.

Two years later I noted strange saplings under the trees of the ridge. I couldn't believe that hackberry trees would grow where they had never grown before, since they are trees of the bottoms and the canyons and never grow on the high sandstone ridges. Now, however, there are hundreds of these hackberry trees along the ridges. Sometimes when the tree under which they sprang up is cut down or dies, they shoot up into the sun to vie with the postoak and the tough blackjack.

When the seasons are wet, the autumnal blackjacks are fantastically colored. The leaves are scarlet, yellow, and slightly mauve at the same time. During this time when they stand along the ridge tops and along the sides of the hill, they shine in the sun like hordes of painted warriors. This is one of the tranquil periods of life on the ridge. An indescribable peace seems to come over everything during the day when the sun has lost its intensity of summer; a profound peace of which the patient blackjacks are symbols. Life is fully aware and vital after the languor of the summer, but quiescent; even the prairie breezes are stilled, and the leaves do not break the silence.

When the sun slips into the prairie and adds orange and its own red to the mad coloring of the ridge, the cold air creeps up from the creek bottom. The blackjacks then become expectant; their black boles become blacker, and the whole ridge becomes filled with mystery. As the moon startles the world over the east ridge, the questing howl of a coyote sets others to howling in every direction, but later there will be the hunting cry of distant hounds. When the moon frees itself from the trees of the east ridge, as though it would see better what is going on, the leaves resume their glory—a rather dimmed glory.

I believe that no one has ever written a poem about a blackjack, and I am quite sure that there are no songs about them. As a matter of fact, they go by any number of names, such as scrub-oak, jack-oak, and Cross Timbers. Under the last name they were more or less glorified—at least mentioned in the history of the state of Oklahoma. The following is a summing-up of the historical significance of the tree, which indicates that which one readily suspects; that at least they have always been respected if not loved.

From the *Oklahoma State Guide:* "Interesting and important in the history of Oklahoma is a north- and south-trending strip of rough

country known as the Cross Timbers, varying from five to thirty miles in width across the central part of the State. From Washington Irving's *A Tour of the Prairies* on through the accounts of such trailmakers as Randolph B. Marcy, escorting gold-seekers to California over the southern route in 1849, this belt of matted, tangled undergrowth, stiff-branched blackjacks, shinnery .... made a deep and unfavorable impression..... On a government map of 1834, the Cross Timbers is designated as the 'western boundary of habitable land.' "

My blackjacks of the Osage are not a part of the Cross Timbers of the central part of the state, but they have the same reputation and are just as careless of man's opinion. The blackjacks of the region are cursed by the cattlemen because they harbor screw-flies and other winged pests and because they shade the grass on the sandstone ridges, which is not so good as the limestone grass in the first place. When they are thick and their black, lancelike arms are interlaced, they are almost impenetrable by day and dangerous by night. Range cows penetrate to the center of such strips to drop their calves, and often have screw-worms for their instinctive caution; they cannot be found readily to be treated. Cowboys with bleeding arms and legs, and with torn shirts flapping, come out of such strips swearing, after hours of hide-and-seek with half-wild steers. Some of these steers are never gathered and, with the seasons, become wary and very wise. When they hear the shouting of the roundup, they sneak away through the trees with the stealth and the incredible silence of a bull elk in the pine forest. They freeze like a buck deer and allow the dodging, sweating cowboy to ride within a few yards of them. Their freezing is more remarkable than in the case of a deer's instinctively taking advantage of his coloration, inasmuch as most of them now have the telltale white faces and brick-red bodies of pure-bred Hereford sires and grandsires.

I live on the south edge of the ridge where it is fairly open, but to the north, and spreading out along the north line of the ranch, the typical strip country obtains. The blackjacks are so close together that one seldom sees the dog go down on a covey of quail, and hears only the roar of the wings when they are flushed. This is the area of good sportsmanship where one must be indifferent to the price of shotgun shells and must be satisfied with small bags. It is a perfect area in which to lose an impetuous Irish setter pup among the winter-rusty leaves of the running oaks.

The first time I lost a red puppy in this strip it was quite unintentional. I blew the whistle until the old dogs were circling close to my legs and looking up into my face with that earnest questioning which only dogs can accomplish. There was a tall gray postoak standing like a dignified scoutmaster with the blackjack scouts crowding around him. I sat with my back to it and waited. The old dogs curled up on each side of me, cocking their ears at every sound; they would look intently toward a tree where a nuthatch was loosening bits of bark. They were extremely anxious that the puppy should be found so we could continue our hunting.

I felt that as soon as the puppy became as worried as we were, she would work out the maze that had been our trail for the last two hours. We had been waiting at the tree for an hour when we saw a red streak going full speed through the trees. There was only a glimpse, but one could see that the red streak had its beautiful red plume between its legs. The old dogs ran to overtake the puppy, and I whistled. The blast was for the puppy, but the obedient old dogs came back, looking into my face, and the puppy stopped in her tracks.

I went toward her talking softly, but when she saw me coming, the hair on her back raised and she started away with her bushy tail also protecting her belly. When I stopped, she stopped; and I began to talk soothingly to her. Suddenly she must have caught my scent or the familiar scent of the other dogs. Her tail was raised like a banner, and she allowed herself to pant joyously. I could feel her heart beating wildly as I patted her, but for the remainder of the afternoon she annoyed me by stepping on my heels.

From that afternoon on, being lost in the strip became a part of the training of each red puppy I have owned. Some have been more ingenious than others and have either back-trailed themselves or eventually worked out my trail, but they have all been effectively impressed. I have never had any trouble with runaway dogs, but often they come down in the running oaks when the leaves are as red as themselves and I can't find them. However, they always come back to report to me periodically.

In the heat of the summer we shun the strip. It is the habitat of timber rattlesnakes, and every fly that torments man and animal lives there. In the summer the breezes that sing across the prairie, joyously and refreshingly, become entangled and die there, and sweltering, breathless heat remains dominant.

In the hard days of the old Reservation, every white man had to have a permit issued by the agent. When girls were brought in from Kansas for domestic duty, the family hiring them had to see that their permits were up to date. These and others employed by the agency had to have special permission to enter and remain. These permits allowed them to live for a certain time in the Reservation, employed at certain work, but they were not allowed to remain in the Reservation after death.

This constituted a problem. As in other places in the history of the early West, a man was not always anxious to talk of his past, and as long as he behaved himself, he was not too closely questioned. When such people died on the Reservation, there was no known connection between them and any living soul on earth. The agent must scratch his head and look again at the regulations concerning such matters, then ask the government carpenter to make a coffin out of wood. There was nothing to do but let the dead person lie until a coffin could be knocked together and a man hired to haul the dead man to the Kansas line, there to turn him over to the outside world for identification. There he could be shipped off in the train or buried in one of the little towns along the border.

The situation was not too urgent in the winter, but things had to be done with speed in the summer, in preparation for the two-day trip by lumber wagon over the sandstone-ledged hills and the prairie. Before the bearded, not too happy freighter started with his load, one last gesture was made to the decencies. The body was placed on a bed of blackjack leaves and decorously and tenderly covered with them. In some manner the cool leaves of the blackjack on a terrifically hot day protected the body to a certain extent from the effect of the heat. In any case, the best the people of the Reservation could do for an unfortunate brother in a hard world gave rise to one of the two practical uses of the tree.

We cannot make posts of them, and their grain is twisted and useless for lumber, but they make a hot fire in the fireplace either green or dead, and the smoke is as pleasant in its way as pine smoke, especially to one who can associate it with so many pleasant hours.

When I approach the little sandstone house after a day in the field, dragging heavy feet, the odor of the smoke which is often whipped to the ground by the restless autumn winds floods me with happiness. Inspired by the scent, the whole day comes into review; from the odor of the leaves and the earth in the frost of the morning, to the last red flash of a setter emerging from the russet running oaks with a bird in her mouth, just as the sun slid into the prairie.

Sometimes I leave a kerosene lamp burning so that I shall not be compelled to grope about in the darkness of the interior. When I return after nightfall, it is the only thing that breaks the blackness of the ridge. Its dim, apologetic beam falls into the tree by the south window and becomes an upland will-o'-the-wisp.

When I first came out to the blackjacks, I held the belief that every comfort and every pleasure that depended upon some definite action of labor was all the sweeter. After ten years I have found this to be quite true in a daily life of practical compensations. I have never felt that my solitude, the absence of servants of any sort, and the absence of people in general, except for occasional visitors, was dearly bought or that the labor necessary to attain comfort was ever onerous. Only in supplying a great fireplace with wood have I failed in my original plan.

To feed a fireplace six months out of the year with logs three feet long is hard work for one man with only a two-man saw and an ax. My fireplace is insatiable, and I must cut enough wood in October to last through the winter. In September the days are still too hot for wood-cutting, and even in October the sun hangs on one's back, and the sap that oozes from the green blackjacks attracts all the flies in the country.

Also the duck season begins in October, and when the Mississippi Valley flight is on, there is no time to be lost in such practical activity as wood-cutting. The flight may last several days or a week, but there are always those days when one must go out anyway with the eternal hope that the vanguard of the flight has appeared on the prairie, or after the flight has come and gone one goes out with the hope that that which was thought to be the flight was not really the main flight after all.

I have attempted to use local men at the other end of my saw, but that method has never worked out very well; they want to sit and talk about cattle and horses and grass, and I keep looking at the sky for V's of geese.

I had a young man come over to help me, but his thoughts were certainly not on wood-cutting. The first morning I was impressed. He had just come back from the C.C.C. camp and he showed me with pride how he had learned to carry an ax in the hand as one walked, with the blade down and forward, not over the shoulder in the manner of the ignorant past. He carried the ax from the house to the wood-cutting grounds almost perfectly, but somehow my methods of the benighted period of pre-C.C.C. were more effective in the felling and chopping of trees. He lasted two and a half days, then hitchhiked into town.

To have the Longleys cut my wood from the north strip is much better. There the blackjacks are so thick that the sapling postoaks haven't much chance for full growth until they are cut away, so that the sapling can reach the sun and the air. Even though a hundred running oaks spring up around it, the advantage remains with the sapling as it fights for, and wins, a place in the sun. To have the Longleys cut in the north strip has many advantages.

During hot, dry summers, when the breezes from across the prairie out of the south die in the blackjacks or reach my house only as the little wavelets that roll gently along the sandy beach as remnants of the great waves that have broken offshore, I am determined at such times to get my next winter's wood from those trees to the south which interfere with my comfort. When the cool weather comes, I get everything ready, then go down to the point south of the house, full of business. I stand for a while, then start marking the trees that ought to be cut—the slanting ones and those that seem to be diseased, with black tree blood running from their sores. In the end, however, I find that I have marked only three or four, and am sitting, wondering at the beauty of the others. There is one, for example, that seems to be growing on a flat sandstone rock without visible soil support. This tree seems to symbolize a biological triumph indicating a glorious destiny for its species. One cannot cut a tree that has struggled so magnificently through winds and cold and curling heat, to stand erect on a sandstone rock. When I look at this tree, I always feel that Paul Sears, famed botanist and friend, should be here to appreciate it with me.

Many of the other trees south of the house that have caused me to swelter during the hottest summers are left standing for other reasons; perhaps because they are so symmetrical, or so straight, or because a last year's nest of a red-tailed hawk looms like a brush pile in one of them, and the redtail always comes back to add a little more trash to his home.

The bulky nest of a savage-eyed hawk or the nest of a biologically triumphant crow seems natural and in harmony among the ruthless and savage blackjacks. Even the nest of the ruby-throated hummingbird, like a lichen-covered eyecup on a lichen-covered limb, seems proper and harmonious, but I cannot visualize the nest of a park or city garden bird in them.

The brown thrasher that comes each spring to sit in the top of one of the five within the fence seems to sing with the thrill of the danger he might feel, balancing on the topmost twig of the savage tree. The mockingbird that comes later in the summer to sit delicately balanced on the top of one of them seems as out of harmony as a canary that has escaped his cage to flutter about the garden with pounding heart. This is only the impression which the rugged, primitive blackjacks inspire. Certainly the mockingbird sang along the ridges long before the white man came to make towns and gardens; it is a matter of associating him with other birds often seen in parks and gardens, sitting on telephone poles or swaying in the tops of Lombardy poplars.

The blackjack-covered ridges are like a water hole on the desert where animals and birds come to drink at certain times of the day, depending on the habits of their enemies. The ridges rising abruptly from the prairie offering shade and concealment, and even water, though man-produced, are in effect oases. In the winter the birds come for shelter to the ticking brown leaves, and in the summer to the shade of the glistening green ones. These, however, are indigenous birds, since most of the winter residents stay along the creek bottom among the briars and heavy brush piles.

During the autumn and spring migrations I see strange birds that come to rest on my ridge after their long flights. Besides the northern robins flying home from the South in the spring, there are white-crowned sparrows, myrtle warblers, vireos, and many others strange to the blackjacks. Their chatter and bits of halfhearted song cause me to drop whatever I am doing and go out with the glasses, since an unfamiliar note strikes to the very bottom of my consciousness, so well do I know the accustomed voices. At such times I see birds that breed in the hard loneliness of the Hudson Bay region or in the cities and the gardens of the Great Lakes—birds which I must travel hundreds of miles to see otherwise and know only through books.

Of course, the most thrilling migrants are the ducks and geese from the Far North. The Canada geese seem to use my ridge, pointing south, as a beacon, when they come over in the autumn, and they fly low over my little house, which, except for its composition roof, looks exactly like a whimsical arrangement of sandstone to them. They often sit on the ponds of the ranch and settle on the prairie to rest en route.

In the spring the snow geese that seem to fly at night on their autumn migration fly back north leisurely during the daylight hours as well. Their whiteness is so startling above the blackjacks that even the setters notice them and whine eagerly until they are out of sight.

One extremely hard winter a snowy owl drifted to my ridge, during a year of no rabbits in his own northern domain, I assume. He was like a naked man in a city street, his whiteness screaming his presence to the world of blackjack and prairie. He must have had very difficult hunting even among the many rabbits of the ridge, at least until a heavy snow fell for his protection. The bluejays, titmice, and even the chickadees tormented him during the day. One night as I was riding home, he became a ghost to my horse, as he silently flew out of a tree over our heads. I was almost left in the running oaks before I could get my range pony soothed. Eventually the crows hounded the northern ghost-bird from the ridges, harassing him from daylight to darkness, then picking up again the next morning, like hounds picking up a lost trail.

If my country was once heavily forested, it might well have been with blackjacks and postoak, standing on the standstone cap rock which has long since been eroded and is represented now only by my sandstone ridges covered by the remnants of the forest, and now struggling to survive like an animal at bay. I, being ephemeral, cannot comprehend their struggle as a species, spread over hundreds of years, against the groping fingers of erosion, but must see them as the eternal backdrop to the drama of my ridges. I can see only the struggle of the individuals against winds and drought, fire and disease, and sometimes I think I can see evidence of natural disintegration, especially of those in the stage of senility. They seem to go fast once they reach this stage, falling victims to the virility of other growths, to insects, woodpeckers, and high winds. After seeing their aged ones fall, they do not seem so awfully eternal, even though the Osage hunters who went to fight with the French against Braddock and George Washington might have rested under one of the many that shade my ridge.

Just as I had felt awe in thinking of the span of several hundred years which my blackjacks were allowed as individuals until I saw evidence of their mortality inspiring me with confidence and greater feeling of intimacy, so did I feel awe in the thought of the thousands of years allowed the ridge itself. But after finding evidence of its mortality, I felt that even the backdrop and the stage were actors in our little drama, and the sense of intimacy grew with the finding of the evidence of that which had been academic knowledge.

One summer, during a severe drought, a great prairie fire swept up over the ridge, running before a high south wind through sere bluestem stirrup-high. It devoured all my outbuildings and darted its orange, snake's tongue at the little sandstone house without effect. The dogs and I gave way before it reluctantly and retreated to the ranch house for help. It was finally stopped at the canyon, and in the running oaks north of the house, by the men from three ranches and by the aid of the labor crew from the railroad, who had followed it from its point of origin at their line, snapping at its flanks like buffalo wolves.

I did not return to the ridge until the next spring, after the heavy winter and spring rains. Although the charred grass and debris had been washed away, the earth was still barren of life; only the surviving blackjacks stood like potted plants on the floor of a theater stage. Every dent and bump and wrinkle of the earth was brought out by the spring sun, and every stone lay discovered like a dead fish on a dry lake bed.

I took my tape measure and walked along the crest of the ridge. I measured the exposed parts of the roots of the charred bluestem tussocks and found that the life of my ridge had been shortened by nearly one-half inch during one terrific agitation of nature's balance. The hairy fingers were feeling their way up its flanks, and I, the ephemeral one, had seen them groping.

I
SPRING

▌▌▌▌   JUST-DOING-THAT MOON

THE OSAGE SAY THAT THE MOON IS A WOMAN AND THAT SHE MAKES HER appearance twelve times a year. With this periodicity and the tremendous effects she has upon the earth and its children, it is natural that she should be a woman. When she attains full glory and dominates the ridges, there is never any disturbance by the male element, and all is tranquil as under the soothing hand of a great mother. Grandfather the Sun has gone to rest, and even Father the Fire is dim in her presence, as though out of a traditional understanding and deference, like a great warrior in camp where woman is supreme.

At dawn she leaves, they say, as a good woman should, taking her children, the stars, with her, so as not to disturb Grandfather the Sun when he takes over the male world of daytime. She goes on silent moccasins and with modesty befitting a woman.

Each one of her twelve appearances has special significance, and the Osage have designated them and given each appearance a name characteristic of its significance to their bit of earth. They knew nothing about Janus, Mars, or the Caesars, Julius and Augustus, but they knew about the Moon Woman and her influence upon their earth.

Spring comes to the blackjacks in March, and, roughly, this period is the Osage Just-Doing-That Moon. This is the time of great restlessness in nature; and when they said that the Moon Woman was "just doing that," they made a futile attempt to describe her actions. She is like a pampered, tempermental woman who changes from tears and tragic weeping to ecstatic laughter within the hour, during this period of change from winter to summer.

For days the hot winds blow from the Gulf or from the semidesert of the Southwest, bringing lassitude and causing people to look hopefully toward the northwest for clouds, seeking relief, yet fearing the form which relief may take in this whimsical Just-Doing-That Moon.

When nerves are on edge and the enervating heat has sapped vitality and the body is sticky with unseasonable sweat, people grow short-tempered and morbid and are possessed with the fear of impending danger, and there is resentment against those ceaseless winds that seem so purposeful in setting the stage for disaster.

They sometimes die at night only to take up their blowing again at sunrise. I have gone to bed at night hoping fervently that the next sunrise would bring tranquility and that the meadowlarks would sing again from the fence posts. Often I stand watching the light against the southern horizon, hoping that the wind will change or that rain will come before the prairie fire reaches my south pasture.

At such times the air is filled with the smoke of burning prairie grass, and the cowboys must leave their work to fight the fire with wet sacks and backfiring. When helpless to stop it, they turn it off toward some wide road or highway, canyon or creek. After they return to the ranch house with red eyes and blackened faces, the tracks of the water wagon across the charred prairie glisten in the sun until rain comes.

After darkness brings calm, the Moon Woman may not appear with her full benignity to soften the effects of her tantrums, but the kindliness of her reign is felt, and, though the acrid odor hangs in the air, the fires that move against the distant hillsides fascinate all who look at them and compensate with beauty and peace for the heartbreaking day.

When the winds move into the west, clouds of dust from the grassless plains and the wheat fields of western Kansas, Oklahoma, and Texas creep like fog over the blackjacks, making ghosts of the trees and producing a silence that is sinister. The winds seem to die under their heavy burden, and the dust rolls in under its own impetus, shutting out the sun and disembodying the voices of the restless range cows and unhappy calves. The crows caw and flap by my windows like somber spirits of the half-lighted world.

But if every first moon of the spring were like this, Just-Doing-That Moon would have little significance. There are always the hot winds from the south, and the winds from the west and the southwest, but during some springs the rains come often and in abundance before the winds have blown themselves out. For several years there has been no dust rolling in like poison gas, making the early weeds of the prairie into queer animals in the eerie light, but you never know what will come; you can never guess what Just-Doing-That Moon will do from year to year.

During the wet springs the hot winds blow steadily for several days, then suddenly the clouds mass in the northwest, and a breath from the spring blizzards in the Rockies rolls in to meet the unseasonable heat carried from the south; rolling over the hot air, it soon seeks by its weight to settle to the earth, and the former is pushed up by the pressure. This is the time when hope for relief struggles with fear in the hearts of the children of the earth. Spiraling winds fall in funnel-shaped clouds to the earth and roar like a freight train over subterranean cavities, and man and his houses become playthings of the wind's madness. The air of the interior of buildings, finding that there is no pressure on the outside because of the vacuum formed by the whirling winds, explodes like dynamite to fill the vacuum that nature will not tolerate and crumbles the brick and steel as though they were bits of paper.

While the fantastic funnels play over the prairie and blackjacks like toe dancers, touching here and there, the rain comes down in torrents, whipped by the crazy winds. Sometimes hailstones fall and bounce or, shattering, add to the Wagnerian drama. When they have lifted into the clouds again, or have worn themselves out by frantic whirling far away to the northeast, the cold air has displaced the heated layer, and man counts the cost of the destruction of life and property.

Great clearings are made through the blackjacks and resemble the preparatory work for some superhighway, or the trees that have not been blown down stand stripped and jagged like those in a battle zone. The air, after these maniacal displays, is usually seasonal and fresh, and the tree toads sing their evening chorus; the meadowlarks sing, and the blackbirds flock to the blackjacks to bow and ruffle their feathers in their nuptial ritual just before sunset.

During the dry springs the people forget their fear of tornadoes, but Just-Doing-That Moon may bring them again as she listens to their prayers for rain, or she may drench the earth until the ravines and the canyons roar, and the creeks and the rivers become yellow and chocolate-colored and lap at the spans of the bridges, carrying away crops and outhouses and other things that man in his confidence has built within their domain.

Often the spring is so wet and cold that the grass is retarded, and ranchers must wait until the warm sun starts the growth before they can receive the great trainloads of cattle that the cowboys poke out of the stock cars and drive to the pastures. Just as often, however, they must wait for rains to start the grass and fill the ponds.

One year when some poor cattle came to my pastures too soon, the Cowhand said, as he watched them move about nosing the dead grass of the past season, "If it don't rain purty soon, we're gonna hafta put sticks under them Arkansas'." Then, after looking at them with contempt, he continued, "I don't know what the ole man paid fer 'em, but looks like to me they ain't never gonna dollar out."

Not only do the years vary during the reign of Just-Doing-That Moon but no two days are alike. One may be mild and sun-drenched, with the earth almost spongy underfoot, with the prairie lying in emerald undulations in the clear light, the little wet-weather brooks talking merrily and the prairie pools glistening, while the cardinals say exactly what I feel about such days. The cardinal song with the liquid notes of the red-winged blackbird and the silly cheerfulness of the meadowlark make a queer, irresponsible chorus. A day when the white-face calves romp with tails high about their placid mothers; a picture-book spring day.

The next day may be squally, with clouds racing across the sky in opposite directions—clouds whipped by crazy winds high above, their edges raveled like torn shawls. A day of uncertainty and ominous playfulness of the winds above; winds that seem to circle in confusion, not knowing whether to blow north or south, driving the clouds like a befuddled flock of migrant birds.

I watch the mad cloud game with a feeling of unrest, knowing that the conditions are right for the formation of the dreaded funnel which might drop to the blackjacks at any moment and dance its tarantella of destruction across the country.

During one period of my life I was fascinated by these frenzies of nature and used to watch the distant funnels move wantonly across the prairie from a safe place on the edge of a cave-spotted canyon. One day as a boy, as I sat on my pony at the point of a ridge, I watched a tornado wipe out a little town of the Osage. After the storm, which had held me fascinated, I rode down into the valley among the debris. The people had recovered from their fright and were standing in groups, each with his dramatic story to tell. There were mattresses hanging in the tall sycamores along the creek, and, as I rode to investigate this strange thing, my horse shied, and I saw the first dead man I had ever seen.

The blackjacks have shed their brown leaves of winter by this time, and they etch their bare branches into the afterglow as the very red sun sinks slowly into the prairie. It is during this time that the vultures come back from wherever they go and circle high above the prairie. The people say that when these birds appear, there will be no more frost, but to me their appearance seems to be based on their knowledge of the habits of range cattle. Range cows will struggle through the winter only to die as the first grass appears, and the weakling calves die and make the vultures' food supply abundant.

I am quite ready to believe that they hunt by sight. If that is true, the fact makes of them a remarkable bird, inasmuch as they must be the only bird or animal of the ridges that can penetrate protective coloration. Certainly a dead cow or horse can be seen from the air, but there are many small animals that die in their natural environment. Death imposes its own special body conformations, but many animals also die and retain natural positions. Those animals sprawled out in death, no matter how protectively colored, cannot escape the eye of the vulture; but I do not know what leads him to those in natural positions. Perhaps the coyotes and the opossums find them through scent, pull them about until they assume the outlines of death, so that the circling vulture might descend to his feast. The omnivorous coyotes and opossums are first-rate assistants to the scavenger-in-chief of the ridges.

I must assume that the vultures have no well-developed olfactory sense, but certainly I do not know. I believe that the Osage told Audubon that they do not have. Perhaps the high development of an olfactory sense in a bird that remains high in the air much of the time would be useless, inasmuch as scents lie close to the earth; and if the bird hunted by scent alone, it would seem that he must fly close to the earth to catch the currents. Flying thus, they would give little pleasure; hanging against the upper currents, or circling against the blue of the sky, they are the most graceful of the large birds, with a beauty in flight that is fascinating. On the rare occasions when I see them perched in a quarreling circle around a newly made hole in a carcass, I never linger long enough to become disgusted.

I never remember them except with pleasure, since they do not obtrude as the zopolotes do in Mexico. I feel with the others of my country that they are the harbingers of spring. With all their unpleasant habits, I sense no unpleasant associations when they appear in their purposeful circles, calm and conservative in this unstable season. I forget their nasty habit of using regurgitation as a defense weapon and man's use of them as unpleasant symbols in poetry and political cartoons. Their pariah role was made necessary for their existence in the great drama of the species, and their sharp eyes, their featherless, obscene heads, and their glorious power of flight are necessary adjustments to that role.

Since they cannot go out with assurance that their hunger will be satisfied when hunger inspires them, they often gorge themselves with food, until they are unable to lift themselves from the prairie if there is no wind into which they can launch themselves. In this helpless state they could be taken by their enemies easily, but apparently they have no enemies among the birds and animals, and man seems to be quite indifferent to them despite their size. Bobcats sometimes destroy their nests in the cliffs along Bird Creek, not for the purpose of using them for food, but to oust them from likely bobcat dens.

I have no fear that they will ever come to sit on my roof like so many glum patients in a doctor's anteroom, since the food supply of the ridges is limited in normal times by the deaths. Only in case of catastrophe would they come in great numbers, as indeed they have done during one month of my life among the blackjacks.

Robins come to the ridges in flocks now, that American thrush that was named for the redbreast of England by the early settlers and has nothing in common with him except a reddish-brown breast. There are robins on the ridge all winter, despite the inevitable "first-robin" stories in the papers every spring, but I don't know whether they are the indigenous ones or northern robins that have stopped here. There may be a complete change in my robin population during the winter, or my residents remain and the northern robin hops over them to more southern regions. I have noticed that the groups and families of the same species do have a certain respect for each other—respect for range and food supply. Invasions usually are the movements of one species into the domain of another. They seem to feel instinctively that the species to which they belong should not be handicapped in its struggle to survive, and they tend to spread little by little into other regions if their numbers become momentarily greater rather than attempt to displace members of their own species.

This is perhaps a primitive, undisturbed tendency, and when a species reaches the stage of development which man has reached, hopelessly bound by his own artificialities, it will find that survival demands intraspecies struggle. Man, become dominant, has triumphed over his enemies among the other species, with the exception of the insects, and now finds himself struggling against himself, encumbering himself through the protection of his unfit and worrying over the matter of reconciling his primal tendencies with his dreams.

The distances are greater now since the leaves have gone from the trees, and the vistas are strange and sometimes disturbing, especially when a light appears far across the night prairie, or a speck of white gleams in the sun through the black branches of the blackjacks far to the south. I suddenly feel that the earth is becoming a little crowded.

Soon, however, the tassels start on the bare branches, to grow into dangling blooms, and the new grass begins to show among the copper-colored grass of the last season. On the very tops of the ridges where the sandstone is near the surface and there is little old grass to hide it, the tender, green shoots become green stripes down the backs of the ridges.

The crow becomes secretive now, and one must be quite observant to see the beginnings of the bulky nests in the blackjacks. They are built with ingenuity and are made to look exactly like last year's nests, with no evidence of freshly broken sticks. They are made a little ragged at the under edges so as to appear as the battered, weathered nests of last year should appear. The builder is quiet now; extremely conservative and silent. He flies low against the spring winds among the black boles of the trees, showing himself as little as possible. He pretends to be utterly disinterested in the happenings of the blackjacks, and only if a giraffe appeared suddenly would he give way to his instinct to be first with the dramatic latest.

He spends much time at this season walking precisely over the recently burned spots on the prairie, picking up things to eat; early slugs perhaps. He is omnivorous and will eat anything from grain, fruit, fish, and carrion to the eggs and nestlings of other birds.

The crows do not fly in flocks during this period, the mated pairs staying to themselves. Their nests are never in colonies; as a matter of fact, they are usually far apart. One year a pair built in a tree just outside the corner of my fence, and I didn't notice the nest until I saw them sneaking in with food for the young. I never knew whether they had assumed that I should never think of looking for a nest under my nose, so to speak, or whether they had misjudged my absence in Washington. In any case, they figuratively sweated with nervousness until they got the young ones away. I even got the impression that they were force-feeding them, which in the case of nestlings is almost impossible, since they will eat several times their own weight within a few hours.

The whistling of the cardinal becomes more persistent and confident, especially on the days when the earth is fresh and there is no wind. When rains come and the clouds have melted and the tree toads become ecstatic, he will whistle clearly to the world that spring is here. But, like man and the other species, he is susceptible to the moods of the earth. When the winds hiss through the coppery grass of last season, and only the titmice and the early wrens throw their joy away on the mad whims of Just-Doing-That Moon, the cardinal sits huddled up on the lee side of a tree trunk and whistles with half a heart, not believing that which he wants to tell the world.

If the moon shows herself during this period of her madness, she almost makes the world forget her tantrums. Her smile may be cold, and the bare branches of the trees cast their shadows over the grass so that they look like fretted iron. The coyotes will invariably greet her with choruses from several directions and from varying distances, disturbed like poets who can't write poetry.

The great horned owl floats up from the creek bottom like a dark ghost and booms out over the ridges, frightening life into even greater silence. Sometimes he seems to carry on conversation with other owls, far and near, through a series of booms and screams, caring little at such times whether he frightens possible prey into long-held rigidity. The owls do this when they are not hungry and not hunting seriously, it seems; simply one of their expressions satisfying some playful urge perhaps. During the remainder of the year their booming is the serious weapon of the hunter, and this ridiculous, ghoulish shrieking and irresponsible booming could be associated with their nuptials; if so, a description of this symbol of wisdom and dignity bobbing up and down and ruffling his feathers, and bowing in the moonlight as he snaps his beak, ought to be tremendously interesting, if not disillusioning, to those who insist that the owl is filled with wisdom and dignity.

I am not an ornithologist and my interpretations of those things which I see constantly among the birds about me are for my own pleasure. I should like to be accurate for my own satisfaction, but I seldom compare statements and conclusions of others with my own, owing chiefly to my laziness in the matter of fine-print scholarship. I have watched the nuptial dances of many birds and animals—perhaps the word "antics" would be more proper in the case of the latter —and, after appreciating them as nuptial displays, I have gone about as far as I can go. Why some of these dances are so prolonged and so emotional and elaborate, I cannot guess, and no one has been able to guess for me—at least to my satisfaction. Nature is so lavish in her desire to prolong the fighting existence of the species that she sees to it that millions of germs are released and millions of eggs laid to assure the development of one or a few individuals. She must build up an excess of sexual emotion in the species during certain times of the year to insure that her plans will be carried out with emotion left over, or, rather, she builds up the emotion so that the very little needed for the actual contact between male and female will be certified, the other to be used up in fevered nuptial activity and preparation.

Naturally I wondered about the owls that came to the ridge every March to scream at each other like outraged witches or boom back and forth at each other to disturb the peace of the heavy spring nights. One day I saw Louie and asked him to come out and tell me what my owls were doing and saying. He had told me that he could call them up and talk with them and that the best time to do it was in March.

Louie came out about dusk. We drove down as far as we could into the creek bottom, then walked down into the tall timber. Louie noticed me in my attempts to find some place for concealment. "You don't hafta hide, that-a-way," he said. "Them owls don't care 'bout nothin' when they do this here big talkin'."

He chose a sycamore log and sat with his back against it. He pulled his plug of tobacco out of dirty paper and offered it to me. When I refused, he looked at it critically, as though wondering how long it would last, then bit into it and jerked his head from side to side like a dog tearing at a carcass.

We sat for some time, then he said, "Moon's comin'." It was a typical March moon, red and large and startling. The coyotes began their song to it from the hills on the west, then stopped as suddenly as they had begun. Then far down the valley an owl boomed. In the darkness Louie's Indian face was indistinct, but I could smell him in the heavy air; a mixture of wood smoke, fried pork fat, and tobacco.

The tree toads set up a chorus, then stopped abruptly just as the coyotes had done. The silence became heavy but not expectant. It seemed that all life had left the earth. It was too early for the grass-roots songs of the insects; too early in the season.

I heard Louie spit, and he seemed to take in a tremendous amount of air, then he sang out, "Hoo hoo, hoo hoo, hoo hoo-o-o-o-ah." There was a long silence, then from quite near there was an answer. Immediately his "hoo hoo-o-o-o-ahing" became confidential and assumed a conversational tone, a coaxing, seductive tone; and the answers were in the same tone.

I could see several owls against the moon, which was now above the tree tops and was smaller and had turned from brick-red to silver. They sat against the moon like storybook owls, and occasionally one would become agitated and walk along the limb of a sycamore, then peer down at us with some misgivings. They talked among themselves and with Louie in that confidential, conversational tone, but did no bobbing and fluffing as I expected them to do. One would fly silently away, and then he would come back, or another would join the half-dozen already there, but there was no shrieking and no distant booming at each other as they were accustomed to do on the ridge. It was a convention of owls with a deep common urge but lacking the confidence to express it. The convention was chairmaned by an obliging, detached Cherokee, who was perfectly willing to let time and moonlight flow over him on silent owl's wings, while his thoughts played indolently elsewhere.

The horned larks come back to the dusty roads leading from the blackjacks to town. They fly in front of the car and do acrobatic stunts just ahead of me; aerial maneuvers that would indicate the expression of some annual sexual emotion. They are always along the road and always ready to fly up and keep just ahead of the car.

The prairie chickens come to the ridge for the last time in flocks to feed the acorns. They come in from the high prairie to the north; low into the wind, sometimes just clearing the roof of my house. Later during this time they begin their dances on the green tops of the high prairie hills.

Despite the flow of time that changes the earth and its inhabitants every year, every season, and every day, and the progression of life, there are certain things that happen with regularity and become symbols of the seasons. The appearance of these things gives me confidence in the impression that things are permanent, since I cannot see the subtle changes that go on about me. We men want to cling to the things we know and bind ourselves with tradition, even though constant adjustment in all forms of life is imperative to survival.

Each spring I watch for the first shoots of the bluestem and for the faint yellow-green tint that indicates the tassel blooms of the blackjacks and the postoaks. I listen for the chatter of the swifts that come out of nowhere, to resume their life in my chimney with their colony of nests, and each morning I stand out in the yard listening intently for the distant booming of the prairie chickens. When I hear the snow geese or the Canadians fly over my little house in the night, I always feel a sharp sadness over my earth-bound condition. Visions of pebble-edged lakes, arctic willows, and tundra come to me as I listen; then all is flooded with the contentment that I feel in knowing that things are happening at the appointed time and in the accustomed manner, and all is well. Man does not want to be swept on with the silent, relentless jungle river of time, moving so imperceptively past his familiar landmarks. While he resents monotony, he feels safer with it and seems to fall into routine instinctively. Monotony is not imposed upon him by the natural forces but is sired by his own biology and lack of imagination and unintelligent interest in things about him.

Since he has been relieved by his phenomenal development from constant watchfulness to protect his life, he has lost much of the zest for living which the ever alert lower species have, but is still urged by the other primal instincts, and fights with the other species against the flow that carries him on.

When spring comes to the ridges, even though it comes with female madness, I am not so sensitive to the flow. The return of familiar things at the appointed time gives me confidence and a feeling of permanence, and time seems to become slightly sluggish with the new hope and the awaiting of the glory that never quite arrives.

During this season of vague hopes and vague plans and the return of bubbling life to the ridges, there was a man-arranged certainty—the visit of Les Claypoole.

Les had lived on the Beaver Creek ranch for thirty-eight years, more than half of them since my father's death. He never had a written contract with my father, and our names never appeared on an agreement. The rental money was due each year on the first day of March, and on that date he appeared with the check. A blizzard howled across the prairie one March first. The trains panted idly behind great drifts, and the telephone lines sagged and broke with the weight of the snow, but he forced his horse through the storm to the nearest telephone and eventually got a connection.

"Say," he shouted, "I don't see how in hell a man's gonna git into town to do business; she's raisin' hell up here."

"It's bad here, too," I answered.

"Yeah, but how in hell's a man gonna git his rent paid?"

"Well, you'll have to wait until the thaw comes—no hurry, is there?"

"Reckon not, but the rent money's due today, and a—I don't see no way in this world to get there with it, lessen a man's to wait a few days—that all right with you?"

"Certainly; wait a week if you want to."

From the way he was shouting through the phone, I imagined he was trying to shout above the roar of the wind around the wooden railroad station.

He left the saddle in 1902 to start his own outfit on the Beaver Creek ranch, and for thirty-eight years he saddled his horse every day and left him standing in the shed, ready. Even after he bought his first model-T Ford he kept his horse saddled, ready for any emergency, so powerful was the habit formed during the hard years when he made a hand driving the great cattle herds to Dodge City during the days when a cowboy slept in his wet clothes and used his saddle for a pillow.

His face was like weathered granite, and his steel-gray eyes and his silence, as he looked at his great gold watch with the hunting case, caused me to feel like a guilty schoolboy when I was late for a meeting with him. He wore a big black hat of the early days, and it was the first thing he put on as he sat on the edge of his bed at four o'clock each morning, catching it behind and not in front. Then he took a chew of tobacco.

After he had started the fire in the kitchen stove, he did his morning chores, then washed, with great snorting and sniffing, and dried his face and hands on a roller towel hanging behind the door. He went to the radio, put on his glasses, and dialed until he found the station at Wichita, Kansas, which had a program of cowboy music. When the volume filled the house, he would look up and say, "HOTdam." Sometimes if his stomach was in good order, he would get up from his chair, wave his great black hat, and do a buck-and-wing on the pine flooring, giving a Comanche yell as he finished.

When he first got his radio, he spent all his leisure time dialing and looking expectantly at it over his glasses, but no cowboy music nor the romantic lure of shortwave could hold him after he had opened the great gold watch and clicked the case shut with finality at nine o'clock each night.

"Them fellers got my money fer this here thing, but they ain't gonna make me lose no goddam sleep over it," he would say with a throaty giggle that sounded like "kek, kek, kek."

He would drive up to my gate with a flourish, push his great hat forward, then say something about damned fools living high up on a sandstone ridge.

"Your pa sure would be proud of you," he once said, "lettin' your grass out and not a hoof of stock of your own."

We had our traditional dinner of steak and beer, then would sit and talk about the many things that plague men; about the poor quality of farm and ranch workers, and neighbors who won't do what they say they'll do; about fences that must be replaced since the last flood, and the price of cattle.

After we had discussed the important things in life, and just before nine o'clock, he would turn to me with a lewd twinkle and say, "Bin doin' any good with the town gals—oughtta be some purty high-steppin' heifers about town, you bein' so clost."

At nine o'clock he would get up and go outside and look long at the sky, then come back in and say, "Well, where's my stall?"

The last time he came to see me, he didn't come to pay rental, but he came the first of March out of habit. His presence gave me the usual feeling that all was well and regular and that things would go on as they had been going, with that regularity that gave man confidence even when the constant changes worked within him as well as around him.

But Les was upset, and I was slightly shocked that anything could affect his down-to-earth reasonableness. After a long silence he said, "That new neighbor, fella that moved in after I left, is a-plowin' with a goddam tractor, and him a-settin on that hilltop, and not enough pasture fer a goose to git fat on." He continued: "A tearin' hell outta good limestone grass that never in this world'ull come back." Then, after a long pause: "Can't git nobuddy to do nothin' anymore—like it oughtta be done. The sorriest set of goddam road lizzards in this world. They lope around in them tin lizzies, load up with a herd of empty-headed heifers that oughtta, bigod, be in bed, er a-heppin' their mammys tu home, and they go to them roller-skatin' outfits and roll around in a goddam circle all night. Nex mornin' course, they aint worth a steer's tit—as fur as workin'."

He yawned and looked at the clock, then said: "Kek, kek, kek, bigod; you bin a-goin' to Washin'ton so much your're a-gittin' to be jist like them biscuit-eaters up there—why don'cha set that clock the way it oughtta be set?"

"That's war time," I said.

He tapped the great gold watch with his reptilian-like finger: "This watch's bin a-carryin' the Lord's time fer fifty years, and I don't aim to hev it carry no other. What-cha s'pose the Lord hung the goddam sun fer if He aimed to hev man a-monkeyin' with His time?"

IV

THE PLANTING MOON CORRESPONDS WITH THE MONTH OF APRIL AND IS the shortest name in the Osage calendar. They say simply, "Wah-Pee," and that includes all the rather involved ceremonies of planting and growth: the collection and care of wild lily roots, the gathering of wild onions, and the preparation of the symbolic robes for the children.

All this is woman's work, the female children of the earth planning with Mother Earth and the Moon Woman for the coming of the fruits of the earth; preparing for the nuptials of ageless earth and Grandfather the Sun and all his male manifestations. Certain ceremonies were performed and songs were sung, and often, as they sang their planting songs, the April rains would slant from the sky with a solitary cloud as their source, while the sun, still present, made the raindrops sparkle with life.

Old Ee-Nah-Apee told me one time in her slow, broken English: "My son, you asked about this here Wah-Pee, what we call Plantin' Moon. Some time we call it woman's moon—that's what we say; woman's moon, but we just say that 'cause it's Plantin' Moon. Some time we call Just-Doing-That Moon, crazy woman moon too, but it ain't that.

"L-o-o-o-ong time ago we used to have them bags, I guess you call it, made out of grass. We put corn in these here bags, and we put them on our back; we tie them too with buckskin strings on our back. We go there with long pole in our hand too. We stand there at that place where we gonna plant that corn. We stand there with that pole in right hand, and we look at Grandfather the Sun. We have cleaned all them weeds and stuff off from that place where we gonna plant this here corn; we make little opah, hehn? What you call it hills, hehn?

"Purty soon womens go to them little—hills, I guess, and they make hole with that pole on south side of that there hill. They used to say Grandfather sure would see them holes in them hills on south side, that-a-way. We put corn in them hills, in them little holes; and when we have all of 'em with corn in it, we put our feets on it. We stand on them little hills and make drum against the earth with them poles and sing purty song."

She would then sing the song for me, and, though it fascinated me, I am not sure that I remember it very well, so I have gone elsewhere for a free translation of it:

I have made a footprint, a sacred one.
I have made a footprint, through it the blades push upward.
I have made a footprint, through it the blades radiate.
I have made a footprint, over it the blades float in the wind.
I have made a footprint, over it the ears lean toward one another.
I have made a footprint, over it I pluck the ears.
I have made a footprint, over it I bend the stalks to pluck the ears.
I have made a footprint, over it the tassels lie gray.
I have made a footprint, smoke rises from my lodge.
I have made a footprint, there is cheer in my lodge.
I have made a footprint, I live in the light of day.

When she had finished, she would look at me with a new light in her eyes and then laugh as though she were embarrassed by recalling such primitive things that the tribe was now attempting to put away forever. "That was a l-o-o-o-ong time ago," she would say in a patronizing manner, but even so she had lived in those days, and she had great happiness in recalling them.

"Which foot, mother," I once asked her, "did you use to cover the corn?"

"Like always for Chesho it is lef foot, and for Hunkah right one."

She referred to the grand division of the tribe represented by Chesho, the Sky People, and Hunkah, the Earth People, the Sky People being the peace division and the Earth People being the war division.

We do no planting on the ranch, except in a small way. We sometimes plant small fields to kaffir for barnyard feeding and lespedeza in thrown-out fields that are slow in coming back to bluestem. I often have kaffir planted in little half-acre clearings for the prairie chickens and quail. Naturally it is never harvested but left for their harvesting.

I do little planting, then, but that planting song of the Osage runs in my head when the Planting Moon comes and the earth bursts into life and fantastic promises. Rain squalls come often and hang from the sky like some diaphanous drapery while the sun shines.

The Planting Moon could be called the moon of promise, for with it comes hope eternal, and the character of my soil on the sandstone ridge is forgotten. The ground seems rich and fruitful in my yard as I dig with the sharpshooter spade. I dig more holes than I can ever fill with plants because the earth invites digging, and the feel of it and the odor of it inspire dreams. I plan a garden in the savage blackjacks each spring. Sitting in the wheelbarrow with my tools lying about, I dream of the garden beautiful as the wrens sing ecstatically about me, and that garden is a real ambition as I berate myself for the years wasted.

The wrens, however, as they flit nervously here and there exploring every upturned vessel and every cranny in the eaves, realize the dreams about which they sing in a nest and family, but my dreams fade with the song. One year they built a nest in the pocket of my leather jacket which I had hung on the fence as I delved happily. I had to break up their plans for a home, but I did so on the theory that inasmuch as they are incessant nest-builders anyway, this nest in my pocket was only an overflow expression and had nothing to do with the harsh business of life; an ornamental expression very much like the manuscript which lay neglected on my desk.

The very last brown, wind-agitated leaf of the blackjacks is pushed off by the buds, but the trees are not bare. They are now overdressed, rather like some frill-loving country girl at a fair, with their bloom tassels dangling. One sitting under them can feel the cool little bits of moisture on face and hands, sap oozings that attract a beelike fly which comes to buzz among the branches.

My plants are in the ground by the time the Planting Moon is well over. I have planted more vines, the inevitable morning-glory, and more roses along the fence, which I visualize as a future bombardment of color, of scarlet particularly. I have planted more of the indigenous trumpet vines and, with fervent hope, more honeysuckle.

One year the yielding earth inspired me with such hope and to such activity with the sharpshooter that I made two excavations; one a small one of heart shape in the front yard, and one large rectangular one just off the kitchen door. I had no idea why I was digging them when I started, but later, when I struck a stratum of hard sandstone in the heart-shaped one, I knew it would be a fish pond, with the run-off from the front porch to supply it. The large one had me guessing. The Cowhand rode by one day and, after looking at it for some time, said, "Everbody oughtta have 'em a 'fraid hole in this country."

"That's right," I said, but I kept the secret—even from myself. Only the Planting Moon knew why I was digging. I had no intentions about making a storm cellar without help, but the Cowhand is practical, and I always like to appear practical. Naturally when the Planting Moon passed with its freshness, its earth-scents, and its extravagant promises, I left the tools leaning against a tree; and the excavation, which had reached a depth of two feet, shone like a wound for several seasons. When the hard rains filled it with water, the mallards came flying to it, to squawk and flap and play like city children at a fireplug. They soon had the water green with droppings, and feathers floated on it like rudderless boats.

I had no mosquitoes in the blackjacks until I made that excavation. They gave me an idea; I thought I might cement it and pipe the water from the kitchen-porch roof to it, and keep minnows there. I could seine chubs from the ravines to put into it, have minnows for fishing, and, of course, rid myself of a mosquito breeding-place.

Under the influence of one of the Planting Moons, I filled it with rich soil from the creek bottoms and planted roses there. The other excavation, the inscrutable heart-shaped one, I filled with grass-cuttings, leaves, and ashes from the fireplace, then planted a Chinese elm. Its growth was incredible, and its vitality so great that its leaves hang in yellow glory long after all the other planted trees have lost theirs.

During this moon I can hear the prairie chickens booming before I get out of my sleeping bag, and the bluebirds start cleaning out the tree boxes, and talk weakly and sadly about the leaves that the squirrels have placed in them, and fuss about the way the flickers have widened the holes, thus making them less habitable for bluebirds. I could never discover anything cheerful about this classical symbol of happiness, except his color. Their songs are filled with injured innocence and pessimism. One day I rushed out of the house with the 22-caliber rifle when a bluebird was expressing his extreme happiness from a fence post. I had thought that a blacksnake might have found his way to the nest, so filled with tragic resignation was the bird's voice.

If the gods of the Osage still influenced the people of the blackjacks and prairie, there would certainly be a most pretentious ceremony when the long cattle trains come screaming into the little loading-pens and stand panting from their exertion as the cattle bawl and the cowboys shout as they unload them. Sometimes the dust clouds float up like smoke, and sometimes the mud squeeges under cloven hoof and sharp boot heel, leaving a quagmire where no grass will grow that season.

Instead of a planting ritual wherein the Osage prayed for good yields so that the camp could be fed and made happy for another year, the cowmen would petition for just the proper amount of rain and sun and a top market. They might possibly have a ceremony more like the Osage buffalo dance, which was a prayer to Wah-Kon-Tah to see that the great herds kept to their migration routes, flowing north and south with the seasons, and at the proper time dot the plains with yellow calves as long as the seasons lasted.

I can visualize the cowmen riding across the early-morning prairie to a high spot where the prairie chickens dance and where the goose grass is like a green velvet ceremonial rug. There would be three cowboys riding ahead carrying standards topped by symbols. The middle one would be a dollar sign, and those on each side, the sun symbol for fast growing and, on the other, the crooked lightning symbol for frequent rain. Arriving at the spot, the riders would sit their horses in a great circle, while a very old cowman, with his weathered face and shrewd eyes, would stand in the center with outstretched arms as the priest. He would, of course, face the east as the sun came up over the prairie's rim, while specially designated dancers would dance around him in groups of four, representing the four seasons and the four directions. The leading group would be dressed in Hereford bull skins with the horns attached and resting on their heads, symbolizing fecundity and strength. The second group would be dressed in cowhides with the dollar sign painted on them, the third with the lightning symbol on their cowhides, and the fourth bearing the sun symbol. I see the high priest dressed in a robe of bluestem grass, wearing a crown with dollar signs instead of points or stars, and bearing a wand in each hand with the symbols of sun and rain at the tips. The chant would be accompanied by weird strummings of guitars in the hands of three cowboys.

But the Planting Moon has lost her significance over the blackjacks and prairie. She comes to weep shallow tears to freshen the earth; she laughs and dances in her exuberance and sets the ridges athrill with bird song and tree-toad chorus. She turns the prairie to emerald where the snow goose sits to rest and feed on his way north, gleaming exotically in his whiteness like some gigantic growth of prairie fungus. But her rains and her warm, invigorating sun nurture the great herds of cattle that are brought in to fatten on the bluestem at this time.

However, she is still temperamental and hysterical. One year she screamed unreasonably across the blackjacks in a great blizzard that brought snow which drifted across my road, and I was snowbound for three days. I sat at the window by the fire and watched a lone lilac bloom thrash the drift that covered the bush, like a bird fluttering to escape a trap.

The cowman turns out when the grass has colored the prairie again and the winter feeding is over. The "cake houses" are empty and the feeding grounds deserted, their long feed-troughs dark against the greening earth. Soon the bare earth of the feeding grounds with its incipient drainage system is covered with weeds and curly grass to hide the scar caused by hundreds of milling cattle. The Planting Moon abhors sterility, and when she can't hide trampled earth with bluestem, she does so with weeds, buffalo grass, sticker-weeds, and cockleburs.

This is the season when the mockingbird comes back to the ridges and sings tentatively, shyly from the tops of the blackjacks, and the first notes of the chuck-will's-widow comes plaintively from the east ridge as the moon rises, but not with confidence yet. If the red-winged blackbirds come to the head of the canyon to spill their liquid songs throughout the day, I know that the spring will be a wet one and that the water holes will be replenished at least until after their nesting season. The brown thrasher comes to sing from the tip of the trees, late in the afternoons and early in the morning, with his jerky imitation of the mockingbird.

But the Planting Moon is not athrill with sunshine and tinkling brooks; with gamboling lambs over flower-starred meadows in my part of the world. Such days are rare. Sharp winds obtain with squalls of rain, and, high above, the indecisive circling of ragged-edged clouds that may mean disaster. These purposeless clouds are painted gorgeously by the sunsets if they have not clashed and set up conditions for tornadic winds by four or five o'clock in the afternoons. They hold the pinks and flame color long after the sun has set, their high speed ever changing the color pattern.

Long after the coyote chorus of twilight, they sail across the face of the Planting Moon, wiping the silver from the ridges momentarily. With the moving clouds and the sharp stridulations from the grass roots, the hope-filled chorus of the tree toads, and the scented earth, there is the impression of virility and stability, and unconquerable hope.

Realizing that each day in each season is distinctively individual and that there is never a repetition, as the balance swings delicately with the flow of time and the subtle changes through earth's progression, the reappearance of the species on schedule to sing and mate during the Planting Moon gives the assurance that man cherishes. I see only the accustomed things happening and am thrilled with the other species by the all-absorbing hope. I do not remember those heavy thoughts about each day bringing me closer to the end of bird song, saddle-creaking, moon shadows, and the coyote chorus; I am filled with romance and youth; the ten years have made no difference when the Planting Moon comes to the ridges.

I sometimes remember that ten years ago, when I first came out to the blackjacks, I actually got up on April mornings and ran through the rain and the wind or through the dewy grass, leaving a dark trail; or that I rode out onto the prairie to see what the ragged, wind-maddened clouds would create to feed to the point of saturation my *joie de vivre*.

But the fact that the biological changes within myself have changed my attitude and tempered my intense desire for action does not come to bother me during this time. If I simply get up and stand out in the yard with the moist wind in my face and listen for the booming of the prairie chickens in the medley of meadowlark song and the doleful whistling of the upland plover, I do not sense the change in myself any more than I can actually see the change in the earth and its species.

Each year several blackjacks die, owing to wind, lightning, or drought. They are blasted thus in late spring or during the summer, but they usually do not actually die until midsummer. They express hope, too, in their attempts to bloom. They cover themselves with pale tassels, forgetting the fatal blasting in the pulse-quickening hope brought by the Planting Moon. But the leaves that come are pale green and soon fade and wither as the heat of midsummer creeps over the ridges.

There is one old postoak on the west point that has been declining for the last ten years, but still puts out his tassels each Planting Moon. But each year the tassels on the higher limbs wither in midsummer and do not have the vitality to bloom the succeeding spring, and thus his vitality retreats from the crown downward, until the lower limbs only are capable of putting forth dark-green leaves. Lower and lower creeps the life-force in him, but each Planting Moon inspires him with hope.

He is like an old man who once had a great shock of shining hair, but who is now bald on top, with only a graying fringe around the edges of his skull. His disintegration is natural, and I watch him closely. I have watched the saplings creep closer to him and grow larger and larger each year, as his vitality dims and he relinquishes his dominance over the earth about him. That which he needed and took in his virility some three hundred years ago, that which he gained in his virility and held against all in his maturity, he can no longer hold in his senility; and the life-forces that sustained him are being used by several running oaks, three sapling postoaks, a fast-growing hackberry reaching up to his middle, but which was stationary at eighteen inches during my first five years on the ridges, taking advantage of the life-forces of the earth as the old tree relinquishes them in its struggle with the other saplings. One of these saplings will survive the struggle to take his place when the old tree makes his final clutch at life and puts forth his last pale tassels some future Planting Moon. Then the pileated woodpeckers will come and tear out his old heart, looking for disrespectful grubs, and vines will cover his white bones without reverence. The battle of the saplings and the grasses, relieved of his suppressing shade and his all-devouring vitality, will become fiercer, until some running oak or one of the sapling postoaks survives, reducing the others to another long period of waiting or to death as it reaches out for the life-forces its virility requires.

This old oak is my Symbol Tree. The evidence of his mortality, a disintegration which I can see from season to season, gives me comfort and returns to me that sense of importance which I lost after coming to the ridges to live; that swaggering importance of *Homo sapiens* fresh from the magic of steel and concrete.

He also serves as a concrete example of the relationship of all things that spring from the earth and helps to anchor my thoughts about man's relationship to man and to the earth from which he sprang; thoughts that tend often to circle indecisively like a flock of sandhill cranes high above the prairie.

The new hope that comes to me now after ten years in the blackjacks, I express by my deep appreciation of the far horizon and the bubbling life and throbbing earth. The fact that I accept the miracle tranquilly, and stay close to the little sandstone house when the ragged clouds play their mad game, is never put up against my mad desire for action of ten years ago; my desire to struggle playfully against the madness of the elements. The hope that comes with the Planting Moon is all absorbing, ignoring man's limitations and scoffing at experience quite often. Senility puts forth its last tassels, and life overflowing with emotion exuberantly expresses the force within; even to overflowering in artificial ornamentation when maturity is reached.

The biological changes within myself during the last ten years have dimmed the glory of moonlight, dulled my sensitiveness to the waving of a grass blade or the movement of leaf shadows perhaps. They have dulled my high pleasure in driving snow, lightning display, and in driving or riding madly across the prairie to keep in sight of the wolf hounds, but the keen emotion which I feel in watching every spring the dance of the prairie chicken never dims.

Every morning before sunrise during the Planting Moon, when the rain is not falling, I drive the station wagon out onto the high prairie and back it close to a dancing ground, placing it between the dancers and the sun, and wait for the birds to gather. I stop before reaching the ground to let the endgate down and raise the rear window. In this way when the car is backed up to the dancing place, you can have complete freedom to take notes or use a camera, if you do not make any noise or carelessly stick a hand or arm out of one of the windows.

The prairie chicken has been slow in adjusting himself to man and man's mechanism. During the oil exploitation in my country he was almost extinct. A few clung on to their range in the middle of the great ranches and lived out the great frenzy of oil development. He has only just now come back to a nice balance with his food supply, but he has not yet learned that a car may carry hunters with guns, and instead of freezing effectively in the grass of the prairie that so well protects him, he will only squat and keep his head above the grass to see what is going on. He knows that a man on horseback may be dangerous and that a man on foot usually is, but his failure to see danger in the cars that travel over the prairie may prove to be quite important to his future existence.

Before the white man came to the Osage these grouse populated the range to the point of saturation and on April mornings filled the prairie with their booming as they danced on the high hills.

Naturalists sometimes call the nuptial activities of birds "antics," but the nuptial ceremonies of the prairie chicken are much more than antics. They are true dances which have fascinated most of my visitors to The Blackjacks, people who are not particularly interested in wild life. These dances have something of the same early-morning fervency of an Easter sunrise service on a mountain, with the advantage, of course, of not being cluttered with a breakfastless mob.

On the high prairie hills where the prairie grass is short, and the early-spring grass or late-winter grass covers the highest points of the hill with emerald, the dances begin just at sunrise. To these spots the cock prairie chicken comes every year on early April mornings. He flies there just before sunup and starts his dance slowly and tentatively, like a participant in the Osage social dances. When he seems to be sufficiently warmed by the emotion that the mating urge inspires, he begins to dance with great fervor and sends his sonorous booming over the heavy currents of the spring prairie. One seldom sees the hens, but they seem to be sitting about in the tall, winter bluestem which surrounds the dance grounds, demurely watching the glorious male dancing for their benefit.

Each cock has a beat, and he will dance up and down this beat which is a straight line, inflating the saffron sacs under the long pinnate feathers on each side of his neck until they change color and resemble small oranges. As he inflates these sacs, he makes a sound which is something like "ooh den doo den do-o-o-o-o-o" and which has a ventriloquisitic effect on the heavy morning air. His wings trail and his tail shapes itself into a fan and stands erect, while the pinnate feathers on each side of his neck stick up above his head like horns. His head is lowered as the sacs on his neck fill and glow in the pale light of morning. He takes a few short, mincing steps with his head down, his wings atrail, and his tail erect, then stops and prances in one spot, lowers his head and shakes it slightly as the climax comes. The resulting rolling, sonorous booming can be heard for a great distance, and he may repeat this several times before going back along his beat to repeat the procedure at the other end of it.

There may be four or five, or there may be twenty or forty, cocks dancing on the same dance ground, and the result is a rolling, booming sound that is the expression of full-blooded life, and this sound, with the sad whistling of the upland plover and the irresponsible song of the meadowlark, makes up the theme song of the early-morning April prairie.

Sometimes when the cocks have brought their wings back to normal position and have lowered their tails, and the pinnate feathers again cover the saffron sacs, now deflated, they will cackle like a domestic chicken and fly straight into the air to the height of two or three feet out of the sheer joy of living. If the ventriloquial sound of their booming has misled a searcher, this flying into the air with inane exuberance will certainly attract his attention.

After they have danced for several mornings, the fights occur. One cock will come too close to the beat of another, or they may suddenly decide to run at each other. At first there is bluff, then they lower their heads and, with beaks close to the ground and pointed at each other, they peck tentatively, then back away. But suddenly they will fly into the air; much higher than two game cocks, but in much the same manner, except that they depend more on their beaks than on their heels, which are undeveloped. If a slight prairie breeze springs up before the dancing is over, barred feathers from the fighting cocks will float over the grasses.

Later, the hissing of the breezes through the dead grasses of the last season will bring to their consciousness the danger that is ever present, and they seem gradually to become sober and more alert. The sun, barely peeping over the prairie's rim, sets up the little breezes and restless currents, and, as the dancers become more calm and alert, the least little noise will frighten them, and they will be off, alternately flapping and sailing far across the hills.

I have been much interested in the impressions which these nuptial dances have on people of divers interests, and for that reason I take casual Blackjack visitors out on the prairie during the season of this activity. All of them express surprise that birds and animals should behave in such "a human manner," but not one of them has failed to be impressed as we talk about the experience over coffee under the Blackjack. Like all sex-inspired emotions and actions, the dance has a fundamental appeal to man and inspires the same interest in some of my visitors, who are usually bored by nature, as does the eternal drama of sex in literature, on the screen, and in music.

I have watched this dance every spring for years, and, as in the case of the Osage dances, I have never grown tired of it. Every spring, along with the renewal of the dance, comes a renewal of my intense interest; as fresh as the urge that inspires it in a greening world filled with renewed hope.

One of the men who had photographed the last heath hen cock on Martha's Vineyard explained to me how the last heath cock in all the world had come up to the old dancing ground, to strut instinctively before hens that were gone from the earth; the last dramatic gesture of a species, with only the eyes of cameras hidden in the bush to record the farewell.

I passed the first Planting Moon in the blackjacks, expressing in action the wonder of being alive. I planted roses, wisteria, ivy, lilacs, honeysuckle, and the indigenous trumpet vine. I was thrilled with my solitude and with the madness of that particular Planting Moon. I splashed the station wagon through the east pasture over the road I had just made, when the winds whipped the rain across the prairie. I enjoyed the drive from town over the dirt county road and through the slush and mud of my private road, when the sheet-lightning played over the prairie and there was some doubt whether I could get through.

I was proud of harmony with the life about me. I became a part of it as I had wished. The fox squirrels were the first to ignore my presence. They lay along the limbs of the yard trees in catlike poses or played over the roof. They even became accustomed to the two Irish setters and worried them into a frenzy.

The coyotes trotted nonchalantly over the ridge at dusk or stood off and yelped at the house when the first lamp was lighted and gave out on the dark trees. On rainy mornings I often saw them sneaking down the canyon from the wrath of Tony of the ranch house at the head of the canyon, but we lived in harmony.

I saw a bobcat's track in the ashes where I put the garbage, just outside the west gate, and the prairie chickens came in flocks of forty and fifty to feed on the acorns during winter months, sitting in the trees around the house. Once when the setters were in town, a skunk walked into the house through the open door. I heard the dry clicking of his claws on the cement floor and looked up from my book. We looked at each other for some time. He had caught my movement in looking up from my reading. If I had had hackles, they might have risen, but instead the back of my neck tingled where racial hackles once grew. The fear of discomfort in men and animals is really great. I kept my immobility consciously and he kept his instinctively; the fear, however, was on my side, as there was none in his innocent self-assurance.

Assured that I was harmless, he went into the kitchen, and I could hear him tearing the paper from the garbage box, the bacon wrapping. He stayed so long that I continued reading for some time, then I heard his claws ticking against the cement, and he passed on out into the yard. I got up and closed the door.

Naturally the setters didn't like this harmony of life on the ridge. They cursed the coyotes from the safety of the woven-wire fence and worried when the prairie chickens came whishing in great flocks to settle in the trees. They slavered as they watched the squirrels jump from tree to tree, eternally hoping for a misstep.

Thus for over a year I lived as a part of the balance. There was no shouting and no firing of guns around the little house. But a strange thing happened; I, under the influence of the following Planting

Moon, broke the truce. I brought pheasants, chickens, and guineas to the ridge.

Man is under the same natural urges as the other species of the earth. He mates, he fears, he struggles to survive, and he expresses himself in song and in play; he goes even further and acknowledges the progression of life through his dream of God. But why can't he be satisfied without responsibility? Perhaps it is the primal urge to protect his mate and young diverted into other channels when mate and young are lacking or not in primal need of his protection.

In any case, with all my plans to become a part of the balance of nature on the ridges, I brought conflict, after the period of a year. Perhaps my position was unnatural, living as I did, not from the ridge, but feeding myself artificially from cans brought from town and food from the ranch. I was not a part of the economic struggle of the ridge which results in the balance, and therefore I was really an anomaly, as far as my own survival was concerned. After bringing pheasants, guineas, and chickens to the ridge, I had to fight for the survival of my charges against my predacious neighbors, which was probably a more natural state and in the end more satisfying than the "friends and neighbor" idea. I became important to my predacious neighbors; the presence of my charges whetted their desires and sharpened their cunning. We learned more about each other; we found ourselves in struggle now and pitted our wits against each other and saw no more of each other in repose. We had greater mutual respect, and I became a part of the struggle and remained a part of the balance through my strength to protect my flocks. Thus, I achieved a greater harmony with my environment and found that there is no place for dreams in natural progression, and it seems to me that I had realized for the first time that with responsibility come enemies.

 LITTLE-FLOWER-KILLER MOON

THE OSAGE CALL MAY THE LITTLE-FLOWER-KILLER MOON. IT MIGHT SEEM
that there is a paradox here, but actually the little flowers die during
this month. They wanted to indicate that the thousands of little
flowers that sprang up early in the seasons of Just-Doing-That Moon
and the Planting Moon pass away at this time to appear again the
following year.

These little flowers are those that grow close to the earth and even
appear before the grass has begun to sprout, in some years even before
the snows stop falling. These are the Johnny-jump-up, spring beauties, and hundreds of others that I cannot name which grow on the
ridges and on the burned-over places and on the prairie, where they
make the black, desolated spots gay with their beauty.

The spring beauties cover the blackjack ridges with their striped
petals, and among them appear little blue and yellow flowers. They
are so profuse that they give the impression that some spring festival
of the gods had left confetti there.

Thus when the grass has covered the ridges in May, the weeds
begin to grow and flower: the tall, waving spiderworts, the black-
eyed Susans; and the little flowers that came first to cover the earth
must pass away. The flowers of this moon are the tall flowers that
wave above the grass and not the earth-hugging little flowers.

The crows are quiet, and the bluejays are not so conspicuous as
usual. This is the moon of the songsters and the season when the
little ones are breaking their shells all over the ridges and in the

bottoms. The birds that have spent the winter away are back now: the scissor-tailed flycatcher, crested flycatcher, phoebe, mockingbird, field sparrow, brown thrasher, oriole, and yellow-billed cuckoo. During this moon the quail begin to whistle and the prairie chickens can still be heard at sunup.

Life is beginning, and there is no outstanding event by which to mark this season; an outstanding stage in the creation of life, since it is the time for the blooming of all life. Only the fading of the little flowers seems to be outstanding in the world of vocal, bubbling life.

But still the Moon Woman is temperamental. The funnel-shaped clouds may come. There may be too much rain or too little; too much cold or unseasonable heat.

I watch the marsh hawks through the glasses as they build their nest in the tall winter grass at the head of the canyon. The ash-colored male carries material from across the prairie but does not fly directly to his nest; he alights on a spot removed from the building site, then, assuring himself that he is not being watched, goes on to the nesting place. When I am visible, there is no work at all; the birds will neither come near the site nor indicate in any way that they are in the least interested in it. The redtails, on the other hand, bring material to the old nest in the blackjack south of the house and carelessly patch their last year's home. The male will bring sticks for an hour or more, then rise and circle high in the sky, screaming his delight in having so little to do of domestic labor.

His mate will join him in his high circling at times, and the two of them will play a game of aerial tag, though it is always she who drops back to work first. The marsh hawks also take time off to play high against the blue, but most of the time only the male plays and expresses his joy of living by flying in circles. This is a nuptial flight and a sort of expression that takes the place of song.

The Osage used the redtail in one of their most sacred rites. His skin was used as the outside of the Wah-hopeh, or medicine bundle. Wah-Kon-Tah had given him a red tail, and they did not need to paint him with the sacred color of fire and sun; even a sacred eagle feather had to be painted or dyed red.

The female coyotes are secretive and find some limestone ledge under which they can dig their dens; ledges that protect their whelps so effectively that few men take the trouble to dig them out. Each season there is a den south of my house, and during the whelping period and all throughout June and July my chickens are not molested. The coyote does her hunting elsewhere for fear of reprisals. Not until August, when the whelps are large enough to hunt on their own, must I guard my flocks against this particular family.

I watch her through the glasses when she brings food to the den. Her course is circuitous as she approaches with a half-grown chicken or a rabbit. Reaching a high point, she will stand for many minutes looking over the country, with the prey laid carefully at her feet. When she is satisfied that no danger is near, she turns off from the direct line so as not to make a trail to the den by constant use; she usually comes along the limestone escarpment where no scent will hang and where there will be no lasting impression of her treading. Before she enters the den, she has another look around, then disappears quickly. So as not to arouse her suspicions, I must watch only on very still days or on those when the wind is in my favor, and I am so far away that I cannot hear and therefore do not know whether the whelps make any sound at her approach, but I feel quite sure that they do not. The whimpering of baby animals and the hissing of nestlings to express hunger and impatience are the only stupidity I have ever discovered in nature.

One day after she had trotted away from the den with obvious purpose, I came back to the pens and chose a half-grown white Plymouth Rock, one of the flock I had that year for the purpose of experimenting with the owls to determine whether they depended more on their acute hearing in their hunting or on their sight.

I turned the befuddled chicken out on the prairie near the den, as near to the den as I dared go with my heavy scent, then lay behind some buckbrush back on the ridge to watch. A white chicken on the prairie can be seen from a greater distance than a bay, sorrel, or palomino horse. Any strange sound or the least movement may make a dozen widely differing species freeze in their tracks until they know the nature of it, but a white object appearing suddenly seems to stop all life with a jerk, like the stopping of machinery.

I was very much amused by the actions of the chicken. He would walk very fast through the grass, then stop and crane his neck to unbelievable lengths in inane futility. He would run a few steps in the direction of the house, then stop, stretch his neck, and run back in the direction from which he had come. Soon he started singing a worried little song, the chicken's song of fear, as he raised and lowered his hackles repeatedly. He had lost his racial memory of fear from above, as he didn't cock his eye at the sky once.

I was growing tired of the game and was wondering what I should do next, when the coyote appeared. She came up in an easy little fox-trot with what looked like a gopher in her mouth. The chicken thought she was a dog and, under generations of the protection of man, had no instinct to protect himself against a strange dog. As he stretched his neck even higher, his fear was vague and general, and he began to sing his little song again. The coyote couldn't have missed seeing him, but she pretended that he wasn't there. She went through the same ritual of precaution as before, except that she varied her direction to the limestone escarpment. When she reappeared a half-hour later, she trotted away, absolutely ignoring the easy and very desirable prey.

I had to drive the chicken back to the pens, and it was like herding a stubborn steer on a slow horse. The stupid chicken insisted on run-ning in circles, and I was compelled to run and head him off, until he eventually flapped helplessly in the grass from exhaustion and then squawked frantically all the way back to the pens under my arm.

Every full moon seems to inspire the dog coyotes to yowl and yap, but during this time they send up their quavering questioning at sundown and again when the moon appears. Their song is the long wolflike howl that expresses the yearning of all life and seems to be asking Little-Flower-Killer Moon what it is that disturbs them.

A month after I had broken the truce with the predators, I had built my chicken houses and, as a guard against the rapacious Cooper's hawk, had stretched inch-mesh wire over the tops of the pens. The first attack upon my charges, and therefore on me, was made during this moon by the skunk.

In my sudden enthusiasm for responsibility, I had sent to North Carolina for some "H-D" eggs. They are pit-games that are black, occasionally occurring with red saddles and hackles, and have red eyes that look like coals of fire. The man who first imported the eggs from England paid a hundred dollars for them, and when he placed them in the incubator, he marked them "H.D." for the purpose of identification.

The H-D is a fighting bird bred from the jungle fowl by the Romans, for the pit, and thus found his way to the blackjacks through England. They have been weakened through inbreeding, and the hatches are bad; the chicks often appear with toes spread in all directions and with weak legs. But when they grow up, they are strong and active, and the cocks are ready to fight anything that walks or flies—even myself. I was very proud of them.

I came home late one night to find that the mother hen that had been hovering a brood of H-D chicks was gone, and the chicks, unharmed, were scattered all over the yard, frozen, in the grass roots, in the corner of the fireplace chimney, and under the rose bushes. They screamed with intense fright when I handled them in order to put them into a basket, though ordinarily they were accustomed to being handled.

I then opened the door of a little coop where I had some half-grown H-D's and found all six of them dead and headless. There among them, curled up comfortably in a corner of the coop, was the skunk purring contentedly like a cat full of milk. He had dug under the side of the coop with some trouble and had killed the young H-D's from sheer lust, after carrying away the mother hen and scattering her chicks all over the yard.

I didn't hesitate. I was so annoyed that I held the muzzle of my Smith & Wesson to his head and emptied the cylinder, glorying in the nauseating musk odor that hung on the heavy air of night, transforming its glory with the sharp explosions that broke the silence of the ridge into a symbol of the mighty power of *Homo sapiens* when aroused and announcing his entrance into the struggle.

The fact that this skunk might have made several visits to my charges for food, and escaped each time, is obvious. He need not have been the indolent victim of my wrath, but he let his lust, that had nothing whatever to do with his necessity to survive, lead into excessive killing and urge him to remain abnormally with his victims.

Not all skunks are lustful killers; as a matter of fact, he is the only one in all my experience on the ridge to express himself in this manner. He was abnormal just as some men are abnormal. When conditions are right, there are sexual abnormalities just as there are among men; and there are killers among animals just as there are among men, and if the social conditions which man imposes on himself were extended into the so-called "animal" world, even the most careless observer could say that the "purity" of nature is an illusion.

It was during the Little-Flower-Killer Moon of my second year,

when I felt that I had to assume some responsibility, that my interference brought tragedy into my woven-wire inclosure.

I had lumber left over from the building of the chicken and pheasant houses, so I built several bird boxes and placed them in the trees
inside the yard. I intended to attract crested flycatchers, flickers, bluebirds, wrens, and titmice. I wanted as many birds as possible as close
as possible, so that I could watch them from my windows or hear
their voices throughout the season, but, like the many dreams of man
based on the hope and the desire to progress toward some reasoned
felicity, my plan did not take into consideration the realities of the
earth drama.

I placed the boxes just so, with little landing platforms, and roofs
projecting over the entrances, then waited. The bluebirds came first
and raised a family before the Little-Flower-Killer Moon had arrived,
but the Bewick's wrens ignored the boxes altogether and built in the
drawer of the wash table under the locust. The crested flycatchers
came and built as did the flickers.

Then one day I heard mourning from the flycatcher tree. I saw the
birds sitting helplessly watching the box, from which the back half of
a blacksnake was writhing. I had to shoot holes through the box with
the 22-caliber rifle to kill the snake and, in so doing, killed the
nestlings.

This tragedy was repeated in the flicker box and in another flycatcher box, until I had to tear them down. I could have put tin "collars" around the bottoms of the trees, but this concentration of the
ridge's drama discouraged further experiments.

This tragedy always brings up a paradox in the beautifully worked
out balance in nature through the use of protective coloration, immobility, and silence in the hunted and the predacious alike. Thus I
am eternally puzzled about the inane cries that nestling birds make
when they hear their parents alight on the tree or when they have
gone a long time without food. These cries are not dainty little infant
cries but reptilian hissings and croakings which grow in volume as
the nestlings grow, until I can hear the rasping hunger cries of the
nestling flickers and flycatchers, not only in the boxes in the trees of
the yard but in the hollow trees outside the fence, as I sit reading or
working in my house.

It is these petulant, greedy, absolutely useless cries of the nestlings
that bring the slithering blacksnake purposefully through the grasses

and up the tree with the smugness of a skunk. Like the skunk, he shows an absolute indifference to anyone who may be watching him, and, like the skunk, he is dangerously armed but less effectively.

The blacksnake, simply and inscrutably, with utmost unconcern and with the sureness of fate, wriggles up the tree, ignoring both the presence of man and the distracted cries and the sharp beaks of the parent-birds. Other species, attracted by the cries of the parents, usually arrive to join them and scold helplessly; exactly like frightened and perhaps thrilled people who come to watch a neighbor's house burn or wonder at a sudden death on the street; frightened and excited because of their own vulnerablity but thrilled with the drama. There is little of mass defense instinct against the outlaw inasmuch as there is no physical defense whatever. Albeit, the screaming and swearing of five or six different species of birds have in them much of bluff, indignation, and self-righteousness.

If I do not appear with the 22-caliber rifle until the snake has most of the foreport of his body in the box, and his tail coiled about it, he has already begun to swallow the nestlings, and I must shoot through the box. However, I usually hear the first alarm calls and shoot the marauder out of the tree before he has reached the nest.

My feeling of tragedy is keen at such times, but there is certainly compensation to the hunter when the long, black body relaxes his hold and falls like a piece of rope to the ground, and the hunter can count the hits which were effective.

Often when I have gone back into the house, I look through the window to see a crow alight heavily in the top of the tree of tragedy and with close-drawn feathers stretch his neck and look down at the box. Crows are always present when something exciting is afoot, but they do not dare to come close to a man with a gun. There seems to be a sort of kindred feeling between the blacksnake and the crow. Both are robbers of bird's nests and hen houses and both are diabolically black, and they seem to respect each other. The respect on the part of the snake could be fear, since the crow is very ably armed with a strong beak and uses a flock-defense which has as its weapon nerve-shattering swearing. A snake does not dislike crow's eggs or nestlings, but young crows are usually practically silent even when hungry, and a crow's nest is always made to appear deserted. As a matter of fact, the whole species seem to have vanished from the earth until the nesting season is over for them. Furthermore, April days, the season of the crow's nesting, are entirely too cold for the blacksnake. Thus they have nothing to fear from each other but certainly have much in common.

The crow's nestlings seem to escape most hunters, and I could never quite understand this, especially since the species seems to be tipping the balance dangerously by its numbers. The crow undoubtedly owes his triumph to the interference of the white man, and perhaps the effects of this scale-tipping may come later, and man may not recognize it when it comes; it may come in the form of some insect pest freed from its old enemies in the natural balance which were displaced by the multiplication of the crow, which was due in turn to the landing of a few zealous Christians on the bare shores of Massachusetts, whose crops augmented his natural food supply.

One hot May day I was lying on my porch reading. I had been subconcious for some time of the subdued talking of crows; lazy conversation, like that of people on their front porch fanning themselves on a summer's evening. Soon I heard a note of excitement, then the pitiful cries of a pair of flickers. I raised up so as not to frighten the crows, and, obscured by the rusted screen of the porch, I saw several of them sitting nonchalantly about the hole in a tree. With cocked heads they were giving the hole their full attention. A snake's rear half writhed happily from the hole, and they were watching him at his massacre with mild interest; perhaps with a slight expectation that there might be something edible as a result of the slimy business. They had made no outcries, as any other birds would have done, at least as any hole-nester would have done, but talked about it calmly as though they appreciated the excitement that had turned up on such a hot and unpromising day.

England in May is no more inspiring than my country during this time. The rain comes not in great crazy storms but gently. The prairie undulates in the green velvet of the bluestem, and cattle dot the hills, while mauve cloud shadows move indolently over them and across the canyons.

The mockingbird has begun to sing with more assurance, and the dickcissels from the fence posts, and from the bottoms come the poignant, soul-stirring song of the wood thrush. This bird stirs me like moonlight on the desert, and to me his song is the loveliest of all bird song; even more poignant than that of the nightingale, and more mystical and disturbing than that of the clarín of Mexico, disembodied in the eternally dripping jungle.

Often I ride down to a point on the edge of the canyon just before sundown and sit listening to this indescribable song that seems to express all the yearning of the human spirit; the song that asks the eternal question "Why?" so softly, so sadly, so submissively, as the day ends.

But this is the busy season on the ranches; the calves must be rounded up, castrated, branded, and "shot" with serums. Neighbor comes to help neighbor "work" his calves during this time, until all the herds of the country have been worked. Such co-operation in this sparsely settled ranch country is traditional, and the tradition is faithfully and eagerly kept alive. When we see smoke rising from the prairie miles away, we rush to it in force, just as every cowboy on the ranches is ready at all time to help roundup, "receive," or work calves when his neighbor calls.

One morning at daybreak I went over to help a neighbor work calves. I was not necessary, but I felt very much that I wanted to work calves that morning. I threw my saddle in the station wagon and drove the short distance across the prairie, arriving there before my neighbor had arrived from town and before most of the cowboys had arrived for the day's work.

Red had ridden up from the ranch and greeted me as I stopped. He came up to me smiling broadly, then winked one eye and motioned with his thumb like a hitchhiker toward the stable. I got out and followed him inside. He reached into his brush-jacket pocket and pulled out a bottle of whiskey and handed it to me.

"I don't believe I want a drink," I said.

"I'll take your'n," he said, as he held the bottle to his mouth and threw his head far back.

"That won't last you long the way you're drinking it," I warned.

"All I aim to do is kinda drown them cobwebs out from last night; shore felt rocky this mornin'." He put the bottle back in the inside pocket of his jacket and said, "Hell, I'm ready to ride." He looked at me shrewdly. "Say, you ask the Ole Man can I go with you to kick 'em outta the runnin' oaks in the east pasture—I don't care about nobody knowin' I got a bottle with me, and a ole boy's shore gonna need it fore the day's through."

We set out stirrup to stirrup through the dewy bluestem toward the east pasture. The sun was just coming up to take charge of a world as fresh as mint flavor, appearing suddenly with the glistening blackjacks etched in its red like an inlay, like some cloisonné conceived by a whimsical artist. The crickets were still chirruping in the cool shade of the grass roots, rather rapidly as though they would finish before the sun should discover them and impose grass-roots silence.

A white-face with a calf at her side trotted off into the east with her stupid head high and her eyes bulging as though she had never seen a man. We turned instinctively and followed her very plain trail through the dewy grass, knowing that she would join a group. Her trail ended with a band of cows and calves under the possessive eye of a massive, curly-headed bull. They stood and stared at us with bovine opacity of comprehension.

Red pulled his horse back on its hind feet. "Say," he said pointing, "see that postoak on the other side of that openin'? I bet ole Boots here can daylight that pony of your'n."

I smiled at him. "You must be feeling good."

"Hell, I am..... Come on."

"This is not my horse," I said, "and he'll get enough work by noon; imagine I'll have to change horses this afternoon. This old pony's not used to carrying 185 pounds every day—working under that weight."

"Hell, that ole pony's as tough as whet-leather..... Come on."

"No; you'll burn that firewater up soon enough. Better enjoy feeling good while you can. When you run out, you'll feel like the devil."

"Guess your right. There's the east-line fence; better start gatherin'."

We picked up small herds here and there through the blackjacks, rode around and picked up singles, and soon had a herd of bawling, agitated cows and calves with the indolently moving bulls, bawling and stopping to paw the earth. As we rode behind them, Red tipped the bottle again and carefully put it back in the inside pocket of his jacket.

I said, "Takes a lot of drowning for what you did last night."

He smiled at me. "I'm as pure as a lily. I shore had some fun though. Went to this dance—didn't hardly know NOboddy, but after I had me a few snorts, I shashays up to a ole gal a-settin' along the wall. I bet she'd tip the Fairbanks at two hunnert. I walks up to her and I says: 'Lissen, sister, I'm fixin' to cut loose with a little plain an' fancy in about a minit and aim to have yu hep me.' She kinda smiles and says, 'Don't guess I know yu, do I?'" He attempted to imitate her with an unconvincing falsetto and then continued: "I said, 'That's all right, I look wooly, but I ain't got no mange and I'm gentle an' playful as a kitten.'"

"Well, she gits up and kinda paces towards me with her arms out, and we tangle. I aim tu tell yu we do-se-do'ed. When we set down she said I shore was a good dancer, and I tole her I wasn't no prize, but I'd be in there a-sweatin' an a-tryin' when the music finely give out. I put my hand over on her laig and said I was goin' out to find me another snort, and I shore would be back. Iffen she'd a-had a tail, she'd a-wagged it.

"When I got to the door, I seen two-three bunches of ole boys with bottles; under a big elum tree, about the corrals, and by the well. I tangled with the well outfit cause I kinda felt dry fer watter anyways. When I got back to the door, I squalled like a bobcat and done a few fancy ones up to that ole gal. I knowed she'd be a-waitin', couldn't do nothin' else, cause I was 'bout the only one drunk enough to tackle her. After them last snorts she looked purty good."

"How long did the dance last?" I asked.

"Yu know when yu come a-drivin' up this mornin', I'd just got in." He laughed reminiscently, then said: "She musta slipped some of her harness; them ole tits of her'n got tu floppin' and ever time we'd swing your partner, I'd duck my head." With his laughing, his shaky hands, and the restiveness of his lathered horse, he couldn't finish making the cigarette with which he had been fumbling for some time, so he let it fall, and I offered him one from my package. He laughed to himself, then said: "I cain't hep thinkin' about that ole gal; boy, she was ready to ship. She could a-stood flat-footed and a-whupped a houn' pup out from under the sofy with them tits."

Soon the little herd that bawled with uneasiness before us joined others driven by other pairs of cowboys, and, as the herd grew and moved slowly toward the roundup ground, they became a mass of red backs, flowing like viscous fluid. Cows would ride each other as they moved along, and the movement, excitement, and body heat of the mass seemed to excite the sex urge of all, and the bulls were continually rearing their massive shoulders and great white faces above the level of the massed backs, mating willy-nilly with the cows;

forcing their biological services on some that attempted frantically to get away from them.

Red and another cowboy rode through the herd at the roundup ground and roped the calves to be worked, dragging them out of the milling herd. Others waited to brand, castrate, and "shoot" them against epidemics. I waited to throw Red's calves as he dragged them one at a time out of the herd by leaning over, catching them by the legs on the opposite side from which I stood, and flopping them, then holding them while they were worked. A kicking range calf can break a man's leg or arm with his flying feet, even when he is properly thrown with his flailing legs away from the one handling him.

Red was throwing rather a large loop, and the man working with him was dragging out most of the calves. The sweat rolled down his face, and his eyes were bleary, and he was glad of relief so that he could sneak behind one of the pickup trucks and renew his courage.

The women from the neighboring ranches had baked cakes and had brought salads to the ranch house. They were busy, red-faced, and happy in the kitchen. The owner had killed a fat calf and had sent him back to the house to be prepared for the noon meal.

We lay sprawled on the grass in the yard about the house at noontime, with faces scrubbed to a strawberry red, waiting for some shy little girl to come out and announce that the food was ready.

As I lay on my back watching the white clouds float by and listening to the happy song of the meadowlark, the weak, contented song of the dickcissel, awaiting those magic words, "Well, I guess it's ready," I wondered if those clouds were not a little more pleasing, the distant blackjacks more fascinating with their shellacked leaves in the May sun, when I was hungry and a little tired from physical exertion. It seemed that the voices of the birds, and even the metallic, lazy groaning of the windmill, inspired a readier and keener contentment, and my thoughts skipped with warmer enthusiasm and more quickly from one pleasant thing to another, like a hummingbird in a boundless garden.

II
SUMMER

VI   BUFFALO-PAWING-EARTH MOON

THE BUFFALO ARE GONE FROM THE BLACKJACKS AND FROM THE HEAD-
waters of the Cimarron River, where the Osage once hunted them.
Here, in my country, they have been displaced by the white-face bulls,
and the roaring of those great curly-headed brutes as they walk ar-
rogantly across the prairie is the dominant voice of June. They stand
and paw the earth, lifting sod high above their backs when the ground
is damp and raising dust clouds when it is dry, with their noses close
to the earth as they bellow and roll their eyes angrily. As the buffalo
once were, they are now the lords of the range, and there is no other
animal to dispute their position; not even myself when I am afoot.

But, with all his bellowing and his lordly air, the bull, being a male,
is therefore a compromiser and a bluffer. Often when a challenge is
answered by another bull, they start approaching each other, stopping
to paw the earth and bellow, then continue their approach toward
each other, bawling their warnings. When they come close, they stop,
like two barnyard cocks, two dogs, or two men, to appraise each other,
then slowly circle. They stand higher in the shoulders and they lean
toward each other. If they are fairly well matched as to size, they may
bluff in this manner for some time, tentatively lowering their heads.
Then one of them will see something far off, and he will immediately pretend great interest, the interest growing, until eventually he
will pretend that he must go to investigate. He does not do this precipitately, since to walk off would be to expose his vulnerable flank or
shoulder. He moves away with his head to his foe—slowly, a few steps
at a time, stopping at intervals to show the other that he is quite
willing to fight—then walks away when some distance separates
them if the other does not push the fight. They sometimes get to-

gether, however, and as they warm to the battle, they forget the bluffing and attempt to kill, cutting each other rather badly at times.

I saw a very large bull accept the challenge of a smaller one, and when he found that he could outthrust him, he was very anxious to fight; he would run at the smaller one when he could catch him off guard. The small bull would only lower his head to meet the terrific charge and in this way protect his flank, but he was pushed ingloriously over the wet and slippery ground. Certainly he made male excuses to get away, but the big bull knew his advantage and was thus inspired to greater male effort to vanquish him.

Unlike the range stallion, the range bull does not attempt to hold a harem together. He is not only polygamous but an insatiable philanderer. He roars his impatience and bad will toward all things as he goes from one group of cows to another, nosing each one until he finds one that is ready to accept him. If another bull has already claimed the cow, he does not fly into him as his great parading and bawling might lead one to believe he might do. The two tentatively push each other around a bit but keep the restless cow in the corners of their eyes, breaking to follow as she walks away. They spend most of their time attempting to frustrate each other.

It was during this season that a painted bunting came to my yard one year, and his visit was so unusual that I can remember the details. He is an extravagantly colored bird that is seldom seen except in the tangle of vines and other growths along the river bottoms. Even in these places he is rarely seen in our country. He looks as though he had been colored by a whimsical child who had amused himself by daubing the cardinal colors in patches without blending them. Thus with his harsh, contrasting coloration the painted bunting certainly asks a question that I can't answer. Why such coloration that is not the least protective in our country? One might imagine that he had been swept out of the jungle, where such coloring is protective, by some hurricane and had settled down here on the ridges, miraculously escaping destruction in this high, open region of blackjacks.

I am surprised to find that the Osage have ignored him, since he is not used either in the old or in the new religious ceremonies. He is designed to be man's symbol for something, and I am disappointed that the Osage have neglected him.

This is the season of shining green, whispering breezes, and distant, lilac-tinted hills that turn mauve after sunset. During this season each day is very much like the one that preceded it; days filled with throbbing life and earth-scents; days when the sun is not yet too hot and the winds not yet too hot and persistent. June is not much affected by drought even in drought years, since the inevitable spring rains have moistened the earth.

But during the wet years this is the season of floods that wash out bridges and roads and tear at the grassless spots on the prairie. The clouds form quickly and become menacing, and the deep-throated roar of the thunder warns of Wah-Kon-Tah's anger as he lashes at the earth with lightning. The rain comes in sheets, and the planted trees of my yard bow before the wind, while the rounded crowns of the blackjacks boil in angry protest. After a few minutes or an hour the clouds have rolled on to the southwest, and the sun shines on a world fresher than ever, with the meadowlarks leading off a chorus of bird song even before the last drops have fallen and while the thunder still growls in the distance. They sing accompanied by the dripping of the water from the leaves and by the roar of the feathery water rushing down the canyon in front of the house.

I always associate this month with the religious and other ceremonies of the Osage. I think it is an association of my childhood; at this time they came in from all over the reservation and camped by our house on the hill and in the creek bottoms to receive their interest on the money which they received for their lands in Kansas.

I used to visit the camps with my father and watch the activity among the rounded lodges, rounded in harmony with the rounded hills of the reservation. There were deaths during these encampments, and I was often awakened from sleep at the hour before dawn by the death chant from the hills across the creek. And there were the June dances and the occasional weddings to impress me with the sacredness of this Buffalo-Pawing-Earth Moon to the tribe.

Their religion, their concept of God, came out of my blackjacks, out of the fears inspired by the elements, and it was colored just as the animals were colored for perfect adjustment. Of course, it was the result of man's imagination and his dreams and fears. Even though primitive man had the distinction among the animals of being able to think, he was not by reason of his mental powers the "insurgent" which some anthropologists choose to call him. His mental processes were still under the influence of the natural background, and the

Osage religion of Wah-Kon-Tah was as much a product of the black-jacks and the prairie as the physical man.

During this time I am always aware of the god that came out of these ridges as the concept of man, and I like to visit with the people who conceived him and watch the changes under the flow of time, just as I watch the changes in life about me and the changes within myself.

It is during this moon that the Osage hold their traditional social dances that in the dim past had some religious meaning; they were interpretative of the swelling life of the prairie earth that carried the frenzied bawling of the bull buffaloes along with their own drum rhythm and the chant of their singers. The Buffalo-Pawing-Earth Moon is also the earth-singing moon, the moon of life-thrill expressed by many voices.

The dance, called the Ee-lon-shescah, or men's dance, is held about the eighteenth or twentieth of June at the Village. This village is the home of one of the physical divisions of the tribe, called Wah-Hah-Koh-Lee, or Thorn People, because they chose to live in the brush of the creek valleys when they were removed from their original home in Missouri near the present city of St. Louis. The dance is also held about the same time in the villages of the other divisions of the tribe, except that they plan the time so that there will be no conflict. Out of the five original physical divisions, there are only three active at present. There were many clans, but these physical divisions had nothing to do with clans. Following Indian custom, they were descriptive of habitat in nomenclature, just as names were given to their children to fit their characters. There were the Seh-Tah, the Lowland or Little Osage; Pah-Solé, the Big-Hill People; Sah'n-Solé, the Timber Plateau People; Wah- Hah-Koh-Lee, the Thorn People, and the Nonceh-Waspi, the Heart Stays People, or those who stayed in the original home.

The dance being a social one, some of the neighboring tribes are invited to participate and may expect gifts and at least sufficient flour, coffee, beans, and potatoes to supply them for the four days of the encampment. The whole tribe acts as host to these visitors, but the theoretical host is the man who is called the Drum Man, he to whom the drum authority has been given. He has eight advisers, Teh-tah-hah'n, two Whip Men, who see that everyone dances and does the proper thing while dancing, two Water Boys, and two Tail Dancers, who arise from their seats to dance a sort of encore after each dance. There are ten singers, one of whom is the leader; they beat the rhythm and sing and are seated around the kettledrum in the center of the dance ground, which is usually shaded by an arbor of fresh willow branches. Besides these there are four women who are designated as Makers of Bread, but they simply oversee the cooking and employ Negroes and whites to do the actual cooking and serving. The man who cries the dances is the Wah-tze-piah, or Town Crier.

I go out to the Village to pay my respects and give the Drum Man some money as a token, since he has the responsibility of feeding the visitors and the expense of the ceremony. This is usually on the first day of the dancing and during the morning before the dances start. However, I often spend the day talking with the old men in the shade of the houses or lodges. Most of these old men do not dance now, and they sit and tell stories during the period when there is no dancing; they never grow tired of watching, even though they do not participate. Here I pick up many stories of the jealousy between the Peyote factions, and laugh with them over the stories of dignified men being humiliated. I like the sound of their voices and the graceful movements of their hands as they talk, in this setting of colorful activity.

One afternoon as the dancers were being dressed by their women, some members of the East Moon faction of the church were talking just outside the lodge of one of the dancers while he was being dressed. It was very hot, and the sides of the lodge were tucked up, and we could see him sitting on his blankets as his wife dressed him, holding the hand mirror up to his face as she tied on his scalplock made of buffalo-tail tuft and wild-turkey bristle. He was the son of a fervent West Mooner.

One of the old men started to talk about the young dancer's grandfather, pretending that he was not aware of the young man being dressed behind him: "He sure was a great man," he said very seriously. "When I was little boy, I used to look at him and say, 'He sure is big man.' He used to walk straight like oak tree; he kinda talk from w-a-a-a-ay down deep, seem like. I said, 'he sure is great man'—that's what I said; like that..... 'He sure must be great man,' I said. Us little boys used to play in place where he gotta come to his house— all-a-time he come 'long that-a-way. When he come 'long he wave his hand and say, 'get outta my way'; we sure would run. He sure ack like he big man.

"He used to talk big too at meetin'. He used to say he sure was great man. He say when he go to Wash'ton peoples look at him; everbody sure look at him he said. 'Look at big chief,' they say—he say that's what them peoples in Wash'ton say. When I was little boy, I say to myself, 'He sure mus be great man.'

"Some Sioux mens come one day. Big mens, I guess; chiefs, maybe. They din't come to see him; they come to see our Chief. Theys all settin' 'round talkin', and this man come 'long all dressed up. He come 'bout hour late so everbody see he's big man, I guess; at same time all dressed up. He got on buckskin shirt with scalps on it, and bear-claw necklace too. At same time nobody say for him to come. He stood and look, and make himself very tall, seems like. He point to place he gonna set in circle, and make some young mens move over. They wasn't hardly no room, but he make them young mens move, and he put his blanket down there. He set down and fan with his fan. He look proud, and kinda frown, and set straight. I was little boy; I say to myself, 'He sure mus be great mans.'

"They talk long time there. They talk about how white mans takin' Sioux land, and they say maybe its purty good thing if Indians go to this place Mexico. Purty soon this man stand up and say he want to say few words, and everbody look at him. He talk long time 'bout how great he is. He ack big and say he have presents for them

Sioux, and I guess they think he's some chief. He sure talk long. I said, 'He mus be great mans with that paint on his face and them feathers and scalps.'

"He had one of them eagle feathers in hair; them feathers like what is under tail of eagle—soft one, ain't it? It sure was purty. It was painted pink like they do them little feathers from under tail of eagle. I don't guess he din't have no right to wear that; at same time I said, 'He sure mus be great mans'—I was little boy; I don't know no better, I guess. Them Sioux din't know no better either, I guess.

"Seem like he talk lo-o-o-o-ong time. He frown and ack very proud, and he make his voice big, but I don't guess he said nothin'; only talk 'bout him bein' great man. Purty soon when he talk, little louse cr-a-a-wl up that soft feather, ain't it? Cr-a-a-wl, cr-a-a-wl up that feather. Purty soon when that louse get on top, that feather bend. That louse was too heavy and that feather bend. At same time he finish his talkin' that feather make bow, ain't it? That little eagle feather make bow with louse ridin' on it—sure was funny."

The group laughed heartily, and one of them kept saying, "He sure was big man, ain't it?" While they were still laughing, the young dancer, now fully dressed, arose suddenly and walked with dignity toward the dance ground, his dance bells tinkling. No one noticed him, apparently. When the young dancer had vanished and the laughter had died, another told a story about one of their own East Mooners:

"Ole man got too much, I guess. He come outta church and was settin' under big tree. He set there long time. Purty soon red bird come 'long; seem like he set in that tree and look down at ole man, nen purty soon he start singin': 'cheer, cheer, cheer, cha, cha.' You know how they sing that-a-way. Ole man he look up at that bird, and that bird keep doin' that. Purty soon he flew 'way. Ole man got to thinkin', I guess. Purty soon he went got his drum, and set there long time. At same time he couldn't hardly see nothin' 'count too much peyote. At same time he think he can make song like that red bird. I guess he think Wah-Kon-Tah sent that bird to give him song.

"I come outta church and I seen him settin' there. 'How,' he say to me. 'Come here, my son; I got song I gonna give you.' I set down by him, and he beat that little drum and went: 'tze, tze, tze, tze.' I hole up my hand. 'Naw,' I say, 'I don't want it.' "

Again there was hearty laughter, and the talker said, "Ole man sure was full too much peyote."

The dancers are sedate as they dance from their benches toward the center of the dance ground and around the drum. They wear colored, silken shirts, broad beaded belts, leggings, and moccasins. From their heads a scalplock quivers, and an otter skin hangs down their backs almost to the ground. They keep straightening this while dancing as a woman might arrange a stray strand of hair. Some of them carry little hand mirrors, and nearly all of them carry beaded quirts in their right hands. Some carry eagle-tail fans in their left hands.

Those of the Buffalo clan imitate the buffalo bull as they dance by standing straight and often backing up and making an explosive sound like the cough of a bull buffalo. Those of the Eagle clan sway their heads from side to side as they bend over, just as the hunting eagle moves his head while he flies high in the air looking for prey. The Deer clan members lift their feet high and prance gracefully like a rutting buck, while the Bear clan dancers lumber around the drum without ostentation, and the men of the Panther clan slink softly and crouch as they dance.

The lead singer lifts his voice in a falsetto, then, as the drum starts with its rhythm, the other singers join him. The Osage dancers, being host, arise from their benches, straighten their otter-skin tailpieces, and move slowly with the rhythm toward the center and the drum, followed by the visitors. When the dance ends and the dancers have gone back to their benches, the drumbeats start again, but this time only the Osage Tail Dancers arise and dance out from their benches; the singing stops just as they reach the drum, and they stop, often with an uplifted foot on an unfinished beat.

For four days they dance thus, once in the afternoon for several hours, and again in the evening; then on the afternoon of the fourth day they have the Smoke Dance, or Give-Away Dance, during which the singers honor some of the families with their own song. When this family song is sung, all members of the honored family present, both men and women, whether participating in the general dancing or just watchers, leave their seats and dance very gravely. Sometimes, as they dance, tears come to their eyes as they think of some relative recently passed away or of the ancestor in whose honor the song was originally made.

When they have finished, those of the family who wish make gifts to any guest they desire to honor. It may be a gift of silver dollars to one of the singers, a blanket, cloth, or even a horse, which is led into the circle and his halter rope handed over to some favored guest or to an Osage of some other clan or family. Formerly most of the gifts were horses, but now silver dollars are given away more frequently.

I have never grown tired of watching the dancers. I remember them from the time I was a little boy, holding my father's hand—a time when they wore nothing except breechcloths, moccasins, silver arm bands, and scalplocks and carried hand mirrors and war axes. Now, only the older men are tall and straight; then they were all tall and lean. But for all the fat bellies and fat, flabby arms and gorgeous costumes, the dance is grave and the figures graceful, and in its dignity and fervency the dance is still a prayer. It is still a prayer to Wah-Kon-Tah of the old religion, notwithstanding the symbols of Peyotism with which they adorn themselves.

I am always impressed when the singers sing the "Song of the Red Horse." In this song there is simplicity and joy and a poignant fervency which affects me deeply.

Some years ago when my father was young, a man was given a horse at one of the Smoke Dances, a beautiful horse, red as blood, and shining in the sun as he quivered from the excitement induced by the jingling bells on the dancer's leggings and the swarming color. The man took the halter rope and was immediately overcome with joy when he realized that the wonderful horse had been smoked to him. He stood a moment in the silence, then he made a song—a song that sang itself from the depths of his heart:

> I heard singers sing song of his father.
> I saw red horse shine in sun.
> I saw sun shine on flanks of red horse.
> I saw his shining ears point to heaven.
> I hold rope in my hand.
> I hear my heart sing.
> Red Horse is mine.

I am suddenly aware of the changes in the earth's surface, especially when I find that I must change the trail that leads to my little house, because a ravine has been gradually eating toward it practically unnoticed. When it comes within a few feet of my road, I must do something immediately, or one day I shall find my road to town blocked.

As I change the road or attempt to delay the erosive progress of the ravine, I think of the dynamic nature of earth and its drama.

But this changing of the earth's face is quite slow compared with the drama represented by the relentless movement of Christianity. I feel the earth's drama all about me, but the conflict between Christianity and the old religion of the Osage forces itself upon my attention, although it is not so obvious as the other conflicts; not even so obvious as the slow wearing-away of the earth, but certainly much faster-moving. I become suddenly aware that I am watching a conflict that has been happening since the beginning of time, but, strangely enough, I am only aware of it at odd moments.

I have been intrigued for the last ten years with this cleaning-up activity of militant, devouring Christianity; the cleaning-out of the machine-gun nests of the native religion, and the gradual roundup of the guerrillas left in odd corners as the advance sweeps on. As I watch with my sympathies fired and my sense of the dramatic inspired, a new force makes it appearance and seems intent on conquering the conqueror, Christianity. The natural, slow-moving local drama, wherein the original paganism of the blackjacks had to adjust itself through Peyotism to Europeanized Christianity, now becomes a tragedy in the wild confusion of adjustment to the new force of natural science, mechanically conceived.

This new force has crept into the homes of the white men and into their souls and seems to be crumbling the self-confidence of triumphant Christianity, thus allowing, oddly enough, the religion of Wah-Kon-Tah–Peyotism to survive longer through the weakening of this self-confidence.

As in all the triumphs of Christianity, the native religions linger longer in the country; so does this native religion of Wah-Kon-Tah–Peyotism take its last stand in the country, in the hearts of the older men of the tribe who live quietly on their ranches over the old reservation. With these older men the old paganism will pass, and Christianity will creep into every corner, vying with the mechanical conception for superiority.

I feel that I have been extremely fortunate to be a witness to the last struggle of a native religion, and certainly my daily life in the blackjacks has been influenced as much by this struggle as by any other struggle for survival. The passing of a concept of God seems to be almost as poignant as the passing of a species.

And thus in the adjustment of the Indian's concept of God to that of the Christian's, he has put behind him the old religion of Wah-Kon-Tah and has accepted Christ, but talks to Christ through the Peyote button. In Peyotism there is both the old religion and Christianity, but there are many things which the old men do not wish to talk about concerning the old religion. They say that it was good at one time when the Osage people were strong, but now it seems it is not strong enough to stand up against the Christian religion, and therefore its medicine is bad and should be forgotten. Since it failed before the stronger religion of the white man, it can do no more than cause death; it has nothing to do with living, now.

Spotted Horse sent his second son out to see me because he had heard I was attempting to get some sacred bundles for the museum. He drove up to my fence in a gay convertible. He had no desire to give me his father's message, since he believed it to be quite unpleasant. We sat on each side of the fireplace and talked desultorily, then he said abruptly, "Ole man wanted me to talk to you about Wah Hopeh. . . . . Wah Hopeh Bundle what they call sacred bundle."

"He says for me not to open one?"

"Yeah, he says you must not open one of them bundles. He says you alltime ask too many questions about them bundles, he says. You oughtn't to do that; it's bad. He says you'll sure die if you fool with them things. Osage have put them bad things away, he says. He says we must follow word of Moonhead now."

"It's all right to have sacred bundles in the museum?"

"Yeah, I guess that's all right, but what he says don't fool with them bundles. You mustn't open it and you mustn't handle it either, he says. You sister mustn't handle it either, he says. This is way he says; he tole me to tell you this. He says only one that have word—have authority to put bundle in museum, is only one that mus handle it. No one mus touch it only that one. That one mus put it in one of them glass cases and ever'body leave it alone."

"All right," I said, "but we have to have some of those bundles there."

"Ole man tole me to come talk to you now, but he says he wants to talk to you sometime about these things."

"All right."

We sat for some time looking into the fire, then he said, "I guess he wants to talk to you." He got up suddenly, picked up his big black hat, and walked out. He slid his great bulk under the wheel of his car and drove off, his whole manner showing the relief which he felt in having given his father's message.

MOCCASIN PRINTS

The confusion into which Christianity and mechanism has thrown the Osage Indian, the man who was a part of the balance of my blackjacks and prairie, is only a part of his tragedy. The old men lament the destruction of their social structure, but they are more concerned over the consequent end of the tribe as a unit, the sudden rupture of their record, and the loss of their individual immortality.

The "insurgent" man of my ridges, through his ability to think, has projected himself into the future, beyond the disintegration of his body. He has the benefit of two progressions, physical and mental or spiritual, and he wants to live beyond the final disintegration in both: in his descendants and in the thoughts or consciousness of his descendants, urged by the mysterious earth-force toward some objective beyond his comprehension.

Formerly when they went into senility like the Symbol Oak, they made the same pitiful gestures toward survival with the last pale tassel, with the last breath, and then passed into the virility of their saplings, assuring the continuance of their species. But now their consciousness points out to them the end of their race, the end of their god, the complete assimilation of their children, and the end of their immortality. It is the sheet-water of oblivion that washes their moccasin prints from the ridges and agitates their last thoughts.

It is because of these thoughts in the head of Eagle-That-Gets-What-He-Wants that he often asks his wife to send for me during this moon of soft, dreamy days. The talk is on the same subject and varies little, but one day I took notes as the old wife began the conversation.

When she was settled on the floor with her things about her, she said slowly in English, "He says he wants to talk to you. He said when he is gone young people might forget things. He wants you to write these things down." She picked up a piece of cloth and set one of the pink ribbons against it; held it from her for a moment, then began to work the ribbon into the cloth. She continued to speak in English as the chief sat with his eyes closed as if attempting to remember.

"Seems like now these things will not be remembered by the people who will follow, if you do not write them down in book. The old people used to tell these things to their children, and they would tell them to their children, and these things would be remembered for many years. They would tell them many times, and they would be remembered for thousand years—I guess." She looked over at the chief and said, "Hehn?" He seemed to be asleep, and she continued: "Now, seems like we must put these things in book. Ole people used to talk and the young ones listened, but we got to be like white man now, I guess." She sewed on the cloth a short time, then said in Osage to the chief, "I want to tell my son here about the way we did things, hehn? I shall tell him about Tze Topah."

The chief looked up and said, "Tell him that about Tze Topah. . . . . I am thinking about what I wish to tell him."

She turned again to me and smiled: "He said to tell you about the way we used to do things. I will tell you about Tze Topah, who was chief of Little Osages. He was his uncle too." After fumbling with the varicolored ribbons, she continued: "Tze Topah was chief of the Little Osages. He was a great mans. One time he said to himself, 'I am getting old; soon I shall die.' He wanted the people to remember him and the things he did. He always fasted for seven days in January and in July, so that he could have beautiful dreams; so he could talk to the trees and they would talk to Wah-Kon-Tah for him; so he could talk to the buffalo and they could talk to Wah-Kon-Tah for him.

"One time when he was fasting, he heard a buffalo bull singing— he was singing, 'I go west, I go west; soon I shall go to the west, and you will never see me again. Soon I shall go west, and you will not have covering for your bodies. Soon I shall go west, and you will not have covering for your houses. Soon I shall go west, and you will not have food for your relatives. Soon I shall go west, and you will live no more in the light of day.'

"When Tze Topah heard this, he crawled to the top of a hill and looked far out on the prairie, but he could not see the bull. He wondered about this. Seems like the song went away in distance, like the bull was going. Tze Topah was very hungry after seven days. He had heard many things and had seen many beautiful things, but the song of the buffalo made his heart heavy.

"He was so weak that he must crawl on his belly, but he could see a lo-o-o-o-ng ways. He saw some cows and some calves—buffaloes they were. He shot a fat cow and ate the tongue and liver, and he felt better. He made a song about this as he lay on his back, but I do not remember about this." She turned to the chief and said in Osage: "He made song about cow making him happy, hehn?"

"No," said the chief. "Calf of cow made song; Tze Topah heard calf singing." He cleared his throat and sang for a moment, and, when he was finished, he laughed and looked at my secretary, perhaps from slight embarrassment.

His wife continued: "He says the calf sang; do you understand? Calf sang song like this: 'I can't find my mother, except her head.' That's what he sang, that little calf, and Tze Topah heard him sing that song when he was lying there on his back, full of buffalo tongue and liver—seems like. Every January and July he made this fasting, and he would tell the people about these things.

"He would look at the sun and when there was a small circle around it, he knew that he would kill his enemy; but when the sun had a wide circle around it, he knew that he would only take horses.

"But what I wanted to tell you; he was going to die from being old. He spent many hours telling the people what he knew, and about the things he had done when he was younger, so that they would not forget about him when he passed away; so that they could tell their children about the great Tze Topah. But there was one band of Little Osages camped far away on the plains. Seems like they had been away for a long time, and Tze Topah was worried about this. One day he caught his horse and rode several days to this camp of Little Osages. When he was near that place, he took his war clothes and his paint from the war bag, and dressed himself in his clothes and painted his face. He looked in water to paint his face, I guess, hehn?

"When he was dressed, he rode into that camp and sang a song that he had made for himself. He rode through that camp many times and sang that song. He sat on his horse very straight, with his shield over his arm and his long bow in his hand, with a red eagle feather on the end of it. I forget about that song, but he sang that all the people should get up from their robes and come out of their houses. He sang that all the people should stop their work and come and bring their little children, so that they would know that he was the great Tze Topah. He wanted them to see him and know who he was—that's what he sang. He wanted the older people to see him and he wanted the little children to see him so that they could tell their children and the children of their children, and the great Tze Topah would be remembered as long as Osages had tongues to talk and their children turned their ears to them.

"That's why he wanted you to come this morning. He has been thinking about Tze Topah and he has been thinking about everything that is happening to the young people. Soon they will be white men and women, he says, and they will not remember very long what the old people have said. He says his picture which that white man painted—that one that talks so much—is in the museum and that is good. But he says that the things which he says ought to be in book, so that his words will live."

When he is quite well, he sometimes sends his son out to The Blackjacks to tell me to come, either to his ranch house or to the big spring located on some of his land in the eastern part of the county. This spring is shaded by hickorys and blackjacks, and there he sits and dreams while his wife prepares the feast over an open fire, cooking all the old foods of her people.

As we sit in the shade by the spring after the meal, he will tell me little stories of animals or repeat some of the stories which the grandmothers were accustomed to tell little children on long winter nights long ago. We also talk of the politics of the tribe, and during these talks he usually takes from his shirt pocket under the folds of his blanket a creased paper which he hands to me, and which is often a personal letter from some official of the United States government; he watches my face closely as I read it.

When his chronic arthritis confines him to his chair in the corner of his house at the ranch or at the Village, he usually wants to talk about the things which he wishes people to remember about him. He realizes he cannot depend upon the father-to-son method of history impressed on the minds of the succeeding generations by constant repetition. He knows that his passing, and the passing of the other older men of the tribe, will be the symbolic passing of the tribe in so far as the old order is concerned, and he feels that he will be cheated of that very precious immortality which is the tribal memory.

This worries him when he is ill, and he becomes at such times very anxious that I write down that which he has to say. He wants to live in the memory of man through the agency of word symbols of the white man and through the paint of the artist.

His habit, when I bring a secretary to put down his conversation, is to repeat everything he has said many times before. The tendency to follow the method of transmission of the history of his people by constant repetition is very strong. I cannot lead him; I must wait until he has said what he wishes to say, and then lead into that which I seek to know. His repetitions vary little, and then only in the very trivial phases.

He has a great sense of humor. He calls his place where a big spring flows down the ravine by the old house "Hollywood," for some reason of his own, and when he mentions the name, he smiles with appreciation. He had a big red-faced Irishman working for him, and he called him "Delicious," because of his apple-like complexion.

Sometimes when he is quite ill sitting in his chair, with his legs wrapped in a blanket, he taps his cane on the floor gently in the rhythm of the drum and closes his eyes to better see the pictures that float before his mind. These pictures are often of himself as a little boy being brought into the government school at the agency, where he saw his scalplock fall to the floor at his moccasined feet, after having been cut off close to his head, and where he was given white boy's clothes to wear. There are pictures of a very frightened little boy with nine other Osage boys and girls on a train going to Carlisle in faraway Pennsylvania, under the care of Major Miles, whom they called "Thick Hand." It was on that train that he saw his first black man, and from whom he shrank. He remembers that the ten little Osage took the basket of fruit which a train "butch" held temptingly before them, settled themselves around it, and ate heartily, while the butch, half-afraid of them, hesitated to express his injury until the Major came back to the car and paid for the fruit. There is another picture of a little Osage boy riding out on his first buffalo hunt with a resplendent uncle as leader of the hunt and of the arrow which he had shot and which quivered in the side of an open-mouthed calf.

It makes him very happy to look back over the road which he has traveled; back to the days before the white men had crossed his road with their own roads to the confusion of his people. He says that he is out of that confusion now and that his feet are straight and true along the Indian Road and that he can see its end ahead of him. He says that, when he was a little boy, he used to think that where the prairie and the sky met was actually the wall of the world and that all trails ended there. Now he says that he knows this to be true and that the meeting of the sky and the prairie is really the end of his road and that he can see where he is going because the distance is so short.

But who will know that he, Eagle-That-Gets-What-He-Wants, now chief of the Osage, will be held in the memory of his people; that he will be brought to life again for many years around the fires of his people, as they talk of their great past and of the men who made it glorious. He is ready for the end of the road, but the uncertainty that his moccasin prints will remain makes him very unhappy.

He keeps repeating to me the story of how he was given the authority as chief of the Little Osage. He seems to think more of that authority which was given in the traditional manner than of the honor in being the elected chief of all the Osage.

After Carlisle he stayed with his uncle, who had received the chieftainship from Tze Topah or Nopawollah. He stayed with his uncle because his father had died during his absence at school. When his uncle died, there were several old men sitting about, and they cried in the old way. They knew nothing of Peyote in those days.

"My uncle passed on," he tells me. "When I saw him there, it seemed that my heart was so heavy that it pulled my head down. I said, 'I am alone now. I do not want to stay where there is so much sadness.' I said, 'There is only Three Striker left of my family.'

"Soon the old men stopped their crying, and I looked up. It had been some time since my uncle passed on, but when I looked up, he was sitting on his robes. He was talking; his voice seemed to come from f-a-a-a-ar away like man in cave. Soon he turned his eyes to me. They were like eyes of buffalo skull lying on prairie for a long time. He said to me, 'Go to that trunk and bring me those papers you find there.'

"I went to trunk and opened it. There were many papers, but there were certain papers there. I took these papers back to him; I was afraid. He reached his hand which held the papers to me. I wanted to back away, but I stood still. His hand did not shake as it had done before he passed on, and his voice was steady when he said to me: 'I turn over chieftainship to you. I give you authority to carry Father Fire. These old men who sit here have heard me say this. These old men will know that I have done this.' "

The young chief was very sad. He was afraid he could not carry the great responsibility of chieftainship. And as he rode back to his relative on Rock Creek, he thought of the many things which a chief must do. He thought about what his father had told him about learning the white man's ways at the white man's school.

The picture of the little log cabin which the government had built for his father on Mission Creek was in his mind as he rode along. He could see his father again standing in the one room, where his own hunting dogs lay about him, sleeping, as he entered with the lariat rope coiled around his neck, and with his saddle and buffalo-hide blanket in his hands. He had come from herding his father's many horses as he did every day, and, as he stood there, his father had said to him that he wanted to talk.

"Son," his father had said gravely, "I have been to house of Striking Ax. The head men of the Little Osage are meeting at that place. I have listened to their talk. They say that what Government said to us is not true. They say there that what Government said to us about having our own land if we left Kansas is not true. I heard them say there that white men are coming here too. They will come like flood water on river; they will run over everything. When I think about talk I heard there at house of Striking Ax, I said I have made a mistake. I said I have been preparing my son for things that will never happen. There will be three boys sent away to school from Little Osage. That's what they talked about there. You will be one of those boys. I want you to learn to speak as the white man speaks, so that you will have easier time when white man comes."

As the young chief rode toward the house of his relative, the pictures passed through his mind like clouds across the sky. He recalled that it was the next day after the talk with his father that he rode behind his father to the agency, where his scalplock was cut off and he was given white boy's clothes and put on the train at Arkansas City, Kansas, to be taken to faraway Carlisle in Pennsylvania.

And as he rode along that day, a voice very much like the voice of his father kept saying to him, "I have made a mistake; I have been preparing you for things that will never happen.....I want you to speak as the white man speaks," and he knew now that what his father had said was true—that he must learn to speak as the white man speaks and learn what the white man thinks and why he does certain things. He must know something of the white man's God, so that he, too, could benefit from the strong medicine of the white man's God, for the benefit of his people.

He felt very much alone as he rode along, and his thoughts and the sadness that sat heavily on his heart with the memory pictures drowned the reality of things about him, so that he was at the corral of his relative's place before he was aware of it.

But that night when he could not sleep for the heaviness of his heart and for the pictures that crowded his mind is vivid in his memory. He could not pray to Wah-Kon-Tah for relief then, as today he could pray to him with Peyote songs. In those days you did not pray to Wah-Kon-Tah for aid but for the weakness of your enemies so that you might overcome them, or you asked Wah-Kon-Tah why he had done certain things to you; why he had brought you sadness and grief. In the old days you asked Wah-Kon-Tah these things, then went out yourself to right the wrong and propitiate Wah-Kon-Tah so that he would let you alone, so that you could take care of yourself. If he had known about Peyote that night as he lay in great sadness, he could have unburdened his soul by singing his prayers to the Peyote button, and Wah-Kon-Tah of today would have given him some satisfaction through a voice or a sign.

So he lay through the night on his robes in the corner of the log cabin of his relative, Three Striker, with his heart like a great stone within him and with tears that brought no relief.

The next morning it seemed that everything else was shut out of his mind but the voice of his father, saying, "I want you to talk as the white man talks." He realized that he could not do this. At Carlisle he had talked with others who spoke the Siouan tongue, but he was too shy to speak English, and his mind "pushed it away." Now, he must learn to face the white man so that he could be a worthy chief of the Little Osage. He said to his relative, Three Striker, "I shall leave my horse at stage station. I am going to Elgin for train there. I shall go to Haskell school." Three Striker said nothing, but watched him as he rode away.

When he arrived at the stage station on Hickory Creek, the white man there said that the stage had gone. Happiness and sadness were so mixed in his heart that he didn't know what to do. He rode on then into the agency and came to the Village. He tied his horse to the stakes of Striking Ax's lodge and went in. Striking Ax had his wife feed him, then as they sat on their robes he told Striking Ax that he had made up his mind to go to Haskell so that he could learn about white man and his ways. Striking Ax was a distant relative, so he had a right to know these things and he had the right to advise him.

After some time Striking Ax said: "No, I want you to stay here. I want you to stay here until I get back. I go to talk to parents of a girl. I know this girl will be suitable wife for you."

Several days later he came back and said: "I have given my word to parents of this girl. Parents of this girl have accepted my word. You must think of marriage now."

In his talks the chief usually skips the actual ceremony of his marriage, because he believes that it is not important to his immortality, but when his wife is present she likes to talk about it and usually takes over the conversation. She wants me to know that the modern ceremony is much different from the one she went through many years ago, and she likes to relive it in detail and to deplore the changes which white men and mechanism have brought.

VII BUFFALO-BREEDING MOON

QUITE OFTEN DURING THE MONTH OF JULY THERE IS NO RAIN. DURING the years of drought it is naturally more unpleasant than during the years of wet weather, when the earth is moistened by the rains of spring and the gushing floods of June; but July, the Buffalo-Breeding Moon, is always hot, consistently the hottest month of the year.

Again the white-face bulls take the place of the bawling, mating buffalo here in the blackjacks, their mating frenzy causing their sides to work in a bellows action and their tempers to become even shorter in the heat.

The bird chorus has almost ceased, and only a few of the more independent singers ignore the blazing sun and the hot shade. The dickcissels sit on the fence posts or on a swaying weed and sing with some cheer but weakly, the cuckoo croaks with petulance, and the flycatchers—the kingbird, crested, and scissor-tailed—build their nests on the ridge, but only the crested is loudly vocal in anything that resembles song. It is definitely not a song but a happy burst of enthusiasm which expresses happiness very well. The scissortail does a few acrobatics over the house which are accompanied by chatter, but their long scissor-like tails make of these nuptial flights a graceful action. With the kingbirds they are the most tyrannical of birds, and there is no marauding crow or hawk that cares to linger in the vicinity of their nests. They fly above them like a pursuit plane attacking a bomber and dive on their backs with definite effect, the larger birds flapping away as though escaping hornets.

The quail continue to whistle cheerfully all through this month, especially during wet years when they sometimes raise two broods, owing to the fact that the earlier ones have been drowned out or because of the plenitude of water and dew. The cicada and the field sparrow, of course, sing all summer.

As the world of the blackjacks falls into somnolence that reduces life to a murmur, I watch the plants that I cared for so tenderly, and for which I had such hopes during the Planting Moon, curl and turn yellow. I watch this with indifference now, though I should have considered it a minor tragedy in May or June. The water in the tank under the run-off spout sinks so low that the dogs can scarcely reach it, and I must put a pole in it so that the squirrels can climb out if they lose their footing while reaching down to drink. This water and the water in the spring are the only waters on the ridge during dry years, and the birds of the ridge and some of the animals visit them sometime during the day or night. Of course, there is a pan under the pump, but I can never remember to keep it full. One day when I returned to The Blackjacks after being absent for several days, I found that I had forgotten to put the pole in the tank, and the water had evaporated incredibly. There were eight drowned squirrels in it.

When the hot winds blow and the vividness of life fades, there is no comfort under the Blackjack, and there is no relief to be found in the house. I stick to the red leather chair and moisten the couch with sweat. Even though from day to day I do not wear my clothes at all, the heat makes my body drip, and I can neither read nor work for the sweat splashing on the typewriter keys. Paradoxically there is some comfort in lying out in the sun. I cannot give the reason for this, except that the pleasure seems to come from the absolute abandonment of all effort to escape the heat, meeting it by yielding to it. The escape alternative is fishing. I pay little attention to fishing signs; I go simply because I happen to be in the mood for fishing or to escape the heat by physical action. Here seems to be another paradox. Tie a horse in the sun and he suffers terribly with the heat, but he can graze over the prairie in the same sun and remain perfectly comfortable.

I throw things into the station wagon, go into town to get ice, and then drive over washed-out feed roads and cattle trails to some creek bottom where there are clear and deep holes of water. I always take the dogs along, which, of course, makes of me a very careless fisherman.

These creek bottoms are hotter than my blackjack ridges. No prairie breeze ever penetrates there, and the cicada chorus is deafening; but in action I am defeating the heat. Once the tackle is assembled and I am whipping the water with a little black gnat with a red tail, and the reel is singing, I am a true fisherman and triumphant. As I approach the big holes along the bank through the weeds, fighting spider webs, gnats, and mosquitoes with my left hand while I fish with my right, the heat is forgotten. When I am wading upstream up to my middle, I am entirely too happy to think of the heat. The setters worry a little at such times and swim back and forth across the creek; but there are always unorthodox perch to take the flies of unorthodox fishermen.

Later, as I cook my fish, the mosquitoes start their nocturnal hunting and the cicada chorus becomes sharper. The bullfrogs sit on the half-submerged logs and croak their love songs, monotonously and dolefully, as though love were a duty instead of the cosmic disturbance that it is during the Buffalo-Breeding Moon.

I can sleep in the station wagon or on top of it, and I invariably choose the top, since mosquitoes fly close to the earth; also the air is fresher. However, I do not entirely escape either mosquitoes or heat even though I am far above ground prowlers. At least the cicada chorus leaves off at complete darkness. During full moonlight the witchery is so disturbing that I cannot sleep, and I sit and dream while the bullfrogs and the horned owls drown out the hum of the mosquitoes and the stridulations from the grass, the frog attempting to impress his female with a love croak and the owl attempting to frighten the nocturnal prowlers into careless movement.

This is the month of visitors to The Blackjacks. During this month I talk more than I do all during the year. This is the season of beer and talk under the Blackjack. My visitors leave the hot cities with tingling anticipation in their hearts and arrive to strip down to their shorts and make themselves believe that this is the very kind of life they would like to live. They find the garden sprinkling can suspended from a postoak, filled with cold well water, a perfect shower and the absence of an outhouse a complete liberation from city conventions. From the running oaks a man can enjoy the freedom of all outdoors and think up telling points to be made later under the Blackjack, around the green table when we talk cabbages and kings.

Often several arrive at the same time, and I must manage to find sufficient chairs. The green metal table is moved out in the shade of the Blackjack and a tub is filled with cracked ice and beer, and I begin to feel the inspiration to cook. I enjoy the very thought of food when there are others about to share my delight in it; cooking for one's self is rather an uninspiring chore.

If there is no venison or bear left over from the last hunt in my cold-storage locker, there are great cuts of choice beef to be served with spaghetti, or I fry a chicken for each person present, or roast a guinea or a pheasant for each person, but always have spaghetti. One week I had nothing but spaghetti and eggs and did not grow tired of them.

I, like all men who have advanced beyond the water-boiling stage in cookery, am very proud of the things which I do well—cooking beef, frying chickens and young guineas, and roasting ducks. I have gained a reputation as a cook through the rather underhanded exploitation of nature. Visitors from the city are always intensely hungry in the country, especially since they cannot go into a cafe at will and order a meal, and the realization of this always makes them conscious of food. Also there is something about country air, even though in July it may be like the breath of a panting dog, that sharpens the natural urges. But the great trick is delay. I wait until the first or second pangs have passed, then leave my chair at the table and with an announcement, the expansiveness of which implies limitless beef and beer and piles of spaghetti, that dinner is about to be prepared.

Of course, the chorus of volunteers is wisely squashed when I recall to their memories that which I have said many times—that this is a one-man outfit and that there is not sufficient room in the box kitchen. Standing in shorts and cowboys boots at the kerosene stove, I am happy. The sweat pours from my face and body, and I have a towel around my neck and a glass of whiskey and soda or a bottle of beer at hand, which the hungrier guests keep supplied as an excuse to see how the food is coming. Only people who have never visited The Blackjacks ever come into the kitchen to offer advice, some visitor who has reached the egg-frying or the spaghetti stage in the beautiful art. Such a visitor is very deftly discouraged by whatever method then presents itself.

Then as the sun slips behind the blackjacks, fired to a deep red it seems by its own uncontrollable heat, we sit around the table and silently eat, except for a few desultory statements or the expression of an afterthought by someone who had neglected to express this particular idea during the heat of some discussion earlier in the afternoon.

This freedom, sitting at table in shorts in the middle of a great expanse of blackjacks and prairie, with nothing in sight to recall the screeching and the clanking of the mechanized world somewhere beyond the wild ridges, inspires primitiveness in my guests. I can see it in the glow of their faces and the manner in which they toss the beef bones over their shoulders to the dogs; by the manner in which they pat their naked bellies as they stretch in their chairs after the meal; in the wholehearted manner in which they belch; and by the unaccustomed profanity in their conversation.

The interest in the New Deal and international affairs dies with the day, and they simply sit, pat the setters, and ask about the plants and the trees as they watch the distant prairie hills darken from lilac to mauve. They always straighten in their chairs when an old dog coyote howls his eternal question to the scorched red moon hanging in the trees of the east ridge.

Once as several of us sat thus about the table covered with the remains of a meal and empty beer bottles, and my visitors were floating idly on the swells of their virile dreams, a great bull walked with deliberation along the front fence, bawling belligerently. A man from a very large city, pale from his endless, sedentary work and smothering domesticity, asked about the habits of cattle.

When I had finished about the business in detail, he said, "You mean to tell me that those fellows"—he pointed to the bull—"do nothing but walk around looking for a new love affair?"

"That's right."

"And you said there are about twelve cows to every bull in this pasture?"

"Yes, about that proportion, I should say."

His eyes twinkled mischievously, he smiled roguishly at us, and said, "I hate the bastards."

Once two of my guests continued their discussion after dinner and sat over their whiskey-and-sodas in the moonlight absorbed in world affairs. I became sleepy and arranged my bed in the swing. I was soon asleep, and the voice of the one championing the New Deal faded away at last.

I had been looking toward the northwest for days for an accumulation of clouds that might swing over my blackjacks and revive my parched ridge and stop the oven-hot winds that sang relentlessly through the leaves of the trees and hissed through my screen porch. My nerves thirsted for relief from the terrible monotony that was broken only temporarily by the nights. I even dreamed of the smell of rain and the sound of its sluicing through the gutter spouts and its tattoo on the tin roof of the front porch.

When I dozed off in the swing as my friends were talking heatedly, my last thought had been of rain; not expectation but hope. Then in the early-morning hours I heard thunder. I got up quickly and put on my boots, then started rolling my mattress so that I could carry it in. I awakened to full realization suddenly as I stood there in the bright moonlight. One of my friends had been pounding periodically on the metal table to stress his points concerning the British rubber policy.

The Cowhand is my most frequent visitor during this time. He rides up to the fence from working the pasture and ties his horse to it at the point where I have one of my trumpet vines. A cowboy has a delicate respect for women, a profound respect for fat cattle and strong cowhorses, but the only vegetation he respects is bluestem grass.

He clanks up holding his hat as a fan, sits down, and starts rolling a cigarette. I am always glad to see him. He takes his whiskey straight and his beer in three gulps and a "hagh" from the bottle.

We talk of horses, cattle, and the hard life of a cowboy on thirty-three dollars a month, house, and chickens, and deplore the exclusion of hogs and a milk cow in the arrangement. He likes ale better than beer with fried chicken and spaghetti, just as I do, and he likes square-dance music on my tinny phonograph.

He tells me the news of the country; those things that happen in the everyday lives of people living far apart; tidbits that travel from ranch to ranch and from farm to farm by some unknown agency and are never heard of in town. This very mysterious spread of information concerning local lives is like the spread of some epidemic, like influenza; one is not aware of the carrying agency. The Cowhand seldom goes off the ranch except in roundup time, when he goes to help the neighbors, or when he makes his infrequent trips to town, but his information is current.

He sometimes turns his horse loose in the yard and stays the night, especially after afternoons of beer and food. He saw me bring out sheets for the bed on the couch. "Hell," he said, "don't go to no trouble to be puttin' them things on my bed, I ain't got no use fer 'em. The woman gives me hell about sheets; she won't put 'em on my bed a-tall —says I tear 'em with my goddam toenails. I kick like a bay steer, anymore."

He likes to tell me about his plans for his family, his dreams, and the possibility of his quitting the saddle.

"A ole boy ain't got no business a-cowboyin' when he's got a woman and kids to kinda look after; a ole boy's wages ain't gonna git it done. Tell yu what a ole boy could do; and they wouldn't be nothin' crooked 'bout it either. Take these dogy cafes now. They's many a ole cow dies durin' droppin' time, and leaves purty good cafes without a mother. A dogy cafe like that ain't got a chance in the world agin' coyotes and starvin' if they ain't found and tuk care of. A ole boy like me could watch durin' droppin' time and take them little dogys home and give 'em melk from a bottle like a kid; first thing yu know, he's got him a herd to start on."

He looked at me and then continued defensively, "Them little dogys 'ud die anyways iffen a ole boy didn't take care of 'em—he could kinda go fifty-fifty with the boss."

"I'll bet you do most of your dreaming in the saddle, don't you," I asked, "as you're riding the pastures? I have some of the damnedest dreams in the saddle."

"Hell," he answered quickly, "my ole tail's in the saddle but my mind's in Arkansaw. I do a lotta studyin' 'bout things and a-dreamin'. Time I git to the corral at home, them cattle I bin a-doctorin' fer worms is all mine, and I got the woman all dressed up in fancy doo-dads. It's a comedown when a ole boy goes in the house and the woman tells him they ain't no more beans, and payday not comin' along fer a week."

The reason I get all the gossip of the prairie at this time is due to the fact that my neighbors have little to do in this season before shipping time, for the calves are growing and the cattle becoming fatter and fatter every day, and haying season has not yet arrived; the waving meadows of bluestem not yet ready to put up. Before my meadow was leased, my neighbors would drop in to ask about my hay and perhaps bid on it, and they usually stayed for several hours talking of cattle and markets and incidentally letting drop little tidbits of scandal; some woman or girl "cuttin' up" a little, or about a neighbor who is attempting to introduce sheep into our cattle country, and how "he thinks he's cuttin' a fat one" by so doing. Their hopeful predictions about sheep are always true; they have not been successful thus far in this part of the country, and with my neighbors I am contented that this should be so. The bawl of cattle is a part of the prairie's rugged force and lure; the petulant bleating of sheep on a cold, damp day is nerve-racking. My coyote-hunting neighbor said, "Sheepmen are hell for shootin' coyotes—the bastards even poison 'em."

One wind-scorched day a rancher from the north drove up in his pickup truck to ask about my hay. We sat under the Blackjack and talked for a while, then I asked him if he wanted a cold bottle of beer.

"No, don't reckon I do," he said. "Cain't drenk that belly-wash; might take a drenk with you—if you ain't got any, it's all right."

"Sorry," I said, "not a drop; don't drink it in the summer."

"That's all right; don't need it I reckon—man's better off without it. I tell yu though, it kinda heps a man along. Take me now; I can take two, three slugs, and I got the purtiest wife and the smartest kids in the country; I got the best grass and plenty good watter, and the fattest goddam cattle in the United States—hell, I cain't even git outta debt on beer."

Thus the Buffalo-Breeding Moon with its heat is a season of suspended action in the business of life, like a midwinter month in the North when snow and cold restrict action and confine men to the fireplace or the kitchen. The people of my country are not so much restricted, however, as they are made restive by the heat. They go from shade to shade for conversation and watermelon-eating or go into town to sit under electric fans and drink beer.

Of the noctural hunters, the great horned owl is the most important. He strikes fear into the hearts of the guineas with his booming and freezes the life of the grass roots and the running oaks. Only the nonchalant skunk carries on with his turning of cow chips looking for beetles, to feel suddenly the sharp talons of the great bird in his back; his blackness is of no avail, and the two white stripes running down his back, like the scalplock of the Osage warriors serving as a challenge to all enemies, only advertise his position to his deadliest enemy. But even when the white stripes are rudimentary and he is almost completely black, the keen ears of the great owl can detect the faintest crack of a stick or scratch of a claw. The owl accepts the challenge of the white stripes and takes advantage of the utter disregard in which the skunk holds all things not edible. He seems to enjoy the porklike meat of the skunk.

I don't know how often these ghostly hunters of the moonlight strike skunks, but I have shot them when they gave off very strongly the skunk-musk odor, and I have heard the dramatic struggle startling the silent nights as I lay in my bedding roll. When an owl strikes a meandering skunk, the musk defense of the latter seems to concern the great bird very little, but it invades every square inch of the ridge like some heavy, suffocating gas.

During early evenings usually just before dusk, when the first fresh exhalations of the grasses and the leaves come like a pat of encouragement at the end of a midsummer's day, the leaves of the blackjacks begin to sigh pleasantly in a breeze that comes for miles across the prairie from the south. Then nighthawks join the colony of swifts that live in my chimney in insect-chasing low over the tree tops. The nighthawks, called bullbats because of the sound made by the air passing along the edges of their tremendous mouths as they dive on their prey, seem to come from nowhere very suddenly. As they dive, a blowing-across-a-gun-barrel sound is heard, and this in the early day was interpreted as being similar to the voice of a bull. There is no reason why they should be called "bullbats," since they are members of the goatsucker family, and, further, there is no logical reason why the family should be called "goatsuckers" either for that matter.

There are two members of this family that come to the blackjacks in summer along with the nighthawks: the whippoorwill and the chuck-will's-widow. They are somber birds as they sit during the day on fence posts or on the ground, where they become a part of the leaf shadows of the trees. They are dull and gray with dirty white edges here and there. The nighthawk has white on the wings so arranged that they look like holes in his primaries as he flies in the late evening.

These three goatsuckers are colored like night-flying moths and are as mysterious as the dusk in which they fly. The song of the classical whippoorwill and that of the much less classical chuck-will's-widow are the theme songs of dreamy moonlight nights of romance. The bitter-sweetness of the whippoorwill's song lends itself to the thrilling mystery of romance and mating, while the constant repetition of his own name by the chuck-will's-widow is like a ritual of which he is growing tired; like the prayers of a weary Arab beggar to impress the almsgiver. This ritual will come from the depths of the blackjacks for hours at a time, long after the poetic voice of the whippoorwill has ceased.

Because these three shadowy birds of mysterious dusk and moonlight witchery were clothed somberly for the purpose of protection, because they were, with the exception of the nighthawk, seldom seen, and because they were not dressed in startling reds or blues or yellows and did not show themselves in man's gardens and sway among the apple blossoms in ecstatic song, they became the subject of gossip, and they carry the stigma of man's gossip in their family name: goatsucker.

It might have been due to the fact that a herd of goats traveling through weeds and grass will stir up insects which fly into the air above them, and just as barn swallows follow a man on horseback or afoot to get the insects he disturbs, so do the nighthawks, or, better, his cousins the nightjars of England and northern Europe, follow and circle above the herd of goats. It seemed perfectly logical to man that if a milk goat failed to be consistent in her yield, she must have been sucked by the birds flying above the homing herd. Wasn't the bird's mouth large enough and shaped for sucking goats? Wasn't he a mysterious ghostlike bird of the dusk as well? He was undoubtedly one, with his cousin the visible whippoorwill, but certainly the latter when seen was not associated with the voice of sweet mystery that came out of the moonlit woods of America.

The very large, pileated woodpecker, the one often mistaken for the practically extinct ivory-billed woodpecker, comes to my ridge to rip open the dead stumps of the postoaks. He tears an old, half-rotted stump to bits, looking for larvae, as effectively as I could so so with a hay hook. He shouts to the world that he has come, and his terrific cackling and his large size, with the startling red crest, make him conspicuous, and there is little wonder that at one time he was almost extinct in the Osage country. The Osage say that the white man was jealous because he could make more noise than he could and forthwith shot and ate him.

Every time I stop in the field to pull cockleburs from between the toes of my setters, or pick them from their plumelike tails and flanks, I think of the Carolina parakeet, which used to eat them. Every time I must prick my fingers in cutting them from a horse's tail or mane, I wonder what combination of things brought about the parakeet's complete extinction. The white man's plow and his abandoned hog pens increased their food supply. Their exit as a species from the earth's struggle must have been as sudden as that of the passenger pigeon, but without the dramatics attending the heath cock that danced his species into oblivion on Martha's Vineyard.

In ordinary years when the heat of the Buffalo-Breeding Moon creeps over the ridges, the vesper sparrow stops his evening song, the blue grosbeak becomes silent, and even the dickcissel, the sun-worshiper, stops his song from the tops of swaying weeds or from fence posts. There is only one voice of musical pretensions during the periods of heat that does not sharpen it to a knife's edge, although always associated with the hottest days. This is the song of the little spartan with the pink beak and the long tail, the ever present, the ever singing field sparrow.

During this time the voice of the crow is lazy like the indolent conversation of people, and the bluejay is subdued, while the croak of the yellow-billed cuckoo is one of petulance and protest. The bluebirds express their classical happiness with pettish little voices as they hover in great numbers over the birdbath, like bits of azure paper picked up by a whirlwind. Often the quail whistles until August, but soon this cheerful voice ceases, and the little field sparrow carries the burden of expressing the joy that is in living. His voice expresses the joy as he shells the seeds from the grasses in the yard, while the sharp little talk of the hummingbird, as he thrusts in and backs out of the flowers of the trumpet vines, expresses the spirit of life that the pitiless sun cannot subdue.

The growth rings in the sections taken from my postoaks indicate that there is a cycle of weather over the ridges which brings drought every six, seven, or eight years; this would perhaps explain so many interesting things to me about the earth, the little area of earth where I live, if I but had the wit to know why this is so. Sections from trees two and three hundred years of age tell me the facts but give no hint as to the reasons. They even tell me that, about the time of the American Revolution, a great prairie fire swept my ridges; probably set by the Osage to frustrate a war party of the Pawnee or Cheyenne horsetakers. That is all they will tell me. However, I have confirmed their evidence that drought comes to the blackjack ridges periodically, and I have passed through two summers of such drought.

One summer my pastures were the symbols of desolation. The sky was like a brass bowl inverted upon the earth of the ridges, shutting out the air of the universe. The water of the creek shrank into green scum-covered holes. The recently brought in "dust-bowl," government-sponsored cattle bawled distractedly as they strung out toward the muddy water holes, raising a cloud of dust on the brown prairie, which had been emerald only a few weeks previously. Crows sat ominously, like the raven on the bust of Pallas, on the glaring white limestone above the last moisture of the sun-cracked mud of the spring water hole below the house. They watched the air bubbles that meant crayfish digging down into the cool mud away from the sun.

The turkey vultures circled eternally. Even I could locate the hide-shrunken carcasses far out on the south pasture when the heated air currents became whimsical.

Cottony "dry-weather clouds" came in the afternoons only as a symbol which made of their vanishment a tragedy. Sometimes they coalesced in the northwest, spat a few drops that seemed to hiss as they hit the hot earth, then melted into the hot sky; melted even as the thunder growled in the distance.

The cuckoo was silent; he who croaks on hot days and is locally called "rain crow" because, they say, that when he croaks, he calls for rain. The very monotonous, happy voice of the dickcissel was not heard, and another priest of the all-subduing heat, the field sparrow, was silent. Only the rasping, piercing voice of the cicada kept on mercilessly, the true heat-chanter, the choir leader of drought's hell.

Then the grasshoppers came in force. They ate every leaf from my locust trees; they stripped the Chinese elms, the mulberries, and devoured every wilted, dusty weed, every half-yellow grass blade and shriveled rose leaf, until there was nothing left that was or had been green except the English ivy on the fireplace chimney and the leaves of the blackjacks.

One morning I found that they had eaten the ivy to the ground and had begun on a hoe handle. The trunks of the leafless trees were baked by the sun until the bark was scorched, and today they all have long, gashlike wounds reaching from top to bottom of their main stems.

There was no way to stop the hordes. Instructions were sent out from the Department of Agriculture to spread poisoned mash in a certain manner. One of my neighbors tried this and poisoned a flock of turkeys. I did nothing but wonder what would come next.

Each morning, however, the leaves of the blackjacks glistened in the morning light and cast their ragged shade on the brown earth. The shade was deceptive, as it offered no relief from the heat, but it was protection against the pitiless sun, and the glossy green leaves felt cool to the touch. There they stood throughout the drought, gloriously green; a symbol of life-everlasting in an expanse of brown desolation.

The sun shot up each morning out of the blackjacks of the east ridge, like a rifle-range target-marker; without conventional rays, dulled by the heat haze on the horizon, it came to stare at a world that had had no respite during the night, a world past protesting. As it climbed the sky, it was a disk of white-hot metal, standing for hours, it seemed, in one spot before moving on with agonizing slowness through brassy space. Then, as it descended, it seemed to stand still again to send its burning ray-fingers into the grass roots to dispel every shadow, every possible refuge.

It set up little currents over the brown prairie, which danced madly in whirlwinds, lifting crisped grass blades and broomweeds to gyrate in the prairie dust.

And each day the glass climbed, from its low at about 90, relentlessly degree by degree until it reached 112, 113, or 115 at four o'clock in the afternoon; then slowly by half-degrees it descended, reaching 100 long after darkness had fallen.

As the grass and even the weeds curled in the pitiless rays of the sun, and the cattle bawled with thirst, the vegetable gardens and crops were eaten by the grasshoppers or shriveled by the bake-oven winds. It seemed that a special destroying agent of nature had come to persecute her children, and imaginations were acute.

Under large tents spread in vacant lots in the small towns, the sweating people came to sing and pray to an apparently heedless Deity for relief. An instinctive fear spread over the dusty prairie as the insufferable heat and drought lingered with human purposefulness.

Evidence of a prairie lycanthropy appeared. An old dog coyote with a bobbed tail was declared by some to have supernatural powers and came close to becoming a werewolf, embodying the spirit of this inescapable tragedy purposefully arranged by whimsical nature to persecute man. He might have been a wandering lobo from the west, magnified through the shimmering heat and by man's distress, with his deeds distorted by man's heat-deranged imagination.

However, notoriety did come to a drought fear-vision, when a woman in one of the small towns was frightened from her kitchen garden by a monster that looked like an armadillo. He was good for several stories in the local papers. He was at once a diversion and a subject for ridicule, yet the nonbelievers as well as the believers wanted him to be real, so great was the distracting, purposeful heat, so nearly was modern, literate man's soul shriveled to the point of appreciating atavistic symbols.

On the prairie that is half sky and half undulating earth, where the evil-dispelling sun at one time during the day finds every grass root, mystery cannot live long. When a man can sit on his front porch and see for miles, he has few illusions, and mystery can approach no closer than the range of his vision. So when the first rains spattered on the dust to end the great drought of that summer, man's cycle of the seasons returned to accustomed behavior, and he again became the self-sufficient master of all about him, and "Ole Bob," supernatural old dog coyote or lobo, missed fame as a prairie werewolf.

VIII

YELLOW-FLOWER MOON

IF THE OSAGE HAD KNOWN ABOUT GOLD AND HAD NOT BEEN SO CLOSE TO the creative earth, they might have called this the Golden Moon for aesthetic reasons. The flowering weeds are predominantly yellow during this season, the blues, reds, and purples having passed or faded into pastels, so that the prairies are softer and mellowed. Yellow is very definitely the color of August; even the bluestem seems old-gold-washed at a distance, especially when blooming. There are the pastel blues and lavenders of the thistles and other flowers, but the sunflowers and the prairie goldenrods are glowing yellow. Yellow butterflies predominate, and the goldfinch comes to the ridges to tear at the thistle and to find something in the heart of the sunflower.

In the dry seasons, if the drought is not an extraordinary one, rains come in August, and the world that seemed dead springs into life again. The cattlemen have a new interest in life as the first warm rains come out of the northwest and from the east as well during this season. Though the air that was hot and dry may become steamy-hot with the rains, the earth is moist, and the green scum is washed from the water holes, and the discolored ponds become clear again.

If the market is right, fat cattle may be shipped at this time, and ranchers begin to analyze the virtues of the spring colts running on the range with their mothers; still long-legged, playful, and skittish, they begin to indicate what types of horses they may become.

There is zest and hope in the air again, even though the glass may creep up to the hundred mark each day. Bare-backed hay crews come to mow the meadows and bale the bluestem, and there is much activity and color. The women select their canned fruits to be taken to the county fair in September and cull their flocks. The cowboys look forward to the local rodeo and listen to talk about Cheyenne and Pendleton roundups. They discuss the possibilities of the bulldogging and the calf-roping, especially the match roping, where two cowboys are pitted against each other for prize money, and to win bets they have wagered with each other or the bets of backers.

A young cowboy came to my house one day with badly suppressed excitement. We sat for some time talking of hay and cattle, but he was not much interested in either just then. I asked him about his family and about the rains in the western part of the country. There had been rains, he said.

"Sure hadda good'un other night—sure a good'un; Beaver Creek got out of its banks and come up about the barn."

"Your dad contracted his calves?" I asked.

"Yeah, man from commission house in Kansas City, takin' 'em for eight, come time they're ready to ship."

He got up and walked over to the fence, picked up a new weed-cutter and felt the blade with his thumb, then said, "Say, reckon a fella could borry your saddle; if he'd take good care of it?"

"Well, I suppose so," I said. "If you're the one who wants it—I'm sure a man could borrow it."

"The ole man didn't know I was comin' down here and if he'd knowed I aim to ask you for your saddle, he wouldn't a-let me come. That'un a-mine ain't much 'count for ropin'. I bin aimin' to git me a new one, but seem like I don't git 'round to it. Mostly I ain't got the money for the one I want. I figgered you might not need your'n 'til after the rodeo, if a fella'ud take good care of it."

"You going to enter?"

He became a little embarrassed. "Yeah, I guess so." Then a little later his pride almost expressed itself. "Yeah, got me matched a-calf ropin'—Mr. Daniels' puttin' up the money to rope me at ole Red."

"Why, he got a championship belt at Cheyenne," I said.

"Yeah," he said with a catch in his throat. His emotion was choking him.

During wet years this is the month when I start working the setters in the strip north of the ranch house. If there are puppies whelped in March or April, they are now ready to learn that life is earnest and that cottontail rabbits and field mice have no part in the serious business of life; that terrapins are not sufficiently important to be barked at; and that young pheasants are in a special category and are not to be pointed, accidently killed, and carried about shellacked with puppy slavers.

If there are no puppies to be trained, I take the old dogs and walk out to the strip, carrying the 410-gauge for the purpose of giving meaning to the process of conditioning after the long summer idleness.

The young birds are now large enough to fly strongly, and the rains have left water-filled depressions so that the dogs can cool off as frequently as they wish. The grass and weed seeds are rather a nuisance as well as the heat, but by taking them out two or three times a week, and staying a little longer each day, they soon lose their summer's fat and become hardened by the time the quail season opens in November.

Training Irish setters requires more patience than training the ordinary intelligent horse in most cases, though I had one that was a natural retriever and surprised me by bringing a bird the first time I had her in the field. The bird seemed to be as large as the puppy, and her wobbly puppy legs became entangled in the grass, but she held on and laid the bird at my feet to look up at me with her roguish eyes lighted and her little pink tongue hanging out in an expression of her importance and happiness.

These setters are such beautiful dogs that their specialization in the field was almost forgotten for a number of years when they were being bred for the bench. They are erratic, temperamental, and very sensitive; that is, the females are. I use only females for hunting; I don't like the male attitude in the field. There is something about their virile ruggedness and hardheaded aggressiveness that fails to fit into my pattern of shooting. My male attitude won't tolerate male cockiness, and therefore I use females, who pretend that they don't know more about quail hunting than I do.

Even though it may take two or three years to properly train some of my puppies, when they are trained they remain well trained, and I have never had one that was gun-shy, nor have I ever had one that was not a perfect companion around the house as well as in the field.

Each year there is a period of autumnal weather, a kind of first notice of the approaching autumn. The stridulations of the insects have an autumnal sadness and the birds begin stirring. The setters become quite restive and keep asking why we don't do something about it. The ragged, half-molted bluejays come to the yard to see if anything has happened during the days of midsummer quiescence, and a pileated woodpecker comes to look over the postoaks for winter storage, cackling his presence.

These exhilarating days are short-lived, and soon the heat settles again, and the days seem hotter than ever.

The upland plover start their migration at this time. As in the case of the robin, I am not sure whether the ones that breed here begin to move south or whether the voices I hear during the night as they pass over the ridge are those that breed in the north. At one time these birds afforded wonderful shooting, but something happened. They must have passed through some cycle, as they were not seen in great numbers on the prairie of my country for years.

Occasionally I hear the voice of a curlew, but not often. If one rides out on the prairie after a week of heavy rains during this season, one may see them. Like the thousands of toads, they seem to come with the rain.

One Yellow-Flower Moon the swifts disappeared from my chimney and were gone until the rain came. I have no idea where they went and do not understand why they don't do this every year.

The young prairie chickens wobble as they take off on their flights across the prairie and seem to be unpracticed in the alternate flapping and sailing flight of their species.

This is the time of reburnished hope; the hope of the Planting Moon that was tarnished by the heat. The days are not cool yet, and the hot days of September are to come, but there is something in the air like whispering, a tingle that has no definite source.

And this is the day of youth on the ridges. The broods of birds and animals have reached that stage when they know more than their parents and laugh at their elder's caution. Immature quail refuse to freeze as I ride by but stand and look with unconcern, or, if the setters are with me, fly up into the trees and stretch their necks at the dogs like the dusky grouse in the Rockies called by the natives "fool hens." The young roosters, tailless and insufficiently feathered, stand on the fence posts or the wheelbarrow handle and challenge the world in a scratchy, gurgling crow. The ridges are full of sophomores, whose parents are dull and stodgy and annoyingly cautious.

But owing to this new bubbling in life and the conceit and glory of youth, I must be more watchful than ever. The young horned owls flood the blackjacks each moonlit night and crowd the guineas off the trees, then catch them when they hit the ground. The lanky young coyotes might appear at any time of the day, sneering at the traditional coyote hunting hours and conditions, and take a chicken from under my nose; and young bobcats lie on the lower limbs of the blackjacks and wait for the far-ranging flock of turkeys. They wait for and catch the sophomores that leave the protection of the flock to chase some especially delicious great yellow grasshopper; they wait not like a shadow, dappled by the slightly moving leaves as the old ones do, but with their jitterbug tails twitching with excitement.

The young mallards, however, are like teen-agers crushed by the ideas of dominant parents. They are seemingly backward and very good. They follow mamma in a column from place to place like convent girls following a nun. They have no ideas of their own. This may be due to the fact that they don't sprout juvenile wings like the other fowls but must wait until they are fully grown before they can have wings. Without wings one doesn't dare have independent ideas. And, of course, they are very graceless; they stumble over everything, recover, shake their incipient tails, evacuate, and carry on with the best of imbecilic good humor. They would even stumble over contour lines if they knew about them.

But what compensations for this graceless, earth-bound youth when the strong wings of maturity come and carry them through the air at seventy-two miles an hour—I have "clocked" them in a plane—or they become free to swim, dive, and express their perennial joy of living on some pond or lake! There is nothing that enjoys life like a mallard; not even a bird dog, a range stallion, or a mockingbird. It is a shame he can't sing.

In a world where each family is a unit, or at best a flock is a unit for the assurance of survival, there is no youth more favored than a duckling mallard. Of all the domesticated mothers of the ridge, the mallard hen is the wisest, the clearest thinker, and the quickest in correct judgment. At the moment when a mother duck is engrossed in a fresh pan of water with her greedy ducklings, she has her eye on the circling but harmless turkey vulture, high against the blue sky. Or she will suddenly herd her family to the buckbrush when a shadow, flying low among the blackjack trunks, zooms suddenly into the lower branches and becomes invisible.

The chickens may have missed the shadowy Cooper's hawk, and the pit-games, the turkeys, and the guineas who have their eyes and ears open for ground prowlers chiefly may have become frozen where they stand with their broods still busy about them. The sharp warnings from the mothers which send the broods scurrying into the grass roots, where they immediately become bits of stone, leaves, and tufts of grass may come too late, since the hawk's method of hunting depends upon his position in the tree and the movement of his intended prey.

At such times the turkey hen will stand and watch, having nothing to fear for herself on account of her size, while her little ones lay hidden; but the guinea hen will set up such a piercing cackle, in which the whole flock of adults join her, that the blue-gray shadow, his nerves a bit jumpy, will drop from his hiding place and fly swiftly away, low over the grass, losing himself immediately among the boles of the blackjacks.

The clumsy ducklings cannot freeze where they are but must stumble to the thick growths of buckbrush for safety, led by their frightened mother. Her loud quack is emitted when the shadow first appears, before he has taken up his position in the tree, so that she and her flock are moving while he is in movement and are well hidden by the time he has taken his stand. I have also noticed that the loud quack of the duck is a signal not only for the young but one of fear and for the purpose of attracting my attention. This latter statement is an opening for ridicule, I admit, but I have a great respect for the wisdom of the wild mallard mother.

Before the fence was built around the yard, the flocks had the run of the place whenever the pen gates were left open. As is my custom now on hot nights, I then slept out in the yard on the south side of the house under the tree which my friends had already begun to call "the Blackjack." One night I went to sleep slightly swaying in the swing, with the dogs lying on either side of me. My 12-gauge shotgun, loaded with No. 2 shot, was leaning against the tree. I slept nude, with a sheet at hand to pull over me toward morning.

I was awakened by the dogs barking with conviction. I saw them in the light of my flash-torch standing some hundred yards away with the hair erect on their backs. I took the gun and walked toward them, flashing the light in a circle, thinking I might catch the eyes of a coyote, but knowing that he would undoubtedly squat in the long grass so that I couldn't see him. I called the dogs back, and they were quite willing to respond inasmuch as they had no heart for fighting with a coyote. As a matter of fact, they would be no match for him.

Later I was awakened again. The dogs were standing where they had stood before. This time I ran through the long grass, passed the dogs with my light and gun, believing that I might force the coyote to show himself, but I got no glimpse of him. After I had got to sleep again, I was awakened by some movement under the swing. I flashed the light, and there was the mallard hen with her ducklings around her, and with absolute faith and contentment showing in the very intelligent eye she tilted toward me. She had quit the pen on the second alarm. My loud laughter seemed to crash the silence of the night, and the dogs came up to look into my face.

It was just before dawn when I was awakened again by the frantic barking of the dogs. This time as I shot my feet into my slippers I thought of the duck under the swing, and with my gun ran, not toward the dogs, but in the other direction, to the chicken pens. I was in time to see a coyote making for the gate at full speed. He had apparently been disturbed as he was about to enter the door of the chicken house. I hadn't brought my flash-torch with me this time, so could not see him well in the early-morning light.

When they heard the shot, the dogs left off their barking to the south of the house and joined me, then to my surprise struck the trail of the fleeing coyote, perhaps encouraged by the gunshot. I realized that, as soon as he was out of sight of me, the coyote would turn on them if they stayed on his trail. I ran back to the house and picked up the 30-06-caliber rifle and ran after the dogs. I saw them coming back to me, but I kept on, knowing that the coyote would run across the prairie in circling back to the south again.

I caught glimpses of him as he loped leisurely toward the head of the canyon, looking back over his shoulder, and after I had fired twice at him he speeded up and looked straight ahead. He was running as I wanted him to run—along the rim of the canyon—so I cut across and ran to the south end of the ridge, and, as he came into view, I fired several shots at him, turning him twice, so that on the second turn he ran back north, I running and firing until my gun was empty.

He ran on, a yellow streak across the prairie, and I stood watching him out of sight over the rim. The barrel of my rifle was hot. I had lost one of my slippers, and my bare foot was bleeding. The grazing cattle stood gazing at me as I stood naked and gleaming in the dim, early-morning light of the prairie.

I had spoiled an old coyote trick—one of them keeping the dogs' attention while the other raided; but I had done some very poor shooting chiefly because I hadn't washed my face. I am never able to see well in the mornings until I have washed my face in cold water.

When I had limped back to my little house, the mother mallard was making a terrific fuss over a pan of water which I had set out for the dogs, and the ducklings were all attempting to get into it at the same time.

I have never had any trouble raising guineas and pheasants when I left them with their natural mothers. A pheasant hen can cause her brood to literally melt into the grass, joining them in invisibility when danger comes. A chicken foster-mother is either too slow-witted or else doesn't have the right note in her warning. The Cooper's hawks take half of the guinea brood of a foster-mother, one at a time. In common with the crow and the bluejay, the guineas can overwhelm an enemy by numbers and noise, and, like the jays and crows, nothing strange escapes their notice. They make a terrific din over a shirt hanging on the fence if they have not noticed it there before, and, when they find a snake or a terrapin, they make such a noise that for my own comfort I must go out and do something about it. Very few predators have the heart to attack little guineas when they are protected by the raucous guinea flock.

From my experience in attempting to stock the ranch with pheasants I learned why a friend's father in England had asked us to shoot only pheasant cocks on designated days. The ring-necked pheasant is polygamous, and the older cocks are very jealous of their harems. Because of their age, experience, and fighting power, these old cocks gather the hens to themselves and keep the younger ones away. The disgruntled younger ones stay about the edges of the flocks and spend their time attempting to lure some of the hens away. If successful, they fly off with them to new territory, which means in my country that they must fly across a great expanse of prairie to other growths of blackjacks or to the creek bottoms for the cover which is necessary to them. This is one reason why my flock never grew, but, of course, this does not answer the question of what happens to them. My Cooper's hawks and great horned owls, coyotes and bobcats, are energetic and certainly well established, but I am sure that they did not account for the flock of twenty-five or thirty which seemed to disappear suddenly after four years on the ridges. Some romantics say that the birds planted in this country move gradually toward the North and West; toward China, from which the original stock of ringnecks were brought. They point to the fact that the states of Oregon and the

Dakotas are well stocked and hint that those birds planted in my country ultimately make their way to these regions.

I have lost several pit-game cocks that have stood against coyotes. During the poetic hour of dawn, tragedy comes to my flocks in the summer when they range away from the house. Awaiting them as they forage is the motionless Cooper's hawk in his position on the lower limbs of the blackjacks, and well hidden in the buckbrush the coyotes also wait. When either the Cooper's hawk or the coyote charges, the flocks freeze or come squawking back to the house and to the protection of my guns. All except the H-D cock. The Cooper's hawk will not attack him, since his prey is usually the half-grown guineas, turkeys, and chickens, but the cock will go to the rescue of any fledgling that is struck, even though he is never quite quick enough to stop the hawk. When the coyote charges, he will meet him halfway, but, of course, he is no match for the wolf.

No matter how hungry a sophomore coyote may be, he seems to have fun killing and jumping high in the grass to locate the half-grown, frightened chickens, the guineas having flown into the trees and the turkeys having finally composed their wits and scattered in every direction. He pays no attention to the terrified cackling of the hens, stopping only when necessary to snap the neck of an audacious H-D cock or when the guineas have brought him to his senses from his orgy. At such a moment he looks toward the house, and if the dogs have not joined the chorus of cackling and squawking, or if he does not see me, he will start to collect his kill—the young

chickens only, leaving the old cock lie. He will pile them up on a spot under the ridge out of sight of the house, then carry them away two or three at a time, taking them by the heads. However, if I appear, he will squat in the long grass until I leave, then slink away to return later. Sometimes he will run and not depend upon squatting, and in so doing he will put a ridge or a growth of trees between us as quickly as possible, stopping to look back when he reaches the crest of the last ridge, just before he drops out of sight over it.

In order to protect growing fowls, one must have a shotgun within reach at all times. Even as I type this line, my 12-gauge shotgun loaded with No. 2 shot stands within reach. No. 2 shot is heavy enough to take care of both the day and the night marauders, although a rifle would be much more effective in rare cases. I have learned never to place two guns within reach; for instance, a rifle for coyotes alongside the shotgun, even if one rarely gets in proper range for the shotgun. The attack from bird or animal comes with such suddenness that there is no time for thinking; successful action is a matter of co-ordination. Once I grabbed a broom that I had carelessly set up in the corner of the room alongside of the 12-gauge, ran out of the door, and covered a vanishing Cooper's hawk beautifully. He lost himself almost immediately among the boles of the blackjack, but I could hear the cries of the half-grown guinea he held in his talons until distance blotted them out. Completely filled with chagrin, I could neither swear nor laugh.

If man had hair on the back of his neck and along his spine, his hackles would rise just as those of animals do when fear comes and the reaction is quite involuntary. Whatever muscles or nerve action causes this involuntary raising of the hair in response to fear, it comes to man only as a tingling sensation, since he has no hair to raise.

I have this hackle-raising sensation when I am awakened in the dead of night, in the profound silence and darkness of the blackjacks, by the death squawk of a guinea, pheasant, or chicken. I sit up in bed stunned, and the back of my neck tingles. There is no definite action until thought comes. But even after I have become a reasoning animal, the tingling continues. After I have my slippers on and my gun and flash-torch in my hands, this manifestation of fear is still present. I note as I run through the yard gate with the dogs that the hair on their backs is raised, and I hear growls rumbling in their throats, and they begin barking at about the same time that my neck-tingling sensation has left and I have begun to reason about the nature of the enemy that has made the attack.

But how sinister is the blackness that fades back from the power of my light, as I attempt to "shine" a pair of eyes on the ground or in the trees. The blackness of the mysterious, drama-charged night steps back reluctantly as the beams play here and there and the macabre shadows dance in the now expectant silence. The dogs, having left off their barking, methodically test the air currents but remain close to me as our minds go through the process of elimination. If the marauder is a skunk, he will show himself, carry on in his bloody work with unconcern, or come toward us to investigate in undulations of black and white. In the latter case we all retreat; we do not want the sharp, piercing musk odor lying over the ridge for the remainder of the night in case he misinterprets our intentions. He will probably stop at the fence, but there is no guaranty for this. Being one of the most whimsical of animals, he may suddenly turn off down the ridge on other business.

If the visitor is a bobcat, he is far away with his chicken by the time we appear. If an owl, he is also far away, tearing savagely at his prey on some dead stump of a tree in the creek bottom; and, if an opossum, I can "shine" him in one of the trees and shoot him out, or, by circling, see him sneaking away and kick him into feigning death, thereafter breaking his neck by placing a stick on it, standing on each end of the stick, and pulling him sharply by the tail.

The bobcat is a very close relative of the lynx and looks very much like him except that he is smaller and, living in the canyons as he does, dark gray in coloration with a hint of the dappling of leaf shadows. As a matter of fact, a bobcat skin placed on the ground under the trees becomes immediately a part of the sunlight-and-shadow pattern of the ground and is difficult to see again if one turns the head for a moment. Just as the coyote's yellow-gray blends with the yellow, copper-colored grasses of winter and oddly enough with the golden-green grasses of summer, so does the bobcat blend with the leaf shadows of the canyons and the blackjack hills. There is a hint of yellow in the hair for the sun-splashes of the dappled shade. This also blends with the winter grasses, just as the darker hair, which blends with the shade-patches of the summer leaves, also blends with the somberness of the winter woods.

One does not see a bobcat except when hunting them with trail hounds at night, and even then they do not always tree but may run the ridges all night. I have seen them in the daytime only when hunting quail, and then only when they were caught in an incautious moment of nerve failure. Well protected by their coloration, they most certainly would be passed up as they crouch in a tree or by a cliff face. However, often unnerved by the presence of bird dog and hunter, they break and run, and while sometimes peppered with bird shot, they are rarely killed in this manner.

Like the lynx, they seem to be ill proportioned, with a ridiculous stub for a tail and great feet that might be serviceable to a cougar. A romantic trailer in the snow might thrill himself with the idea that he was hunting man-eating game.

A bobcat loves turkey meat, and he has a mysterious instinct which guides him when I am absent with the dogs. He can tear the inch-mesh chicken-pen wire and climb with ease over the woven-wire fence of the yard if there are turkeys there, and he can carry a full-grown gobbler back over the fence. He comes, like most night prowlers, just after a shower, and, like the great horned owl, on moonlight nights when bobcats look like moon shadows. If he kills more turkeys than he can eat at the time, he will carry the others away from the house and meticulously cover the carcasses with leaves to await his return, as a bear might do with a sheep. He has no coyote tricks; he is powerful and silent, with his mind deep in the groove of savage instinct, and his protective coloration, as in the case of all big hunter-cats, serves him as a hunter primarily. His only enemies, with the exception of man and his hounds, are screw-flies and bacilli. His deep silence is broken only on damp spring nights when he goes awooing, and his great scream-growl comes up from the head of the canyon to startle me from sleep and the dogs to frantic bluff-barking.

SHEILA

One day the Cowhand roped a coyote and came riding up to the house with it struggling on the end of the rope. It was a whelp that had not yet learned that the high, vertical projection of a horse's back is man.

The whelp pulled steadily, and, even though her eyes were protruding and her tongue hanging out, she made no sound. I decided to keep her. I hadn't had such a pet for years, and I thought I might learn something from her by watching her at close quarters. We put her in a wire-mesh portable coop, and I called her "Sheila." I knew an English girl named Sheila who had red hair and coyote eyes, but certainly she never knew it.

I fed her canned dog food and kept water available, but she would sit all day looking out, her yellow-green eyes filled with hatred and courage. She made no noise at night, but I am sure that she stirred about in her close quarters. I couldn't study her very well during the day, since, as soon as I appeared, she became perfectly quiet.

One morning I found that another coyote had come up to the cage and had bitten at the wire, then, finding that this was no good, had begun to dig under, only to be further foiled by the mesh covering the bottom of the cage. I then began to consider one of the empty chicken houses, since I realized that if the visitor were the mother coyote, she would sooner or later convince herself that the young one could not be freed and would bring her poison.

I'd had such a thing happen once when I was a little boy. I had taken four nestling bluejays at the time they were ready to leave the nest and had made a cage for them which I nailed to the fence. I wasn't sure what they should be fed, so I left the feeding up to the parents. Daily they came to the inch mesh and gave the young ones food. For two weeks or more they did this, and the young ones had grown long tails and were as large as the parents. I had begun to compliment myself because I knew that I could begin feeding them almost anything that the grown birds ate; it was the nestling diet about which I was doubtful.

One morning I came out to find the young bluejays stiff and dead. They had all stiffened the same way as they died, and I realized that the old birds, having given up the case as hopeless, had brought their young ones poison.

Thus I was worried about Sheila, although I saw no evidence that the mother had been bringing food to her and pushing it through the mesh. Each night Sheila had a visitor, and each night the visitor dug at the ground around the edges of the cage, but oddly enough neither I nor the dogs heard anything. The visitor often tore savagely at the wire, but this was done so expertly and so quietly that we were not disturbed. I wondered why the dogs were unable to get the scent, even though they could not hear the sound of digging and of wire being chewed.

Sheila developed screw-worms in a wound she had received when being dragged along the ground by the Cowhand. I got some remedy such as we use on cattle and horses, but to get the liquid to the wound took some doing. I had to hold her head against the side of the cage with a stout stick, then drop the medicine into the wound from above, and the stick was soon fang-marked where she snapped at it when it was inserted. She would snap the stick with incredible quickness.

She never became accustomed to me. She watched every move with her savage yellow-green eyes, and I had to be careful about allowing my hands to come near the mesh. She seemed to be waiting for just such an opportunity.

Her wound healed and I fed her, cleaned her cage, and watched her very carefully, but all I saw were two unblinking eyes filled with indomitable spirit and savagery. All this time she made no sound; from the time that the noose first fell over her head until the night she died, she remained silent and, in my presence, motionless. Only her head moved as I moved, or she transferred her gaze quickly to the dogs if they happened to come up. They would not come near the cage ordinarily, and, after a few days of worrying about her, they paid little attention to her. The chickens and turkeys came up to the cage but ignored her, as she did them. Even the guineas forgot about her, and eventually the visitor that I assumed was her mother came no more, and she was left alone with her unrelenting hatred.

Coyote whelps may be tamed and be made to follow their masters about, even ludicrously wagging their tails, though they can never be trained to respect man's vested interest in the barnyard fowls. In order to make pets of them, they must be taken young; dug out of the prairie den as a matter of fact. Sheila was hopeless as she was taken after she had begun to hunt for herself, and I wanted her only for the purpose of study in any case. She taught me nothing except the fact that even at her age her mother was still interested in her and had made valiant attempts to save her. She also confirmed my experience that coyotes suffer and die in silence and thus do not endanger the other members of the band by calling for help. I am sure she did not call for the aid she received from the visitor.

It seemed that Sheila willed to die. There was nothing wrong with her that I could determine. When I fed her that morning, she watched my hands for the one false move, her terrible eyes steady and intense. She watched me as I left the cage. I turned as I reached the gate of the yard, and she was still watching me. Her eyes aroused no sense of pity in me; they only inspired admiration for her courage.

As I went back to the typewriter, I began to plan to have a collar made for her, with my name on it so that I might have some interesting data in case she were later caught by trail hounds or by one of my neighbor's packs of running hounds, after I should have freed her. I wondered if she would stay in the vicinity where she had suffered such humiliation.

When I went to her cage again that evening, she was dead. Everything about her verified this except her eyes. They still stared savagely at the world, and because of their never dying quality of hatred, I poked her body with a stick before opening the cage, even though my reason made me quite sure she was dead.

The tree shadows from the sun and the moon are hourglasses. I am not only pleased to be able to tell the time of the day and night by them but they give me an anxious sense of flowing time. They make me feel that I can't live long enough or fast enough to appreciate fully the things of the earth about me. As the day shadows lengthen with the descending sun, they stretch their long fingers toward the east from which the day has come to the one that is to follow before I am ready for it; before I have lived the one that is falling off into the abyss of the past behind the west-ridge blackjacks completely.

Even when the sun was so agonizingly slow during the great drought, I was not really so unhappy as I pretended to be. I really loved the tragedy of it; I enjoyed being histrionic and poetic about it, though I did not wish to exaggerate its hell. I expressed its sinister influence on life exactly as I saw it and felt it, but I got pleasure out of my persecution, not as a sublimated martyr, but as a spiritual masochist.

Owing to the biological changes within myself, I am now not so likely to wait for a roaring blizzard to go visiting across the prairie, or wait in town until a storm is at its height to push the station wagon through the flooded dirt roads to my little house in order to enjoy the reflected sheet-lightning on the prairie pools and accept nature's anger that seems to be concentrated on me crawling along through the night. When I first came to the blackjacks, I enjoyed battling with the elements and went out of my way to do so.

One night, during the Yellow-Flower Moon, as I came from town in the fury of a storm, my headlights flashed suddenly on the sunflowers that lined the road as I slithered through the water-filled ruts, and they kept me in the trail that I couldn't see. When I had to stop momentarily, the wagon swayed in the terrific gusts and the thunder cracked about me. When I arrived at my little house, slipping and sliding, with the rear end of the wagon attempting to take the place of the front end, I was too excited to sleep and watched the frenzy over the blackjacks until it died.

I love every manifestation of nature, though now, like an aging player, I am not so keen to get into the game to become a part of the struggle; and though during the last years, when I take things more as matters of fact rather than as miracles, there is still never a moment of boredom, and the tree shadows tell me that I must live intensely if I am to get the last drop of juice from the glowing orange.

From the Bible, I believe, came the statement that "it is not good for man to be alone." That might not be the correct wording, but the meaning is clear that man should not be without woman. I accept this generalization without quibbling, and, being a naturalist, though I do not wear the fraternity pin of the order, I do not believe in sublimation of natural urges. The greatest beauty in nature is produced through the activity of mating; bird song, nuptial dancing, and antics; majestic antlers, nuptial plumage, insect chorus, and glossy pelage, while the greatest—no, not the greatest ugliness, but ugliness is often the result of inhibitions and prohibitions.

I tried an experiment one summer. I took a young rooster just after he began to crow and allowed him to run with the other flocks, but keeping him strictly away from his own kind. He soon began to harass the young guineas both male and female in a most disgusting manner. And one summer I succeeded in saving one lone poult from the bobcats and coyotes. It grew into a fine turkey hen but the only turkey on the ridge. The next spring she became confused and would squat at my feet when I went to the pens to feed the flocks. A queer sort of primal embarrassment came over me, and I associated her with a depressing ugliness until I could get a gobbler.

But one cannot appreciate what it means to step out of natural background where one has lived alone, with only the voices of the ridges, into the society of one's own kind. One being fresh and alert one's self sees only freshness and beauty in others. How beautiful are women in the soft light at the dinner table and on the dance floor, and how wonderful the music. How heavenly is the scotch-and-soda, the wine, and the taste of a cigarette, and how interesting the conversation of men, no matter on what subject. How clearly one seems to see the social, economic, and political problems through the spectrum of one's own freshness, and how much greater is the magic of the indefinite "They" who have made the wonders of civilization; the magicians who have brought forth the radio, television, chrome-bright mechanisms, skyscrapers, and electrical gadgets. And how beautiful is romance, filling every cell of one's capacity for emotion, and how delightfully inspiring to ornamental expression.

But the excitement of living, and the eagerness to fill each day with it before the shadow-fingers fall across the canyon east of the house, is not enough for man it seems. First, I had to have responsibility and disturb the balance of the blackjacks; then, after a few years, I extended my activities beyond the ridges. I became a member of a business committee which had as its duties the administration to a certain extent, and the conservation to a greater extent, of the oil properties and the grazing lands of the Osage tribe. I had to appear in Washington two or three times a year to represent them before the houses of Congress and in the offices of the Secretary of Interior, represented by the Indian Bureau.

I believe that a mate and a family could not have satisfied my bubbling urge for responsibility, since I went further and allowed myself to be appointed as a member of the State Board of Education. I was "axed" from this board, fortunately, before I had neglected my blackjacks too much. There was a rumor about that I intended to introduce Latin and Greek into the schools, but my "axing" had, in fact, a political significance. Under the influence of a natural background freshness, one can go too far.

My life in the blackjacks being naturally sympathetic to conservation, and my deep feeling for the flow of time, along with my primal urge to cling to landmarks along the jungle river of natural progression, and, lastly, my sympathy with the old men of the tribe who feared the missing of their immortality, I felt that conservation could be very well stretched to cover some oil portraits of the older men. This was real conservation, since these old men would soon pass away and with them the Osage as he was, the era and the type passing with the individuals. It was not difficult to obtain the co-operation of the head of the Art Project of the P.W.A. and then get the approval of the Commissioner of Indian Affairs and of the Secretary of the Interior.

Soon after my return from Washington, one spring, I was notified that the money for a museum, to be called "The Osage Indian Museum," was available and that an artist would come to the Osage with instructions to paint twelve portraits, which were to be hung in the museum.

The artist arrived, and we made out the list of those whose portraits we wanted. We made a list of twenty-four, since I knew that we could get only some of them to sit. We also found that, unless I went along with the artist, the old men would not pose, and it became necessary for me to drive into town from The Blackjacks each morning, pick up the artist, then drive out to the ranch home of the subject. I attempted to make definite appointments, but if the whim came to the sitter to leave before we arrived, he would be gone and no one seemed to know where, and at such times we should be compelled to drive back to town or catch someone on the spur of the moment.

This was during the Yellow-Flower Moon of the great drought, when the sun climbed monotonously above the blackjacks and the glass climbed each day above the hundred-degree mark. The roads leading to the Indians' homes were marked by clouds of dust, and along them the yellowed leaves of the corn rattled in the hot winds. It was a time when the old men wanted to sit on their raised platforms under their structures of fresh willow and sycamore boughs and dream while fanning themselves with their eagle-wing fans. It was a good time to think about their youth or sing to themselves a Peyote song, while the cicadas sang their songs of heat.

We found some of them a little short-tempered, when we were lucky enough to find them at home, and, as I wiped the sweat from my face, I had to rekindle their interest when time came for the sitting by assuring them that their portraits would hang in the museum; that people would come many hundreds of years later to look at them and know that the Osage once lived here and were great people and that the old men who had their portraits there would be known by those who would live many years after they had passed away; that the people a hundred years from then would look at these portraits and say, "So these are Osage—we know now that they lived and that which people tell is true; that they lived here and were great people."

After two visits to Claremore's house on a hill in the Hominy country, we found him at home. Only a few members of his family were there. His black servants were busy with little chores about the place. A woman was cleaning the long table in the screened-in summer house where they had just eaten. His old wife walked about leaning on her cane; she was half-blind but still attempted to direct the ménage. A daughter sat swinging her feet from the raised platform under the shade of the fresh branches of the roof, while Claremore sat in an old rocking-chair in the dense shade of the summer house. He made little figures in the dust at his feet with his cane, raising his head occasionally to look far across the valley where the heat shimmered.

"This man has come to paint your picture," I said. "You said we could do this thing today."

"Tomorrow," he said, without looking up.

I turned to his daughter. I realized that she now played the chief role in the family, since the old wife had become enfeebled. "This picture is for the Osage people and their children for a hundred years. He need not be disturbed; he may sit where he is. It is hot, but we have come here three times in the heat. What will people say when they look at these pictures many years from now, and Claremore is not there?"

"Poppa don't want to today; he says you mus come back."

"No, we can't come back in this heat again. This man must go home soon—it is too bad."

"I guess you can come back tomorrow. He says that will be good, if you come back tomorrow."

"People's memory is short. If they do not see that picture there, they will say that there is no Claremore. We will not be there a hundred years from now to tell these people that there was a Claremore. We cannot say to these people that Claremore once lived here but he did not have his picture painted because it was too hot. These people will shake their heads and say there was no Claremore."

The old man turned to his daughter and said, "Go to that trunk—bring my things here."

"It's too hot to dress," I said; "let him sit as he is."

"He wants to dress," she said.

"He'll smother."

"Yeah, I guess he will."

As the artist arranged his easel and examined his brushes, the daughter and the old wife kept bringing things out of the trunk. The wife wanted to supervise the proceedings, to exercise her traditional prerogatives, but she could scarcely see. Finally, she stood before him leaning on her cane and holding a hand mirror so that he could see himself as the daughter dressed him. She took off his shirt and started to help him with his pants, then turned to me and said, "How much is goin' show?"

"Just the upper part, from the waist up."

She combed his hair and placed an otter-skin bandeau on his head. She brought a buckskin shirt from the trunk and shook it, then slipped it over his head, and as it fell about him he smoothed it gently. It had a dozen or more scalplocks sewed to it in two rows in front. When she opened the paint box to paint his face, he put up his hand, and she placed it back in the handbag. While he straightened the scalplock-bedecked shirt, she placed a bear-claw necklace about his neck. He took the mirror from his wife and straightened the bandeau, arranged the tailpiece, turned his head from side to side, then, handing the mirror back, said, "How."

As the artist worked, the old man sat very straight, and the sweat rolled down his face, while the daughter fanned him with an eagle-wing fan, and the old wife sat in her chair and rocked gently. After an hour of posing, a Negro servant brought a tin of water, and he drank it in great gulps. For three hours he sat thus while the artist got the detail of his dress, so that on the following day he would not be obliged to dress. However, he insisted on dressing the next day and

128 ←

sitting stoically while the sweat dripped down under the bandeau and made dark patches on his buckskin shirt.

Abott and Pitts were members of the Osage Council, and they both lived in the Hominy country. They agreed to sit, but we had to make several trips to their homes before we found either one of them. We found Abott on the streets of the little town of Hominy and took him back out to his ranch with us. His ranch house is inclosed by a woven-wire fence six feet in height. Near by in the shade of some pecan trees is the conical Peyote church. He is not an old man, but his membership on the Council and the Peyote church on his place indicate his importance.

"My," said the artist, "you've got a nice place here, Mr. Abott."

"Yeah, like white man, ain't it? Built fence to keep white man out, but it ain't no good; can't keep white man out. Can't keep myself in either, I guess."

"Why do white men want to get in?"

"I owe 'em money—that's what they say."

He turned to me. "I got my clothes, but I guess I don't need 'em." He said to the artist, "Ole man, I guess this'll be all right." He felt of his brown shirt.

He posed out on the porch where the breeze played, bare-headed and with his hands folded across his stomach. He looked like an East Indian diplomatist with the golden-rimmed glassses which added to the high intelligence in his face and the humor which shone in his eyes.

After a half-hour of posing he said, "Pitts gonna dress?"

"No," I said.

"Guess I won't dress. I got good dance clothes. Pitts ain't gonna dress?"

"No."

"He gonna wear blanket?"

"Don't think so."

"It's sure hot, ain't it?" He addressed the artist, "Ole man, I gotta shashe." The artist was not an old man, and he winced when Abott thus addressed him.

He came back in through the back door, stopped at the dresser and poured powder down the front of his shirt, then came back to his posing.

He said suddenly, "Ole man, when you come back?"

The artist looked at me hopefully, then said to Abott, "Why, I thought—we have just begun. I'm in a place where I can't quit now."

Abott got up and walked over to look at the canvas, then went back to assume his pose. He looked at me: "Ole man's purty good, ain't it?"

I had told the artist about Abott's great sense of humor and of his ability at repartee. Now he suggested that I keep him talking so that animation would show in his face.

When the posing was over for the day, he went around to look at his unfinished portrait. The face had been painted in and part of the shirt, its odd brown having been caught perfectly by the artist. He gazed at the canvas with approval, then he turned to me and said: "I sure oughtta dressed; be better if I dressed. Pitts gonna dress, I bet."

"No," I said; "I don't think so."

"When you goin' to Pitts' house? He said he ain't gonna dress, ain't it?"

"That's what he told me. We'll go to his house as soon as we are finished with you."

"Ole man oughtta paint Pitts with goggles, ain't it?"

"Why?" asked the artist.

Abott extended both arms and closed his hands as though he were driving a car. "He's always goin' some place fast," he said.

"Must be a busy man," said the artist. "Do you suppose we can ever get to paint him?"

"Sure," said Abott. "He don't do nothin' when he gits where he's goin'; jist stan' 'round town and look at high-heel gurls."

The next day Abott was waiting for us. He sat and struck his pose before the artist had his things ready, then he looked at me and his eyes twinkled, "Pitts ain't gonna be home I bet."

"He said he would."

"Said he would he home?"

"That's what he said."

He thought for a minute, then he said, "I got good dance clothes—sure good'uns. They at my son-in-law's house. I tole 'em to bring 'em here."

"You won't need your clothes. You're all right the way you are. It's a good picture—will be," I said.

"You like it?" he asked.

"I think it's going to be good."

The artist stepped aside, squinted at the canvas and then at Abott, then said, "you want to have a look, Mr. Abott?"

Abott stood for some time, then remarked, "That shirt's sure good."

"Don't you like the face?" I asked.

"Yeah—it's too what-cha-call-it? It's like white man that lost his money. Maybe someday when I look at it, I shoot myself. White man got my money long time ago, but maybe when I see this face I remember it and hafta shoot myself."

When he had taken his pose again, the artist looked at me, and I said to Abott, "This artist wants more twinkle in your eyes; think I'll tell him a story about you."

"Yeah, go ahead," he said, and his eyes shone in anticipation of a good story, even one about himself.

"Well," I said, "I suppose you have guessed that your subject, Mr. Abott, has financial difficulties. He was given a certificate of competency by the Secretary of Interior, but later he asked to be restricted again. There are still some questions about alleged obligations. He was continually hounded by creditors wherever he went, and he could find no peace. People would come up to him anywhere in public and ask for payment; they would follow him to the agency when he went to get his check. He was afraid to walk down the street, and he was afraid to stay at home.

"One day he was walking down the street in the town of Hominy, when he heard a man call to him. He began to walk faster, tapping the pavement with his cane, but he could hear the hurrying steps of the white man grow closer. When he realized that the white man was quite near, he reached into his pocket without looking back and handed him some money. Later this same man, after overcoming his surprise, overtook Abott and handed the money back to him and gave him eighty dollars more. He had been attempting to see Abott for several days in order to pay him rental on some grazing land."

Abott's face lighted up, and the artist worked very fast. Abott laughed until his belly shook and said, "That's sure right."

"Again," I said, "when he was walking down the street of Hominy, a grasshopper happened to fly in from the country and lighted on his shoulder. You know the kind; the big yellow ones that plop against our windshield and flow? One of these lighted on his left shoulder. He increased his speed a little, and turned his head slightly as he said, 'Pay you next week.' "

When the portrait was finished, Abott was reluctant to have this unique diversion ended. "When you gonna paint Pitts?" he asked as we were leaving.

"Tomorrow, perhaps."

"Maybe I come over there," he said.

Nonceh Tonkah was at this time the only old man who wore the scalplock of the old·days of Wah-Kon-Tah and the war path. He was a diehard; he believed in the old ways and had nothing to do with the Peyote church.

When we went to his house in town, the glass registered 112 degrees above zero. He was very courteous and seemed to be flattered that he had been chosen one of the group whose pictures were to be hung in the museum. We got the electric fan out and connected it up on the porch, and with the air from it hitting his face he sat up straight, but he was very nervous, and he was very much amused by the whole thing. He kept making remarks in Osage.

He said to his hovering daughter: "Ask this white man if he wants my head when I pass away?" He laughed heartily, then said, "Ask him if he wants my head to put on wall like that of buffalo?" Later he said, "Tell this white man he must send his daughter to me. For this picture he must send his daughter—that is Osage way." He laughed with appreciation, but no one laughed with him, as they did not understand what he was saying. His daughter was patronizing. She believed that perhaps this was not good humor for a strange white man.

He was done in profile, and his portrait shows a classic American Indian contour that would not be out of place on a coin.

The chief of the Osage has all the characteristics that a great chief should have. He sits at the head of the council table listening with dignity, and, when he feels called upon to speak, he does so quietly, in measured tones and with great effect. He walks with perfect carriage under his eighty years, unhurried, like a true child of the earth. When he rides, he sits in the back of his Lincoln-Zephyr with his wife beside him like a king on parade, though with more naturalness, since he is never on parade. He has this inherent dignity when riding through the streets of the towns of the county or through the blackjacks and over the prairie.

When we drove out to his ranch and asked him to sit for the artist, he agreed without question. He was above indicating discomfort from the heat or from possible illness. He smiled at the artist with his eyes laughing. The artist immediately felt his great dignity, so he decided that he must do a full, seated figure out on the porch where the light was constant and where the chief could look across his own fields to the hill where his father was buried.

When we arrived, he was wearing a light shirt with pink ribbons through the cuffs, dark trousers, and with his blanket tied about his waist. His hair fell in two braids down the front of his shirt on each side. He wore shoes instead of moccasins. As we talked, his wife brought a blanket, half red and half blue, and draped it over a straight-backed chair on the porch. As she came back through the room, he arose and followed her into the back of the house.

When he appeared in the doorway a half-hour later, the artist jumped to his feet and said, "Ah." His wife had dressed him in his best finery. In his hair was an under-tail feather of an eagle, colored pink, and the two braids fell over his shoulders in front. He wore a silken scarf about his neck and a bone necklace. His shirt was mauve, and he sat on the red-and-blue blanket which his wife had placed for him, draping it over his left shoulder so that it fell over his lap and hung down on the opposite side. In his left hand he held an eagle-tail fan with a buckskin handle which was fringed. The sweat was already beginning to run down his face.

He sat for three hours squinting in the bright light of the dazzling day. Occasionally he fanned himself, but there were no stirrings or grimaces to indicate the terrible discomfort of so much clothing.

The artist worked silently, stopping only to wipe his flushed face with a towel. The dogs stirred in their flea hunts under the porch. The chickens under the bushes made odd noises in their throats as they held their mouths wide open and allowed their wings to hang carelessly. The cicadas were subdued, contenting themselves with rasping little laments to the heat-god. A pet crow which the chief's Negro chauffeur had taken from the nest and tamed hopped upon the porch beside me and, with mouth open and wings dropped, cocked his head and looked at me impudently. I flicked my sweat-soaked handkerchief at him, and he swore terribly. The chief laughed and the artist laughed, and then, as if the spell had been broken, the latter laid his brushes and palette aside and wiped his glowing face again. The chief arose and walked into the house where his wife waited to undress him and lay each article away with tenderness and precision in its accustomed place in the long trunk.

When we arrived in town, the mercury had reached 116 degrees, the highest temperature on record at the agency. When I reached The

Blackjacks, my glass registered 103. I pulled off my clothes, wrung the water out of them, then threw them on the grass to dry.

I sat for the remainder of the afternoon on the porch looking out across the head of the canyon to the east ridge where the still-green blackjacks stood on the drought-yellowed ridge's backbone like the hackles on an angry, tawny beast.

For four days the chief went through the agonies of dazzling light and intense heat. Each day I sat on the end of the porch and watched the heat subdue life. I watched the leaves of the vines and the locust curl so as to offer less surface to the burning sun and noted each day that they were growing paler and that each day there were more yellow ones. These let go and floated to the ground with a very dry rattle, which is absent in the falling leaves of autumn. Under the trees, the planted trees, the prematurely fallen leaves protested in dry little crackles when a restless current disturbed them. But the black-jacks, the sun-worshipers of the far ridges, turned their leaves edge-wise to the sun, and there was no surface for the rays to burn, and their sun-metalized foliage clung to them and remained fresh.

The gold-washed grasses of a normal summer had turned to lifeless yellows and browns, and I realized how much green meant to the happiness of man, its freshness and restfulness making the world what it is. To raise my spirits as I leaned against the corner post of the porch, I looked up to the vibrant green of the blackjacks on the ridges and wondered why the Amer-European had called them use-less. But he has recently called Latin and Greek useless as well and is leaving them out of the college curriculum.

These are my thoughts as recorded in my diary of these four days while the chief posed. I had nothing else to do but sit and think, set off on an idle cycle of thought by chickens, leaves, and air currents.

When the portrait was finished, we stood about and looked at it. I noted that the background was yellow, but I thought nothing of it at the time. Later, however, I remembered that the artist was a very sensitive man, and he also put suffering in the face where I saw no suffering. As a child he had been in a pogrom in Russia and later had undoubtedly read Fenimore Cooper.

There was something in the face that hurt the chief's dignity. He looked at it for a long time with his eyes smiling in courtesy and kindliness.

The artist put his brushes away, wiped his face with the towel, then extended his hand and said, "Chief, I'm finished. I'm not coming back tomorrow." He repeated this, making a meaningless gesture with his hands and shaking his head, "Not coming back any more— not coming back tomorrow." The chief took his hand in his very limp one and smiled graciously. He allowed the sweat to fall from his face to the folds of his blanket, and he said in English, which he used very rarely, and strangely enough with a Chinese accent. "No come?"

"No—finished; see—finished. Go away, no come back." As he said this, he waved his arms and shook his head.

"You mus come back," insisted the chief. "I wait tomolla, you."

"What for? Finished—see; all through." He smiled indulgently.

The chief started toward the door, and I could see where the sweat was seeping through his heavy blanket. He turned and raised his hand, "Come back tomolla; I paint you." He smiled very happily and disappeared within the door.

The twelve portraits were finished, and the dauntless artist kept his good humor. As a matter of fact, neither he nor I could indulge in temperament when such indulgence was the prerogative of the Osage sitters—a prerogative which they exploited in all its phases and to its elastic limits. Only the women sitters were detached and calm and punctual. They threw their blankets over their shoulders, over their everyday apparel of shirt and shrouding, gathered them in front, and sat with folded hands. There was a third woman on the list, but she outdid the men in temperament.

When we arrived to paint her, I introduced her to the artist by giving him an account of her famed girlhood beauty, while she looked down modestly at her feet. It took her a very long time to dress, and when she finally appeared she was dressed in all her finery. She wore valuable ornaments and heirlooms and had touched up her still rather attractive face. She posed like a queen.

She couldn't wait to be invited to look at the canvas but got up suddenly and walked over to have a look, with her ornaments jingling. She stood for some time, then turned quickly and fled back to her room and later appeared in her ordinary clothes. She frowned and scolded all during the time the artist was painting her husband. She chased the dogs off the side porch with the broom, and I could see by their injured-innocence expression that they had been accustomed to daydreaming there without molestation. When her grandson asked for money, she refused to give it to him, and I could see that he was accustomed to receiving when he asked. Knowing the indulgence of Osage grandmothers, I was also surprised. Once when she passed behind the artist as he worked, in the sudden housewifely busyness which expressed her unhappiness, she frowned at the back of his head and said to herself, "O-skee-kah," which means in Osage, among other things, liar and horse thief.

Later, one May day when the prairie was emerald, and mauve cloud shadows moved indolently across the campus of the agency, and the smoke from the separate camps of the four Osage clans arose in a semicircle around the new museum, we celebrated its opening.

If we could have saved for posterity the picture of the descending sun shining through the strips of beef strung along the drying-poles; the women busy around the kettles; and the dancers of the four clans coming together for the first time in many years to dance to the earth rhythm of the drums like befeathered and gorgeously painted gods, then posterity would need to ask few questions. If we could have saved the picture for them of the old men who, though dressed, were too old to dance but sat with closed eyes around the dance ground in dream-thought; or if we could have saved the picture of the dancers who, as they danced, saw nothing except that which was in their hearts, there would be little need to attempt to have their souls painted on canvas.

III
AUTUMN

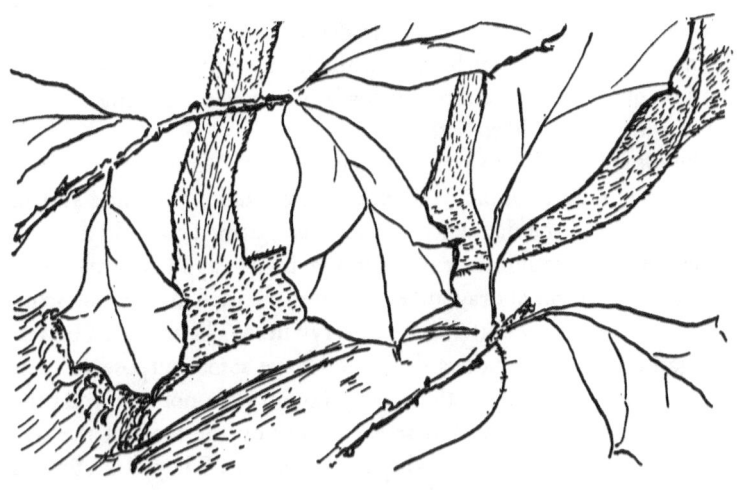

IX

DEER-HIDING MOON

THE DOES AND FAWNS FED AS USUAL ON THE SIDES OF THE BLACKJACK ridges in the early mornings and in the later afternoons, and they lay in the sun among the running oaks during the day on the south sides of the hills so that the sun would hit them on chilly autumnal days. Their habits changed little, but the bucks seemed to disappear at this time of the year. They stayed in the very thick timber, and one could find saplings where they had rubbed their itching antlers in their urge to scrape the mosslike covering off their new adornment. Little strips of this covering could be found hanging to the saplings and the bushes, where a restive buck had scraped and thrashed. This "velvet," as the hunter calls it, has the appearance of gray fungus-like mold on bread or cheese, and it peels after the antlers have hardened; then the bucks scrape it off. It was difficult for an Osage hunter to find them at this time.

I asked Little Panther why they hid at this season, and he said, "'Cause they 'shamed I guess. They don't want women deers to see 'em with that thing on its horns, I guess. They sure hide good, too."

To use this characteristic of the buck as a symbol of September would seem to be the only negative in the whole of creative Moon Woman's manifestations. The Osage sensed a lull in creation, but this activity of the deer would correspond to the activity of the bull in Buffalo-Pawing-Earth Moon—a preparation for intense activity in creation, yet, in the case of the deer, obvious only through his absence from his summer haunts, while in the buffalo evinced by his domination of the scene through his bellowing and pawing and his challenging the world to battle.

The Osage seemed to overlook the fact that September is also a period of intense creation, of intense insect activity. The flies swarm in the middle of the day when the sun has warmed the cold air, and the wasps hum around the eaves. Strange insects fly in swarms across the ridge, and flocks of dragonflies pass over the yard in their bouncing flight, and the yellow butterflies are everywhere. The monarch butterflies gather into tremendous flocks and have some purpose in their actions for the first time in their lives, though I am not sure what the queer antics signify. They chase each other on the level of the tree tops in some kind of nuptial display, I imagine. They also cling in groups to the leaves of the postoaks, and, when they close their wings, they are like prematurely dead leaves. They also fly high against the sky at this time; in thousands, as though they were migrating.

Thus many insects and especially the dawdling butterfly have creative purpose during the Deer-Hiding Moon. As a matter of fact, I imagine that if the deer, as in the case of the buffalo, had not played such an important role in the life and religion of the Osage, they might have called September the Little-People-Going-Away Moon, which would have included both birds and insects, since most of them are gone by the end of this month.

They seemed to treat the insects and the reptiles as though they were below the notice of great hunters. They honored only the spider in the invertebrate world, but his honor is high. They seemed to recognize only those forms which I honor with my interest, and for much the same reason. They have made the spider, whose web one cannot escape in summer and autumn, into a symbol. A conventionalized spider is the symbol of a secret society of women at present, but at one time it was the symbol of a clan.

The story goes that one group of the children of the earth, a clan division of the Osage, had been slow in adopting a symbol suitable to great warriors. The buffalo had been chosen by one clan, the eagle by another, and the panther by still another, until all the animals of great strength, grace, courage, and other necessary virtues that a symbol of the Osage must have had been adopted by other clans.

The left-out band then went along the roads of the earth searching for a fitting symbol. When the animals heard that a band of the Great Osage were traveling the roads of the earth looking for a symbol, they presented themselves one at a time, desiring very much to have this great honor. Each one was very courteously discouraged, and the children traveled on and on along the roads of the earth.

One day they met a coyote, and he said, "Children of the earth, where are you going?" and the leader of the band answered, "We look for a symbol."

The coyote said, "Take me, O children of the earth; I am brave and cunning and fleet."

"You talk too much," said the leader, and they went on their way. They met a skunk, an owl, and many others desiring to become a clan symbol of the Great Osage, but to each one the leader had an objection. The objection to the skunk was obvious, and the owl carried the evil spirit, as every little Osage boy knew.

The children of the earth were growing very tired and were disappointed when suddenly the leader walked into a spider's web stretched across the road. He wiped his face with his hand and scolded, his temper being short from his long, empty search, "You little black thing, get your house out of the way of the children of the earth; we must have our eyes to see; you allow your house to blind us."

The spider said, "O children of the earth, all things come to my house and some break their necks therein, but you are only blinded for a moment."

"Get your funny house out of our way," said the leader with great anger.

"Where do you go," asked the spider, "that you need to see more than is before you?"

"We search for a proper symbol for our clan; we must have clear eyes to know this symbol, but you blind us with your funny house."

"Take me," said the spider.

"You little black thing," answered the leader, "have you great courage and strength like the buffalo; do you furnish clothing to the children of the earth and covering for their homes? Do you fill their bellies when frost comes to the inside of the lodge? Can you fly like the eagle; do you have the beauty and the courage of the eagle and furnish feathers for the ceremonies? Do you have the strength and grace of the panther; do you furnish soft skins for the children of the earth?"

"No," insisted the spider; "but I shall make a good symbol for the children of the earth."

"Ho, ho, take your house from our faces and get out of our way, you little black thing."

The spider then said, "You do not ask me why I should make a good symbol for your clan, then I shall tell you."

"All right," said the leader, attempting to be courteous; and the people hid their faces with their hands so that the spider couldn't see them laughing.

The spider said, "O children of the earth, you have come a long way, but your travels are ended. I shall tell you why you should take me for your symbol. You see me; I am a little black thing, you say, but, when you come to my house, you must stop to rub your eyes and clean your faces. I am a little black thing; I have not the strength, the courage, the beauty of those you talk about, but remember this: wherever I go I build my house, and where I build my house all things come to it."

Thus the spider became the symbol of one of the clans of the Great Osage and is now tattooed on the backs of the hands of the women who belong to the secret society, which is select. This symbol also appears on the backbone of my books, and I also wanted to adopt it for my brand, but it was too intricate.

It has always seemed to me that, of all the arthropod activity during the latter part of August, and September, the spiders are the most active. Their webs form delicate lacework and needlework and shine in long strands like tight wires stretched from tree top to tree top. They float in tattered strings across the roads and shine as they stretch across the tall grass of the prairie; they form little funnels around holes in the earth and span the space between my books and the wall.

The katydids continue their loud, metallic stridulations which began in August, and the sparrowhawks flock to the ridge.

Man could undoubtedly learn something from the drama of my ridge about the things that make for war. It seems to me that the species fight only as a last resort over food supply and in the protection of their young. They are sometimes misled by their fear, just as men are, and plunge to death battle over fancied wrongs and danger—fancied encroachments on their food supply and danger to their young—but they seem to want to live and let live, except those, of course, whose food supply consists of other animals. Even with each other, however, they desire peace if possible. The species of the ridge have only one reason for war against each other—the physical one divided into three parts: food supply (economic), protection of young (invasion), and battles over mating within the species. The predator's invasion of my chicken pens and my domain is just that—invasion.

Man's wars, on the other hand, have the added forces for war in religion and ideologies; while mating, if one discounts Cleopatra and Helen, is confined in man, as it is in the lower animals, to murders and individual battle. However, the basic cause for man's wars is economic; even ideologies grow out of economic pressure. Man the thinker must understand these things before he can effectively save his young manhood from the battle's slaughter in every generation. He must understand these things and constantly make the adjustments that nature demands, to at least postpone his wars and make peace contemporaneous with the life of the strongest national units. This matter of the destruction of a nation's virility every generation is so very important that man cannot afford to dream about ways and means of long peace periods but must work toward that end in harmony with the natural progression in life of the earth.

He fumbles toward the natural processes, but he seems to find there what he wants to find. The Nazi sees the law of survival and elects his own unit as the surviving unit without trial by struggle. Through the ages philosophers who have gone back to "nature" have found the obvious beauty and harmony which is the climax of the natural struggle; they have not noted the shavings and the cuttings and the cast-off inferior parts on the factory floor; they have seen the perfect, shining mechanism.

If the communist and the socialist go to the ants and the bees for their communal economics and division of labor, they fail to see them as a part of the whole drama.

When my wasps, who are very much like the bees in their cycle of life, fly high above the blackjacks at this season of Deer-Hiding Moon, carrying on with the dizziest kind of nuptials, they are carrying out an agreement with the great balance which gives them their right to exist. Their economic and social arrangement is the necessary adjustment to this demand of the natural processes. After the dizzy romance high over the blackjacks, the jaded drones and workers die, and the impregnated females or "queens" then conveniently hide in crevices of stone and under the roots of trees, perhaps under my eaves, and hibernate until spring revives them, when each sets to work building a nest in the ground or elsewhere, depending upon the habits of the species. They all build of self-manufactured paper or adobe their houses of cuplike cells—three to begin—in which they lay their eggs. They feed the grubs when they hatch, then build more cells, and the grubs become "workers" because of the nature of the food they have had—honey and masticated insects—and they take over the domestic duties like stepchildren, while the "queen" continues to lay eggs in each new cell which the "workers" have built.

This is the role assigned to them as the price of their survival. Very interesting to the man squatting over their activity, but what a stupid mechanization and standardization if applied to the socioeconomy of man. Gone would be the beauty of mating and romance and ornamental expression for perhaps 90 per cent of the population. What a terrible price to pay for existence. Only wasps, bees, termites, and ants form such communities for the purpose of adjustment to the balance. As long as man survives by his power to think, he ought certainly to avoid such a ridiculous price for his existence.

There is nothing duller than the routine work of bees, wasps, ants, and termites; long processions of workers carrying burdens like coolies, all day, each day, making of beautiful life a mechanical precision, like a factory. They say, of course, that life is a factory, and perhaps it does bear surprising resemblance to mass production; but it is hidden behind my blackjacks, behind my bluestem, my roses and morning-glories, and its noise drowned out by bird song, wind in the leaves, rain on the roof, and the querulous song of the coyote, and I prefer not to go to my ants, bees, and wasps to be reminded of it.

I am sometimes ashamed of my lack of knowledge in entomology, but only at times when a spider with gorgeous color patterns lowers himself almost in my face, or when a moth as mystery-colored as a whippoorwill flits across my vision at twilight. Sometimes a large insect, nameless as far as I am concerned, attracts my attention by his odd coloring as he clings to the trunk of a tree. I can only stand and wonder about him in my complete ignorance of his identity and his role in the drama of life. At such times I am as one with black cowboy Joe Barkus, who is handy man on the ranch. I am just as limited as he is in expressing my wonder and my interest, and I am usually quite contented to accept his picturesque characterizations. One day he and I stood together looking at a large insect which had a seemingly senseless and certainly a gorgeous color pattern. I was thinking over and over again, "Extravagant bug," my thoughts imprisoned like a caged squirrel on a treadwheel. Then Joe spoke for both of us, as he pointed a crooked black finger at the bizarre bug and said, "Ah declah'h, he done look like he got red fedders in hees ace."

The only other insects I am aware of are those that intrude upon me and disturb my comfort, such as the little fellows that seep in through the screens to swarm about me as I read under the kerosene lamp; almost invisible little pests that I could not possibly identify if they were brought to me on slides. I know the vicious deer flies, the morbid screw-flies, the common housefly, bottle flies, and the large horsefly that sometimes makes a mistake when I go out to take my shower, scented and glistening with perspiration. I don't mind smelling like a horse at such times, but I feel with some satisfaction that such a stupid fly will not last long in the severe struggle for existence.

I am fascinated by the black widow spider that has now taken over my coyote-, owl-, bobcat-, and opossum-depleted hen houses, but I don't know much about her except that, as a well-supplied, dominant widow, she impresses me as being truly American. I let her live with the idea that I shall watch her and learn something, but I always forget her, and what happens to her when the cold weather comes I don't know. Since she has already eaten her husband earlier in the summer after mating and goes into widowed hibernation, she isn't of much literary interest.

The scorpions move about in the table, chair, and bear-rug shadows of my lamps before a change in the weather but cause me practically no discomfort. Once when I brought some half-decayed wood into the fire on a cold winter night, one hibernating in the heat of the wood warmed up in the fire, relaxed, awoke, and distractedly ran out of the fireplace and up my pajama leg as I sat reading. I mechanically slapped at my thigh and then jumped up with full consciousness of what had happened, dancing out of my pajamas. The sting feels like a needle heated to a white heat over a Bunsen burner.

One of the red setter puppies likes to watch the logs burning and spot the scorpions as they come out, stiffening into a perfect point. She has such fun at this perversion that she points beetles during the summer, expecting me to crush them. I wish she were as steady in the field.

One night a centipede fell from the walls of the porch onto my bed, and, as I brushed at him in my sleep, he stung me. My arm swelled and turned bluish-green; the discoloration reached halfway to my shoulder. I marked the end of it with a pen, then watched it, resolved to go into town if it crossed the ink mark. I had to keep dipping my arm in salt water to clear it up.

The tarantulas crawl heavily about the yard with a ferocity that belies their manners. I have seen dragonfly-like predators attack them and kill them with ease, then fly off with them piecemeal; and my half-grown chickens used to kill them after a moment of excited chatter, then eat them while they were still quivering.

I am always poking my face into spiders' webs as I come out of my doors; especially the webs of the nocturnal ones that await the night-flying insects. Some of these are beautiful, even iridescent, with the early-morning sun making jewels of the collected dew. Stretched between the house and the locust trees, they are as large and as perfect as pieces of Swiss lace.

The butterflies float like the thoughts of a lively child over the grass tops. The monarchs, the tigers, and the black tigers flutter and sail about without purpose, but the little saffron-colored ones alight daintily on the damp spots by the pump with obvious purpose, while the little white ones seem to be eternally hunting something in the grass roots. Sometimes in the early autumn the monarchs fill the sky by the thousands, like leaves lifted by a whirlwind.

I have mud-dauber wasps, yellow jackets, black, red, striped, and red wasps with black wings. The latter will back all the way across the yard dragging the body of a victim much larger than himself through depressions that must seem like mountain valleys to him, through grass that surely must seem a forest, and up the sheer face of a rock wall, steeper than any mountain man ever scaled. He will occasionally leave his burden in a little bare spot, while he flies about to get his bearings, like a scout plane, then alights again to continue the laborious backing and dragging of his victim to the distant nest.

The cicada is certainly a part of my life in the blackjacks, as are the crickets and the katydids and the grasshoppers. He is the leader of the heat chant in the long, dry summers. He is large and not unattractive, and I believe he does no harm; meaning, of course, that he does not disturb the economics of man, or in any way interfere with his plans in the cattle country. His voice of heat is really a love song, since only the males are vocal. He must surely produce such a state of nerves in the female with his montonous buzzing that she yields from sheer weariness.

He is larger than most of the insects and certainly he is much louder and definitely lives much longer. His song is unique and is produced in a unique manner: by a drumhead or diaphragm in the sounding organ which is vibrated by muscles of the thoracic cavity.

The roundabout, evasive manner in which most insects propagate has always been a source of amusement to me—like a Rube Goldberg mechanism. The cicada lays her eggs on the limb of a tree. These eggs hatch and the larvae fall out of the tree, and when they hit the ground, they bore in and stay there for years. The cycle from egg to the fully developed love-sick heat-chanter is said to be seventeen years. The larvae live in the ground, eating roots and vegetation, and at this stage they may be harmful. The sudden and mysterious passing of some pampered plant may be due to cicada larvae.

After many years—some say seven, some say more—the larva emerges in another form. He is now an ugly, mud-colored pupa with only the impression of ridiculous little wings that are really wing sheaths. The whole insect looks like a wax model made by some meticulous Chinese artist, then carelessly dropped in the mud. This ugly, wingless creature—he may also be called a nymph at this stage, but to me he looks exactly like a pupa, or at least the way a pupa ought to look—crawls across the ground after coming out of the subterranean nursery, leaving his hole topped with a sort of dirt chimney. He climbs up the bole of a tree, the stem of a weed, the curbing of a well, a hoe handle, a fence post, or anything that is handy and erect. If he climbs a tree, he will sometimes crawl out and hang downward from a leaf, clinging there with his very strong legs. Most of the time, however, he stops midway up the tree as though too fatigued to go higher.

I have said that, in common with universal ignorance, I am not aware of insects until I am stung, crawled over, or buzzed into weariness. Those that give me deep pleasure, like the grass-roots choristers, just remain romantic voices of the night. They express my queer feeling about early autumn with their sad, end-of-the-seasons stridulations and express my happiness in being alone in a fresh, dewy world after an earth-cleansing rain that came in the night. But most of them are nameless as far as I am concerned. A strange note or action by bird or animal will send me prowling about the ridge for hours until I find the source and the reason and set me to worrying for several days if I fail.

Thus the cicada has forced himself on my attention both by his size and by his vibrating drumhead. He has actually gone so far as to drown out conversation with my friends under the Blackjack; and the knife-edge he gives to drought-weariness with his rasping, monotonous song—a theme song of imminent disaster like Wagnerian music—gives him an importance equal to that of the coyote, the great horned owl, and the bobcat.

So I have learned something about him. I have watched the pupa come out of his hole with his little wing impressions and body of muddy wax and climb slowly up a tree trunk until he is about on the level with my eyes, then stop. He is a muddy shell humped like a bull buffalo, and with bulging eyes; a shell that is vital and quivering. To watch his transformation is an all-day job demanding extreme patience, and a convenient stump or a chair is contributive to the interest.

The mud dries quickly, and he turns from chocolate color to shale brown. No matter how dead and drab he may look there on the black trunk of the tree, there is ever the impression of quivering life somewhere inside him. Soon the thing shakes a little, pulses a little, and then after a while the shell begins to split down the back. After several hours the split reaches from the proboscis through the head and back to the abdomen, and there is a double pair of folded wings that look as if they might be gelatin. When the wings are freed, they begin to quiver, and continue to quiver until the transformation is complete. Slowly the body emerges as an exact replica of the pupa case except for the coloring and the vitality that manifests itself in reflected light from every facet and segment.

The insect crawls out of the pupa husk and sits on it, quivering slightly, and the folded wings that had fitted into the wing impressions on the husk now slowly unfold and gradually harden from gelatin to a clear-veined pair of wings on each side. When the wings have reached full size through unfolding, they are held above the body and vibrated for hours more, until they are completely dry and hard; then the cicada leaves the case and flies swiftly away with the most disagreeable cry that sounds like "zzzzzzZIT."

When he sings, one can see the thorax vibrate as he clings to the limb of a tree, and with all this noise one might think that he had many enemies, but apparently he has but few. Perhaps because he is too large for most birds to handle, or perhaps his speed is too great and his dodging too artful for the capacity of most insectivorous birds. I have seen scissor-tailed flycatchers get him on the wing, but their success seems to be in the art of diving at him as he passes their tree. Kingbirds and crested flycatchers catch him in the same manner, although the crested flycatcher seems to make a specialty of hunting him out among the branches of the trees. When disturbed thus, he will fly out with a great clatter and buzzing.

I have no devastating migrations as in the case of voles and lemmings or like the field-mouse migration I saw in California when heavy rains and snows in the mountains filled a San Joaquin Valley lake that had been dry for years and sent millions of mice out across the highways and the fields.

Sometimes in a rodent year the pack rats will overrun the ridge, building their brush-pile houses under rock ledges, in hollow trees and under tree roots, in my abandoned chicken houses, and under the galvanized tank in which I catch the roof run-off. They carry away anything that is loose and put it on the trash heap they have built; like the crows, they love bright things and will struggle along with very large objects simply because the objects are bright.

The pack-rat prize on my ridge is a bright air pump which I had for pumping up pressure in my gasoline stove. When I was away for several days, they gnawed a hole in my box kitchen and somehow, after great struggle, got the prize through. Seeing on my return the unmistakable evidence that rats had been in the kitchen, I began looking in the proper places for such bright things as spoons and the air pump. Just as I had given up the pump as being lost, I found it shining on a rat's house in one of the chicken houses. This particular pump seemed to affect them as a lamp affects a moth; they couldn't keep away from the kitchen, and they managed to get this lovely bright pump once more but gave up the struggle halfway between the chicken house and my kitchen, leaving it shining in the sun.

During the years of rodent migrations—there has been only one bad one in the ten years I have lived at The Blackjacks—the great horned owls come to the ridge in greater numbers and sit on the dead tops of the postoaks, and even on the ridgepole of my roof, breaking the night silence with their great booming, freezing the drama of the blackjacks. During one year of rodents, tragic squeaks could be heard all during the night, and the dogs kept insisting that something ought to be done about it.

During such invasions the chickens escaped disaster from all except skunks and opossums. The coyotes and the bobcats like fat pack rats when they can catch enough of them to make the hunt for them worth while. Field mice to these two are like oysters, serving only as cocktails or as appetizers, but in the year of rodents they live easily and leave my flocks alone. I have seen a coyote so busy hunting field mice, jumping high above the grass tops to pounce on them, or standing on his hind legs like the fox in a fable to better see the course of the mice in their runways, that he failed to see or scent me. In one year of rodents I had a setter puppy that ecstatically hunted field mice, ignoring both quail and that forbidden glory, the cottontail rabbit.

Sometimes the rabbits are everywhere, and then in other years one sees only a frightened one occasionally. When this happens, the balance of the blackjacks is thrown out rather seriously, and strange tragedies occur. During the years of no rabbits, my flocks must be guarded both day and night. The shadowy bobcats become bolder and the coyotes more impudent. The blacksnakes, having no young rabbits to prey on, are a greater menace to the birds. Some of the species of the blackjacks are forced to change their diets and endanger their lives by trespassing on the domains and the food supplies of others. If one could trace the effect on the balance of nature during one year of no rabbits, to the minutest bacilli, he would find a drama so bloody and far-reaching that he would hesitate to credit his own findings.

During the rat invasions there is little harm done, and the pack rat is rather a gentleman compared with his cousin, the city rat. He lives on grains and, I believe, is not in the least carnivorous; at least he does not eat my little chickens. One cold winter, however, one of them established himself under my galvanized tank and, during the night, cut half the English ivy from the fireplace chimney, where it had struggled with and barely beaten two summers of drought. I caught him in a trap, then destroyed his house of green ivy, sticks, and can lids.

The grasshopper invasion, on the other hand, is in effect as bad as a periodic vole invasion in Europe and the Norwegian lemming phenomenon. These locusts come in the drought summers and strip everything green in their path. They grease the windshields of the cars on the highways with their spattered bodies, clog the radiator honeycomb, and cause overheating of the motor. My turkeys, chickens, and pheasants used to stand in the shade uncomfortably wriggling their necks like a man with a tight collar, so full were their gullets from the overflow of their crops.

Man as an agitator of the balance in his economic business of life has also tipped the scales by introduction of species from other continents, who, in their original habitats, were kept in balance by natural enemies and limited food supply but who burst like steam from a safety valve in America, where their enemies were absent and their food supply abundant, enabling them to harass man by their numbers and overrun the habitats of indigenous species. He has introduced insects and birds to kill economically harmful insects without considering the biological or economic result.

The English sparrow, introduced in 1850, now overruns every city from coast to coast and has even seeped into Death Valley. The starling, introduced in 1890, is overflowing the regions of his original plantation along the Atlantic Coast and is lapping farther and farther west like successive wavelets on a shore. I have neither sparrows nor starlings here at The Blackjacks, and none of the imported insects as far as I know. The sparrows and starlings have survived by taking up city life, where the hawk as a potential enemy comes seldom, although I have seen a sharp-shinned hawk perched on the flag pole of a building in New York City—nonchalantly, too, as though he were accustomed to it as a hunting station.

I shoot every half-frightened sparrow that is attracted to my martin or tree boxes, but this is not an important duty, inasmuch as the blackjacks are a bit too wild for them, especially since the chickens and other fowls are gone. No starling has ever visited the ridge.

My drama of the blackjacks has its original cast. Its heroes are the coyotes, the crows, triumphing through quick and perfect adjustment to man and his mechanisms and through the lack of serious challenge by some form of insect life, the great horned owl, the bobcat, and the prairie chicken, through the removal of the small farmer by the growing ranches, and the subsidence of the oil development, and the absence of the workers who follow the industry on its whimsical jumps from place to place over the world. For the drama the unconquerable blackjacks form the eternal backdrop.

The air seems charged and there is anticipation of wood smoke, frosty mornings, and whirring wings. The dogs come to me every afternoon at about three o'clock and demand the daily walk with the 410-guage. There is nothing to hunt yet except doves, but we have never elevated them to the status of game.

Occasionally I go to the little divide north of my house, stand in the opening there, and do some wing-shooting. This is particularly good sport, since doves are fast-flying birds and in this case cannot be seen until they are over the stand, and they must be dropped before they disappear to the rear. I do not care to shoot doves in any other manner.

The sumac turns scarlet on the sides of the ridges and sometimes holds its glory until the blackjacks turn. The woodpeckers start to chatter about hiding their winter stores in the holes and under the bark of the trees, and the crows are vociferous and restive, the bluejays ubiquitous. The idle hours of plenty are fading and the days are closing in. Symbolized by the buck scratching his antlers in preparation for his appearance as a swollen-necked, shining, glorious male, the Deer-Hiding Moon is a moon of purposeful activity.

When the rains come in the latter part of the month, they are followed by the first autumnal cold, and, despite the days of exhilarating air and genial sunshine, there is a definite sadness. There is no sadness in the bird-talk, and the flocks that are leaving seem to be happy and filled with joy. The sadness is in the air that exhilarates; in the sad songs of the insects which in the summer are definitely gay and irresponsible. They sing all through the day, not just on cloudy days and during the early mornings and the late afternoons and nights, and the song is very definitely the song-of-the-end-of-the-season.

As I stand enjoying the gold-washed prairie stretching for miles to the south, and note the beginning of change about me, I see a beer cap shining in the sun and under the Blackjack, where the green table stood, a rusted bottle-opener. There are little pools of cold water in the seat depressions of the metal chairs, and under the locust by the kitchen there is a box of empty beer bottles, their once-bright labels rain-spotted and faded.

An end-of-the-season feeling comes over me; an expectancy that is not unpleasant yet not happy; a feeling of delicate, indefinable bitter-sweetness as in the silence that follows laughter that has been disturbed and cut short before it was finished.

I also charge myself with neglect which is vague, and the end-of-the-season feeling jerks me up, bringing to my consciousness something quite intangible that I have left undone through my summer indolence. This feeling is far from definite, but it interferes with my placidity. I am sure that the mournful songs from the grass roots sharpen the feeling. I have often wondered if it could be a racial memory of great activity in the storing of the caves in man's dawn history with food and hides; a racial memory-fear in man's heart akin to the tingling at the back of a man's neck where hackles once stood on end, but having its source in the primordial fear of cold and starvation instead of fear of night prowlers.

This feeling lasts only a few days, and, when the first real cold comes, it is drowned in the emotion of expectation. The first blue-winged teal stop on the ponds and the prairie pools, and every gun in the cabinet is taken out and oiled. I buy all the outdoor magazines I see displayed in town, and I turn through my sporting goods catalogues and page shop. I become restive and am unable to sit at the typewriter; my thoughts are a series of anticipations, and under the influence of them I walk up and down the cement floor of my little house or around the yard.

How much of my excitement I transmit to my dogs and how much of their excitement, badly suppressed, originates in their response to the changing season I don't know. I do know that they keep their ears cocked for sounds in the house, and every metallic sound that only remotely resembles the mechanism of a gun inspires anxious crowding to the doors and the windows. If I appear at that moment, they dance about me and bark with excitement, Micky whirling in a ridiculous manner, and Bridget attempting to walk on her hind legs.

As the hunting season approaches, the little associations of the summer lose their significance entirely.

The perch will take a black gnat now, and the holes along Bird Creek are clear and very calm under the leaf shadows. Dried sycamore leaves float on them, subject to the slightest breath of breeze in their sailings. The bass fracture the surface when the horse's feet disturb the grasshoppers along the bank, and they land stupidly in the water. Nature is not so careful about them now, since they have bred and assured the continuance of the species; they seem to become progressively more stupid as the season advances and certainly more sluggish.

The cicadas' chant high in the elms, hackberrys, and sycamores is deafening above the placid holes of water, and they sometimes fall and spin frantically on the water, sending concentric wavelets toward the banks with the dead sycamore leaves riding them. I have never seen a bass strike one, but they will take my red-and-white "river runt" or my "broken-back" plug if I can cast them just so under the half-submerged tree trunks or rock projections.

But while waiting for the festival of the blackjacks, when they become madly colored in carnival before winter's repentance, and all the activity of guns and dogs drowns the milder thoughts, I sometimes go to the mountains for rainbow trout. Nature never made a fish more beautiful or more satisfactory. I have never caught the golden trout of the east slopes of the Sierra Nevadas, the almost legendary trout of Lone Pine Creek, but I have tried. But even under the emotion of the legend concerning their rarity and their beauty, I still think that whipping the dashing, feathered mountain streams for rainbow places one a step closer to paradise.

Sometimes it is a change from the harassing sun and cracked earth of drought to daily afternoon rains and water shining everywhere—days when the rains come down in whispers as one slogs along in wet clothing, dragging heavy wading boots; back down the garrulous stream, with the trout in the creel wonderfully cold and pleasing to the touch. Damp, cold afternoons when the range sheep bleat with pettishness from the mountainsides, and the Rocky Mountain jays follow in the pines to tell the world of your coming.

I thought camp to be around each bend of the little stream one afternoon but found each time nothing but the stream winding on, marked by its willows, and the mountains brooding in the dull light with their wispy collars of clouds and their burden of discontented sheep. My creel was full and I was hungry and cold, and I couldn't keep my pipe going. The whiskey flask was empty. Somewhere in that mournful half-light would be pine smoke and food and warmth, but it seemed to move on and on as I moved toward it, like a prairie horizon.

Then suddenly I came on a Mexican sheepherders' camp. They had eaten, but the pot of mutton was still hot, and there was tortilla dough left. As I sat and ate, they talked of the weather and of sheep but mostly of my comfort, with the wonderful manners that Mexicans have. Their questions were not disconcertingly direct but were assumptions pleasantly expressed and carried no obligations. The suspicion of native Americans would have made me uncomfortable until I had succeeded in satisfying them by establishing my association with something or someone of which or of whom they knew, and approved, nullifying their courtesy even though satisfying my hunger through sincerely extending it. They might have saved my life had it been in danger, even sacrificing their own, while my Mexicans would have shrugged their shoulders and stared placidly at my passing, but somehow the boiled mutton and tortillas under the dripping pines was one of the meals that remains in my memory. Here was the satisfying of hunger associated with understanding, human kindness, and perfect courtesy. and one did not care if the bright smiles came only from the teeth.

During the latter part of this moon the blackjacks give the relief from the hot sun which they have been promising since June, and their shade is now comfortable. No matter how hot the sun beats down during the day, the nights are now cool, and the dew sparkles in the early sun. The goldenrod covers the prairie, adding yellow-gold to the old-gold of the bluestem blooms.

The life-cycles are ending, and the seeds for the new ones have been sowed. Again things happen in the accustomed manner at the accustomed times to give man assurance, making bright again the illusion of permanence.

X DEER-BREEDING MOON

 IF I HAVE NOT FINISHED MY WORK AT THE TYPEWRITER WHEN THIS MOON comes to the blackjacks, I must push it aside. If I attempt to carry on, the writing suffers; it loses so much in such a mysterious way that it is often useless and insipid. I do not always recognize this at the time, but it hits me in the face later, and I feel embarrassed. No winter mallard can be happier than I am from October to January. I often get up in the mornings and run down the ridge with the dogs until I am exhausted, from the sheer love of action and the feel of the frosty air in my face. This would certainly be an odd display if there were people here to see it; an odd expression of spirit in a country where everything is done from a sitting position, either behind a wheel or from a saddle. When a cowboy plays, he runs his horse, but he is as clumsy on the ground as an eagle or an airplane. I appreciate the feeling which inspires a cowhorse to buck on a frosty morning.

The squirrels are busy at this time of the year, and they bark during the sunny afternoons along the creek bottoms and over the ridges. There are only the big fox squirrels on the ridges, but in the bottoms the gray squirrels cling high in the tall, white sycamores and redoaks. The black squirrel is seldom seen. He is the black phase of the gray squirrel, and it is the skin from the scrotum of the black that the Osage use for their love medicine. The scrotum has much significance in itself, and it forms the bag into which other ingredients are placed.

The buck goat has been the symbol of male intensity and salacity since before the time of the Romans, but the Osage have always admired such qualities in the boar squirrel. I have spent many hours watching them during this, their rutting season, and their mating seems frenzied and tireless. There is little of the delicate nuptial display found even in the prancing of the stallion, with mane and tail flying in wild beauty. The finesse of the boar squirrel is the finesse of the buck goat. One will take a sudden fancy for some female, and if she does not yield immediately, he will chase her through the tops of the trees until he catches her, then go back to chase another one that he has seen slipping around to the other side of a tree as he flashed by. It is not uncommon to kill fat and slovenly squirrels that have been castrated in the nest by jealous old ones.

And this is the moon when the whitetail buck used to step out of hiding to stand with head high, neck swollen, and new, polished antlers shining in the sun. Deer-Breeding Moon is also called New-Horn Moon.

The buck is restive and eager with the mystery that floods him, and he is often sullen and may be dangerous, seeming to lose respect for all things. He may appear in places he has shunned before and walk with dignity across the highways in front of cars, and he is much more likely to attack a hunter at this time than is the much larger mule deer of the Rockies. He always reminds me of a cocky young man who is so filled with the wonderful biological glory of virility that tradition, experienced judgment, and caution become dimmed, and he alone struts in tingling superiority.

Unfortunately the whitetail buck is gone from the blackjacks. There are no mountain fastnesses with dark, inaccessible canyons or forbidding swamps in my country, and the open prairie and blackjacks cannot protect him from the mechanized invasion. He and the wild turkeys may come back—may come back as the prairie chicken has done with the enlargement of the ranches.

The quail have reached the adult stage now, and their scent has returned. During the summer, and certainly during the breeding season, they seem to have lost their scent. I have stood with my eye on a well-hidden nest, not able to see the mother bird because of her perfect blending with her surroundings, but knowing that she was there, while the dogs nosed about with never a hint that there was the scent they love so much in the tuft of bluestem. Even on damp, cool days their scent seems to be dead during the nesting season. The nests not only have no scent for dogs or coyotes but they are so roofed and harmonized with the surrounding vegetation that they cannot be seen by the marauding crows. However, the crow and coyote are quite smart enough to watch the birds and spot the nest when one or the other of the birds leaves or enters. Of course, after the little ones hatch, they can run immediately and thereafter become bits of bark, stone, weed shadow, or grass when they freeze on the danger signal. I have surprised the hens with their downy chicks when only a few hours or days of age and have heard the signal from them and have seen the little, intangible bits of life run in all directions or melt into the earth, where they squat. The mother bird will flutter away, pretending that she is crippled, beating her wings against the ground in order to lure me away, and certainly fooling the dogs. At such times I turn back on my tracks for fear of stepping on some of the chicks.

A steer, a horse, or even a coyote or a man for that matter, will never step on a tuft of bluestem or a weed as they walk across the prairie; instinctively they avoid them. The quail and the prairie chickens both build their nests under weeds or grass tufts and even along the edge of cow trails, and they are safe from the hoofs of animals and the foot of man. Only cars crossing the prairie will roll over the nests of prairie chickens.

Thus the trails of the blackjacks and the prairie are jagged and crooked, while the deer and cattle trails along the canyon sides of the Rockies where the ground is bare or the grass tufts sparse are as even and flowing as contour lines. To follow a cattle trail back to my little house, on heavy feet after a day in the field, is almost as fatiguing as walking in the entangling grass; as unrhythmical as walking railroad ties.

This is the season for the cutting of wood, and I load it and haul it over to the house in the station wagon after the woodcutters have sawed it into three-foot lengths. The hauling is much the easiest phase of the wood-getting business.

All woodcutters as they wipe the sweat from their faces, even on a rather cold day, will sooner or later bring out the trite statement made by an early-day wit: "They's one thing 'bout a blackjack; it's a double heater; once when a man's a-cuttin' it and agin' when it's a-burnin'."

An old woodcutter came one October to cut my wood. I showed him where I wanted the trees cut from around some postoak saplings and helped him with the two-man saw until his helper came. We sawed, then rested and talked, to resume sawing after we had emptied our pipes. While we were sitting on the log, he said, "A book-writin' feller like you don't seem like'ud have any business a-cuttin' his own wood; a feller like you 'stead of wastin' time a-writin' books oughtta git out and run fer sheriff."

"Wouldn't have a chance," I said, smiling.

"I guess you're kindy like me; don't know much 'cept what you're workin' at. Take me now; 'bout all I know is hard work. 'Bout time I'se feelin' my oats when I'se a kid of a boy, and hardly knowed better'en to spit agin' the wind, and orta bin gettin' a little schoolin', I gotta steppin' high like a buck deer. Married me a little ole ignorant gal and figgered I'se cuttin' a fat'un. Hell, I didn't know nothin' and she didn't know nothin' to learn me.

"I do a heap of studyin' sometime and figgerin' what makes the wheel turn, as the feller says, but then, hell, I spit on my hands and take to whatever I'm a-doin' after a little, and figger that the good Lord'll take care of things th'out no aid from sich as me."

The clear, starry nights are filled with the voices of the hounds. I lie in my sleeping bag and listen as they run the canyons and the ridges. Often they run so close to my little house that my setters are disturbed and join the excitement. At such times as the cry of hounds fade in the distance, an old dog coyote will sit on the point of the ridge south of the house and howl defiance, swearing at them with all his rich vocabulary.

I much prefer visual hunting. Trail hounds have little appeal for me, but their masters are the most interesting group of hunters of the blackjacks. They are true dreamers and poets. Lone hunters often sit by their fires on the point of the east ridge all night, looking into the fire and listening to what they believe to be the sweetest music in the whole world as it comes out of the mysterious darkness. Man, free from domestic worry and the slavery of the business of life, sitting out under the cold stars by a lone fire—a man who quite often has only keys and knife to jingle in his pockets and who invariably lies to his wife about the price which he pays for some hound which has caught his fancy.

But they love talk. They tell others of the feats of their hounds, and I have often sat about a fire with several hunters listening to each one singing the praises of his hounds; men who from the medley of voices seem to know which voice belongs to which hound as well as they know the voices of their children.

They boast of some favored hound's prowess and will not admit that the favored one sending his voice through the night might be on the trail of a rabbit or a wandering opossum. And they will not have it that a coyote started is not always a coyote caught, although the only evidence they have may be splotches of blood on the white hairs of the hound's throat and chest. I have enjoyed many a hunt from my bedding roll, but I have also heard the sharp, inquisitive baying of confusion which seems to end most of them, and invariably the coyote has the last word as he sits on some point of vantage taunting his trailers.

During the early days of this month the Southwestern Wolf Hunters Association holds its annual meeting on lands belonging to the chief of the Osage. Here they hold a four-day meeting complete with a bench show and the cast each morning at daybreak. The several judges are mounted and wear red coats which are distinguishing marks and not borrowed tradition.

Men and women afoot, on horseback, in cars and pickup trucks, stand shivering in the darkness of the early morning, while the hounds stand in line held in leash by owners and handlers and face the master of the hunt and other officials, including the judges, all on horseback. The names of the men entering the hounds are called off, and the number of the hound, which is painted on either side in red paint, is called. When all is ready, the rules of the hunt are read and word given. The hounds break for the timber, and many of them start baying in the excitement of anticipation.

For hours they run and mouth through the blackjacks, and the men in cars halt in some spot along the dirt roads to listen and watch, then, as the mouthing fades, they move on to a new spot. If they are lucky, they may see the coyote cross the road nervously looking back over his shoulder, and then, when he has disappeared, see the hounds cross in a flood.

I sat on the point of a hill one morning at one of these meetings and listened to one persistent hound, apparently running in circles in the timber below me; the five or six others having left the point, I was alone. The hound seemed to be halfhearted or acting like a pup on some cold trail. Soon, however, just in front of me the coyote came out of the timber and stood a moment looking back, then moved his ears and tested the air, as he looked around the open space he was about to cross. I remained still and he didn't see me, although he was not more than fifty feet away. He stood there as though attempting to make up his mind. He was panting slightly. He kept looking back at the timber he had just left, where the lone hound was working out his trail.

Then the hound appeared, and his voice became more certain and excited when he saw the coyote, and he began to move his tail in a ridiculous circle as he rushed toward him. The coyote stood and watched the approaching hound with steady gaze, raising his brush slightly. Then, when the hound was almost upon him, he ran across the opening in front of me, and the hound came on behind him. The coyote was only loping, and the hound's nose was almost touching the long hair of his hind legs, but he made no attempt to run faster or take hold of the coyote. They simply loped across the opening, the hound yapping and the coyote with his mouth open and tongue out as though he were laughing.

I didn't report the number of the hound to the owner. He would have received excellent marking if a judge had heard him in his persistent and lonesome trailing, but his playfulness as he loped easily behind the coyote across the opening might have embarrassed the owner if he could not have thought of some reasonable excuse for such flippancy.

A man who boasts that he has the greatest fighting chickens and the best hounds in the country came into the barber shop one day and started talking about the performance of his hounds the night before.

"Them dogs of mine," he said, "musta run a cat clean out of the country last night; either that or, by dogy, they's after a smart ole wolf that took 'em all night to catch—they wasn't in yet when I left."

Someone said, "Maybe they didn't get him."

"Hell, that's what's the matter; they had to run him before they could catch him. They'll catch him all right; I got the best hounds in the country."

A cowboy raised up in a chair, with the lather foaming on his face, and said, "Damned if you ain't. As I'se comin' in this mornin' I seen your dogs a-eatin' on one end of a dead steer and a coupla coyotes a-eatin' on the other."

"Yeah, I guess you did," sneered the dog-owner.

The cowboy sat straight up, and the barber stepped back, with his razor held high and to one side, as the cowboy shouted, "Hell they ain't—I'll bet you fifty and take you out there."

We get weather reports over the radio with storm warnings to cattlemen of an oncoming blizzard. During October, however, I am interested in these warnings chiefly as they affect the flight of ducks and geese. When the news comes that there is cold and snow in the north, I get out my 12-gauge and drive out onto the prairie to watch the ponds from some high point with the glasses or ride around the pastures to visit the ponds of the ranch to see if there is any sign yet.

By the time these storms reach our latitude they have deteriorated into cold rains, but with them, or just before them, come the main flight of ducks and geese out of the Far North. When I hear the first rustling of the blackjack leaves as I sit by the fire with the dogs, I go outside to listen and wait for the wind to grow and the air to become colder, holding my hand out to feel if there is a cold mist. On such nights I can't read and my favorite programs on the radio seem dull and sparkless. Even the dogs sense my excitement, and they leave the fire to come to me and offer their paws as though they think I need some special manifestation of friendship. From the time I have been old enough to hunt, this expectancy of cold rain during this season has submerged all interest in other things.

I listen until the icy winds sing around the eaves and puff explosively into the fireplace, and I can hear the trickle of rain or the whispering of mist if the wind dies. I stand outside looking into the north, then go back to the fire and examine the guns and look again at the shells in my hunting coat. Finally, through habit, I turn on the news at ten o'clock, but I hear nothing. If I am in bed when the first V of geese fly over the ridge like an excited pack of hounds, I jump up to run out and gaze into the blackness, shaking a little but not from cold. During the night I can hear the mournful whistle of the plover and the honking of brant and geese, hour after hour, like the lament of refugees following the way my ridge points out to them.

Long before daylight I am up and making coffee and sandwiches by the light of my kerosene lamps. When all is ready, I step out into the cold rain and start off in the station wagon for the high prairie. The unhappy expression of the setters fails to touch me as I close the door and leave the house in their care.

Even with mud and snow tires the station wagon labors and slips and sways through the mud of the natural roads, and the slowly falling rain slants into the windshield. The muddy water splashes over the headlights and obscures my vision. The hissing of the windshield wiper is futile.

Soon I leave the road and drive across the prairie along some rutted feed trail until I reach the first pond. I sit in the wagon and wait for the light, then walk carefully behind the dam. If I hear no splashing or goose chatter, I pull a broomweed and, holding it in front of my face, look cautiously over.

Sometimes geese are very canny and sometimes very stupid. They will often become frightened at the slightest blowing of a strand of hair over the dam and then fly directly over the spot where the hunter is hidden. At other times they will sit while the hunter looks at them and gauges the range. Most of the time, however, they match the wary wild turkey in their own wariness. Many times when the wind was in my favor I have been sure that they have not seen me or heard me, but still I have not always been able to get near them. On other occasions I have crawled through the broomweeds and the dead bluestem for a quarter of a mile to get a shot at them. At such times they mistake me for a coyote and feel quite safe in their element. I do not say that they are unaware of my crawling through the weeds; it is simply a case of mistaken identity. One cold, foggy morning I crawled into the middle of a flock of mallards feeding at the shallow edges and inlets of the pond. I couldn't believe it when I found myself looking into the steady eye of a greenhead only a few yards away.

I drive from pond to pond, then at noon go back to a pond which they use all during the season, sit in the wagon, and watch the sky as I eat my lunch.

Driving back to the little house through the frozen muck of the road, hungry and almost always wet, is just as much a part of the glory of the day as the actual hunting. The dogs meet me at the door, sniff my clothes, and dance about me happily without a sign of having been injured or neglected. I build up the fire and change my clothes, then sit for awhile with the flame dancing on the red glass in my hand as I lose myself in recapitulation. After my meal I draw the ducks and string them up on a wire on the front porch, then back to the fire to fall asleep as I dream. At such times I wish for a magic wand to make my clothes disappear and cause me to float to my sleeping bag.

Full glory comes to the blackjacks at this time. They shine with profound tranquillity in the sun, expressing gaiety by their multi-colored magnificence and grandeur by their incredible dignity. On moonlight nights I leave the fire to go out to stand among them. In the eerie light they have lost their brilliance, but their colors are distinguishable and their serenity more complete. I stand in the silence with emotion that hurts and cannot be relieved by expression, either by word symbols or by physical action. Then when the cold, mystical silence is broken by a coyote howling from the point of the ridge, I wait for him to stop and go back to his earthy business of hunting; then I go back to my fire. In his long quavering cry he, unencumbered by artificiality, has asked the question for both of us and expressed as well as it can ever be expressed that which wells in both our hearts.

When we go bear hunting in the mountains, it is during the latter part of the Deer-Breeding Moon, but during this moon following one of the great drought summers, the Deerslayer telegraphed that the bear had come down out of the Guadalupe Mountains. We learned that there had been a drought in the mountains that year when we arrived at his ranch, and the bear had come down to ravage the valleys in their hunger.

The Deerslayer showed us the skin of a big cinnamon he had killed the day before, and he struck the attitude of injured innocence which men assume when their vested interest has been disturbed. This great cinnamon bear had taken his sheep, and he was pretending to be upset over the loss, but one could read in his hunter's face that he would gladly give a dozen sheep, with a few Iowa bucks thrown in, if he could get another chance to shoot a cinnamon charging down the mountainside as he had shot this one.

We saddled the horses before daylight the next morning, while the hounds whined and gave voice to their excitement. I was given a little mustang just brought in from the range. The little fellow was as tough and as hard as the mesa over which he had been roaming for months. In the cold of the early morning he shivered when the saddle was thrown on him, and he shivered again when I put my 30-06 rifle in the scabbard; and when I climbed on him, he stood irresolute with his tail tucked between his legs, snorting as though he had shucks in his nose.

For a mile or more he kept his head practically on my chest and seemed to want to travel sidewise, but when the hot sun shone over the mountains he slowed down. We rode along the sheep-mesh fence until we came to the place where a bear had dexterously separated the wire and left a few of his bristles. The mustang was not interested and stood with his head down as we examined the spot.

The bear had come into the sheep fence, killed several sheep, and then had gone out at some other place, so we found it useless to put the hounds on the trail here if we could find the exit and a trail that would not be confused with the scent of sheep.

The higher the sun climbed, the more indifferent became the mustang. When I kicked him with my spurless heels, he moved his ears back and gave the impression of being drained of all his power to break a walk.

We couldn't keep up with the others, and I realized that I was doing more work than he was, so I gave him his head and hoped that we would not jump the bear that day but on the following day, when I should have a real horse under me.

We had to climb up the south sides of the mountains where the tall pines refuse to grow and where only shinnery, cactus, and sage shine in the sun that plays there.

I forgot about the bear, believing it was too late for a run anyway and the scent certainly killed by the heat of midmorning, and began to please myself with the topography. From my backbone of a high mountain ridge, I could look east over a series of tawny hills bare of everything except grass; sheep range. A long, tawny range, sharply cut against the horizon, lay like a slumbering stegosaurus, the igneous dike that formed its backbone resembling the spine armor.

The sun had killed the voices of sheep and bird, and over everything lay midday silence. As I slouched in the saddle, I fell under the spell of the soporific scene and the rhythm and was soon creating an airplane which in some manner received its power from the air and was perfectly aligned, and, like the wings of a gull or a vulture, it automatically adjusted itself to the vertical currents of the upper air, thus coming to earth only when the pilot chose to do so, with or without power. Flying around the world, one could simply set some gadgets and go to sleep when tired, to resume the guidance of the plane when he waked up.

I was just about to receive the applause of an admiring assembly of civil and military aeronautical experts when I realized that the rhythm had stopped and my dream with it. The mustang that had fired me so with such hopes that he might be an eager bear horse during the early morning was now, under the shade of a Douglas fir, supporting himself on three legs and resting the fourth. I listened for the others, and I could hear their horses' hoofs on the stones of the side of the mountain below me. I felt that we could not possibly pick up the trail now, this late in the day, and was considering the possibility of cutting across the ridges to the ranch. As I considered this, I looked at the ground where we were standing, and there in a bare spot where the deer had stamped the soil loose was the fresh imprint of a bear's foot. I took my rifle from the scabbard and looked about me. Seeing nothing, I turned the mustang down the side of the mountain and motioned to the others to come with the hounds.

We put the lead hound's nose on the track, and immediately the pack started off with a great clamor, and we were off along the backbone of the mountain behind them, dodging the trees and tearing through the growths of live oak. With my head low over the neck of the pony I separated the clutching live oaks with my gauntleted hand as a prow cuts the water. All three of us were in time to see the bear reach a tall Douglas fir just in front of the hounds, jump around to the opposite side, and climb to the top swiftly.

While we were skinning him and wondering at his size and porky fatness, I realized that the little mustang under the spell of my excitement had kept up with the others. The other two horses were heaving like bellows, and the foam slid down their bellies and hung, while the mustang was dark with sweat but not too spent. He stood with his head lowered, as though the smell of bear didn't bother him in the least. He shut his eyes and seemed to go to sleep.

He would not carry his share of the meat or hide, and we had to get D to go for it in his wood wagon and haul it to his house so that we could pick it up later in the truck. When we drove up to D's house, he was standing by the carcass talking to two other men. He kept saying, "It's got a foot like a man; sure has—just like a man."

Our regular hunts, however, came late in the Deer-Breeding Moon, just before the deer season opened, so that we could hunt with the hounds up to the day before deer hunting started.

One morning we climbed on to a divide that shouldered against Holdup Peak and stopped to play the glasses over the rimrock. There were three of us: the Cowwooly, attempting to keep the jittery Satan quiet as he looked through the glasses; the Old Timer, squinting with his cold eyes at the talus slopes and sitting straight on a tranquil little buckskin as hard as steel and as philosophical as a camel; while I stood beside Hereford ready to take the glasses, my saddle-dream of the last two hours snuffed like a candle's light by the winds of expectation preceding the storm of exciting action.

The granitic mass that is Holdup Peak threw its morning shadows far across the canyons and divides, and the Douglas firs had begun to whisper ever so softly in the first sun-born currents that stirred like drowsy spirits. The hounds lay about us, only old Floppy, the lead hound, looked expectantly at the Cowwooly busily attempting to keep Satan faced toward the rimrock while he kept the glasses on the strikingly black spot on the gray talus; a spot very black against the granitic slivers, and blacker still against the old-gold of the shaded aspens.

The bear had been watching us as we wondered about his identity, and, just after I took the glasses back, he began to climb straight up the peak, using the aspen growth as cover. He had heard the horses' hoofs against the stones and had stopped there to watch us but then seemed to realize that he was not protected in his blackness against the gray and old-gold, even in the shadows of the peak.

Hereford sensed the excitement, and his legs seemed to spring against the hard, disintegrated granite of the divide's backbone, as he followed the deerlike Satan up the divide to the shoulder. The hounds also felt the excitement, but, like the horses, could neither see nor scent the bear. Several of the younger ones gave voice tentatively as though they would test their voices for the impending race.

We reached the wild, deep canyons on the sliding, clinking talus, then the Cowwooly stepped off of Satan and clamored up the sliding rock toward the aspens, dragging old Floppy along by the collar. When we heard the first deep mouthing of Floppy, the other hounds bounded up to join him, and Satan did a dance around the pine sapling to which he was tied.

It was planned that the Cowwooly should scramble around the shoulder for the purpose of getting to the saddle on the other side of the peak before the bear came over, and thus turn him down the big canyon. I was to ride along the timber line to the edge of the canyon and, by listening to the hounds, determine which way the bear was going.

I rode Hereford hard over the fallen pines and across the slide rock at the heads of the little ravines, and soon we were alone, the Old Timer having taken another course.

I found the projection of an escarpment. I left Hereford flecked with sweat foam and heaving sides under the shade of a pine. The sweat dripped from under my hatband. I sat looking out across the savage, untouched wilderness, with the sweat evaporating so fast in the high, dry air that the last drops felt like ice water on the back of my hands. A Rocky Mountain jay cocked his head and scolded me, then flew away to report to the others. A rock was dislodged and clinked against another far down the canyon, and later, climbing slowly up the other side, I saw two mule-deer bucks. They climbed slowly and seemed a bit baffled, since they could detect no scent, and kept stopping to look back toward the sunny side of the canyon directly under me where they had been bedded down. When they stopped, it was always in the shade, behind a bush or the trunk of a pine, where their rusty-blue-gray coats blended perfectly.

As I watched them, I heard the faint voices of the hounds far up the canyon. As they grew in volume, I realized that I had chosen correctly and that they were coming down the canyon and would pass somewhere below me. The bass voice of old Floppy grew steadily in volume, and the keener, higher voices of the others were the chorus.

Bear hunting, with its frenzied action and the deep voices of the bloodhounds echoing from the savage walls of the mountain canyons, awakens every nerve to incautious action. Somewhere ahead of that excited chorusing was a great black beast whose ancestors far back in dim time once hunted man, and man has a racial memory of having been the delicate, thin-skinned hunted instead of the hunter, which adds zest to bear hunting; the racial memory of the scratching and sniffing at his cave barrier is still deep in man's soul. Such memories are the heritage of the hunted and not a part of the primeval instinct of the hunter.

Soon the voice of old Floppy bounced up and down the canyon like mild thunder, and I sat with every cell alert; I sat choked with emotion as the "music" filled the canyon.

The volume reached its apex just below me, and, as it broke, I rose and went back to Hereford. He shied from the intensity that filled me, and I immediately conveyed my excitement to him. He seemed to forget his caution at the edge of the canyon and plunged down the steep sides without the least hesitation. The dust boiled about us as we slid, his fore legs stiff and his hind legs slanted under his belly as brakes. He grunted and sighed but kept sliding. We came to a precipitous wall that reached to the bottom of the canyon, and I had to step off and lead him until we found a way down. I tried to make him go before me, but he would not, so I went ahead with the reins in my hand, sliding down amid tumbling rocks and dust clouds to the bottom. If I could have stopped on my way down, I dared not do so, since he would have tumbled helplessly over me.

When we reached the bottom, we stopped to drink at a cold stream, but this was done rather mechanically, since everything was shut out of my consciousness except the thundering music of the chase, just ahead of us down the canyon. I put Hereford into a dead run along the canyon floor.

Then the chorusing ended suddenly, and we stopped to listen. Hereford's breathing made the saddle creak, so I got off and walked to one side, attempting to hear above the thumping of my heart. As I drank at the stream I thought I had heard rifle shots down the canyon, but paid little attention, and only now I realized that they might have had some significance. I sat down and lit a cigarette. All life and sound were gone from the somber canyon; all except the beating of my heart and the slight creaking of the saddle as Hereford breathed. Suddenly he pricked his ears and looked up the canyon, then I saw the Cowwooly and the Old Timer coming toward me.

"Where'd he go?" asked the Cowwooly.

"Don't know."

We sat there for some time listening, but the silence was complete. The Cowwooly looked over at me and said, "Wasn't you shot them shots, then?"

"No; farther down the canyon."

We rode on along the canyon stream, and in a few minutes we came to a deer hunter's camp. The bedding-rolls and pack saddles were strewn about, and the horses were in the corral. A Mexican cook came up smiling with delightful graciousness.

"Buenos días," he said.

"Buenos días," we answered.

The Cowwooly was the first to see old Floppy lying in the shade of a tree, panting, with his red tongue touching the ground as he lay looking at us. Without a word, the Cowwooly rode one way and I the other. We circled the camp but found no tracks or sign that something had been dragged. We came back to where the Old Timer and the Mexican were talking. He turned to us and said that the Mexican was alone according to his story; that the hunters were looking for deer signs somewhere so as to be ready for the opening of the season on the following day. He turned back to the Mexican and asked, "Nobody shot a bear that came down the canyon, verdad?"

"No, señor."

When we started on, Floppy arose slowly and took his place at Satan's heels, then one by one and two by two the others joined us as we turned up Holdup Canyon toward camp. We rode in silence.

Probably an hour later, the Cowwooly turned in his saddle and said, "That chollo's a goddam liar."

The long shadow which the mountains cast were being absorbed by the twilight, and, as we rimmed out, we saw the smoke of our camp, standing straight in the still air like a fakir's rope.

The disappointing climax of our hunt did not occur to me forcefully until I had left the saddle and was sitting on a log watching the flames curl around the blackened pot. With no soothing rhythm to smooth the sharp edges of reality, the sudden silence in a brooding canyon that had smashed the highest pitch of emotion suddenly seemed tragic to me on this last day of our bear hunting for the season.

Sometimes when the Cowwooly and I sit alone, a little gas explosion in the pine logs sends the sparks high into the air, and we hear the thud of running deer in the outer darkness, and sometimes we catch the glint of their eyes as they stand, fascinated. I should not wonder what the Cowwooly is thinking when upon examination I find, after hours of looking into the fire, that I can recall nothing definite about what I have been thinking; the thoughts are disconnected and cannot be put together and brought back clearly at the time. The sight of a fire is like a very pleasing odor; it perfumes and strengthens the memories associated with it. On gazing into a fire I am often thrilled with the memories it brings back to me of other fires and other places.

The urge to tell stories or talk around a campfire must be the poor substitute expression of a deep emotion associated with racial memories which cannot be expressed—a substitute expression which softens the poignancy of futility and dulls the sharp edge of unhappiness. Face to face with primitive disturbances, we are all like those who have surpluses of creative spirit but cannot sing, dance, paint, interpret on instruments, compose, or write. With no medium of expression the depths of our souls remain unguessed and unappreciated, even by ourselves, even as the dawning soul of our ancestor, with his hairy arms over his head, gazing into the wonder of a fire, which sensed dreams that could be expressed only in fear and poignant emotion.

When the Cowwooly changes sides to the fire, I get up to push a half-burned log into the flame. Our fire-dreams are then broken, and our talk is of the daily obstacles that thwart man and distort his designs; of the fundamental things of living far out in the folds of the brown, sterile foothills with two children and a woman who is not well; of wrangling over line fences with cattlemen and hauling water in a fifty-five-gallon drum from a well seven miles away.

The Cowwooly makes no complaint. He believes that a man's work and a man's fun are both pretty hard and that there is little to distinguish between them, even before a fire high in a mountain hunter's camp. Hard luck, work, and a "big time" are accepted as part of life. When a man has to saddle up on a cold wind-moaning night and ride for a doctor, because a man's wife "just cain't pack a boy," or one of the children becomes chronically puny, that is just hard luck, and there is no use talking about it. When a man has to get enough property together anyway he can, and get enough cash to supply the necessities—food, clothing, and medicine—that is work, and work is just as natural as breathing. It often means contracting with a big outfit to gather their "wild 'uns" in the high mountain range; cattle that in many cases have evaded the roundups for years and may never have seen a man; five- and six-year-old steers that hide like buck deer and charge off down the canyon sides through live oak thickets when they are discovered, where there isn't a chance for a man to throw a decent loop, and where he tangles with hell if his pony falls.

Participating in a rodeo is play, and there is a great satisfaction in having a couple of horses like Satan and Hereford; the one as fast as lightning in match saddle races and the other with a head full of cow sense. With such horses a man has a chance at the calf-roping money, saddle races, or even the wild-cow-milking prizes. If you and your horses are good, having a "big time" at a rodeo brings in money.

"Say," the Cowwooly said one night as he squatted on his heels before the fire, "why don't yu write about ole Pete? I know jist 'bout everthin' they is to know about 'im."

"He certainly would make a wonderful story, if all I hear about him is true. . . . . I think it is, but people wouldn't believe it. You couldn't write about him unless you made him talk just as he talks, and I am afraid magazine editors would think it too thick."

"Yeah, I guess they would. Takes know to write, don't it?"

"Takes a queer kind of man and a lot of hard work. I suppose sitting at a typewriter for six or eight hours wouldn't seem like work to you though."

"Hell it wouldn't. Say, sometimes I wish I'da went on in school. Guess I couldda at that, but I don' know. Did I ever tell the why I didn't?"

"No."

"Yu ain't never bin to the Flats? It's the closest water in this country, and they did some irrigatin' there. They's a little schoolhouse by one of them ditches, where they know they's lots of water. I aimed to keep goin' there whin I was a kid, but I—I tell yu how it happened.

"It come a big snow one winter, and us kids gotta buildin' us some forts outta snow and a-pastin' each other with snowballs. We gotta putin' rocks in 'em, and one of 'em caught me up side the head and I keeled over, like I'se dead. I got me a big quartz rock and put in me a big snowball, and wet 'er down till it was ice; I laid it up side a ole kid's head, and he went out like Lottie's eye.

"The teacher come out and made us quit, then yu know how kids is; we gotta throwin' soft ones at the girls, jist in fun and to hear 'em scream. They's one little girl there that said that I hit her with a hard one on purpose, and the teacher said that if he ever caught me doin' it again he'd send me home.

"Nex day the first thing I know, the teacher calls me in and says he's goin' whup me fer washin' a girl's face with snow. I said I didn't do it, but he claimed I did. I tole him I wasn't goin' take no whuppin' for somethin' I didn't do; he said he was goin' whup me. I tole him iffen he'd tell me what girl tole sich a lie, I'd go bring her face to face.

"He let on he wasn't listenin' to what I was sayin' and tole me to git ready. I tole him, hell, I wasn't goin' take no whuppin' for somethin' I never done. When he come at me, I grabbed his goddam stick, and me and him tangled. I didn't do nothin'—I just kep him from whuppin' me. Finely he got tar'd, I guess, and quit, and he shore was red-faced. He said never to step my foot in that schoolhouse agin', and I tole him I shore wouldn't.

"I got on my ole pony and loped home. I messed around and done my chores, and I kep thinkin' about the whole thing and how that bastard 'ud said I was to blame for that face washin'. I was stayin' with some folks, and thay wasn't much explainin' to do. I just said I was goin' quit, and that's all thay was to it.

"I couldn't git it out of my head. I worked hard but seem like everthin' I did, I'd have to be thinkin' about that teacher and the way he done me. Cuttin' wood I shore would make the kindlin' fly when I was thinkin' about it. Hell, I knowed I wasn't no angel, but to be blamed for somethin' I didn't do shore made me mad.

"Seem like I couldn't do nothin' for two, three days but be mad. One night I was layin' in bed. I couldn't sleep for the moon shinin' into my winda anyhow, so I laid there thinkin'. I kep thinkin' about how mad I was, and how I half-wished that teacher's head was under the ax when I was cuttin' wood. I gotta thinkin' about that ax in the yard, and how I'ud been keepin' it sharp. I got up and pulled on my britches and boots and slipped out of the house. That ole ax shore did show up there in the moonlight, and everthin' was just like daytime. I saddled my ole pony, and, as I come by the woodpile, I grabbed up that ole ax and loped off.

"You see, along that irrigation ditch was about the only trees on the whole Flats. They'd been planted there by different teachers and the kids at the school. They was mostly cottonwoods, but they shore was proud of 'em.

"When I got there, I stopped my pony and jist looked. It was kinda scary there; everthin' so quiet in the moonlight. You know how a schoolhouse looks when thay ain't no kids runnin' around hollerin'? And that moonlight made it worse, a-shinin' down and makin' shadows. I got tu 'maginin' thay was somebody standin' in the shadows. It looked kinda purty there too, in the moonlight like that with them trees a-throwin' their shadows, and yu could hear that irrigation water a-gurglin'. I come goddam near to goin' back, but then I got to thinkin' the way I'd been treated.

"I stepped off my ole pony and set in. Thay was maybe six of them biggest trees, and it wasn't long 'fore I had 'em all down. Every time one of 'em cracked down, I couldn't hep lookin' around; seem like everybody in the country oughtta woke up, and it seemed so still afterwards that I got kinda nervous, but I 'ud spit on my hands and take to another one."

After a silence a cold wind came up the canyon and whipped the smoke about crazily, so that there seemed to be no escape from it. He set his hat on the back of his head and yawned, then, standing, spread his hands to the rekindled fire, blinked, and turned his face away. A few minutes later he unceremoniously went to his little suspended tent shelter and got into his sleeping bag.

The flames danced on the tall pines with renewed vigor and on the white cook tent. I could hear the far-off tinkling of the bell on the little blue mare that constantly gave us the location of the remuda.

XI

THIS IS THE TRUE HUNTING MOON, AND DURING THIS MOON ALL OTHER business is secondary to hunting. The blackjacks are still shining fantastically in the sun, and the sumac are less startling in their bright scarlet now, since they have no green background and many of them have shed their leaves by this time. The mallards have come to linger on the prairie ponds or feed along the banks of the creeks, flying to and from the grounds where the cattle are grain-fed. The prairie chickens have begun to fly into the blackjacks from the high prairie to feed on the acorns. The whitetail buck, if still here, would be stepping high with a male musk that man himself could smell at times.

The swifts have gone from the chimney, although they hang on until the mornings are quite cold, and sometimes even after I have built the first fire of the autumn in the fireplace. The insectivorous birds have gone; only the seed-eaters remain, and such omnivorous ruffians as the bluejays and the crows become noisier and much more active, along with the flicker and the pileated woodpecker.

The prairie is still gold-washed, and the seeding bluestem is turning from old-gold to a somber, unburnished copper. There are new and well-defined trails radiating from a point on the east ridge where the cattle are fed during the winter, jagged trails leading down from the point over the rim of the canyon and along the sides to the water at the bottom.

Often the cold, steady winter rains begin in November, and the earth becomes water-soaked. The trucks hauling cake or grain to the feed pens frequently become stuck as they plow their way across the prairie. These rains sometimes catch the cattlemen unprepared, and the cattle which they are wintering hump up in the cold drizzle, and feeding must begin.

One day a friend drove up to my gate with a worried look. He had planned to go deer hunting with me, but I knew that he had come to tell me that he couldn't go.

"Say," he said, "I'm gonna hafta dog it on you."

"Why?"

"I got a carload of corn on a sidin' at my place and the mud's belly deep to a horse in that low place by the tracks. Can't get trucks in there to unload, and I gotta start feedin', the rain comin' like it is. I just can't make 'er, and I sure hate it, but I gotta dog it this time."

"Well, all you can do is wait until it drys up; your cows won't starve. When we get back, you can unload then; surely the railroad people....."

"Yeah, but this cold rain and no feed—liable to hurt a man's calf crop next February. Tell you what I'm gonna do; I'm gonna buy me some sacks and get me some loafers from town, and put 'em in that car a-loadin', drive the trucks up as far as we can, and string them fellas out from the car to the trucks, acrosst that mud, then kinda piss-ant that corn over."

November is divided into two major hunting periods. In the period which includes the latter part of October with the early part of November, we hunt bear and deer in the mountains, then I return to The Blackjacks for the opening of the quail season on the twenty-first. We hunt bear with the hounds until the deer season opens, then we chain the sad-faced pack. We hunt from horseback, and thus our deer hunting is also exciting.

We sometimes go in pairs, one on each side of a canyon or a shallow feeder-canyon, and, as the big bucks break out toward the rimrock, on one side or the other, one of us gets a shot. We seldom have a standing target and very rarely get a shot under three hundred yards. This distance is much the best sport, of course. There is continued movement and scrambling up and down the canyon sides or shoulders of the high peaks. One must sometimes ride hell-for-leather, step off his horse, and shoot at a bounding buck several hundred yards away.

I prefer hunting alone. I saddle Hereford in the early morning, put two bars of chocolate in my hunting jacket, if I do not forget them entirely, and set out. Hereford and I have hunted together for so long that we know each other's habits. We hunt out the sides of the canyons, usually going up the north sides, since the big bucks like to scrape out little beds on the south sides under bushes that screen them from view but where the warm sun can reach them.

It is impossible to see them as they lie watching us, but here again is where fleetness is a curse. Like the hunted coyote frozen in the yellow-brown grasses, or the eagle-hunted jackrabbit blending perfectly with the gray weeds of the prairie, the buck seems to be aware of the alternative defense lying in his great speed and sooner or later calls upon it when his nerves give way. But at such times he does not always break into a bounding run but may sneak along like a gray-blue shadow, with antlers pressed low on his back. However, if he arises from his perfect protective immobility, a single rolling pebble down the canyon is a giveaway, and after such slight little sounds, when Hereford and I are standing like a statue in the shadows of the north side of the canyon, I step off and become tense with readiness.

His great pride at this time of the year, his antlers, are sometimes, ironically, also the buck's undoing as the sun shines on them when he stands above his bed, not yet decided to flee. This happens rarely, however, and even then only an accustomed eye may detect this very feeble, always indefinite heliographic message.

After the buck is gutted and Hereford and I have struggled to hang him above the reach of prowling lynx or bear, we climb a shoulder among the Douglas firs to some growth of yellow quaking aspen. He will stand for several hours pricking his ears at every sound or movement, while I dream to the joyless whispering of the pines and the petulant talk of the aspens. I look out over the tops of the wild pines to the shimmering hills that are like turgid seas solidified. At my feet are the results of the terrific forces of earth's processes; the wild confusion of peaks and ridges cut by the great gashes that are the dark canyons.

This writhing, riven crust does not excite my emotion. The profound tranquillity that is only a veneer is like the peace that comes after an earth-shivering storm, never to stay. One feels the violence all about and knows that the few hours of sunlight are ephemeral. As I dream with my emotions at ebb, I feel that the lengthening shadows are my running sands of contentment. I know about the bloody drama that goes on in the primordial area which my eyes cover, and I know that my presence, as quiet as it is, and my scent, as vague as it may be, are disturbing the immediate area about the aspen grove. As I loll, the pig eyes of a bear may be nervously on me from the rimrock above, or a band of deer may stand frozen, with the grass still hanging from their mouths, watching me; wondering about the confused scent of smoke, cooked meat, and animal odor that comes from me.

I am not smug as I sit there. I am small and overpowered by the primitive forces, but there is no fear. Instead there is the only true freedom that man can feel; the serenity that comes with the absence of emotion and the complete absence of man's pitiful urge to express himself; the only complete contentment.

My thoughts come like the breezes that move through the pines and in their passing leave nothing to disturb; leave no seed that may swell and burst into resolve, demanding action. No matter how sharp or interesting, they are lost with my spirit in my oneness with the earth about me.

How satisfying it is to be free from slavery, free from sad little attempts to express the mystery of disturbing life, and to escape the pain that such questing brings. Thoughts are sufficient—thoughts that pass like camera slides through the mind and are forgotten with their passing.

The shadows lengthen and the breezes that talk in the pines begin to hiss a little with a mysterious and sharp foreboding. A vague feeling of restiveness comes over me, and I have an urge to follow the peaks' shadows down the slopes and into the sunlight again. Hereford will not stand for me as I put the rifle into the scabbard and climb into the saddle. He does not need to be urged to strike a foxtrot down the backbone of the ridge.

We seldom see members of other hunting parties, except those who hunt the deep canyons afoot. On horseback in the high, open country we have great mobility and have the plateau and the rimrock to ourselves. We need not worry about the bullets of other hunters finding us. We make a gesture, however, and wear red hatbands.

One November I was hunting afoot in the Sacramento Range. The dead junipers writhed in ghostly gray throughout the ridge where I hunted, like figures in some Shakespearean fantasy. The heavy growth of pine made stalking necessary. I hunted to the farther end of the ridge where there was a maze of interlaced deer trails and where there were many hoofprints, but there were no tracks of man. Most of the hunters of the other parties hunted close to their camps near water. I had been careful to put on a flaming red shirt, and this, with my hatband, made me safely conspicuous in this crowded and heavily wooded region.

I came to the point where the plateau broke suddenly and sloped precipitately into the great blinding whiteness of the Alamagorda Flats far below. I sat on the point hidden by bushes and waited. I felt a tremendous relief in being out of the heavy forests where other hunters stalked in fevered anticipation and greed and in nervous fear of missing. I felt a slight disgust.

Suddenly as I sat there, I smelled the smoke of a cigar. It was unmistakable. Just a whiff and no more. Instinctively I froze like a buck, and I listened so intently that I could hear the beating of my heart. As I cocked my ear, I felt my nostrils distending. The silence was complete except for the metallic ticking of an insect on the sun-warmed slope below me. I became conscious of my instinctive immobility, but I saw no humor in it. I was a rounded outline at the point of the ridge, my red shirt dappled by the bush shadows. I was in no danger from a hunter, but I thought only of the many gunners on the mountain—the eager, nervous, unaccustomed gunners.

With my senses knife-edged, I sat for some time but could not catch that elusive odor of cigar smoke again. I slipped quickly down over the edge of the plateau and, holding my rifle high so that the sun would glint on it, I made my way around the point to a comparatively open space in the bright sun, then I climbed over the rim and stood in sun-brilliant red for several minutes before going back along the ridge toward camp. I avoided all shadows and heavy growths and wound my way among the glaring juniper skeletons. My hunter's heart melted in fear and the instinct of self-preservation came into play as I became the hunted. It had nothing whatever to do with reason; I was under the control of my own protective instincts and could do little about it except walk boldly back to camp in the sun.

But in the high, open country, where hard riding and long-range shooting add zest to the hunting, the lack of water and the ruggedness also act as obstacles to hunters who like less activity. We must drive down into the open foothills for our water, which we haul in a fifty-five-gallon drum.

One day the Cowwooly and I drove with the empty drum in my station wagon. We left it at the lonesome, shining, groaning windmill in the Flats and drove on to his shack hidden in the folds of the brown, sterile hills. We completed some of the chores which he had come to do; then, as the dolorous bearhound puppies played clumsily around us, we squatted on our heels in the sun against the native-sawed siding of his forlorn little house. Desolated by the absence of his wife and children, the savage brown hills seemed more menacing, and the winds that sang in the eaves were unutterably sad. He worked on a leather saddle cinch. He waved his hand with the leather punch in it over the sage-covered little canyon, the sagging corral and the tin-patched barn, the scattered bits of mechanisms, and a worn-out tire.

"I don't aim to live out my days like this," he said. "I aim to have a little somethin'. If I could win me some big money at the rodeo and git a little a-head, I'd fix up a place fer the woman and kids, and have a little stock around me. I gotta show the woman she didn't make no mistake."

He worked on the cinch for some time in silence. The bearhound puppies rolled and growled in baby make-believe. He laughed as though to himself, then said, "Reckon a person could read too god-dam much? The woman reads ever'thin' she gits her hands on. Reckon she figgered I'se one of them cowpokes in them books; never stopped to figger that 'bout all I had in this world was my butt and my hat."

We sat for some time, each with his own thoughts, then he brightened as he drowned the bothering thoughts of responsibility with a clean sweeping thought that promised immediate action:

"Tell yu what 'les me and you do. I gotta huntin' outfit a-comin' in here 'bout the tenth, way their card reads. Why don't you come back after they leave and me and you'll take the horses and hounds and go up in the Black Range, and catch us a lion. Fill that hack of your'n full of groceries and your outfit, and come back out—they's lots of lions up there."

I knew that there is no closed season on predators, but at the moment I was not thinking, and I said, "When does the season open?"

"Hell," he said, "they ain't no goddam law; lions is premature animals."

"All right," I said.

Filled with the tingling anticipation of a lion hunt as an escape from the things that bind men, he talked glibly all the way back to camp. When we saw a wolf loping up the slope of a brown foothill, he leaped from the station wagon and, with a Comanche war whoop, emptied his rifle at the shadowy figure four hundred yards away. The little native pine shack cringing in the silent sage-gray crease of the menacing brown hills, with its odor of domesticity and its lugubrious wind-songs, was already forgotten.

Just as the mouthing of old Floppy the bearhound is associated with the trampling of the horses in the corral, with the saddling and the last-minute adjustment of cinches, with the smoke of the fire standing straight up among the pines, and Unk, the Negro cook, piddling, humped and futile, so are cold mornings and dogs associated with quail hunting. If there were no dogs waving their plumes over the ridges as they hunt with full-hearted enthusiasm, and no frosty mornings with scented weeds crushed underfoot, and the scent and the feel of the earth, then quail hunting would not be much of a sport.

They are fast on the wing and know how to take care of themselves, and the best of shots do not drop a quail every time. They know how to freeze until the descending foot of man is almost on them, then they flush with a startling flutter like a rocket being exploded from the grasses at one's feet. I have hunted my ridges each year for years, and each year there are the same number of quail. There is a saturation point for coveys, so to speak, which depends directly upon the food supply. Most of the years the grasses go to seed and the food supply is practically constant, but kaffir in patches over the ranch makes the supply sure. The universal food of the ridges are the acorns, and they come almost every year. The quail manage them very well by pecking them into bits that can be swallowed.

One year, the winter of the great blizzard, when the temperature fell to 26 below zero one night, and the earth was covered and glazed over with a frozen crust for weeks, my quail were not caught on the ridges. They went to the creek bottoms for shelter and food and had actually disappeared several days before the cold wave struck. But hundreds of quail were frozen as they slept that year, with their tail points forming the center of a circle and their heads the periphery. They use the same protective circle when sleeping as the musk oxen use for protection against wolves. I believe after that winter, however, they filled their place in the natural balance within the year. At least I noticed very little difference here on the ridges.

Nearly every season I have some preseason idea that I shall use only a 410-guage, but before the season is well started, I go back to my 16-guage, which, though heavier, is certainly more effective.

I hunt practically every hunting day of the season and usually alone. In that way I do not attempt to kill the limit of ten birds. But I note that when I wish to kill the limit for some special purpose, I am not always successful.

Occasionally I join friends to hunt elsewhere, or I invite them to hunt with me at The Blackjacks. At such times when at The Black-jacks, I should like very much to be able to say to them that only double-barreled guns may be used, but somehow I find myself face to face with that old western pioneer spirit wherein a man feels himself free to do as he pleases, and I am sure that such an order or even such a suggestion would be considered an insult. So when I invite people to The Blackjacks for quail shooting I look at their shining automatics and pumpguns with unconcern—I hope. When finally the lock broke on my Parker, I succumbed to custom and bought a 16-guage pumpgun, although someday I feel sure that I shall insist on the use of double-barreled guns only.

I innocently took a pumpgun, which I thought of as a pheasant, grouse, and duck gun, to England, along with my double-barrel, which was scatter-choke, and which I used for quail and partridge. Fortunately I found, in time to save myself embarrassment, that pumpguns and automatics were not tolerated in the field, and I attempted to conceal the fact that I had my pumpgun as one attempts to conceal some personal tragedy. I was already in Scotland, ready to go out the next day for blackcock, when someone at dinner mentioned "that American thing" in referring to a pumpgun. I began to sweat and wondered how I might hide the 32-inch-barrel, full-choke "thing" which I had brought along. When it came to me that, when my things had been unpacked, naturally my guns had been taken to the gun-room, I visualized that "thing" standing tall, smug, and boastful among the modest double-barrels.

The next morning after a rather unhappy night, I went to my host and said with histrionic shyness which I hope was not sullied by the feeling of great relief which flooded me:

"I have a gift for you—I hope you can use it. It's sort of a defensive and not a sporting gun, of course, but I thought perhaps you might like to have it for falcons and eagles—to sorta protect your sheep and things."

"Oh, I say, splendid."

We went ceremoniously to the gunroom, and I handed him the shiny "thing"; then I hunted with my good old double-barrel during my stay in Scotland and England with a clean conscience. I still receive Christmas cards with horses and hounds on them from my grateful host.

I think of quail hunting as the king of sports, except when I am actually bear hunting. But when I am not actually in the mountains hunting bear, and can weigh the two sports without emotion, I find for the quail. To walk all day behind the setters, in rain or snow, or against a cold north wind or a warm south one, or under a too ardent sun, demands the best there is in man and dogs. From the start in the frost when the boots almost ring on the iron-hard frozen ground, and the setters dance with high excitement about you, to the return at twilight, dragging boots clogged with thawed mud, over ridges and across the canyons to the little sandstone house, your heart and pulse and spirit are at highest pitch. There is no room for worry or cares, except the doubtful performance of some doubtful puppy in her first season. For a few hours man and dogs and life are in singing harmony.

When Bill Whitman was writing a monograph on the Osage, he would come out to hunt with me. He had never shot bobwhite quail, and he immediately fell under their spell and was captured completely by the blackjacks and by my setters, who looked like animated fire-balls in the sun. When we were coming in one evening and the little house loomed in the twilight, and the coyotes were howling from every direction, he said, "You know, I feel like a god—a pagan one, of course; a rather tired one, but I have a superior feeling. My blood feels like the way wine tastes, as it rushes through my veins, and it seems that all I have ever felt was important is trivial. Men, other men, of course are plodders, and their work's the work of children to me at this moment."

"Yes, I know," I said.

When we reached the house, we stirred up the fire, and the setters flopped down with happy groans on the bear rug. We sat with our boots off and looked into the fire for some time, then he reached over to the table and picked up a red glass that reflected the flame dance, mixed a scotch-and-soda, and held it out at arm's length. "You know," he said, "it's not right that men should be as gods; we must neutralize this mysterious glory that floods us." And with that he drank.

"That's the only way," I said; "neutralize the glory—then eat steak and spaghetti."

And that's pretty much the way I feel all through the year; have felt through the ten years I have lived on the ridges. Why should I spend the golden hours attempting to express my thoughts and emotions in word symbols when I can't do so adequately. When I think of my books, I think of Anatole France's *Our Lady's Juggler* or the red-shafted flicker that comes in the Little-Flower-Killer Moon to hammer on my empty gasoline drum; alternately hammering and shouting, with spread tail and elevated crest, "wicky-up, wicky-up, wicky-up," to a world busy with its own affairs of the season. Like Our Lady's juggler and the flicker, I can feel the glory with intensity, until the tautness causes something to break, but the resulting artificial expression is pitiful. The querulous yapping of the coyote and the death chant of the Osage do it much better, while the songs of the wood thrush and the mockingbird express it quite pleasingly at least, while I can express the glory in physical action.

Like the juggler, I also feel intensely that I should like to dedicate myself to the glory of living to the limits of my ability with the tools that I have, as he did at the feet of the statue of Our Lady with his balls and knives, but he in his faith believed what the brothers at the abbey had told him—that Our Lady would accept his exhibition as a dedication, since it was the only thing he could do, the thing he did best, and represented the limits of his ability. And she did, as the story goes, step down from her pedestal and wipe the sweat from his brow, as the brothers stood in awe at the entrance to the chapel.

I am afraid that the flicker and I shall never know such acceptance of our poignant attempts to express ourselves.

A good duck day is the day before a pressure area comes in from the north or immediately after it has hit. Often the warm winds blow in gale strength from the south toward the moving cold area, and the ducks and geese flying before the cold must face and fight the strong warm winds from the south. Canada geese often fly very low at this time, taking advantage of the hills, which break the full force of the wind.

A good coyote day is one that is cold and damp, with not too much wind, and earth that is not muddy.

I have almost given up hunting with horses, now that my two neighbors, one to the north and one to the east, who have very good packs, have been hunting from their cars. I don't care fervently about this method, though I do not say that it's not good sport. If good sport depends upon clean killing and danger to the hunter, then car-hunting can easily be classed as good sportsmanship. When you are driving at forty or fifty miles across the prairie, watching and keeping up with the race, anything may happen and sometimes does. I sat with my east neighbor all day in a prairie seepage into which we plunged the car up to the running-board while watching a hot race. I knocked the viscera out of my station wagon during one race and punctured three tires at the same time during another. On the prairie this means that you are afoot and must walk to a highway or to the closest ranch house.

We cruise about over the prairie until we see a coyote, then get as close as possible before letting the hounds tumble out. Sometimes they come out end over end in their anxiety and are so confused that the coyote gains precious time and distance before they are untangled and off.

With this method, where the hounds are carried in the car out to the prairie and taken in after each race, they may have several good races in them; but when hunting with horses, where they must trail behind the horses until the coyote is jumped, then walk back home after the hunt, they are good for only one or, at best, two long runs. Several coyotes may be caught in one hunt from a car, and this is not overdoing it, since there is no dearth of the little wolves.

In hunting with horses we have no traditions as do the British in their fox hunts. There is no traditional thing to be shouted when the coyote is seen, as in England when the fox is "viewed." A horseman may pull his hat down, kick his horse, and whoop, or he may shout, "There goes the son-of-a-bitch," or "He's runnin' like a spotted-assed ape." On the "view" he may simply say, "There's ole shep," then when the hounds have seen him, off go the field in no order whatever; let the best horse or the coyote-wise man arrive at the catch or at least at the kill first.

I had a brown mare, half steeldust and half black Morgan, who enjoyed coyote hunting as much as I did. She kept her ears forward constantly, watching for movement on the prairie as we rode along; she never relaxed. She was built like a quarter horse and was very fast for that distance and always got away ahead of the field. The slow-witted hounds, crosses between staghound and greyhound, always walk with their heads down, strung out behind the horses, and it is up to the man to see the game, then by some signal, usually a shout, quicken the hounds into action, looking for the coyote with heads high and senses alert. If the little mare saw the game before I did, she would jump forward as though she were leaving a track starting-gate, and I had to hold her to a dancing nervousness until the hounds had seen the wolf. On the other hand, if I saw the quarry first, I would snap the reins together, which was a signal for the hounds as well as the mare.

One frosty morning a member of the hunt saw a coyote and pulled his pistol, firing two shots. I was looking in his direction when the mare saw the coyote. She jumped from under my hat, then cut the hounds off from the wolf and made straight for him. I couldn't hold her, so completely was she under the influence of her excitement. I didn't see the deep wash nor did she. She came to the edge and attempted to stop but couldn't, so she tried to clear it. She landed in the middle, then fell over on her back with me under her. I couldn't struggle from under her and she couldn't get up, so we waited for help.

Les Claypoole always said that 'a coyote-huntin' horse was as useless as a coyote-huntin' man—as useless as a boar's tit." He would look at her and laugh, as she danced fretfully among the hounds. "Kek, kek, kek—yu might say she ain't worth killin', but then a horse oughtta be worth as much as its rider anyways; reckon if I had her, I'd sell her for dog meat."

I always like the story about the British hunting lady who at a hunt ball was asked her opinion of a certain diplomatist. She said, "I don't know really, but I rather suspect he'd shoot a fox."

That's much the way we feel in my country. We shoot coyotes only if they are actually killing our flocks or if they become calf-killers. Even then we prefer to hunt such bandits with the hounds. Of course, this prejudice against cold murder is not so deep as it is in England in regard to the fox, but it is growing.

During the days when I believed that shooting at them from an airplane was sport, I noted how quickly they adapted themselves to this form of persecution. They froze when the wing shadows of the plane moved over the prairie or when they heard the roar of the motor; froze like quail under the shadow of a hawk's wing.

My neighbor hunts the country north of my ranch, the illimitable prairie of a very large ranch. When I drive up there in my station wagon, I catch only glimpses of the coyotes running far away up the slope of a ridge and looking back over their shoulders to see if the hounds will come tumbling out, and sometimes I see them cut sharply into the horizon far away, on the last ridge bordering the breaks of a canyon, standing; waiting to see the hounds that they associate with all station wagons.

Next to protective coloration, protective immobility is most important in the drama of survival to the hunter as well as to the hunted. Only those animals and birds which have tremendous speed, or swift, erratic flight as a means of protection as well, ever let their nerves induce them to break immobility when danger or prey is near. A fleet jackrabbit perfectly colored for protection cannot always remain motionless in the face of danger but often puts his other defense to the test—his magnificent speed.

Hunting golden eagles know this. I have seen an eagle fall from the air like a bomb only to lose the jackrabbit prey because he suddenly became a weed or a bunch of grass, even to the keen eyes of the great bird. Then I watched that eagle sail back and forth over the spot, zoom into the higher air, then fold his wings to feign a dive as though he could actually see the prey. If the eagle is persistent, the nerve-shattered rabbit will sooner or later jump to speed away, or become so dominated by fear that he cannot run but jumps in a series of high leaps. In either case the eagle takes him with ease, even beautifully, at the apex of the useless jump.

Antelopes standing on the plains in the green-gray sagebrush blend to invisibility if they do not happen to cut the skyline. If the hunter knows that they are there but can't see them, he can fall to the ground and raise his hat on the end of his gun barrel. Nervousness or curiosity will impel them toward him.

And so it is with coyotes. I have watched them lie down and thereafter have not been able to determine which was coyote and which was a bit of sandstone escarpment or brown-gray weed. Only by standing and watching intently can I eventually be sure that the coyote is neither sandstone nor weed, and if I gaze at him long enough he will flick an ear nervously, then turn his head as though considering the best direction for escape—escape from my steady gaze—and then express in speed the urge of his strained nerves. A coyote's ears are pointed, and sometimes, when he is dissimulating as a part of the landscape, the hunter on horseback may see the sun shine ever so sensitively on the delicate ear tuffs. Cocked ears seem necessary to a full play of all the senses, but they are a transgression of the strict laws governing protective immoblity.

Much has been written about the cupidity of the fox, and one who knows animals would naturally feel that there has been little exaggeration. In the blackjacks the coyote, which has all the fox's characteristics of cleverness with a supplementary few of his own, takes his place. The fox has all the advantages of the literature of Europe, and his fame was brought over in the "Mayflower," and, further, the native American fox has been glorified in his own right; his intelligence has been paraded in fables, in poetry, in sport, and in classical literature in general. He has been pictured with spectacles, in academic gown and mortar board, and his very name has become established in all European languages to imply the highest form of shrewdness. If he were aware of all this, and one who knows him only through literature and one mud-bespattered hunt in England might hesitate to say that he doesn't, he should be most assuredly the cockiest animal in the world.

No matter how great the desire to champion the coyote, the difficulty of being strictly regional is obvious. If one referred to a man as being "coyotey" instead of being foxy, or if one were said to be as shrewd as a coyote, or that he had outcoyoted another, there might be cause for gunplay. Call a man a fox and he accepts the compliment, but it takes courage to call a southwesterner a coyote.

The ill repute in which the coyote is held might point to a humorless southwesterner, unable to overlook a little chicken thievery, since the glorified fox is also a notorious chicken thief. The reason may lie in the fact that the coyote is really a wolf and suffers from the wolf's reputation in the European literature which glorified the fox. Also he is at a disadvantage in never having appeared in literature which colored his virtues and ignored his vices; at least a literature voluminous enough and honored enough to make it classic. I am sure that if he knew this, and again, as in the case of the fox, I am not sure that he doesn't—hesitating even more to say that he doesn't, since I have lived with him all my life and on the most intimate terms for the last decade—he would be smart enough to desire none of the advertising which has made the fox famous.

To the Osage the coyote is a symbol of cupidity and double-dealing, and their stories about him indicate that he thought of himself as a very important animal. In their stories that depend upon dignity made ridiculous as a basis for humor the coyote often appears. He often appears as a warning to the children that they should be considerate of others and that they should never think of themselves as being shrewder than others, since one may be outwitted through one's own vanity. Since they lived in a state wherein their wits had to be sharp and ever ready for use against their enemies of the other tribes, animals, and the elements, these stories were more than nursery rhymes and fables but served as a training for life; part of a military training for success in the eternal battle to survive.

There are many stories about the coyote which the Osage tell their children, and at least two of them have to do with the coon's outwitting the coyote. The Osage children seem to have stronger stomachs than the Amer-European children, as many of these bedtime stories would be classified by the parents of the latter as obscene. If one were to displace the *Decameron* characters with Fontaine animals, he might have an idea of the nature of some of the Osage bedtime stories.

Their constant attempt to discredit the coyote indicates that they really viewed his prowess with respect, yet thought of him more as a jackal than as a wolf. They used him as an indicator that something was astir on the prairie, either enemy, friend, or quarry. Being a know-all of the prairie as were the crow, bluejay, magpie, and squirrel of the wooded area, they watched him carefully and profited by what he told them through his actions. They mimicked his yelping to deceive their enemies, as they mimicked the owl in the woods. He was an important person in the scheme of things, but he hadn't the proper virtues for symbolism.

There are a few spots on the ranch where holes were sunk for oil during the period of frenzied exploitation. Some of these spots have been barren of vegetation for twenty-five years, and some have growths of weeds. Lying about them one finds rusted bits of pipe, cable, tubing, and upright pipes in cement bases once used as anchors for bracing cables. These upright pipes are used now only as stations where the dog coyotes leave their musk-messages. At one of these spots south of my house an old boiler had been left, which disappeared when the Japanese began to buy American scrap iron for their war preparations.

That which was a barren spot is now a yellow wash which will someday be a tributary of Bird Creek. The head of the wash points like an arrow to my house, and the coyotes use its steep sides as cover to approach my chickens.

The old, rusted boiler that stood there near the dry hole for years was like a wart on the prairie; a sore that would not be healed. It became the Cowhand's prison for coyotes. During August, when the unwary whelps were overrunning the prairie, he would practice his roping by catching them and dragging them to the boiler, then he would open the door and shove them in, closing it quickly before they could jump out.

I wondered why a kindly man could be so cruel, and one day I asked him. He smiled sheepishly and said, "Tain't right is it? I dunno, I allus aim to go back and get 'em after ridin' the pasture, I guess. But then I dunno what for—don't know what a man would do with 'em; the bastards."

"You know what you've done," I said, "you and the cattle and the Japs? As long as that old boiler was there with your coyotes in it, the cattle came there, smelled the blood, stamped around it, and bawled, like cattle do. They loosened the soil, killed the few weeds and buffalo grass, and started erosion. That wash started. Then they came for that boiler to send to the Japs, and since there was nothing to hold the soil, the ravine started. Next time you ride by it notice the coyote tracks in the bottom."

"That's right," he said, looking seriously into my eyes.

"You know how sometimes a coyote seems to be laughing at you in the night; a kind of mocking laughter? Well, just before a change in weather an old dog coyote sits on the point and laughs at us over that little deal."

"Yu reckon?" he said apologetically.

IV
WINTER

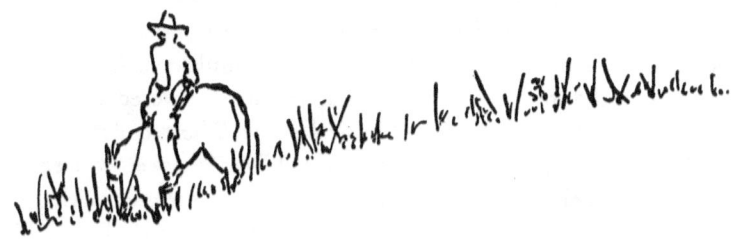

XII

BABY-BEAR MOON

THERE ARE NO BABY BEARS BORN ON THE OLD RESERVATION NOW. I IMAGINE there are no wild bears being born in all the former domain of the Osage.

The ducks have continued their flights south with the exception of a few winter mallards along the creeks. In the days when the cattlemen fed grain instead of cake, they wintered here by the thousands.

The days grow colder and the first heavy snow comes, but, of course, not at the right time, which would be Christmas Eve. When there is a snow at Christmas time, the state papers carry news of the fact in the headlines. The first snow of any consequence, outside of the flurries during November, comes usually before Christmas Day and is gone before the great day arrives.

The prairie is deep copper-color now and remains so all winter. The leaves of the blackjacks are brown and tick gently on calm days but rattle like shot on paper when the wind blows. The planted trees of the yard are bare and cannot be stirred to protest by the cold winds.

The quail sometimes flush into the teeth of a high wind; they turn sharply with it, and their speed becomes doubled. The sun is appreciated now. When it climbs above the blackjacks, life of the ridges moves to the south sides of the hills. The coyotes doze in its warm rays in the long grass at the heads of the ravines, and a smart dog knows that quail are likely to be found under the fallen tree tops or in brush piles on the sun-warmed south slopes. Often the well-fed range cows will not respond to the long howl-like call of the cowboy as he dumps the cake in the feed troughs at the feeding grounds. They prefer to lie comfortably in the soporific sun.

During the long evenings I spend much time by the fire, watching its flame dance on the walls of the house, or just sitting before it in fascination without other light. Its glint on the glass of the pictures recalls the pleasant incidents associated with each one of them. The red-deer heads on each side of the room, the mule-deer head above the mantel, and the bull-elk head in the rear are discovered and made animate by the dance of the whimsical flame. The red deer recalls Scotland, with crooked and gnarled old McCarricker squeeging through the soaked moss of the moors in front of me and talking of the wary "royal" that could not be killed by man. I can still hear his burring talk as the roaring of the stags came to us through the blurry mist. The bull-elk head recalls a white night in Wyoming when I carried the great head on my back to camp, slipping on the new snow and sliding down the mountainside, with the precious head rolling in front of me. I would not leave it to be brought down with the carcass; I had to sever it on the spot and lift it to my back, with the blood streaming down my jacket, and stagger the four miles to camp in the dazzling moonlight while Bill Barron carried my rifle.

After a day of quail hunting, I do not care to read or listen to the radio. I like to recapitulate the events of the day, or I enjoy playing with the details of my more distant memories. I have the motto of my life in the blackjacks painted in Chinese red on the face of my mantel in Roman lettering: VENARI LAVARI LUDERE RIDERE OCCAST VIVERE. It was once the motto of some unit of the Third Augustan Legion and was placed over the entrance of the officers' club at a fort in the Aurès Mountains of North Africa, along the Roman frontier of the first century. It was assembled from pieces of marble lying broken among the tracks of jackals and gazelles. Some of my friends think that the verb "to seek" ought to be added, and even classical scholars have trouble with the contraction "occast." However, I think it a good motto in the original that needs no additions when translated: TO HUNT, TO BATHE, TO PLAY, TO LAUGH—THAT IS TO LIVE.

Man has never been able to say thus and thus is so, or this or that will happen here in this temperamental region of the contact line between the Great Plains and the woodlands of the Mississippi Valley. He does not know how many days will be lulled and warmed by the air from the Gulf coming up the valley, its salt freshness killed by the warm lands over which it travels; or how many days the cold currents of the Arctic will float across the plains from the north. The only time the Moon Woman is consistent in her manifestation would be during July and perhaps August, when she is steady and purposeful. Between July and January there have been variations in temperature as high as a hundred and forty degrees.

One day the titmice were singing all over the yard, and the other winter singers, the chickadees, were making a great fuss about the bear rugs I had cleaned and left on the grass. Both the titmice and the chickadees were worried about these strange things and soon had the bluejays interested. The cardinal, with his crop full of grain from my feed pans, preened, and then started his winter song. Even a meadowlark sang from the prairie. I wore a light woolen shirt and found it too warm and scratchy. It was definitely hot and had been so all during Christmas week. Green flies buzzed about the place where I had dressed some quail, and the coyote hides on the sides of the chicken houses were becoming greasy and had begun to drip a little. I found maggots in the deer head which I intended to have mounted as a gift; I had to saw the antlers from the skull and bury the head.

I spent most of the afternoon hauling wood from the strip and sweated copiously as I loaded and unloaded it, and I killed three scorpions as they ran out of some half-rotted pieces. The earth was calling much as it does during the Planting Moon, and I was considering the line along which I had hoped to build a stone fence and was actually inspired to start the digging for the foundation. This was at four o'clock. I noticed in the northwest a smudge against the steel-blue sky, like a smoke smudge from some burning oil-catchment basin. As I leaned on the sharpshooter, the sweat on my face became icy, and I began to shiver. The smudge soon covered the sky of the northwest. The leaves of the blackjacks began to tick restlessly, and a lone coyote howled like a wolf.

When I went into the house, I carried some wood in with me and made fire in the fireplace, the ashes of which had been cold for several days. Dead leaves sailed past the windows, and the shotlike rattle of the blackjacks became steady. When I went out for more wood—I came back in to get my mackinaw—I had felt sleet grains hit my face; when I got to the woodpile, the sleet was bouncing off the logs. As I came back into the house, the setters crowded past me without the usual permission to enter.

Soon I could not distinguish between the sleet on the tin roof of the porches and the rattling of the blackjack leaves, but the heat of the day was shut up in the little house, and there was no warming-up period, since the fire became effective before the cold could creep in. I could barely see the shapes of the near-by trees as I looked out the window through the slanting sleet. At five o'clock I looked at the glass, and it showed 30 degrees—a drop from 80 earlier in the afternoon.

During the night I had to move into the house from the porch as the snow sifted through the screen and over my sleeping bag. The sleet had given way to snow, and the wind had died, so that I could hear the slight hissing of the crystals.

For three days the snow fell intermittently, then, during the night, ceased, and the moon broke through and made spilled-ink shadows over the ridge. The mercury sank below zero quickly, and before daylight it was 15 below. That night I could hear the trees popping like rifle shots in the creek bottom. I could not see out of my south window over the drift; the north winds came again and caused the snow to eddy there.

Coyote and rabbit tracks were everywhere, and often the trail of a rabbit ended in blood and fur, the cold currents rolling the bits of fur back and forth across the snow. Sometimes at the scene of the tragedy would be the wing-tip marks of a great horned owl, and I saw the great round print of a bobcat, but he had left only disturbed snow and bits of fur; he had carried his prey away to the dark canyon.

One morning I trailed a bobcat for several miles as I came in from dropping feed under the fallen tree tops for the quail. He had meandered along the ridges like a hunting setter and had left nothing uninvestigated. I saw where he had stood for some time near the house when he had caught the tantalizing odor from the chicken houses. He had approached no closer than a hundred yards, but eagerness, indecision, and fear were easily read in the disturbed snow where he had stood. It must have taken quite a bit of will-power for him to turn back into the desolation of the iron-hard world after being so close to his choicest food. The lure must have been similar to that of bacon and coffee to a hungry man. He was apparently haunted by the little house and the wonderful odor coming from the chicken houses for several nights, as I saw his saucer-like tracks all over.

After several days I was able to get to the county road that runs along the east side of the pasture by driving on the high ridges to avoid the drifts and by cutting the wire of the drift fences. The snowplow had cleared part of the drifts along the road, but I had to cut through my neighbor's pastures to avoid others. Living just eight miles from town and with a station wagon equipped with mud and snow tires, I am quite mobile, and I never keep great stocks of food at the little sandstone house.

Before I got back darkness had come, the temperature had risen, and the clouds hid the moon. As I made the last turn to climb the ridge to the house, the eyes of a bobcat shown suddenly in the headlights like two embers from a fireplace, and he was taken so unaware that he sank to his belly in the snow as my lights flooded him; as he opened his mouth in a lip-drawn growl, the prairie chicken he was carrying fell to the snow. He flashed across the beam and was gone. All this happened so quickly in the ghostly night that I was not quite certain that I had seen him at all. Only after I had walked over and picked up the prairie chicken was I definitely sure.

In the years of no rabbits the predators are more active during this time than they are when the ridges are in truer balance, so that my struggle with my enemies goes on day after day and month after month. I can look for intensified struggle when the sophomores flood the ridges in late summer and early autumn, when the balance is out through the scarcity of rabbits and pack rats, and when the blizzards come during the winter months, even though the rabbit tracks make intricate patterns over the snow.

There is a truce, however, among the other species. The bluestem grass takes a rest from its struggle with weeds and running oak and with other grasses, although the battle line between lush grass of the prairie and the short, curly grass of the semiarid zone is some distance to the west of my ridges, swaying toward them during the years of drought and back from them during the years of much rain.

In the years when drought creeps over the ridges, especially after prairie fires during Just-Doing-That Moon, the dominant bluestem seems to waver, and lesser grasses come up as reserves, but disappear when the bluestem becomes refreshed. And during the drought years the short-grass enemy sends its paratroopers far over the lines, and I find buffalo grass in the middle of my pastures as well as strange weeds characteristic of the semiarid short-grass zone. I like to think of them as paratroopers in the struggle between the grasses; and the Cowhand, who is not so poetic, thinks the same thing but says that "they was blowed in with the goddam dust." As a matter of fact, in the ridges' struggle with the hairy fingers of the ravines and canyons, they are nature's reserves, to be brought up when the bluestem fails to hold the sheet-water through injury by too close grazing, drought, or fire, or all three.

I did find true paratroopers one summer in the form of animal life. It was during the second summer of drought, when these two forms from the semiarid zone to the west came to the blackjacks as scouts. They were not on a hunting expedition like the snowy owl, forced by economic pressure to spend the winter on my ridges, but a vanguard of a possible invasion, or, better, paratroopers taking advantage of the desert conditions brought about temporarily by the drought but which might prove to be permanent.

One of these was the roadrunner, the first I had ever seen in the blackjacks; the other, a strange lizzard colored especially for a semiarid environment. I believe that neither one of them succeeded in getting back to the struggle-line. At least I know that the not quite properly colored lizzard was having a hard time of it. Like the imported sparrow and the starling, he seemed to seek the protection of man's work from real or fancied enemies and stayed close to my little house. Perhaps he found a niche somewhere in which to hide. But he spent much time in the sun on a sandstone rock in front of the house, and he didn't blend too well with it, as he most certainly supposed he did. When disturbed he ran to the house and disappeared.

Later I discovered his enemy. I was feeding the chickens in the yard, half-grown ones which I kept in the yard so that I could protect them better from the Cooper's hawks. Suddenly they were thrown into confusion. A blue racer had chased my paratrooper lizzard into the flock and was swinging his head, darting his tongue in anger and confusion. He had lost his intended victim. Beyond the flock the lizzard was still going toward the house—not running on all fours, as I had always seen lizzards run, but up on his hind legs running like a hundred-yard-dash man. The blue racer saw me for the first time and slithered away with incredible speed and grace.

There might have been several of the lizzards on the ridge that year, and the blue racers might have accounted for them, but this particular one not only outran the fastest reptile of the blackjacks but pulled a beautiful coyote trick on him. A coyote hard pressed by the hounds will run through a herd of cattle to confuse his enemy, if they are stag greyhounds, and to kill the scent, if they are trail hounds. The strange, out-of-harmony lizzard had used the chickens for the same purpose.

When the rains came again, both the strangers were gone. I don't know what happened to either of them.

With exception of the struggle between the predators and myself in my attempts to protect the quail and the domestic flocks, the truce is on during the Baby-Bear Moon. The insects have gone, and the insectivorous birds have flown south. Many of the insects are hibernating in the warmth of rotting trees and logs and under the leaves and in the earth.

Migrating hawks come to the ridges to swell the numbers of the indigenous ones. Marsh hawks quarter the ravines. The Swainson's sit on the tops of the blasted trees, waiting for something, but I don't know what, since I have never seen them catch anything. The prairie falcons follow the prairie chickens into the blackjacks when they come

to feed on acorns. They fly on the edges of the flocks, but the birds keep close, if irregular, formation, and they seem to do no more than worry them.

The natural balance of the ridges is very delicate, but if there have been rains during the year and no prairie fires, then there has been no overgrazing, and the natural food is abundant and there is sufficient protection for rabbits and quail. If there have been rains during the summer, then there were no grasshopper invasions; and if there have been no fires, the bluestem holds its own, and the groping fingers of the ravines and canyons lie momentarily defeated.

If the scales are not teeter-tottering from drought, fire, rabbit scarcity, or grasshopper invasion in the seasons preceeding the Baby-Bear Moon, then they are not thrown out during the hard winters, despite the eternal hunting of the hungry predators, unless the winter happens to be exceptional.

The quail and prairie chicken remain in balance with their food supply, as do the jackrabbits and all the other species of the ridges during the wet cycle. The jackrabbits never overrun the prairie because of the coyotes and the golden eagles; the cottontails because of every carnivorous species that walks, runs, or flies. The acorns of the blackjacks, the seeds of the grasses and weeds, and the cottontails are like the canned fruits and vegetables in a farmer's cellar: the symbols of plenty.

I have intimated that my ridges are in their natural state; the state which I believe Paul Sears calls the "climax." His dearly beloved humus, though not too thick on the ridges, but deep on the prairie, has been only slightly injured by the rare prairie fires and the cyclic droughts. Overgrazing on my ridges comes only with the drought years, as we very carefully allow from four to five acres to each cow or steer. We carry that number every year and if the drought comes, or if fire sweeps over the ridges in mid-grazing season—again the fire depending on the drought—we lose, not only in shrinkage of the cattle, but it is often imperative that they be shipped to whatever market obtains at the time.

Before I came to live in the blackjacks, there were patches plowed originally for the purpose of raising corn. I remember it; it was beautiful corn, but, of course, the sustaining soil soon went down the canyon; then small grain was planted, and it was also beautiful for a while, then its sustaining soil went down the canyon during the hysterical Just-Doing-That Moon. Each year she tore at the patches in play and in anger, until even nature couldn't keep cocklebur or curly grass plasters on her sores. Now they are covered with lespedeza, and the bluestem is creeping back.

Recently I have not planted patches of kaffir as I once did for quail and prairie-chicken feed. It does not increase the quail population by increasing food supply, and in the wet cycles it is not needed; in the drought years, like all other plants, it is sapped of life.

Only the crows and the coyotes seem to be agitating the scales by numbers, or rather they did agitate the balance when the white man came with his plow and his flocks. They adjusted themselves to mechanism quickly and with such perfection that it seemed like reasoning. The plow and the flocks increased their food supply, and this, with the fact that they are omnivorous and have few enemies, seemed to make them a favored species. The agitation which they caused in the balance is now perhaps slowing to a delicate adjustment, and they are possibly in harmony even in their great numbers.

Besides the conscious and unconscious enemy of all—man—the crow has only one enemy that I know about. The horned owl comes silently in the night to the crows' roost, just as he comes to my guinea tree, and strikes horror in their murderous hearts. Their blackness to blend with the night seems to be a protection which nature provided with only the owl in mind. They loom in the daylight hours and in the snows of winter, but are organized against all other enemies like a military unit.

The crow spends much of his time during this season on the lower limbs of the blackjacks where the leaves do not obscure his vision so that nothing may escape his notice, either trivial or important. Within half an hour he will shake his tail feathers dozens of times, waggling them like a mallard; he will arrange his wings nervously and fumble with his feathers like a young man fumbling with his dinner-jacket tie before the mirror.

When the pack rats dropped the pump to my gasoline stove, I saw a crow attempting to fly away with it. He could have carried the weight, but he could not get a secure hold on it. They love to collect bright things, and I suppose that this is their form of useless expression, since their voice, while capable of many tones and many inflections, is a military defense code and absolutely utilitarian. Occasionally I go outside to investigate a new sound, wondering what new bird is passing through the blackjacks, only to find that the crows have invented a new code word or that they are using one of the rarely used ones which I have never heard.

East of the ranch house in the strip of blackjacks is the largest crow roost of the three ridges. The dead leaves not only screen them from the cold winter winds but protect them from the hunting owls.

Sometimes, however, as I lie asleep in my bedding roll on the front porch, I am awakened by one of the many tragedies that occur every night somewhere on one of the ridges or in the canyons; often it is the dramatic screaming of a crow.

When shot, and if only wounded, they usually do not utter a sound, hence they do not endanger others that might come to their aid. They remain silent and allow themselves to be picked up, protesting only by opening their mouths. But when attacked by an owl in the night, they scream until the talons of the bird have pierced a vital spot. Sometimes the others of the colony will start an uproar of scolding and swearing, but they do not attack the owl in the darkness; they probably crash blindly into the tops of other trees as they attempt to fly away, or sit closely on their limbs paralyzed with fear.

To be awakened out of a sound sleep by the dramatic screaming of a crow being murdered produces an eerie sensation, especially on winter nights when the dogs are on the bear rugs in front of the fireplace and have not introduced the tragedy by their barking. I believe this is the only time during which I feel any sympathy for them.

The next day the sympathy fades when I see them looking for the owl. They come to the blackjacks and the tall postoaks near the house, and while they talk to each other in their code, they look toward the house as if they think I might be harboring their enemy—with suspicion that seems to threaten, as in the attitude of the early-day hanging mobs. They do not always find him inasmuch as he has probably gone back to the dark canyons along the creek, but if they do discover him, attempting to look like a diseased growth on one of the trees, they give him no peace. They sit on the trees surrounding him, and every member of the mob calls him names as they take turns diving at him, and they seem to be intent on tearing him to bits. However, they never quite touch him.

During this deafening noise, the owl sits calmly, blinking and turning his head from side to side nervously, as though looking for escape. He is not afraid, but his nerves can't take much of this terrific din, and though in flight he offers a better target for their sharp beaks, he will silently flap away through the trees with the whole flock after him, their swearing in crescendo. He seems to see well enough in the sunlight to weave his way through the trees and make his objective without trouble.

When one says that the coyote has no enemies, always excepting, of course, man, with his trail hounds and running hounds, one must exclude microscopical forms as well. Every species has such enemies, and such enemies are a part, a very important part, of the balance, and are not only invisible but mysterious to me. For as long as I can remember, or for as long as old men of the tribe can remember, there has never been a year of no coyotes. They say, however, that the old buffalo wolf, now extinct in the blackjacks, was his enemy; but others say that they were the wolves' little brothers and followed them for the crumbs of the wolves' feasting, as jackals follow the lion. Perhaps man's hounds, guns, traps, and poison are his enemies. If so, he will hold his own. He can outrun most running hounds, play with the trail hounds, avoid traps in a manner that is uncanny, and detect poison in some mysterious manner. He is in gun range quite often but only when you haven't a gun with you. He knows the difference between circling bird dogs and the high-backed running hounds and governs his actions accordingly, which means that he will stand off, just out of range of the shotgun, and watch the bird dogs and me while hunting, or will start running at full speed when he sees a running hound.

He is not a clean killer any more so than the skunk who broke the truce by killing my H-D's, or any other predator, though one often hears people say that lower orders kill only when hungry and invite one to consider the ways of the wild brothers as an example for one's own behavior, just as one is urged to go to the ant for his lessons in social and economic order. In the natural struggle each species is struggling to survive, and the individuals which represent the species and have the responsibility of seeing that the species which they represent survives are the fittest. They are the finished product that has come through the fires of effective self-preservation and natural selection, with all the characteristics necessary for the holding of their place in the balance—planed and trimmed for perfect adjustment.

Hunting for the predator is not an easy matter in the wild state. For every trick of his own his prey has a trick, and for every attack there is a defense; from the shell of the terrapin to the erratic flight of a bird; from nauseating secretions, poisonous stings, and fangs to high speed and thorn bushes. A predator must be as virile and alert and effective as his quarry.

This constitutes hard work, and an animal's tendencies are those of a man: avoid pain, which is really what is meant by "danger," and accept the easier method; seek the less resistant lines for action.

One reason why the lower orders seem to be such clean killers is because they very seldom have the opportunity for a massacre; one momentarily unwary rabbit, one bird out of a flock, one deer out of the herd, taxes all their strength, speed, or cunning, and they often leave part of their prey, just as man leaves food on his plate. But, given easy hunting, they take full advantage of it, not like a true sportsman but like a gunner.

One afternoon a blizzard caught me in town during the Baby-Bear Moon, and I found the drift too much for the station wagon. About midnight the sky cleared and the moon came out, and I knew that all my enemies would be abroad. The next day I followed the snowplow to my east gate, then skidded and plowed my way across the pastures to my desolate little sandstone house.

I felt the atmosphere of murder before I arrived, but I was not quite ready for what I saw, even when I saw a maze of coyote tracks on the ridge. Lying scattered, close to the chicken houses, were the black bodies of my whole flock of H-D's. Their blackness against the snow only added to the sharpness of the feeling of tragedy. The whole ridge was charged with the atmosphere of death; silence, no smoke from the chimney, and the late-afternoon shadows of the trees were ominous. As one who steps into a room where a murder has been committed, I looked about the ridge, knowing, of course, that the sportive coyotes had come during the night.

That's it; they had some sport. They found easy killing and had some sport. I couldn't credit them with vengeance, nor with murder, for that matter, since they hadn't killed members of their own tribe. Their emotions must have been intense and their excitement wild.

The man from the ranch had forgotten to come over to close the chicken-house door, and they knew I was gone with the dogs. There were nine black bodies as symbolic warnings against easy, protected living; the other five had been carried away. My protection and feeding had dulled their instinct for self-preservation and had made them soft and maladjusted to the stark business of existence struggle. They had lost the power to save themselves.

Quite poignant was the fact that among the nine was the pullet that had so successfully adjusted herself during two months of the previous summer. She had contracted roup, and after dosing her with gasoline, since I had no kerosene, I took her to the end of the ridge and turned her loose, saying to myself that there she could not infect the others and that if she survived there on her own she would be brought back to the flock. As I walked away, I felt that I had given her a chance for life, though I held no hope for her.

Some weeks later I was walking along the ridge with the dogs, and I noticed them nosing about as though they scented prairie chickens, and, as I came up to them, I was wondering why prairie chickens should come to the ridge at that time of the season. I found tracks of a domestic chicken in the dry dust, and they were apparently fresh ones; but, since there had been no rain for several weeks, I assured myself that the sick hen had recovered sufficiently to walk about, and in the dust the tracks would appear fresh even if made several weeks past.

Later, I walked again with the dogs to the south ridge, and as we approached the end, I saw them flush something into the trees. I noticed that they did not seem much excited. When I came up to the dusty spot on the ridge, I noted many chicken tracks made there since I had last visited the place. I looked into the trees and finally saw the pullet, frozen on a limb against the trunk of a blackjack.

This was in late August, and I had put her there to die in June. There had been no rain during that time, and it was the season of hunting coyote whelps and young great horned owls. I could not quite believe what I saw; the sick pullet, taken out of the security of the pens, had incredibly adjusted herself to lack of water, to unaccustomed food, and to diurnal and nocturnal enemies. I have no idea where she got her water unless she walked down to the canyon some three hundred yards away, nor what she ate besides weed seeds and acorns. She had developed wing power to the extent that she could fly into the trees when a coyote appeared, and I imagine her blackness was perfect protective coloring in the case of the escape from the owls; but how she learned that a coyote was not an Irish setter or just another strange dog, I do not know.

Even domestic chickens do not have their instincts dulled to the point that they do not freeze when danger comes, especially at night; but how she controlled herself so that she made not the slightest movement when the great owls boomed frightfully around her is beyond my understanding and seems to be asking entirely too much of biological adjustment. One thinks of such adjustments in terms of years and centuries, not of two summer months. But, of course, being an H-D, she was of nature's design, and her quick adjustment was mostly a matter of revival.

Thus the pullet came back to the pens hard, strong-winged, and alert, only to die with the soft-minded flock, under the protection of thirteen other pairs of eyes and ears, and thirteen other instincts for self-preservation, plus the protection of man.

Not all the expressions of the species of the ridges are vital to their survival. Ornamental expression is inspired by the Force among the inhabitants of the ridges just as it is inspired in more privileged man. They have their nuptial dances and their songs, and they all play under the influence of the primal laws, but they also sing and dance and do odd things under the influence of the Force.

The crows, unable to sing or dance, collect bright objects and hide them, then go back to them to enjoy them in solitude. They pick them up and lay them down and turn them over; then they become restive and flip them. They seem to be choked with emotion that they can't express, to the extent that they are almost unhappy.

Pack rats will steal bright things from the kitchen and carry them to their bulky nests; they put them on top, where they haven't the least utilitarian purpose. The squirrels take the empty meat tins and carry them up a tree. They hammer them against the tree for a time, and soon this seems to pall and they, too, grow restive and drop the tin clattering down through the branches, then run down and pick it up again. They let it fall again and go down for it with great alacrity, which seems to grow, until, like the crow, they seem to be frustrated with something that wells within them until eventually they attempt to make the tin stick on a branch. If they fail in this, they leave, but often turn back and shake it frantically as though they sought relief from their emotion by such action. No one of these three can dance or sing, as is well known.

Rabbits and coyotes are inspired by a flash-torch, or a headlight, or by the light shining from my window. The rabbits will gather in such lights and go through some antics almost to the point of exhausting themselves, and the coyotes will sing to a headlight if it is left long enough, or they will sing to the light in my south window when the lamp is first lighted. This has happened only three or four times during my stay on the ridge. They always talk to the moon, and this is ornamental, except perhaps during the mating season, which incidentally is quite definitely a mating talk; a cajoling, eager series of yaps.

My dogs see things in the fire. They dream certainly, but they also lie gazing with their eyes open for long periods, then get up and walk about the room, softly whining as though they were agitated. One night, Biddy startled me by breaking into a long, mournful howl. There was no pain; it wasn't that kind of a howl. She wasn't unhappy, but she was disturbed deep on the inside, and I couldn't help her any more than I can comfort myself at such times.

It seems that the bird song is the expression of mating emotion that has spilled over or ebbed slowly, but I believe that most of my birds of the ridges sing periodically all the time they are with me, long before or long after the mating emotion wells. They sing when the rains come after a drought, and during the first cold weather of late summer or early autumn, which seems to remind them of migration. There are sad little songs and there are songs expressing some kind of bittersweetness which they feel deeply. The ecstatic singing of the mockingbird in the moonlight and the damp woods and twilight singing of the wood thrush have more in them than spilled-over mating emotion. Nature, as prodigal and as lavish as she is in seeing that her designs are carried out, would surely not make use of such prolonged and deep emotion for the assurance of a momentary physical contact. That, it seems to me, would be outnaturing nature.

Such thoughts are absent when the ridges are silvered during the Baby Bear nights and the smoke rises from my jagged chimney like a prayer to the moon. And they are absent during the daylight hours; only when the winds howl over the blackjacks, and it is more pleasant without the lamps, do they swarm. They are always with me—especially are they a part of my saddle-dreams—but more often they are like desert seeds springing up when the conditions are right, perhaps even to bloom, when I occasionally sit all night by the fire. But they come from the ridges and the blackjacks and are a part of my life here.

Every thing and every action on my ridges and among my blackjacks have meaning, and the better I understand the *raison d'être* of these things and these actions, the more intense my pleasure; even if I can satisfy myself with plausible guessing in many cases. Pleasant hours seem to fly, and I am constantly startled with the realization that I have lived here ten years. Yesterday was the great drought, and day before yesterday the iron winter that froze a cardinal on my window sill while I slept. Sometimes there are disagreeable thoughts before the fire during the Baby-Bear Moon.

No twinges in my muscles have halted my stride yet, nor stopped my dawn-to-dark hunting, when fireplace thoughts and saddle-dreams are drowned in the joy of action. The turning of the sumac and blackjack leaves, the first rose and the first morning-glory, and the visits of the painted bunting may have become pale miracles now, since yesterday; but the setters flaming in the pale winter sun, the smell of the earth, the cold feel of my gun, and the explosion of quail from the copper-colored grass will glorify me to the end.

When I am too old to follow the bearhounds and can't hear the coyotes talking to the moon, when my muscles become taut and my joints rusted, then I shall hunt quail from horseback. And then, when my blood flows like a sand-choked, polluted stream, and my heart with its fouled sparkplugs refuses to function with saddle rhythm, I shall invent a self-powered wheel chair and follow the setters, until a befuddled quail flies into my erratic shot pattern and falls. Then, palsied with excitement, I shall wave my gun with toothless joy, tip over and pass on to the next stage, giggling with senile unreasonableness over the thought that they won't be able to find me and spoil it all.

HOLLY AND COYOTES

This is the season when my spirit is disturbed. I do not have much time by the fire during the latter part of the month. I often put the setters in the station wagon and hunt with friends elsewhere, hunting among the blackjacks only part of the time.

There is an added glory in the air that thrills me; perhaps a left-over from the always impending glory that we were made to feel as children by a very energetic mother who followed every detail of the traditional Christmas.

Thus during the latter part of Baby-Bear Moon, I am restive, and I go visiting. I go to talk and hunt with my friends and exploit every spirit-burdened hour as time flows toward the great day. There is an extra, inscrutable happiness as I walk through the grasses, and the setters hunt in wide circles, and a heavy, lead-colored sky spits fine little flakes that promise a white Christmas.

I plan things that never happen, just as nothing happens when the day finally arrives. I plan to go to cedar canyon in the west pasture and get a native cedar for a Christmas tree. I plan to spend a day along the creek bottoms, shooting mistletoe out of the tall trees with my rifle, but I never do these things. I never gather the brilliant, scarlet berries that shine in the dappled sun and make the creek bottoms festive during this season.

I place two candles in the brass holders on each side of the mantel, one red and one green one; then take the dogs in the station wagon and drive into town with a pan of frozen quail at my side for mother's Christmas breakfast.

The cold stars that blink over the blackjacks on Christmas Eve see only a deserted stone house, with a pitiful holly wreath scraping dryly on the front door in the icy little winds. Silent night is broken only by the pagan chorus of the coyotes.

XIIII SINGLE MOON BY HIMSELF

THE MOON WOMAN FLOATS BY HERSELF NOW. THERE ARE NO BABIES OR fruits or flowers, say the Osage, and the Moon Woman is lonesome. She is not so gay and temperamental but dull and moody. Snow may stay on the ground for a long time, and there will be no sun, and the days as much alike, cold and gloomy. This moon is sometimes called Frost-on-Inside-of-Lodge Moon and long ago was known as the Hunger Moon.

Every other morning the long howl of the cowboy calling the cattle is heard from the feed grounds, and the trails leading from the canyon and converging at the grounds become deeper.

The leaves of the blackjacks seem to be eternally dripping, and the earth remains soggy during the day and frozen during the night. It is during the month of January that I become stuck in my own pastures on the road to town. One may pass along a road in the pasture during the day, splashing through the ruts and slipping to the point of stalling, but when one attempts to return after nightfall, the high centers are as hard as iron.

When the winds blow, they seem to come directly from the Arctic, and I am always reminded of the statement made by a pioneer of the Panhandle, where the wind blows seven days a week. He said that there was nothing between his sod house and the North Pole but a barbed-wire fence and that, when his hat blew off, he simply stood and waited for another to roll by. But the picture I shall always remember of Single Moon by Himself is cold fog and eternal dripping.

One day I plowed through the mud for several miles across the prairie to a little farm in a wild creek bottom. My station wagon swayed and labored in the mud, and the snow tires threw mud high into the air above it. Mud-bespattered, I slid down off the hill to the front of the little farmhouse. The sun was shining that day after the morning fog had lifted, and a cardinal was singing there in the bottoms; he sang jerkily as though testing his voice for the spring. I waited for the man of the place to come to me from across the field. I could hear the mud fall off the fenders and the wheels with soggy thumps.

As he approached me, I had a sudden fear that he had sold the colt I had come to see him about; I had heard that he had been offered a good price for it. I asked him immediately about the palomino colt.

"Say," he smiled with importance, "they's more than one of you fellers after that colt; figger if he's that good that a feller 'ud drive through this mud to ast 'bout 'im, by golly I might keep 'im."

"All I wanted to know is whether you had sold him. I want to have the chance to say whether I want him; to say whether I'll beat the price on him."

"Yeah, he's jist a sure good colt; mammy ain't much—ain't never showed much."

"She's not bad—little sway-backed, but she might have pretty good stuff in her for all we know."

"Guess that's right," he agreed; "but hit sure must be on the inside. Well, sir, when she come up a-showin' with that colt, I jist figgered she was fixin' to drop a jackrabbit, but when I seen hit, I jist couldn't believe my own eyes. I begin to figger that if the good Lord aimed to treat me that-a-way, I didn't have no call to treat Him like I bin a-doin'."

"Out of a good stud," I said; "that horse has some of the best colts in the country."

"I aim to git me one more drop outta that mare," he said, "and if she throws another'n like that little dun, I'm gonna let the woman take me back to the Lord, and start livin' right like she says I ain't bin a-doin'."

"Well," I said, "I just wanted to find out what was going on; heard you were about to sell, and thought I'd remind you of your promise. Don't suppose we could see him, do you?"

"I allus aim to do what I say I'll do," he assured me. "Guess the horses is all acrosst the crick—cain't hardly git there in a car, hit muddy like it is. Better stay all night."

"I got to get back."

"Won't take you long to stay all night," he insisted.

Just then his wife came out of the door with her hands under her apron. "Say," she shouted, "you ain't a-gonna try to go back in this mud? Better stay all night."

"No, thank you; I got to get back."

"It'll take you 'til after dark now," she said.

"Yeah," her husband said; "a man might git stuck out there on the prairie."

"No, I think I can make it," I said.

His wife came up with her arms folded across her bosom. She looked at the bespattered station wagon, then said, "Looks like when it sets in to weatherin' it don't know when to quit, anymore."

I started the motor. The man said, "Better stay."

"No, thank you; I got to get back to my coyote den."

"You wouldn't be no trouble," the wife said, "if that's what you're thinkin'."

"No, I know."

"I sure hate to be where there's mud," said the man, "like hit's bin. I got my car put up; I go a-horseback, anymore."

His wife looked up at the bright sun and the blue sky and said, "Sure is purty overhead."

The man spat to the side, "Yeah," he said, "but he ain't a-goin' that-a-way."

My neighbor and I used to hunt with his hounds during this month, but the prairies are usually too soft for cars, and the footing is not always too good for horses.

I am always sorry to leave the blackjacks to be gone for several weeks, but during this month I usually spend several weeks or a month in Washington, D.C., attending to the business of the Osage. They have bills in Congress to be guided, and because they have oil royalties they are, as a tribe, ever on the defensive, so that there are always matters under litigation as well. It seems that they must be constantly protecting themselves against those who sincerely believe them to be a vested interest.

Sometimes some of the older men of the tribe make the trip along with the members of the business committee and members of the agency staff in order to be company for the chief. If there are as many as twelve, they have a special car. Their presence before the Indian committees of both houses is quite effective, as the older men talk with dignity and formality. They soon grow tired of the hotel life, however, and they become annoyed with twittering sentimentalists and press photographers. Their blankets, bandeaux, or black Stetson hats are their everyday dress and they can never quite understand why these things should be of interest to people on the streets and in the lobby of the hotel. They are sensitive to this often brash interest, but they are also resistant and suffer this annoyance rather than conform by changing their traditional manner of dressing.

I stood on the station platform one day as the delegation was leaving for home. They were arranging their bundles and bags in the special car, as I waited for the time of their departure. I had been in Washington for some weeks before the delegation arrived and had to remain for an indefinite period longer. I was utterly lonesome as I stood there, and later, as I shook hands with each one of them, I felt an embarrassing lump in my throat. They were very much interested in their bill which had brought them to Washington to appear before the committees, but it had passed the Senate and had only to pass the House.

They were happy to be going home, but their sudden, whimsical departure and their consciences disturbed them slightly, however more or less the latter might be eased by my staying to see the bill through.

As I shook hands with each one, he said, "Waspi, you stay; good." But each face was lighted with thoughts of home, and I suppose I felt a little out of things.

Just as the porter was about to take up the step, John Abott stepped off and walked quickly up to me, extended his hand, and said, "Waspi, ain't it; good," then with a quick movement he placed a folded sheet of paper in my hand, turned, and rushed back to the car. Looking back over his shoulder, he said, "Take care 'bout that thing for me, ain't it?" He stood at the door as the train moved out, waved to me, and shouted, "You sure see 'bout that thing, ain't it?"

I put the paper in my pocket and watched the train as it disappeared, then walked with low spirits to a taxi. On the way to the Interior Department, I looked at the paper John had given me. It was his hotel statement to the amount of forty-two dollars: room, twenty-one dollars, and à la carte beefsteak, twenty-one dollars.

But not all the Single Moons by Himself are spent in Washington. Often I am on the ridges during the whole dripping, cold month. I am driven inside and spend much time by the fireplace. The hunting season is over and there is no fishing, and the moon shows herself very seldom. She comes out after the great snows that sometimes come during this time; and I find myself waiting for the snows to come with great pleasure, chiefly as a relief, I think, from the constant dripping and the damp cold that penetrates one's clothing; a relief from the ribbons of mud that are my road leading across the prairie and climbing up the east ridge.

With the snow comes activity again. If it is severe, I must carry feed for the quail and scatter it under the fallen tree tops, and I can go rabbit hunting if I care to do so. Since reaching manhood I have never considered this sport, so I leave my rabbits to their natural enemies, to their fate as a food supply for the predators of the blackjacks.

The marsh hawks turn to quail hunting during this time, and I have some sport hiding in the ravines with No. 2 shot and shooting them as they hunt relentlessly. The migratory and the indigenous marsh hawks might be the agency, an important agency at least, that keeps the highly prolific quail in balance, since they seem to hunt quail only during the winter. Having noted their great numbers and their voracity, I decided that I should become that agency for the balance during the autumn, since I can count and take cognizance of the future, while they can neither count nor think. If nature demands such an agency for concentrated action during a period, I shall assume the responsibility, in the name of sport. The hawks are really invaders anyway, seasonal invaders. I am not even sure that the indigenous ones stay on the ridges during the winter. It is not unlikely that they go farther south, allowing their northern brothers to use their hunting and breeding grounds with that subtle respect which members of a species have for each other, even when they have not formed into flocks for protection and are not gregarious.

In any case, they are invaders and I am indigenous, and they are members of another species and therefore my enemies if they do harm to me through their invasion of my range. Nature might even overlook the fact that the quail are not my chief food supply, as long as I regulate my shooting and do not upset the balance in the enjoyment of my sport.

The walls of my little house are of weathered sandstone, uncut, just as they are on the exterior. Hence they are dark and make the room dark during these days of heavy, weeping skies and dripping leaves; but I must stay in the house and attempt to read or work. This is impossible without the lamps, but inasmuch as the evenings are long and the darkness is more sympathetic to lamplight reading, I sit by the fire and think. This is the time when I sum up and collect my impressions of the year to interpret them and otherwise enjoy them. This is the time, the only time, during a year of action that I am able to entertain a series of thoughts and play with conclusions. Saddle-thoughts have a tendency to turn into dreams as sharp rain sometimes turns into soft snowflakes during this month. Fireplace thoughts are clear and sharp but hard to herd together for conclusions because of their sharpness, and must be forced into a pattern quite often, and quite often show the effect of chipping and pressure.

Surrounding me in the house are things made by man. I am shut up in my own den and shut off from nature and sustained by my thoughts and images, which are my intellectual fat stored up in the form of impressions. There is no indecision during the days when the world drips outside and the fire crackles; I must sit and think or read. Whichever I choose I must continue to do, as I find that I can't change from one to the other readily. However, in the evenings I have a third choice—the little battery radio.

I find that the radio is a habit, like smoking cigarettes, but not like the soul-soothing pipe. You think you can't do without the radio, just as you think you can't do without cigarettes, but it is not so difficult as it seems, even when you must give up the newscasts with the rest of it.

I have the third choice naturally during the long evenings, since the radio is not even considered during the day, except on Saturday afternoons during football season and during the Metropolitan Opera programs.

My thoughts then are ornamental. They have nothing to do with earth-law of survival, as I have, with exceptions, leased my range and have no cattle of my own. I have no family responsibilities on the ridges, and therefore my thoughts are not under the influence of the other earth-law, reproduction. Whatever thoughts I might have about either of the two great primal laws, that is, under the influence of those laws, are not in the least burdened.

My thoughts are ornamental and might be creative even though not connected with the primal laws. They might form into images for expressions—ornamentation in word symbols—but I am not quite sure of my thoughts, and I am too lazy to put them up against the recorded knowledge and the philosophy and the analyses of scholars.

The few times I have done this they didn't fit, so I kept them for my own pleasure.

My activities outside are play and therefore come under the influence of the self-preservation law. Animals play for a very good reason and in harmony with biology's plan for the survival of the species—as training for success in the struggle, with the same object as military training, which is for success in battle.

In the play of young animals as well as in the play of their elders, they re-enact in their own element the actions for securing food and avoiding enemies, and the play is regularized. The young play in the same manner as the mature ones play; one for education and training, and the other for relaxation and for constant preparedness.

Where play is irregular and the mature ones express themselves in ways that have nothing to do with survival, then I think they are inspired by some other natural urge, and I believe the expression to be quite ornamental, since it is not urged by the primal laws. I like to believe that ornamentation in action or expression comes from the mysterious Force in the progression. Only the mature animals express themselves thus; never the young in their all-absorbing virility.

However, those expressions which appear ornamental, which have nothing to do with the recognized primal laws of the earth, may be the first appearance of a third urge, made important with the development of man's ability to reason. If the dim, uncertain, often flickering expressions of the coyote, the crow's bright trinkets, the squirrel's meat tin, the wood thrush and the mockingbird's spilling-over in ornamental song, as well as the emotionalism of birds in general, are expressions inspired by this Force, then such expressions might well be represented during the present stage of man's development by the most beautiful art, literature, architecture, music, philosophy, and the highest concepts of God.

I, sitting by my fireplace, must think and manlike must, for my own satisfaction, interpret the things, the signs, the actions, and the voices about me, just as I note every strange automobile tread, or the shoe imprint of a strange horse, not to mention the footprint of a man, in my pastures. The latter would be of high interest, and I could not be happy until I had solved it. In the cases of the automobile tread and the hoofprint, I am never satisfied until I verify my on-the-spot conclusions.

Those things which I see in the blackjacks are a functioning part of the natural drama of the universe; the particular from which one might learn something of the general; and man must be fitted in as long as he is of the earth and must depend upon it and must live under its laws.

Like the play of young animals, children's play represents training as well, and the boy with his games and his tin soldiers and wooden guns and the little girl with her dolls and her mud pies are very interesting after you have watched closely the play of young animals. Also very interesting is the play of men. Acquisitive men, businessmen, and men in general struggling for food, power, and prestige play poker for money and golf for so much a hole. They play competitive games or hunt where the competition is represented by another species. Only those not struggling under the influence of the law of self-preservation, but apparently though certainly not able to escape the law, are more under the influence of the "incipient" law, the Force. These latter play in quite a different manner.

My hunting activity is play then. My dogs are playing when they simulate death battle, rolling over, growling, or rearing against each other and keeping their vulnerable front legs out of the reach of each other's playful fangs. The wrens, spending much time in the bushes, forever prying into crevices and into junk piles, and staying close to man and his cast-off things, seem to have no enemies on the ridges. There are no house cats here. Their play seems to be more colored by the reproductive urge than by the self-preservative one. They build nests all summer; long after they have nested and their young are gone, they carry material to some new, delightful place they have found and sing merrily as they build. When they have finished, they hunt another place, flitting here and there and singing all the while; the nesting play, the singing ornamental, and inspired by the Force, or associative.

The squirrel, not a predator, if one overlooks the diabolism of the breaking-up of birds' nests and other little activities, plays in the trees, always at fleeing from an enemy—simulating the avoidance of capture by his fleetness. The eagle and the redtail soar high in the sky long after their mating season and long before the beginning of the new one. The eagles dive at each other in play as they do when hunting prey. I have often noted that the hawks of the blackjacks that migrate spend much time in the air flying about in circles or standing against a wind high in the blue sky of September.

The crows maneuver in flocks, practicing their military code for protection. They fly in great flocks about their roosting place, to make sure that I or the horned owls are not near. I have never been able to see in their play the defense which they employ against the night attacks of the owl.

The coyote whelps tumble about the entrance to their den, growling and snapping much as puppies play, and the old ones play as the old dogs play, ever keeping their slim, vulnerable front legs out of reach of the other player. When they chase each other as a part of the false battle, they keep their brushes under their bellies for protection and their rear ends low to the ground. And if one wished to know how a bobcat catches a prairie chicken or how a cougar takes a colt or a deer, he might watch a cat or a kitten with a spool. Of course, the cats in the harmony of the balance play much more than lazy old tabby who spends most of his time behind the stove and doesn't worry too much about his food supply.

Just as I train my setters to retrieve by throwing a dead bird into the grass many times, until wetted with their slavers, a cat trains himself by playing with a live mouse, and this is not cruelty but play with a very natural objective.

One who sees a cougar in the wild state not treed by hounds, or caught in a trap, is considered very fortunate, but sometimes by mere chance they are seen. They are perfectly protected by their coloring and glide, with the grace of all cats, like shadows through the woods. The only one I ever saw, I picked up with my twelve-power binoculars on the side of a mountain, against the glare of snow.

This experience was so unique that I am constantly recalling it and have spent many hours attempting to get another glimpse of a cougar unconscious of my presence. I think of it not only as a unique experience but naturally in connection with play in the natural balance, which constitutes a sort of military training, if not for battle, certainly for the struggle for survival.

There had been a snowfall while we were camped in the bighorn country. The big rams had come down from their above-timber-line plateau into the shelter of the forest. I set out alone to see if I could cross a trail. I trailed what I had thought to be two bighorns high up under the rimrock, but they turned out to be two old mule-deer bucks, whose hoofs had not been worn down by great activity and were elongated. Also, their bellies made impressions in the deep snow, like the bellies of bighorn.

I found myself in command of a white snow field across the canyon, when I discovered my mistake, so I played the glasses over it in the hope that I might pick up something. The sun shone brightly, and the woods were absolutely silent and without movement except for the snow occasionally falling from the burdened branches of the trees. I sat with my back against a tree on the north side of the canyon which was in deep shadow, and my clothes blended perfectly with the bole of the tree, and with the gray granite of the rimrock. Of this I was not conscious, however.

As I swept the snow field, I held the glasses on a bit of dirty snow under the shadow of a large pine. I had to know what that spot was. Then there was movement, and I concentrated. It was the writhing tail of a cougar. I felt sure that he was watching me, and I believe I was afraid to breathe normally as I watched with taut nerves. The thought came to me that I should be able to keep my protective immobility as long as he could, then I realized that he wasn't attempting to keep his, with that tail writhing like a snake; and the thrill that came over me was even deeper. I moved the glasses just a little to bring the deer, which I was sure he was stalking, into the field. However, just then he jumped on something and rolled over in the snow, then jumped high and away, like a dog leaps away from a rattlesnake. He put one paw out and struck the object, then sat back exactly like a cat with a mouse. He suddenly jumped on the thing again and bit it, then rolled over on his back and brought it on top of him, as though in mortal combat with it, just as my setter pups do my bear rugs.

I saw immediately that the "prey" was an oblong piece of weaving of some sort, about the size of a saddle blanket. There wasn't anything sinister in this, since I knew that the cougar is only a very swift, graceful, and fierce hunter who is frantically afraid of man, even though very much interested in him as a novelty when unpleasant experience is lacking. He, like most animals, will fight in defense of the precious life intrusted to him by biology, even as the rat or the ant will fight, but will very carefully avoid pain when there are other ways for survival. And, in any case, I could see that the material was not in the form of wearing apparel.

I was so thrilled that I forgot the discomfort of a long-held position and the cold, but I intended to get the last detail of this game in the profound white silence, where the game was the only movement, except for the snow falling from the trees. When he grew tired, he walked off into the shadows and immediately seemed to melt into them, but I attempted to keep him in the field of vision as long as possible. I wasn't sure that he had gone but kept the glasses on the shadow into which he had disappeared. Then suddenly part of the shadow became animated, and he jumped on the "prey" again. I think he must have growled, but I couldn't hear him.

Again he stood above his plaything, then looked off across the canyon, but no special alertness came into his body, and I was sure that he didn't sense my presence. He turned and walked away again, turned his head and looked at the plaything in the snow, then melted completely into the mauve shadows.

I wanted very much to go across the canyon and examine that bit of material with which he had been keeping bright and clean his predatory powers, so to speak, but the canyon was deep, and the head of it high against the rimrock, and my side of the canyon was deep in late-afternoon gloom.

On the way back to camp, however, I satisfied myself with my own interpretation. A hunter's pack outfit had dropped a saddle blanket the autumn before, and the cougar, smelling the "horse" on it, had dug it out of the snow and was compelled to do something about it—drawn to it like a cat is drawn to catnip, or a coyote to aniseed, if not for the same reasons. The manner in which he expressed himself was in play, inspired by the faint odor of the meat which he loves above all other food.

When the rabbits dance in the light of my window, I am at loss to know what the urge is, since it is neither nuptial nor survival expressed by play, so I put it down to ornamentation. But the economically important rabbit, harassed by many animals, must certainly be compelled to keep fit by play, and so he does, all over the ridge. They go streaking across the ridge, then freeze suddenly, or chase each other about until one runs to the protection of the sumac on the side of the hill, or runs into a piece of well casing lying along the fence.

They must keep breeding to supply the other species of the ridges and keep the balance from jiggling, and they must play almost constantly to keep fit for the struggle. So, as a matter of fact, I am not sure when they are playing or when they are enjoying some nuptial ceremony. They might combine the two. I am sure that their thumping is used as a danger signal and is often practiced when there is no danger near, and I am sure that they use this signal in the service of love and romance as well.

I often think of the species *Homo sapiens* who was a part of the balance of my blackjacks. The Osage, while in perfect harmony, assumed that he had two natures; but, of course, he was almost as much under the influence of his natural environment in his man-world of thought as he was in his animal-world of struggle and re-production. His concept of God, springing from his ornamental expressions, was certainly colored by his natural environment and fear of the elements and his enemies. He built up in his imagination the Great Mysteries, and he walked, fought, hunted, and mated in the approval of them. When the Force urged him to expression, he turned his eyes to Grandfather the Sun; the colors he saw under his closed eyelids he put into beadwork, quillwork, and painting, as inspirations from one of the greatest manifestations of the Great Mysteries, the sun, father of Father Fire, impregnator of Mother Earth.

He thought of his tribe as symbolical of the universe, and he divided himself and his universe into two parts, man and animal, spiritual and material, sky and earth, which he called Chesho for the Sky People and Hunkah for the Earth People, because he felt this duality. With his Chesho thoughts, his ornamental expressions, however, he was colored by the processes of the earth in general and by his own struggle in particular.

He gave his own disturbed emotions to symbols having definite outline and substance so that he could "see" them thus and understand them, and he charged them with the emotions within him, so that in turn he went to them to receive back that which he had given them, taking his own shimmering, distorted images that were disturbing his soul and giving them to solid, definite, imperishable objects in an effort to express the urgings of the Force.

The crow in the gathering and storing of bright things was coming close to this transplantation of emotion, as was the squirrel with his meat tin, the mockingbirds and their songs, the coyote and the moon, and perhaps even the wren and his nest-building.

The Osage put their religion into everything they did, or it might be better to say that their ornamental expressions were never quite free from the daily struggle for survival. When they killed their weaklings or their imbeciles, they served two purposes: they left their tribe unencumbered for offensive or defensive action and for complete mobility and they served the survival processes consciously. They also believed that such people carried the evil spirit and could bring harm to the camp other than physical. They did not burn witches after trial and employ the other soul-saving, face-saving rituals of the people of Salem, Massachusetts, nor did they commit mass murder in the profound fear of those things with which the Great Mysteries concerned themselves. They were simple and direct and protected themselves from their fear by simple, direct, and clean action. In their simplicity they were almost as direct, simple, and clean as the processes themselves and not encumbered by the more confused thinking and sharper fears of the more advanced stage of mental development represented by Salem, where man was more able to cut the balloon of imagination from its earthly anchorage.

So the species *Homo sapiens* of my ridges was not very far advanced above the other species of the ridge where his ornamental thought was concerned, even though he was far advanced over them in his thinking when his thought was applied to the laws of self-preservation and reproduction.

He expressed his thoughts in beauty, in handicrafts, and in song and dancing, but he had added another fear to the earth-fears of the elements and of pain which the other species have; he feared the results of his own ornamental thinking and charged the wind, lightning, the tornado, the snake, the screech owl, and imbeciles with his own fear emotions, as well as charms and other objects which were concrete. He could "see" them as he traveled on his way to abstract thinking. These things gave back to him the fear emotion with which he had charged them, as the earth gives back the life with which the elements charge it.

Among the blackjacks, then, indigenous development of the nervous system into thought-processes reached its heights in articulate speech, thought-influenced social and economic organization, artifacts, and the religion of Wah-Kon-Tah. Man of the blackjacks assumed an amphiphysistic state, though he didn't get far from the earth spiritually, and the state was his own assumption.

The amphiphysistic assumption was strengthened by the invasion of the European, but his social and economic organization was destroyed by the Amer-European during his exploitation of the new continent, and his religion adjusted itself to pressure which resulted in Peyotism.

It is quite easy to see the whimsicalities of Just-Doing-That Moon in the old religion of Wah-Kon-Tah. The curling heat of summer, the blizzards of winter, and the sad dignity of autumn were visible as was the uncertainty which the chief food supply, the buffalo, inspired by their seasonal migrations and the uncertainty as to the numbers which grazed away from northern winters. The Osage were always pleading with the Great Mysteries to make the medicine of their enemies, the Pawnee and the Cheyenne, weaker, so that they, the Osage, could feel more assurance of holding their place of power in the skirmishes along the border of their respective ranges.

Man's power of thought among my blackjacks is still colored by the earth from which it sprang and has made its greatest progress under the influence of the primal laws of self-preservation and reproduction, only slightly advanced under the influence of the Force. This latter expression is the shining cicada only just beginning to emerge from the dull, earth-colored pupa, but even when it has freed itself, it is still subject to the laws of the ridges.

My thoughts by the fireplace are Chesho thoughts, purely ornamental. I can get up and walk down to the canyon, where the Carboniferous limestone is exposed and find there evidence of the earth's record through fossils. I can get from my shelves books which give me man's own record of his very short biological history, and I can read the amazing story of the beauty and the ugliness which his ornamental thinking has brought about, his savage and beautiful interpretations of the Force. It doesn't seem strange that these things should be so, when I refuse to take civilized man at his own valuation during the short period of my consciousness. Each generation of civilized man considers itself the ultimate in development and has attempted to fix the values at that stage. To ephemeral man his history on earth seems to be very long, when actually to the history of the earth he is a very recent species.

If I go down to the pond and dip up some mud and water, spread it on a piece of glass, and look at it under my microscope, I see organisms that are in the transition stages from the inorganic, amorphous earth to organisms with definite form. I cannot always say which is inorganic and which organic, but when life is obvious there are many very low forms which seem to be neither vegetable nor animal. I attempt to choose a form which I believe represents the parallel stage in life's development from inorganic earth with man's mental development from the mammalian world. All this is quite unscientific, of course, but it gives me pleasure and is a very great comfort when I return to thoughts about man's present war of ideologies, and his talk of a lasting peace, and the very great mess he has made in his attempts to interpret the Force.

Surely thought and the power to form images are in their very earliest stages of development, and man must be barely emerging from the animal world which he assumes he has left behind. He is incapable of projecting himself into the future to that stage in his mental development when he might bear the same relationship to the mammals out of which he developed that the range horse with flying mane bears to the dust he kicks up and which he spurns.

My thoughts are Chesho, as they should be, and there are no longer Hunkah thoughts of youth and action, when Single Moon by Himself comes to the blackjacks, and I am inside the dark little sandstone house by the fire. My life-force is not needed for the struggle, and it cannot be directed into play, and this energy must be utilized.

Just as the mature animals of the blackjacks use their energy, the life-force which is no longer necessary, no longer completely absorbed by virile struggle, to express ornamentation, so have I, after ten years, reached that stage of ornamentation, and I can now accept that stage in my development with some grace. Then will follow, I am quite sure, the thoughts of senility, and I shall probably worry about immortality—worry about my moccasin prints.

But I must take a hint from what I have learned from the drama of my ridges. When the organism has reached the limits of its growth, has momentarily conquered its enemies, taken from other growths all that it needs by struggle to reach its maturity, then the life-force which is not needed after that part is expended to hold what it has attained may express itself in ornamentation which may really jeopardize survival. They say the great saurians did this physically by the development of useless spines and armor that encumbered them and made adjustment to new conditions impossible, so they became extinct. My Symbol Oak did this during its maturity, about a hundred years ago. It grew queer knots and grain curlicues, which were not diseased, with its excess of life-force after it had taken the sustenance of the other growths around it and attained its maturity.

My ornamental thoughts may have a tendency to become poetic when my radio brings me the war news through heroizing commentators. They may become like a captive balloon cut to wander from its moorings on the prevailing currents, if I permit them, when radio vaudevillians and after-dinner orators speak dramatically of the Four Freedoms and world brotherhood. But I must remember the drama of the blackjacks, man's newness on earth, and his very recent development as a thinking animal. Certainly he is too close to the transition stage to take complete control of himself on the assumption that he has completely separated himself from the earth by the power of thought. Therefore, when he speaks of international brotherhood, he must be charging an abstraction—having reached the abstract thinking stage by a narrow margin—with the emotion built up within himself, with the dreams and hopes born of ornamental thinking. I must not betray my ridges to follow him. As the man of my blackjacks, the Osage, charged symbols, so does the Amer-European charge abstractions.

These dreams of the war-weary people of my unit of society have come to my blackjacks over the air and have become a part of my life. I can't escape them, so I must know the story of these dreams as I must know the story of the horse track or the track of the automobile tread in my pastures. Just as I have the hoofprints and the tread marks, I have the consciously cultivated voice over the radio and the books by people who have had experience with national and international affairs; but neither the voice nor the books are sufficient to assuage my mature worries. As a matter of fact, they often sharpen them, just as the hoofprint and the tread marks sharpen my interest.

While the idea of man's newness on earth and the recent development of his mental power may be consoling to me when I think of his fumbling toward the God-concept, and his careless exploitation of the earth that feeds him, I am not consoled by his fumblings in attempting to create a universal peace from his ornamental thinking rather than from his self-preservation–influenced thinking. With the man-thought-era just beginning biologically, there is little to worry about concerning the future of man and his fate or about his progressive approach toward an understanding of the Force which urges him to expression—if one really worries that far ahead. But when a unit of society, a nation, in constant struggle—an intraspecies struggle—with other nations, leads us to believe that it is applying ornamental thought to the primal business of survival as a nation, then it is natural that sitters-by-the-fire who have learned to think in terms of earth drama, and of man as a part of it, should be disturbed. But this is what the radio commentators and writers of books imply should be done, and if they speak and write for the people of the nation, if the radio voice is the collective voice, then the attitude of the nation is unnatural and highly ornamental, even to the point of jeopardizing its position attained not through dreams but through natural survival power and capacity.

The peace of my ridge is not a peace but a series of range-line skirmishes and constant struggle for survival. The balance is kept by bluff and a respect for that power which backs it up, and it utilizes and protects an area large enough and fruitful enough to sustain that power. The laws of the earth for survival are laid down, and man is not far enough away from the earth to supersede them with those of his own creation; he can only go back to the earth to ascertain where he has diverged from the natural processes.

He may see that his many nationality-conscious units have sufficient economic basis in land and industry, so that they will not be so tempted to invade other units, under whatever ideological slogan they wish to carry on their banners. He may bring about an understanding among nations that have what they need and the power to hold it for the purpose of using the combined power to keep fanatic ideologies, whether religious, economic, or political, in fear of that combined power which must be as ready as the survivor in the blackjacks is ready—to act at any moment.

But he cannot have lasting peace, even though organized warfare seems to be man-created and therefore may be man-controlled. It is quite likely, since man sought protection first in the tribe, then in federation of tribes, and later in the state, that such organization was biological, and therefore the means and methods of protection for the unit were in harmony with the processes. Forced peace, which is the only kind of peace man can conceive of now in his present stage of development, cannot last any longer than the powers that impose it.

Having lived in other lands, I appreciate my nation as the greatest development of a national unit thus far, and, having lived in other lands, I appreciate its absorption in the development of its natural resources and its happy history. However, I do not want its pleasant history to color its attitude toward international relations where other units know and have known only stark struggle for survival, not only with man but with the depleted earth. The tremendous power of my nation can be properly feared and respected, as power of the earth is ever feared and respected, or its power may be made negligible through ornamental thinking applied to primal laws of the earth.

It seems significant that within his unit, the Amer-European has made his power of thought harmonize so well with the earth law of survival, both in his economic and in his social organization, just as the men of the blackjacks, the Osage, did before him. One living far away from the chrome-brightness of civilization, and not completely blinded by it, sees the harmony in the individual struggle and group struggle with the processes of the earth, wherein the fittest attain economic survival and respect the power of each other. This struggle, of course, is controlled and guided by the government of the unit. In the social group struggles one seems to see an urge to overwhelm and supersede those who have attained the higher social privileges under the ideology of social equality. This struggle to survive seems quite natural and therefore can't be wrong, as long as man is of the earth.

I invariably say to anthropologists and others who come to study the Osage: "If you want to understand the old region of the Osage, first study carefully his natural background; then, after you have some understanding of that, his religion becomes clearer to you; when you understand the old religion of Wah-Kon-Tah, then study the lateral and vertical pressures imposed by the invading Amer-European freed of his own European political, religious, and social pressures. You will then see why the new religion developed, the new religion of Peyotism; and you will then have a better understanding of this new religion which is a mixture of the old religion of Wah-Kon-Tah and Christianity."

I think that this holds true as well of the biology of America. Study first the original conditions, wherein the Indian was in harmony with the natural balance; then study the effect of the European freed from the tight political, economic, and social pressures of Europe, running almost berserk on the new continent. His enemies in the Old World were these pressures, and he was suddenly freed from them in the New World, to expand even as the English sparrow has expanded where his enemies are absent and his food supply abundant.

For years the Amer-European exploited his new continent and was so engrossed in it that he took no interest in other units of society, and thought little of his place in the world and of his relationship to other national units. Freed from the ruthless struggles of Europe, he built up his own philosophy of international relations, based on his own economic, social, and political conditions—based on his very pleasant history. He attributed to all other units the contentment and the comfort which were his and attributed to all other units a desire to live in tranquillity and peace, assuming that the peace and tranquillity which he enjoyed was a universal condition which had only to be nurtured by the good will of mankind. This became his philosophy, his ideology.

When the time came, about 1929, which brought to him the fact that a certain climax of his exploitation had come, he became restive, economically, socially, and politically, and began to wonder about his relationship with the other units of the world. This condition was only caused by the end of the "flush production" era of his exploitation, and he must now learn that the layers of his cake under the frosting were also edible. The seemingly sudden end of an era startled him, as a sudden change in cyclic temperature might startle inhabitants of the Tropics, who had been pulling bananas from the trees for generations and then found that the bananas were gone and they must begin to delve. Undoubtedly like the Amer-European who was stunned by the change, the tropical native would stand about for a while feeling sorry for himself and demand changes in government and social structure to satisfy his feeling of injury.

Realization that his economics were vulnerable and, further, that a disturbance among the units in Europe and Asia might upset his accustomed tranquillity, the Amer-European became more and more interested in the relationship among the world units, and finally was drawn into war, where his tremendous power becomes a deciding factor.

Because of the happy history of the Amer-European, and because he has what he needs in his present stage of development, he wants peace. Several of the European units also want peace because they have what they want and do not wish to be disturbed in the enjoyment of it. These national units have this desire in common, and since their desire for peace is based on the fact that they have what they want, and wish to keep what they have, they are aligned against those national units in Europe and Asia who want to expand at the expense of other units and sacrifice peace.

It would seem that when those national units have what they want, and are victorious over those units who have disturbed the peace, they might use the same combined power to enforce peace until such time as they themselves may pass into senility and lose the power to hold what they have. Passing through the stages of virility, maturity, and senility, as does the individual man and all other forms of life, the collective expression of man, the national unit, cannot be permanent if several units who have what they want plan to force by their power peace on the world. Such a peace could not outlast their power to impose it, even if they co-operated with each other as they do during the emergency of war. One or two of the units would begin to decline before the others, and their weakness would invite the encroachment of the lesser, more virile units, just as the decline of my Symbol Oak invites the invasion of virile growths. Even if the power units co-operated perfectly, without jealousy of each other and without the secret treaties and under-the-table diplomacy, the peace interval could live no longer than the unit that first passed into senility.

Nature utilizes every square inch of my blackjacks for the existence of the species, and every spark of the life-force is utilized. When the forms in the stage of senility no longer are able to use the life-force which they acquired in their virility and utilized in their maturity, this life-force must be utilized by virility in its growth to climax. This may apply to man, since he is of the earth. Man's intraspecies struggle seems to be a continuation of the interspecies struggle of my black-jacks. His division into national units in intraspecies struggle may be parallel to the division into species of the lower forms and repeats their interspecies struggle.

His balance-of-power politics might be in harmony with the natural processes and not artificial. As the individual advances into maturity and then into senility, his fears deepen, and he becomes more cautious in the protection of what he has and is prone to compensate for his lack of strength with establishment of artificial barriers for his protection. The national unit is the collective expression of the individual and is urged to protect its weakness in late maturity and in senility. Its barriers are other, stronger units in the balance of power which artificially protect the nonutilized life-force in the senile unit, for their own protection, against the encroachments of virility.

If power units could stop this encroachment, peace might endure with the life-span of these power units, but they are no more able to do this than I, the individual, am able to stop it in the life-balance of my ridges. This transfer of the life-force goes on continuously on my ridges, and the result is the perfect balance of nature. If this is true of the particular, then why not of the general? The difference between the balance of my ridges and the balance of power in the world of man is that man adjusts his balance through organized warfare, and the balance of my ridges is adjusted through a "recognition" of the play of the life-force, through the resignation of senility.

It seems to me that if man desires peace as much as he says he desires it, he might, from the heights of his mental development, also recognize this low of the necessity for life-force transfer. The power units might allow the natural growth of virile units but control their fantastic ideologies, born of pressures. The species of my ridges that do not attain their climaxes remain intensely virile and await the inevitable decline of the senile, no matter how long they must wait, and virility remains always a "danger" to senility.

My national unit manages to control the acquisitive groups within its own structure but allows them natural growth. A society of national power units might do likewise with lesser units and attain thereby a much longer interval of peace.

The fruits of the earth of my national unit flow to the units of Europe, during and after their organized struggles, like the high gales that blow from afar into the vacuum left by the tornadoes of my ridges. This is a part of my unit's strength, but it buys no peace for the world, just as its ideology based on a pleasant history will settle no problems in overcrowded Europe. The leaders of my national unit, trained in the tranquillity of abundance, can contribute only their unit's power to the balance-of-power designs of the ruthless, struggle-sharpened representatives of the European units, if they present only their ideology based on their pleasant history.

Perhaps when the necessity arises, my nation will be forced to forget its ornamental policy in respect to international peace and work under and in harmony with the laws that govern such conditions, expressing effectively its tremendous power in world affairs.

I often go back over the results of man's interference with the natural processes in carrying out his ideas for economic profit, in case I might find there some hint as to what he might be able to do in carrying out his ideas for what he calls lasting peace. Here in the blackjacks I have many breeds of chickens and the white-face cattle. The white chickens and the heavy, short-winged breeds would be the first to go if thrown out of man's protection into the natural balance; only those closer in coloration, power of flight, and alertness to the jungle fowl would have a chance to survive. Only the brown leghorns and the H-D's, constantly alert, strong-winged, and restive, would be able to adjust themselves to the drama of the blackjacks, to prove that man's ideas are not always those of nature. These former are of man's designing, inspired by his dreams for profit: these short-winged, vari-colored fowls and the white-face cattle.

Nature would not be interested in the large white marketable eggs, and certainly not in sterile ones, any more than she would be interested in the white leghorn that laid them. The white leghorn may have the same wing power, the alertness, and the continuous "jitters" that the brown leghorn has, but it would be damned by its whiteness. And even if it escaped with this invitation to destruction, those white eggs would never produce unless laid in holes in trees, or elsewhere hidden from the many egg-eaters of the ridges. White eggs are laid in holes, or well hidden like the glossy eggs of the flicker, or under a grass roof and constantly protected like those of a quail. The red and the barred heavy breeds couldn't last long enough even to lay eggs.

And if the protection of man were taken from the white-face cattle, they would possibly have a chance to survive, but in reduced numbers. In the balance they could not maintain themselves on five acres to the head, and their underslung, meat-packed bodies, so interesting to the cattlemen, would undergo an overhauling by nature if they would become one of the favored species and take the place of the buffalo. This must be done before the buffalo wolves could come back in numbers, and before cougars and black bears came back to their old haunts to sniff at man's tangled wire and junk piles. I think also that nature would do something about their glaring white faces, not only for protection against their enemies, but as protection against the sun and pink eye. If heliographic signals seemed necessary to their survival, then nature woud move the white around to their buttocks, where it could be blacked out by their tails or through muscle movement for the arrangement of the hairs, as in the case of the white rumps of the whitetail deer, the pronghorn, and the cottontail rabbit.

The horses of the blackjacks would survive, just as they survived after the Spanish invasion of the Western Hemisphere. As the horse-loving cougars came back to the blackjacks, the horses would leave and go to the plains and the high prairie, where the cougar has no cover for his hunting and where they avoided him before.

This is what might happen on my ridges if man passed on and there were not other men to continue the protection of man's designs. And thus it seems to me that nature insists on her own designs when the power of man is absent and he can no longer protect his.

Other men will come to my ridges after I have gone and maintain the conditions which exist, because such conditions have economic importance and benefits, as long as they protect the white-face cattle and the bluestem upon which they graze, but what other nations will protect the world peace conditions no longer maintained by power? Can man create a power organization inspired by the Force to suppress the invasion by the now smaller units of the now powerful unit's ranges and aid in adjusting their expansion to their need? Man's collective expression in national units is a new thing even historically, as his advent and his thinking are new things in the history of the earth; and, just as man may be expected to remain a long time, so may national units be expected to exist for a long time; and the unit selfishness and economic advantage must be considered in man's plans to bridge the transition between the decline of the powers that will impose peace and the maturity stage of other units growing into power. The economic benefits of peace must overbalance the benefits of war, since man is very much a part of the earth's processes and cannot dream himself out of them.

As long as my ridges in their present condition of balance and comparative peace are of economic benefit to man as profitable grazing range, then my passing will make very little difference; but if some foul dough-belly, chewing an unlit cigar and squinting his eyes, decides that there would be greater economic benefit in dividing my pastures into town lots, with a belching factory chimney as the Gothic tower of the religion of mechanism, in the center, the peace of the blackjacks would be destroyed. And the people would talk of a miracle, too, as the earth under which I had been laid would boil with my subterreanean writhings.

And thus my thoughts when I must gaze into the fire and there is no action, and I find myself thinking of *my* unit of society, not of the world, but of that unit which protects me and gives me greater latitude for individual action than man has ever known since he first came to the herd for protection. Not even a crow, with his wisdom and his biological triumph, has such latitude, and certainly the poor coolie ant hasn't got it in his "extraordinary social organization."

And when I think of *my* unit, I am being perfectly and naturally selfish, not only about my unit, but about my generation, with my interest faded, though following into the next one. When I feel this way, I wonder how sincere men really are when they talk of the happiness and comfort of future generations, and I wonder how far into the future man's interest in international peace really goes. If it doesn't go any further than two or three generations, owing to the interest in his own immortality through his children, then man of the present hasn't much to worry about in regard to international peace, as the power of the units which can, and probably will, sponsor peace might outlast both himself and his immediate posterity. Mr. Chamberlain, harassed by barbaric screaming and bluff at Munich, expressed in his fear from the corner into which he had been pressed that unprotected feeling which all animals have when cornered when he spoke of "peace in our time." He must have spoken from the heart of man.

When the dripping stops and ice forms on the trees and the snow falls in feather-like flakes, softly, diffidently, I drop my fire-gazing thoughts with the reflection that if man insists in carrying out his designs for universal peace independent of nature, and if they succeed against the designs of nature, there must be a *deus ex machina*.

XIV   LIGHT-OF-DAY-RETURNS MOON

IF THE OSAGE HAD HAD A BETTER OPINION OF THE COYOTE, OR HAD HE been more important in their lives as a symbol or otherwise, this moon might have been called Coyote-Breeding Moon. Certainly he has ever been with them, and with all his cleverness he has aided them as well as plagued them.

But this is really the coyote's moon, although he greets all of them with his great variety of voices and emotions, asking each one of them the disturbing question, "Why?" During this time his voice has a new note in it. The eternal questioning is displaced by tender yearning and the most excited kind of jackal laughing. The warm, damp nights of this moon are filled with his love song.

These are the days when several of them may be seen at one time, and when the hounds tumble out of the station wagon, they never know which one to choose and, by indecision, thwart their own purposes. We surprised four one day on the high prairie and turned the hounds loose on the largest one. Just as they were strung out across the prairie, another one crossed between the hounds and the first one, and the hounds were very much confused, some staying with the first one and others going for the second. Just after this happened they were lost to our view by the escarpment, but certainly all four were mixed up in the race. When we arrived on top, the pack was scattered all over the prairie, circling in dismay with their tongues hanging. They had been beautifully tricked.

Standing in my favorite position with my back to the fire looking far across the prairie to the horizon fifteen miles away through the south window, I saw a band of coyotes cross over the point of the ridge. They were trotting toward the canyon. I could see by the waving grass tops that the wind was out of the south, and this gave me an idea. I got my 16-mm. cinema camera and crawled through the grass toward the upper end of the canyon, the waving tops of the grass blending with my movements.

You never know what to expect when you set out to photograph animals and birds. I have made so many pitiful failures that I have developed a great admiration for wild-life photographers. But in this case, knowing the effect of the mating urge on animals, birds, and men, I knew that the only one of the band that would have its protective senses alert and not drowned by the glory that flooded the others would be the female.

I identified her as soon as I saw them again as they came over the rim of the canyon. As a matter of fact, I saw them before I was ready, and they were doing the unexpected thing—coming toward my position. The female, with mouth open, owing to the unseasonably warm day, would stop occasionally and look about with her savage yellow eyes. Once she seemed to look at me. I wanted her to pass by me, then as the dogs came along, dulled and careless, I could get a good picture. This had to be done quickly, before she got far enough past me so that her sharp nose could get my scent.

She stopped near me and looked about her with a pleased expression, like the smug, pert expression of some belle much sought after at a party and conscious of her own worth. And, believe me, the males acted like members of a stag line.

There was a weed top caught in the tall grasses that hid me and was making a dry little sound as the wind coming up the canyon tried to dislodge it, and this sound was astonishingly the sound of the rattle-snake-like churr of my camera. Never had the fates smiled so understandingly on an enthusiast. However, just as I pressed the little gadget to start the camera, the churring was more metallic than I had thought, and the female immediately became a carven statue, looking straight at me. Even the emotion-doped males stiffened. Then, like a flash, the band was gone, and I stood up to watch them flee up each side of the canyon like yellow-gray streaks. I at least had several feet of exposed film, even though it might seem that the subjects had been posed. I thought I had several feet of exposed film. When I got back to the house on the ridge, I found that I had forgotten to reload the camera after the last attempt at wild-life photography.

One hazy, warmish morning I heard the yapping of the coyotes coming from the head of the canyon. This love talk of the coyotes is the perfect expression of love's uncertainties and male eagerness, and since love is always associated with youth, grace, beauty, and song and sweet sadness, there is something inexhaustibly funny about the love expressions of raucous-voiced or graceless animals.

I took the glasses and looked toward the canyon. I expected to be amused, but what I saw I had never seen before, and, instead of calm amusement, I laughed out. My neighbor's wolfhound bitch, the big blue one, was trotting across the pasture stepping daintily with the running hound's consummate grace. Behind her was one of the fastest and most vicious wolfhounds in all the prairie country, being credited with making clean kills without aid from the pack. Old Buck kept close behind the bitch. Behind him were four male coyotes—one big one in the lead, singing his song of amorous confusion as he trotted, and behind him the smaller ones strung out, stopping occasionally to nose for possible messages, then resuming the eager trot-march across the head of the canyon.

Old Buck would stop when the blue bitch in her apparent complete unconcern would stop to nose among the grasses, and bare his fangs to the coyotes, who in turn snarled back at him. Several times before they trotted out of sight, Buck made a rush at the leading coyote, but the wolf eluded him easily and would circle back when Buck turned to follow the blue bitch again.

I have always known about the truce among male wolfhounds and female coyotes during the coyote's love moon. I have seen the best wolfhounds embarrass their masters by running up to the side of a female coyote during this season, then turn back without harming her, while she, realizing that the hounds are males, makes no effort to run fast but lopes along, looking back over her shoulder like some coquette. She knows when there are females in the pack, however, and she stretches out across the prairie at such times on the serious business of self-preservation.

But this male understanding between old Buck and those love-sick coyotes was something new to me; something new and tremendously humorous.

The Light-of-Day-Returns Moon is the season of lengthening days and the season when Grandfather the Sun again becomes interested in earth and its children. When the Osage say they "live in the light of day," as they do in most of their prayers and songs, they thus express their happiness in the approval of Grandfather.

The cardinals try out their voices in the creek bottoms on warm, springlike days, and the chickadees and the titmice chatter all over the ridges and seem to be little disturbed by the sudden changes in the temperature or when snow flurries and even snowstorms come. New life comes to the blackjacks and the prairie in the form of hundreds of white-face calves. However, these little fellows, with their soft eyes brimful of wonder, suffer much less than the older cattle. On mild days they romp with one another like lambs or lie placidly with their mothers, their white faces scarcely distinguishable from the snow patches that gleam in the sun.

To the original children of the blackjacks the light of day, like all gifts from Wah-Kon-Tah, was held sacred and appreciated, and even now the new war time that makes of the light of day a sluggard affect: very little their routine based on the sun. Their appointments at the agency are not kept on white man's hours, and they bury their dead when Grandfather the Sun is directly above, without reference to the hands of the clock.

And this moon has a certain dripping ugliness like the one before, but the days are noticeably longer, and there is a hint of brightness behind the snowstorms and the cold rains, like the bright spot in the east before dawn, like the light from the heart lighting an ugly face. The brown leaves of the blackjacks and the postoaks begin to drop, and the silence of the bare limbs is ominous yet expectant. There is a cleanliness about the earth like a house prepared for guests.

The earth is alternately frozen and mushy as though being tried out for the hysterical entrance of the prima donna, Just-Doing-That Moon. There is a promise that life will come again and that the Light-of-Day-Returns Moon is in fact the brightness before dawn. It is the transition stage, when new life begins to stir within the earth— not visible, only felt. It is the quivering of the cicada pupa before exploding into diaphanous wings and iridescent facets. It is the mud of the pond before quivering life takes definite form, and it is like the first dim thoughts of man and the first mysterious thrill of puberty.

And it is symbolical of the new God-concept of the men of the blackjacks that flows before and around the pressures of the Amer-European and is kept soft like the bellies of the Osage under the soft living, never to harden into crystals like the old religion of the blackjacks. Fat can be artificial ornamentation, too, although having a basic biological *raison d'être*. Chesho man becomes fat as well as Hunkah man, like religions and philosophies when they reach the mature stage of growth and express themselves by useless ornamentation.

In general, the breaking-up of the tribal organization has caused a state of confusion, and this is carried into the new Peyote religion to make the confusion even greater. Much of this chaos is due to the fact that the descendants of the old chieftains still assume their traditional importance, and there is bitter rivalry between them and the opportunists who speak passable English and imitate the white man's methods of self-advertisement. This imitation of the white man, coupled with the Indian's irrepressible desire for personal prestige, is often ridiculous and often rather poignant.

Deer-Makes-Noise-in-Bush, a West Mooner, came up to talk with me at the grocery store. He was buying groceries for the feast which he would hold at his ranch the next day after a Peyote meeting. As his boxes and packages were being loaded in his pickup truck, he said, "You lissen to them East Moon peoples all time, seem like. You oughta come down my place tonight; we gonna have meetin' there. You see what they do at West Moon meetin'."

"Blackdog's son-in-law is big boss down there, isn't he? He doesn't like me."

"He ain't gonna have nothin' to do with it," he assured me; "I'm gonna be Road Man. Gonna be at my place. You sure mus come, ain't it?"

"All right, I'll come," I said.

The son-in-law was a wizened Osage who claimed the authority over the West Moon fireplaces which the great Moonhead had established at Hominy when he was "tryin' to get through." Being the son-in-law of Blackdog to whom Moonhead had given the authority, he assumed that the authority had descended to him when Blackdog died, but he succeeded in forming a clique only, and many of the West Mooners would not concede his authority and leadership.

I stood at the west-facing door of the conical Peyote church under the trees at Buck-Makes-Noise-in-Bush's ranch and waited for him. The sun was just going down and the cold crept in from the bottoms like some stealthy animal. I knew that he wanted me to appreciate to the fullest the importance which he carried as Road Man, so I waited at the door to greet him and pay my respects.

Soon he came from his house, walking across the bottom toward the church. He was a strange figure in the semidarkness as he walked with dignity. He wore a red blanket, and on the side of his head was the downy eagle feather which grows under the bird's stiff tail feathers. This fluffy feather was dyed red and was worn on the left side indicating the Chesho main division of the tribe, or the Sky People. The softness of the feather symbolized the softness and kindness of the Sky People, also called Peace People. Across his face, with its horn pointing to his temples and its center running through and over his mouth, was painted a red crescent moon, and on each cheek were the jagged fire symbols of the Road Man. He carried the other symbols of Peyote in a beaded, buckskin bag and held the gourd rattle with the beaded handle in his free hand.

As he came up to me, his face glowed with a pride that he couldn't hide, and his body was erect and graceful. He raised his hand in a pontifical salute, then motioned for me to follow him into the church. He stopped suddenly, and I almost ran into him. Over his shoulder I saw the son-in-law of Blackdog sitting in the Road Man's place, with insulting importance. He had a great red heart painted on his face, the Peyote "Heart of the World."

Buck-That-Makes-Noise-in-Bush turned from the door quickly with an explosive "Hagh," like the cough of a buffalo bull, then walked with bowed head back to the house.

In the days of the crystalline religion of Wah-Kon-Tah, which colored their daily struggle for existence in the balance of the blackjacks and the prairie, the Osage must have had some ritualistic greeting for Light-of-Day-Returns Moon, because of its importance in their lives, but I do not know. I have only seen them in the transition period; the period between bluestem and perhaps the return of bluestem; the period of barren spots around the feed troughs, covered with sticker-weed, cocklebur, and curly grass. Perhaps the bluestem of Wah-Kon-Tah will be replaced by the man-nurtured flowers of Christianity in the ultimate assimilation. They have adopted the Man on the Cross, because they understand him. He is both Chesho and Hunkah. His footprints are on the Peyote altars, and they are deep like the footprints of one who has jumped. No bird they know can launch itself into the air, into the sky, without first jumping.

Perhaps He is the Light in the Light-of-Day-Returns Moon; the Light behind the ugliness of man's interpretative fumbling. Perhaps the light of the Light-of-Day-Returns Moon could symbolize the light of man's reasoning after the mammalian darkness of his winter, suggesting that he can still look forward to a Buffalo-Pawing-Earth Moon, with its full light and its creation and beauty, even though biologically still far ahead. The muck of my ponds says this, unless I confuse it—unless I charge it with significance through my thought-images.

It is during this moon of transition, the ending of a cycle and the beginning of a new one, that I begin to look forward to the accustomed happenings of Just-Doing-That Moon that were the landmarks which drowned the feeling of flowing time. But just before the tenth one at the blackjacks there was the hint of a jerk in the rhythm, like the misfire of a sparkplug when flying in the moonlight.

The war came, and with male vanity I asked to be recommissioned in the Air Service. They didn't laugh at me but suggested that I might like teaching cadets on the ground.

I sat in the lobby of my hotel in Washington and counted bellies in uniform, feeling occasionally the hardness of my own. When I got back to the blackjacks, I trotted the half-mile down the backbone of my ridge and back. As I showered, I felt that there had been a mistake.

Later I heard that they were calling pilots of thirty "Pop," and I felt a great sadness. Like the tractor on Beaver Creek that disturbed the conditions which Les Claypoole had fixed for the comfort of his senility, so did the war destroy the citadel of my vanity, forcing me to admit to myself my maturity.

In my shock I almost failed to note that Les had not come to make his traditional visit. Later I went to him.

There were women there in the little room, black-draped, stiff and chalky, sniffling delicately at the casket, and there were a few earth-stained men, clumsily holding their hats, waiting. There was the resignation and dumbness of an old work horse waiting for his collar, as the men looked at the floor between their feet and the women gazed at the casket.

We, less than a dozen of us, knew what the minister would say, because he had to say it; he had no choice, and when he had said it, there was nothing else. This was difficult for the minister. It was more satisfying to feel around for beautiful sentiments about the dead for the comfort of the friends and relatives and spill them with the proper modulations and to feel tragic yourself from self-induced emotion. But he was faced with the shining, self-sufficient word "honor," and he couldn't add to the brightness of that word, so he stopped and we waited. Then he told of an incident of Les's honesty in which he himself was involved, a money matter; and he spoke of honesty as if it were albinism, unnatural and conspicuous among men.

A few big shoes scraped the floor, and eyes were lowered again; a few hats turned in rough fingers nervously. As the minister got further away from frustrating simplicity of plain honor and warmed up with his generalities, I looked at the faces of the men. They knew that Les was honest but they wanted to hear it said by the minister; and their faces said that they wanted someone to express what they felt about it—what they felt about Les's honesty, which was like something that you dug out of the earth, which was hard and useful and indestructible; something put there by God they would reckon. They wanted somebody to tell them why, since they were not unusually touched by the passing of this old neighbor who had lived a full life, they felt so hollow and had such a great sense of the loss of something. It was something everybody knew when he lived but never talked about, but now, since he was dead, they felt it ought to be talked about by somebody who could put it into the proper words; somebody like a preacher.

When the services were over, they walked by to look at the body of the old cowboy, and each one stopped for a moment, as though they were searching the face for the satisfaction which the minister could not supply in the words in which they had placed their hopes.

We followed him through the little town of Hewins, named for his old boss, then onto the prairie, and stopped at a desolate little cemetery on a prairie hill where the winds carry the scent of limestone earth. I imagine the coyotes howl there, too, just as they did at the Beaver Creek ranch.

After ten years of joyous living in rhythm with the life about me, I have reached maturity and the stage of ornamentation, expressed by worry over the peace of the world, the future of my nation, the passing of the landmarks along the jungle river of time. Now I have a deep desire to say, "I have passed by here." It is the great Ego grasping for immortality, like the species around me fighting for life. I shall cling, too, as the last rattling leaf on the blackjack clings during this time, protesting sadly, weakly, in the cold winds busy sweeping the earthhouse for the new life; but my mature disturbances are ornamental clinging, my Chesho part clutching in confusion. Hunkah's immortality is clear and definite and satisfying under the earth-laws of survival, and nature is still interested in me because of my powers of reproduction. I could have immortality represented by the dozens of individuals, without boasting and with mores negligible. In the balance they would choke me off as my life-force waned and as they needed it in their virility, but in civilization they would be patiently impatient, especially if I held unnaturally, under the laws of civilization, economic things of value to their growth.

The great Ego speaks and projects its survival selfishness through the power of thought to the welfare of the world, then back to the welfare of the nation, then withdraws to the Ego these units protect and for whose immortality they will be responsible. If world peace fails, then the nation is in danger. Then if the nation crumbles, the collective voice through which the Ego is glorified becomes unimportant; then the great "I" is like any cornered rat, with his whole life-force concentrated to protect life, no matter how miserable and distorted. When members of the herd or pack are scattered, the individual fights for himself, and there is no time and no overflow of the life-force to be expressed in ornamentation.

I might as well speak of *my* world as I speak of *my* nation; then I would be concerned about my species as it relates to my unit of society and to me.

Thus when all the superstructure is cleared away along with the higher developments in organization for the protection of the species, there stands alone, as he began, the individual, with unsheathed claws and bared fangs; the Ego that is the spark of life and in times of stress always visible. It is like seeing the original granite of earth with the superdeposits eroded.

The great Ego, through his nation, will shout world brotherhood and something about our future generations, if all is going well. But if all is not going so well and he can look back over his shoulder and see the corner, then he will shout about the nation and "peace in our time"; then, when in the corner, he crys simply "Peace."

My Chesho thoughts have then the same roots as my Hunkah thoughts and the same roots as the Hunkah actions in all the species, even though they may be inspired by the Force as an urge to immortality; and, because of the power of projection, I imagine I fear the possibility of the corner and the possible loss of my immortality, on the one hand, and the loss of material comforts, on the other, as well as the glory and power of collective expression.

I am one with the drama of the blackjacks, even in my Chesho self. The books, the magazines, and the voice that comes over the radio to disturb me do just that; they disturb me, because I happen to be at the stage of ornamental expression and under the urge that influences all life at that stage. My disturbance is not inspired by altruism, though altruism may exist in other categories. I can't say that the status quo is disturbed, since there is no such condition possible in the drama of the blackjacks, and the idea of going back to it would be like going back to "normalcy" or Shangri La. I am simply floating along on the jungle river with the landmarks passing, with my Hunkah self perfectly contented, with all parts functioning and healthy, and my

Chesho self confused and clutching, straining for the orgasm, while Hunkah relaxes with assurance.

How dim and simple is the expression of the Force in the coyote, the crow, the mockingbird, and the squirrel with the tin, as compared with the flickering light of my thought attempting to read the Urge in myself, confusing it with shadows and reflections, being able to charge neither symbols nor abstractions with my emotions. To the symbolist and the abstractionist I am lost.

I might well let the wood thrush and the coyote say what I feel, since I can't create beauty more perfect than the materials used. The one can do it so well in song and the other asks the question so beautifully, with aftersilence leaving it so hauntingly unanswered. But my egotism won't allow this. I am not satisfied to feel and enjoy the flood of emotion which earth and the mere fact of living inspires and continue to express the Force-rooted urge in action; I must now attempt to express the subtleties in world symbols, in fear that the people to come will not know that the great Ego has passed this way. I want them to know that I, too, have heard the wood thrush at twilight —the voice disembodied in the dripping woods—that I have heard the coyote talk to the moon and watched the geese against a cold autumn sunset. I want them to be sure that I have heard the baying of the bearhounds bounced from the sides of the canyons and have dreamed to the creaking of a saddle; that I have seen a red rose against a white wall and the morning-glories staring at me with wide-eyed innocence from the fence on fresh September mornings; that I have loved the waving of a single grass blade and have listened to the murmuring of the wind in the blackjacks as well as to its chatter, its moaning, and its hysterical screaming; and that I have been disturbed by its complete absence when the leaves were like metal on moonlight nights, and the whippoorwill filled me with primitive, indefinite longing by the mere repetition of its own name.

My egotism born of the struggle demands, at this stage in my life, that I become an Our Lady's juggler, with word symbols as my poor tools, to sweat at the feet of a beauty, an order, a perfection, a mystery far above my comprehension.